# RESTORING BLAIR HOUSE

# RESTORING BLAIR HOUSE

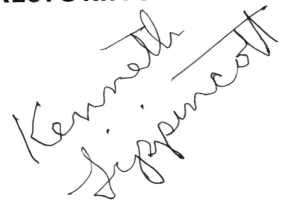

## KENNETH LIPPINCOTT

XULON PRESS

Xulon Press
2301 Lucien Way #415
Maitland, FL 32751
407.339.4217
www.xulonpress.com

Unless otherwise indicated, Scripture quotations taken from the Holy Bible, New International Version (NIV). Copyright © 1973, 1978, 1984, 2011 by Biblica, Inc.™. Used by permission. All rights reserved.

Printed in the United States of America.

ISBN-13: 9781545615225

# CONTENTS

# Dedication

Though bruised and flawed like the characters in my novels, my wife and I as well as our daughters and their husbands are partners. They, more than any other readers, will appreciate what *Restoring Blair House* represents, as they identify with the life lessons and experiences that I share through this novel.

My wife Karen is most important to me. Karen Gustafson, the heroine in the Rock Creek Trilogy is named for my wife Karen and my grandmother Freda Gustafson, who died in childbirth. The Ken Bond family partially reflects my own family history. Katarina Bond is a woman of faith with integrity and loyalty. Her husband is recovering from a heart attack, and they suffer through much difficulty living in a small town. Like my wife, Katarina develops and assumes several ministerial roles as the plot unfolds. Katarina reflects my wife's capabilities and resiliency. Neither Karen Gustafson nor Katarina Bond reflect my wife's tenderness compared to that of Ruth Browning. All three women reflect characteristics of my wife Karen in reflecting the first part of my thematic statement, "Ya know, women have the power to bring out the best in a man..." and that is why I dedicate this book to my wife of 55 years, Karen Rose Powell Lippincott.

My daughters Kristin Becker and Krystal Thomas are the other two most important persons in my life. Both live out the biblical promise for parenting unto three generations. Like their mother, Kristin and Krystal are women of faith, and all but one of my grandchildren have now graduated from high school and are well on their way toward following Christ's lordship in their lives. A partial view of both of our daughters is presented through the Bond's daughters.

The Bond girls help their father deliver newspapers as he recovers from a heart attack, a role my daughters knew well. Also, like my daughters, the Bond girls are a great help to their mother, as at an early age they learn to watch out for other people and to help around the kitchen and with other chores. Today both of my daughters reflect their mother's commitment to marriage and family. In their marriages they effectively bring out the best in their husbands and their children. As grandparents Karen and I cherish moments of watching the Becker and Thomas families as they love one another and seek to follow Christ.

# Restoring Blair House
## Foreword by John Bornschein

I f you close your eyes, you can almost hear it. The wind whistling through the tree limbs nearby with dried, small leaves twisting about on the ground around your feet. Then as you open your eyes you witness the sun peaking, ever so slightly, over the eastern plains. It is a brisk Colorado morning.

As Tim, a hard-working waiter, digs into his pockets to open the door to the Cozy Corner Café, he notices a stranger awaiting him at the entrance. His shoes torn and tattered and his presence ominous. Is he what he seems or this yet another chapter in the mystery of Rock Creek?

Have you ever desired to escape the busyness of life and flee to a place that gives you a fresh start? Many of us have fantasized about starting anew in a small town, shedding our labels and wounds to embrace a new identity with the wisdom of the path behind us. If this is you, then welcome to the small town of Rock Creek, a crossroads for individuals of all walks of life. However, this seemingly remote community that captivates the would be passer-by with intrigue of the simple life is not so far removed, as it would seem, from the quagmire of human interests seeking self preservation at the expense of others. Newcomers are outsiders and strangers in a foreign land–suspicious to all who may dwell there and not everyone is who they seem. While outlanders come and go, not without leaving their mark, we find that even spiritual forces are mutually invested here as two worlds collide.

When the ensuing conflict arises, the town residents will fight for all they have with their friends, family and history at stake.

Kenneth Lippincott has done it again! Prepare to be fully engrossed in this page-turner. This incredible story of forgiveness, redemption and restoration begins just two weeks after the shocking turn of events in **Freedom's Tree**. More twists and deep mystery await as you immerse your heart and soul into the lives of those standing in the shadow of the Blair House.

Unlike other stories, the impact of this adventure goes far beyond the cover and the pages therein. You will be spiritually impacted as you engage in the deeper layers of this journey through real-life scriptural application that will empower you to choose your path wisely. Each of us has the power to bring out the best or the worst in others. So discover for yourself the terrace to truth, justice, grace and mercy as you venture into **Restoring Blair House**.

– John Bornschein

John Bornschein is the Senior Pastor of Calvary Fellowship Fountain Valley, an Executive Producer on "Drive Thru History: America" for the History Channel International, a television host on the Trinity Broadcasting Network, and host of the "Engage in Truth" radio program. John has also served at the United Nations in New York, at the Chaplains Office at the Pentagon, with our Congressional Leaders (including the Senate and House Chaplains) in Washington D.C., with the White House Office of Faith-based and Neighborhood Partnerships and the White House Office of Public Liaison as the Vice Chairman for the National Day of Prayer Task Force, alongside Dr. James and Shirley Dobson and Anne Graham Lotz.

# Acknowledgements

As a young man in college, I had a dream. I portrayed the dream in an oil painting, which became the basis for *The Rock Creek Trilogy*. While I spent parts of forty-eight years writing *Freedom's Tree*, the first book of the trilogy, I completed *Restoring Blair House* in less than two years. Often, I have explained how I took less time to complete my second book because I'm over the hill and I ought to be going faster! The truth—I have had help along the way.

Karen, my lovely wife of fifty-five years, has always been my encourager. She not only helped with the revision and edit of my books, but also she monitored my manuscripts to insure I addressed a woman's point of view. As with *Freedom's Tree*, she assisted in marketing our books locally, by mail order, and during our vacation travels. She reflected to me the true intent of being a partner by giving needed input and by accepting responsibilities. God gave the gift of Karen to me, as He answered my prayer for a godly wife.

God perfectly provided another gift to me through my pastor, John Bornschein. *Freedom's Tree* lacked a foreword, but *Restoring Blair House* does not. I thank my pastor, radio announcer, fellow author, and friend John Bornschein for writing the foreword to *Restoring Blair House*, second book of *The Rock Creek Trilogy*. As Senior Pastor of Calvary Fellowship Fountain Valley, Pastor John challenges all of us to go deeper in our studies and in our walk with God. A young man by comparison, God has used Pastor John as Vice President of the National Day of Prayer, as a consultant to the United Nations, as producer with the History Channel, and more. Pastor John has been an encourager full of grace and mercy.

Last and most significant, I acknowledge God guided my writing just as he provided my wife and my pastor. I have confessed I did not always remember to pray before sitting down in front of my yellow pad or before my computer to work on my book. As a result I would suffer through my self-effort. But most of the time, when I had my wits about me, I did pray for God's guidance in writing my novel, and according to my wife I would surface from my man cave in the basement with a smile on my face and a twinkle in my eye. By God's grace, it is finished!

# Introduction

"Welcome to the valley" was what merchants, oldtimers, and members of the McNaughton Corporation would have said to you had you entered a store and spent some money in the valley. Since Colorado gold and water rights had been a recent issue, the same folk who welcomed you would look at you askance, if they learned you weren't just a visitor, if you had plans to stay awhile. Oldtimers counted you as a newcomer, if they could remember when you arrived in the valley. While Rock Creek Valley is a fictitious setting and the characters of my own creation the storyline has been influenced by my experiences as a secondary teacher and principal. For over forty-three years, I served primarily in small towns, always as a newcomer. Truth has been stranger than fiction.

Times had been tough since the '50's. The state reorganized the school system and towns with one room school houses gave up their little red school house in deference to merging students together for greater opportunities. Interstate highway construction added to the difficulty. It use to be that highways 85/87 carried the bulk of the traffic through the valley, which meant a steady flow of cash was spent daily at gasoline stations, restaurants, and all sorts of shops. For instance in Rock Creek, the grocery store closed as did the volunteer fire department, and the corner gas station was remodeled and became a small convenience store.

Being the middle book in *The Rock Creek Trilogy*, *Restoring Blair House* serves as a bridge to the first book, *Freedom's Tree*, and to the third book, *Defenders of the Valley*. *Freedom's Tree* was a romantic mystery that *Kirkus Reviews* labeled a thriller. It began with arrival from the south of three newcomers on Colorado Day, August 1 and ended August 8, 1980. As the sequel, *Restoring Blair House* continued two weeks later with some characters still fulfilling primary roles, but I elevated some lesser characters and added, perish the thought, newcomers, who arrived from the north. One unanswered subplot from *Freedom's Tree* carried over and became part of the dominant plot in *Restoring Blair House*. While these books are connected, you can be assured *Restoring Blair House* completely stands alone. I'm certain you will want to read *Freedom's Tree*, either before or after you read *Restoring Blair House*.

Speaking of reading, you could read *Restoring Blair House* a combination of ways. I do hope you make predictions as you read and you feast on the words and details. I confess I did a Steinbeck by creating new words like oldtimer and extended the use of the word disciple. Since I wrote this book as Christian fiction, the word disciple became a verb form in addition to its traditional usages. Please do read for the plot line with all its conflicts and climaxes that lead to a satisfying resolution, but also please study the characters, their values, choices and decisions. If you do, you'll discover all are bruised, all flawed, all with secrets, and everyone wants a second chance in this story of forgiveness, redemption, and restoration. Finally, you may choose to treat the scripture that heads each chapter as if it were a pair of glasses for you to view the chapter. I do not teach the scripture, nor do I develop the chapter around it. I use the scripture like a fisherman's bait for the reader to nibble on. Enjoy!

*Ken Lippincott*

# Divine Appointment

## CHAPTER 1

*"... let your light shine before others, that they may see
your good deeds and glorify your Father in heaven."
Matthew 5:16*

"You know, women have the power to bring out the best in a man...or the worst," the man seated at the counter had said.

The waiter stopped in his tracks opposite his only customer. The man had met him at the entrance to the Cozy Corner Café, when he had opened at five this morning. He realized normally, the morning rush would have already begun, but not now, not today. Studying his customer, the waiter noticed he looked disheveled with long chestnut hair in mild disarray. He wore a weathered blue jean jacket, and a slightly wrinkled black polo shirt, but he neither appeared hung-over nor dirty. Correctly, the waiter concluded the man had just slept the night in an automobile or somewhere out of doors.

"What's that you say?"

"Sorry to interrupt your work," the customer casually said with a smile, as he straightened in his seat, "but women are meant to influence us. A wife is to be a full partner."

"How do you mean?"

The customer's hazel eyes briefly twinkled emerald green when he said, "Like in the Bible, the serpent deceived Eve. She ate from the tree of knowledge and offered the apple to Adam."

"What was wrong with that?"

"Eve was made from one of Adam's ribs. She was to be by his side. She wasn't made from his head to be over him, or from his foot to be below him. Adam was supposed to lead Eve. He knew the one rule God had given him, and his job was to teach it to his companion, Eve. When Adam followed Eve into disobedience, he sinned instead of being obedient to God."

"Didn't Eve blame the serpent, and Adam blamed both Eve and God?" asked the waiter.

"Yes and here's another one. God told Abraham that he was going to be the father of a great nation, but then it didn't happen in a normal timeline. When Abraham and his wife Sarah were about ninety, the wife decided to take things into her own hands. She tried to improve on God's plan."

"Not a good thing, I would suppose."

"Not at all, Abraham sired a child through his wife's maidservant, and later his wife became pregnant as God had said she would. The maidservant and her child were sent away, and the consequences of what Sarah and Abraham did continue today."

"What wrong did Abraham do? You said his wife told him to have a child through her maidservant, or was it that he followed his wife into disobedience like what Adam did?"

"Exactly," the customer answered as he leaned forward in his seat, "and instead of waiting on the Lord to fulfill his plan, Abraham's decision was to follow his wife's idea and improve on God's plan. They took things in their own hands, instead of waiting upon the Lord."

"How do you know all this?" the waiter asked.

"It's in the Bible. Do you have a copy?" the customer smiled and asked, again as his hazel eyes twinkled emerald green. Not waiting for an answer, he bent over and grasped a copy from the backpack at his feet. He handed it to the waiter with a printed paper titled, "The Ambassador's Toolkit."

"Well...thank you," said the waiter, "if I had one, it's either long gone or somewhere at my parents' house. Where can I read about Adam and Abraham?"

"Read about Adam and Eve and Abraham and Sarah in the first book of the Bible, *Genesis*. But also read the book of *Ruth* for an example of how a woman can bring out the best in a man, even a good man. Both are in the *Old Testament*," the customer paused and then added, "Also, go to the *New Testament*, the book of *Matthew*, and read about Mary and Joseph, then read the book of *John*."

"Wow, that sounds like a lot to read!" said the wide-eyed waiter.

"I guess it sounds that way, but I think you'll find it very interesting."

"Great...you know, I've been thinking about proposing to my girl-friend. She is drop dead gorgeous, but I wonder if she would help bring out the best in me. I mean I get it that a man has choices to face and decisions to make. I would do anything for her," the waiter reflected.

"But...what else?" the customer asked as his eyes narrowed and the smile left his face.

"She's got me wrapped around her little finger."

The customer leaned forward again and simply asked, "And?"

"She makes me feel guilty. Sometimes I can't do anything right!" the waiter said and added, "Where are you headed?"

"I'm supposed to walk to the church in Rock Creek," and the customer added, "the Bible does say a husband is to lay down his life for his wife, so maybe you should read about Sampson and Delilah too."

"Didn't she cut his hair or something like that?" asked the waiter, and when the customer nodded affirmatively, the waiter continued, "Really, Rock Creek must be ten or more miles down US 85. This is bear country, and you need to be alert. How did you get here?"

"I walked here from outside of Denver," the customer answered, and then asked, "Has a bear caused trouble?" and next, he looked around the empty dining area, before saying "Is business always this slow?"

"To the contrary, I'm usually swamped by now."

"Well, I'm glad we got to talk. I'll be in the area, at least for awhile. I'll check back with you to see if you have any questions from your reading," eyes twinkling, the customer promised. "Say, do you have some cardboard I could put in my shoes. I've worn a hole in the soles of both boots."

"Sure," the waiter said as he reached into the trashcan behind the counter, "here you are. Take the side panel from this box."

One repaired sole for another repaired soul thought the customer, who then said, "Thank you and be certain to read the flyer when you have the opportunity to do so!"

"My name is Tim McNaughton. What's yours?" said Tim the waiter, a tall redhead with a crew-cut and an infectious smile.

"Good name, Timothy, it is good to meet you. Timothy, I'm John Mark Cannikin," the customer replied, as he reached across the counter to grasp Tim's hand, "I'm a cup bearer, living water. Be certain to offer the flyer to others."

"If I didn't have to work, I'd give you a ride to Rock Creek. You could tell me more. Be careful, there's bear on the mesa behind the church in Rock Creek, and ranchers are having trouble with them in the mountains," Tim said. "Will you be staying at the Stage Stop Hotel?"

"No, I've got a light weight tent in my backpack. I'll be all right, and I'll be on the watch for the bear. I'll kill it, if I have to," John Mark said. Grinning as he closed the café door behind him, he immediately headed south out of town down US 85/87, the Valley Highway.

Within seconds, customers from vehicles in the parking lot knocked forcefully at the front door of the café, the most popular eatery in Ridge View. It was where locals congregated to eat breakfast, lunch, and dinner. Elected officials, community service clubs and others met at the café both for official and unofficial business. Decisions affecting the whole valley had been negotiated in the cafe booths, which bordered highway and crossroad frontage. Oft times some met for unsavory purposes and schemes had been hatched here, devilment planned, and foolishness initiated. Often this had been enemy ground!

When Tim heard the pounding, he hastily opened the door, and the crowd that had been waiting outside, entered in. Wiping his hands with the white apron at his waist, Tim said to the first to enter, "Where 'ya been? I've been ready to serve you since well before six o'clock."

"What do 'ya mean, Tim, you never switched on your open sign? It's still turned off," said one customer as the sign flickered, and then produced a steady beam.

"What were 'ya doin,' Tim? And who were the three guys that just left?"

4

"Three guys? I only had one customer," Tim replied, as he removed the plate, silverware, and water glass that John Mark had used from the counter, and held them before the crowd.

"Well, the one guy came out of the door and the two big guys followed after him. They had been blocking the front door."

"We certainly were waiting," another said. "They blocked the door. Nobody could miss the message of their body language. It was clear we were not to approach the door, and I didn't. Each of them must have been nearly seven feet tall. They stood shoulder to shoulder. They blocked the double doorway!"

"Come take a look, Tim. They're not more than a block away."

Tim followed his customers back out the door where all filed out and looked down the highway. Customers pointed in the direction John Mark had traveled, and each commented they could only see one man walking. Most rubbed their eyes, squinted, and looked again in wonderment.

"I know what I saw, and I saw the one leave the café, and the other two had moved away from the door to let him pass by," a heavy set man said with a gruff voice.

"Me too," said another man, "let's eat!"

The rest of the crowd followed, but conversation inside the Cozy Corner Café continued to focus on the subject. Some of the people asked Tim if the fellow had told him where he was going and what he was doing here. Tim replied that the man was just passing through on his way to nowhere. Tim did add he thought the man must have been visiting someone in town and that he had walked to the café for breakfast.

"Don't think so, Tim, he was carrying a good sized backpack," said Red McNaughton, a rancher who owned the local lumberyard and hardware store.

"I'll tail him after I eat," said Bailey, the local sheriff.

"We don't need any vagrants hanging around and for sure, we don't need any more newcomers," replied Red, as he twirled the end of his red mustache.

"Ain't that the truth," several McNaughtons chimed in.

"Here comes the Marlboro Man!" said another customer. "Let's tell Adam Claymore what happened and hear what he has to say."

"Good idea! Isn't he a preacher at the Rock Creek church?" asked an old man.

"Yes, do you remember when he and his wife, Mary, would drive by and she would wave at you like a princess?" asked the old man's brother.

"Absolutely," said Red, "I fell in love with her the first time I saw her, but Adam won her heart."

"Too bad for Adam she died so young," said Bailey.

"Too bad for all of us," countered Red, and all the customers nodded affirmatively.

As one man went to open the door for Adam to enter the café, the rest of the customers gathered around the booth that Red occupied.

"Give him a chance to sit down, before you bombard him with questions," demanded Red, as he took his position on the red leather bench.

Smiling as he entered, Adam put a coin in the newspaper box, removed a copy of the local paper, took off his black Stetson, and adjusted the small red feather in his hat band, before walking to Red's booth. "What's with the reception, fellas? Red, are you holding court?"

"Have a seat, Adam. The boys want your interpretation about what just happened to Tim. And nobody place any breakfast order until we are finished," growled Red. "If anyone is not from here, you will wait, if you know what's good for you."

The eager listeners looked around and an old man reported, "All here live here, Red. We will wait to order breakfast. Right fellas?"

Since no one disagreed, Tim began to tell his tale, "Mr. Claymore, I was going about my duties, getting ready for customers like I do every day, filling salt and pepper shakers, wrapping silverware....."

"Get to it, Tim," Red chastised, "we know you are a good waiter, a good employee."

"Sure, sorry..."

"It's, okay, Tim, tell it like it is," Adam encouraged.

"I was right in the center of the other side of the counter where this guy sat. He looked like he had slept in a car or outside some-where, but he wasn't dirty, just a little disheveled."

"Move it along," demanded Red, who grew more impatient.

"This is important, Red, the guy hadn't said two words to me before or after ordering his food, except he said 'isn't this a glorious day' when I met him at the café door. I was just unlocking the front door. He was looking around at the mountains as the sun made its way down the slope," said Timothy, and then he continued, "You know, it starts at the twin peaks of Huajatolla and moves down the mountain into the valleys. It always seems to pause at the tall oak tree, the Live Oak that looked totally dead until recently and now it has leaf buds."

"I noticed that too!" said the cook, who had joined the group from the kitchen, and then he continued, "Don't worry folks, I've got things ready to cook and nothing will burn."

"Continue," Adam urged. "We all have somewhere to go."

"I don't want to miss anything," Tim continued. "He sat down and ordered breakfast. I served him, and he sat there with his head bowed. I guess he was praying. I walked his way behind the counter. Just as I was directly opposite him, he says 'ya know women have the power to bring out the best in men...or the worst.' I asked what he meant, and he told me about Adam and Eve, Abraham and Sarah. He gave me a Bible he was carrying in his backpack. It's brand new like he passes out new Bibles to people. He told me to read *Genesis*, *Ruth*, and *Matthew* about Mary and Joseph. Oh yeah, he told me to read the book of *John*," Tim finished.

"Is that it?" asked Adam.

"No," Tim said, "it's like he knew what I was thinking about."

"How so?"

"He wanted me to read and pay attention to how the women affected the men. You know about how they help bring out the best or worst in men."

"So, what was on your mind when you were passing by?" Adam inquired with a smile across his face.

"I was considering whether or not to propose to my girl, Heather Ross."

"Meaning the disheveled man, who met you at the door this morning, who marveled at the beauty of the morning upon the mountain, pointed you to scripture that directly relates to your concern, about a choice you are considering, about a decision that will have life-long circumstances," interpreted Adam.

"Yeah, I guess so. Life-long consequences, meaning divorce is not an option for me, so I better get it right," Tim repeated. "That really is significant, isn't it, Adam?"

"Major significance," said Red and several other men in unison.

"I wish I had considered my choice more," said one man, who was then affirmed by a few others.

"Tim, I think the man was being obedient to what God was telling him to do," said Adam.

"You mean God would have the man direct Tim to scripture that would help Tim make his decision," said one of the customers, who had listened intently.

"There's more to it," informed Adam, "Eve and Sarah both led their men into disaster. And the men chose to follow...but Ruth and Mary were positive influences."

"You mean they brought out the best in their men," Tim concluded.

"Yes, but you need to be certain to read the scriptures he told you to read. Do it soon. This is something you must not ignore. How did he happen to be at your door this morning?"

"Adam, he was waiting for me to arrive. I think he camped out somewhere nearby. He said he walked here from Denver."

"Walked here?" Adam questioned, "I wonder why anyone would walk and not hitch a ride."

"He told me why, Adam, he said God told him to walk to Rock Creek and to go to the church there. Your church, Adam," Tim said proudly. "I wonder if he will tell you something, too."

"Cool beans!" said the man who had opened the door for Adam.

"I wonder if he would have said something to me, if I had come out from behind the grill?" commented the cook.

"There's more, isn't there, Tim?" asked Adam.

"He said he would check back with me, and he handed me this paper titled the Ambassador's Tool Kit."

"Then he plans to be here awhile..." Adam commented as he unfolded the paper that Tim had handed him, scanned it, took out a pen from his shirt pocket, and circled several items, and then asked, "Where were the rest of you when all this was going on?"

"Adam, most of us were waiting in our cars in the parking lot," Red said. "The open sign wasn't on."

"More than that, Adam, there were two very tall, very large men standing before the door, kinda blocking the doorway. Everybody saw them, right guys?" a large man said as he looked around for support. "Raise your hand if you saw them!"

"Yeah, we knew not to try to get in," said another, a truck driver, as hands went upward.

"Tell Adam the rest of it," said a different customer.

"I will, Adam, after Tim opened the door and we came in, the open sign flickered on. It had already been plugged in," the larger man explained, "and when we asked Tim about the men outside the door, well, he didn't know anything about them."

"And we took Tim outside to show him the three men walking south out of town on the Valley Highway," added the truck driver.

"We got outside and we looked..."

"All we saw was the one man, all alone..."

"All right, everybody, listen to Adam," growled Red. "Tell us what it means!"

"Okay," Adam paused, "here's my understanding. All of you were privileged to witness God at work. For that, all of you were blessed. I believe God had it in mind for all of you to be a part of what happened. All of you, even Red," Adam said with a smile, as he reached across and slapped Red on his forearm.

Turning directly to him, Adam looked piercingly into Tim's eyes and said, "Tim, God has a plan for you. I think your decision concerning your girl friend will make a difference. If I were you, I would seek God to lead you by you reading the Bible. Do not take this lightly, as I see you are not."

Then back to the crowd, Adam said, "You have witnessed what's called a divine appointment. A divine appointment where a follower of Jesus Christ obediently walked here from Denver to be here at this time to speak to Tim and for all of you to bear witness to what happened. Gentlemen, I think this is only the beginning. And I am supposed to tell you something. I'm going to quote you scripture meant for you now. It's from the New International version of the Bible. *Second Chronicles*, chapter seven, verse fourteen, *'If my people, who are called by my name, will humble themselves and pray and seek my face and confess their sins and turn from their wicked ways, then will I hear them from heaven, will forgive their sin, and will heal their land'" (2Chronicles 7:14).*

Adam returned the paper Tim had handed him, and then Adam told Tim to read what he had circled. Tim began to read. At first he read timidly and then he resonated loudly with love and authority, as understanding came over him, "All have sinned and fallen short of the glory of God. The wages of sin is death, eternal death. But God has provided a way out. He provided a gift, a free gift of eternal life in Jesus Christ. You must be born again," said Tim as he no longer read but said, "Jesus is the way to be born again. Jesus is the way, the truth, and the life." Tim continued, "Adam, I remember what was said to me years ago. Jesus is the only way. No one comes to the Father, but through the Son. Here is what you must do." Looking at the crowd of men, Tim nearly shouted, "You must confess with your mouth that Jesus is Lord. You must believe in your heart that although Jesus died, God raised him from the dead. Jesus paid the price for our sins, and he defeated death! If you believe in your heart and confess it with your mouth, then you will be saved."

Tears swelled in the eyes of the hardest of the men, and others nearly cried, even Red. Adam stood up, asked the men to close their eyes and bow their heads, and then spoke *John 3:16*. He invited all there to accept Jesus Christ as their savior. He said for them to raise their hands, if they had accepted Jesus, and he said he would not embarrass them but would contact them later to follow up on what they had just done. Then streams of tears flowed from Adam's eyes, as he said, "I wish I had been here to see it all."

Then Tim reminded Adam, "Don't forget he is headed your way. He walked from Denver to go to the church in Rock Creek." And Tim spoke loudly to all present, when he said, "Tonight is mid-week prayer meeting at Adam's church. Once, I went every Wednesday. I'm going tonight for the first time in probably ten years."

Next, from the kitchen the cook shouted, "Let's eat. I've got eggs, potatoes and pancakes, bacon and sausage all ready to go. Give your order to Tim and we'll get it out to you promptly. Adam, how about giving thanks for all of us."

Adam prayed and all assembled there at the Cozy Corner Café bowed their heads and listened reverently!

Conversation in the diner differed from the usual this morning. The customers talked about vacation Bible school experiences, Sunday school classes and teachers, summer camp under Uncle Paul and Aunt Mary Eiselstein at Camp Id-ra-ha-je in Bailey, Colorado. Some conversed about when they got married, how they chose a wife, and how God was working in their lives. Several remembered that Uncle Paul never forgot a camper's name and testified of how God was working in their lives. Many spoke about Saturday night Singspirations where churches had gathered together for hymn sings. Some confessed they knew nothing about Jesus, had never attended church, but were curious about what had happened. Also, they wanted to read what Tim was supposed to read. Adam took names and promised to get Bibles to those few. He said he wished there were a Christian bookstore in the valley as well as a Christian radio station, so that everyone could be blessed with Christ honoring music.

In honor of Adam's interpretation, Tim the waiter delivered Red and Adam's order first followed by a rapid distribution of everyone's meals. Two oldtimers pitched in to help Tim and the cook. Tim took the orders complete with table numbers, while the cook kept preparing food. The two oldtimers delivered the meals to the proper tables. Customers sorted out who got what at tables they shared with others. Meanwhile, Adam and Red made plans to flood their pasture land east of the hogbacks that partially surround the town of Jericho Springs, which hugs the mountains to the west part of the valley.

After finishing his breakfast, Red twisted the ends of his red mustache and said, "Okay, let me summarize. You open the first two flood gates starting from the south end and you crank it wide open until the field south of County Road 403 is fully irrigated. It will be the first to dry out. I do the same at the far north end to one flood gate. This should still allow ample water to flow downstream, so we don't negatively affect water pressure in Rock Creek."

"This will take most of the day to complete," clarified Adam.

"Then you and your wranglers will move the mountain herd down to the valley above Blair House near Ezra's saw mill, while I finish flooding the fields down toward folks in Rock Creek."

"Our pastures will continue to produce grass for the winter," added Adam, "and we'll be able to move the mountain herd down here at least a week earlier than usual."

"While you head for the mountains, my men will move your cattle from the pasture at Jericho Springs to the mesa and mine to my pastures on the ridge above the Rock Creek village," said Red.

"Too bad someone torched my trailer, we could have used it as a base to manage the herd," Adam said with a knowing smile.

"Anyway, Rabbit and Barney will lead my wranglers to winter the mountain herd in the pasture we flood," Red said, without acknowledging Adam's statement. He added, "I trust you already told the mayor and council in Jericho Springs that we are moving our herd earlier this year due to the bear?"

"They understood and had heard about the bear. They asked that we move the herd to my mesa and your ridge after school started today, so we can finish before school is out this afternoon," Adam said, and then added, "You are still welcomed to join me in the bear hunt, Red."

"Sorry, Adam, I know you think this is a tough situation, but I'll remain behind to take care of things here. Plus, you will have Pilgrim with you and you've got a gang of solid wranglers. It's not like you have greenhorns working with you. The bear won't have a chance. You will be all right, besides you need to get away for awhile," Red said with a grin breaking out over his face. "I suspect you will want to get back in time to help Karen Gustafson move into the Blair House, and I reckon you will take to heart the advice you just gave to my cousin, Tim McNaughton."

"Our cousin, Red, even if I remarry, and I'm not saying I have any plans, but you and the rest of the McNaughton clan will always be family to me."

"I'll count on that, Adam. We've been through a lot together. Thanks for working with Butch through all this mess with the Night Riders. Our hopes to have all the Blair Estate condemned and declared public domain, seem thwarted."

"I'm glad Butch has been cleared of the murder of Gloria Jones, but one question remains unanswered. Why did she have to die?"

"Don't know...but Adam... you know Butch still faces considerable charges, and Sheriff Bailey fired him. He really blew it when he attacked Deputy Candy and roughed up his girlfriend, Hannah. It's a wonder he is still alive after being shot twice in the back, even with a small caliber pistol. It's hard to believe another McNaughton shot him...and with your Karen's pistol."

"No matter how Butch treated Harper and his girlfriend, Hannah?"

"Don't forget Butch considered Hannah his girlfriend too."

"As well as Gloria Jones," said Adam, who then realized that the discussion had drifted into more sensitive territory and that Red had not answered his earlier question as to why Gloria had been murdered by Sam Gelding. "I reckon you do have your hands full, and I will help with Butch. I know you don't want to hear this, but I believe God is going to use all this to bring Butch back to right relationship with him, Red."

Red smiled and said, "And this is where you tell me that all things work for the good."

"For those who love the Lord," smiled Adam in return. "Red, I won't give up on Butch."

"Thanks, Adam, and I'll do all I can to prevent anything happening to you and yours again," Red earnestly promised. Then both paid Tim their bill at the cash register on the counter near the front door.

Adam told Tim, "You know you shared the Gospel this morning, Tim, and that is what you are supposed to be doing."

Tim nodded and said, "It really felt good. I feel like I'm home once again. Once I started reading what you circled on the paper, Adam, my memory kicked in and it just flowed out of my mouth."

Partners, Adam and Red left the café together, shook hands, hugged, and then parted company with each to do his part. Adam opened his August 24, 1980, copy of the local newspaper and began reading about the pending visit to the valley by a circus and a movie company. Red shouted back to Adam, "I really did see the men blocking the door! I really did, Adam! They wore cowls, as if they were monks or something. Someone said they thought they were angels standing guard!"

\*\*\*

Adam had shouted back to Red that he would see him soon at the pasture. Although plagued by the bear, Adam's nephew Butch and his partner and lifelong friend Red occupied his mind. His first thought focused on the Blair House in Jericho Springs, the primary town in Rock Creek Valley. Located at the base of the mountains on the edge of town, this three-story house stood prominently above other roof-tops in Jericho Springs and occupied half a city block. One dirt road from the west and one from the south converged with County Road 403 before it became Main Street through town. Two creeks merged at the confluence and brought not only two-thirds of the valley's water but also the water deposited gold along the creek beds. While Adam owned the water and mineral rights to the south creek, the wealth brought to the valley from the west creek belonged to who-ever owned the Blair House. Red had organized the McNaughton clan and he formed a corporation to gain the house and all its wealth by attempting to convince the city council to condemn the property. The plan almost worked until the son of the rightful owner appeared on the scene. Although thwarted, their effort to gain the wealth had not ended.

Adam's other thought focused on the activities of Red's son, Butch. Nearly a month earlier, a group, unofficially labeled the Night Riders, had initiated a plan to harass every newcomer in the valley. Their goal had been to motivate newcomers to leave the area prior to the Jericho Springs city council meeting. Since most of the Night Riders were related, they had been recruited secretly as an informal extension of the corporation. Under Red's leadership the corpora-tion had hoped to gain possession of the building, minerals, and water rights to what had been affectionately called the Blair House in Jericho Springs. Without making the connection of the Night Riders to the corporation, at first Adam had endorsed the corporation and had become a member, as his deceased wife was a McNaughton.

Next, before most had been arrested and jailed, members of the Night Riders had set fire to two of Adam's properties. They torched Adam's trailer on the ridge off highway 96. He had rented the trailer to the Bond family, newcomers to the area. Although Butch was a deputy sheriff, rumor had it that he had led the group in the arson as well as activity involving another of Adam's properties. Allegedly,

Butch led or had been involved in the theft and killing of little Andy Browning's ducks. Some of the Night Riders stole the ducks from a farm house that Adam had rented to Rob Browning, Andy's father. The group tossed Andy's ducks into a huge bonfire on Adam's property near Ridge View on the north end of County Road 403. Although both were new to the area, Rob and Ken not only regularly attended the church Adam pastored in Rock Creek, but also the men had participated in one of Adam Claymore's discipleship groups.

Both of these incidents led Adam to distance himself from the corporation when he became suspicious of its connection to the Night Riders. However, the clincher had been the corporation's efforts to coerce the Jericho Springs City Council to condemn the Blair House and make the land, mineral, and water rights available for public purchase. Although the rightful owner had taken possession of the property, the men of the corporation had continued to pressure the council to condemn the Blair House property.

Especially disheartening for Adam had been how readily the community accepted the rumor that his nephew had been the primary suspect in the murder of Gloria Jones. He knew Butch's life had been unraveling, but Adam struggled with the idea that Butch may well have killed her. Butch had attacked fellow deputy Cotton Candy after a school board meeting and had roughed up Hannah Rahab at the Stage Stop Hotel. Butch's abuse had extended to his Cousin Harper, who took revenge by shooting Butch twice in the back. Now Adam wondered what Red might be up to, so Adam prayed that God would do whatever necessary to bring Butch back to himself. While he prayed for grace and mercy, he asked that truth and justice would prevail.

After Adam's prayer, the image of Karen Gustafson flooded his mind. His countenance changed, and he thought about how her influence on him had brought joy to his lonely heart. She had only been in the valley a week, August 1-8, 1980, but Adam knew for the two weeks she had been gone he had pined for her embrace.

# More Divine Appointments

## CHAPTER 2

*"Be alert and of sober mind!"*                    *I Peter 5:8a*

John Mark's walk to Rock Creek had been buoyant. Shortly after leaving Ridge View, he had diverted his trek off US 85/87 when he saw that County Road 403 had a bridge where he could sit and repair his boots. Removing his boots he sat on a brick wall in the center of the bridge where he could gaze at the creek and pond below. At first he just worked on sizing the cardboard to match the inner sole of his left and then his right boot. Finishing, he took in the scene before him. A poetic spot like the Garden of Eden, he thought, a large pond filled by a creek flowing southward. Water held back at a waterfall seemed trapped in the pond as if a brick wall blocked its passage. Not stagnant, flowing water produced a slight roar as it steadily spilled over the barrier. Brush and logs of multiple sizes helped disguise the rock formation. Ample plant life provided a haven for amphibians and fish. John Mark spied bull frogs and trout amongst lily pads, but on the east side of the pond, a knoll had been charred. Sprouts of grass had only recently covered the blackened landscape, he predicted. He looked to the west and saw a farmhouse and barn with a garage. Coming out a doorway, a little boy ran with his dog. The boy's happy shouts and the dog's barking preceded a woman, probably the boy's mother, who had grabbed a broom and chased after both boy and dog. John Mark smiled as Mom had caught them and rolled with them on their meager lawn. Quickened, John Mark prayed for the family's safety and ministry.

Abandoning the county road and not returning to the Valley Highway, John Mark walked along the eastside of the creek bank for miles, until he had discovered another juncture. Nearly midway between Ridge View and the town Rock Creek, the creek converged with another more powerful waterway. He watched the confluence of water, as the more powerful one gradually diminished volume and rapidity. Waiting, he witnessed how the creek that he had followed from Ridge View now dominated the latter.

Curious he climbed above the creek to a highway bridge in time to watch the Sheriff's cruiser enter the Rock Creek village. Removing binoculars from his backpack, John Mark followed the path of the once forceful creek west to a tall elongated mound. A continuous vertical wall extended the mound. Continuing south he spied first one then two wranglers opening what John Mark presumed to be flood gates. Further south he spied a herd of Black Angus cattle being driven out of a pasture and onto a paved road that appeared to lead to a town at the entrance of a mountain valley. With his lariat a drover waved the cattle up another road toward a grand mesa, which extended from the mountains to US 85/87 just beyond the town south of where he stood. As the cattle left the pasture, two other drovers restored the fencing, mounted their horses, and trailed after the herd. Both men, who had opened the floodgates from the creek, parted in opposite directions, one an obvious red head, while the other looked like the actor in the Marlboro Man cigarette commercial. He looked tall in his saddle, spurs probably jingled, and a black Stetson hat graced his crown.

Unintentionally, John Mark looked above the town with his binoculars and caught a glimpse of the Live Oak that dominated the scene before him. It rose from a mound, perhaps a butte he thought, above houses below. He thought it had died until he watched a man and woman pour water from buckets, which they had hauled from somewhere below. John Mark watched as the man sat on a stump before the tree, while the woman sat on the man's lap. Watching them share a kiss, a smile crossed John Mark's face, as he hoped true love blessed both man and woman. Unknowingly, John Mark had discovered Blair House, as he followed the couple as far as he could see, until the house blocked view of them. Quickened, he prayed for the couple and for whatever God had planned for them. He prayed for the house and those that might reside there.

Next, John Mark turned around, faced east, and saw waterways had not only combined at this juncture, but also roadways connected here as well. US 85/87 united with state highway 96, which ended and formed a T. South of Colorado Highway 96, he located the town of Rock Creek, while Ridge View appeared to the north of 96. But what, he wondered, is east where the highway breaks the horizon. As a result, he walked east on 96 toward its crest. He enjoyed the woodland creatures he discovered along the highway including a skunk, which he escaped, a fox in pursuit of a groundhog, and deer resting amongst tall grasses in the shade of deciduous and pine trees. Once on top the roadway at its crest, sadness overcame him. He had discovered remains of another fire. A burnt-out trailer blighted the scene before him and beyond. Another trailer, across the road from the first, appeared dark, lonely, and forgotten were it not for the station wagon parked in the driveway. John Mark marveled at the contrasting scene he viewed with the valley below. Here was loneliness and destruction, while below the ridge behind him appeared to be a thriving setting bordered by mountains to the west, a great mesa to the south, and the ridge on the east. Quickened again, John Mark prayed for those who once lived in the burnt trailer. He asked what had happened would be turned to good, as God had promised for those who were believers. Also, he prayed for the safety of those living in the lonely trailer that remained. With resolve, he continued his journey to Rock Creek and the Church in the Glen.

Rejoining the Valley Highway, John Mark followed pavement to two more tall and elongated mounds with rock walls protruding nearly eight feet above each. The backside of the mound to his left appeared to curl from the highway before the ridge toward the east. Cattails marked the boundary of marshland. He noted a pathway led from behind the mound to the ridge above him, a ridge that had begun outside Ridge View and continued beyond the town before him. The ridge helped create a canyon beginning at the far end of the town. Not only had the highway and creek passed between the mounds, but also the town's water supply stood stored in a tower upon stilts on the south end of the left mound.

Once crossing between the mounds, the creek closely followed the mound on the right, while highway 85/87 passed directly through the little town of Rock Creek. As had been his habit before entering a town, John Mark felt quickened to pray for his own safety against temptation, especially where sin once held a foothold. He shuddered at the thought of succumbing to sin of the past, like a dog returning to its vomit. Confessing his flaw in prayer, he sought protection, wisdom, and discernment. Reminded that he traveled in the full armor of a believer, he proceeded to stride between the two elongated mounds with vertical walls of rock extending skyward from both like a fortress. Suddenly, an old yellow jeep passed him. It carried two rather large men wearing hooded garments, like cowls that monks wear. John Mark watched as the jeep passed through the town and into the canyon traveling south on the highway.

Wind from the canyon brought a sudden chill as John Mark continued walking. He scanned the scene before him, and then entered the town with courage and boldness. To the left, level plain extended a short distance from the highway to the mounds, and then south to rear yards of two houses. A street sign designated what John Mark imagined would be a row of houses on each side of a short street leading from the highway east to the ridge. Beyond the street and the first house, south of the street, he saw what appeared to be three business buildings. Behind the houses and the businesses stood an imposing three story building, which he guessed to be either an apartment house or a hotel. Beyond the three story building, he imagined a parking lot, and then he spotted a grove of trees marking the mouth of a canyon where the highway left the town. Surprised, a gentle wind captivated him as the chilled air mingled with the fragrance of roses. Stunned, chilled fragrance entered his nostrils, tickled their follicles, and dreamily occupied his sinuses. Senses heightened, whimpering like a siren's soft plea beckoned John Mark from the other side of the highway.

Although he had safely entered the stronghold of Rock Creek left of the highway, he had seen little more than the slope of the mound right of the road and the rock wall above it. He had heard her whimpering and the caw of a crow now circled above him. While the crow called harshly, the woman sounded soft, frightened, and vulnerable, as she plead for help. Conflicted, he knew where God was active, evil forces also battled. Was she a snare to dissuade him from his mission, or was she genuinely in need of help?

Multiple sparrows and wrens chased the crow to the water tower above the mound on the left. With trepidation, he crossed over to the right side of the highway and followed the whimpering sounds to the creek, which no longer flowed significantly enough to wash heartily through its channel. At first he did not see her reclining on the log, which extended from the east bank to the center of the creek. Afternoon shadows cloaked her, and he could not clearly see her. Again she whimpered a mournful sound from the shadows where she lay.

Nervously, John Mark attempted humor with first contact, and said with Gaelic accent, "Hello there! Are you a pixie, a sprite, or a fairy?"

"More a sprite than a pixie, more a fairy than a sprite, but alas more Queen Mab than all three," she said as she turned on her side toward him, and continued, "my guess is you cannot clearly see me or you would recognize that I am little more a nymph than a teen, much less a matron but completely a spinster. Are you Lancelot? Will you break my heart, too? Have you come to rescue me? I am sooo very lonely."

"Dear Lady," John Mark said, as he moved down from the highway to the bottom of the creek bank and into the shadows, for he had given in initially to her lure, "I am not Lancelot, but I am here out of obedience. What is your name? Are you Morgan La Fey or are you the Lady of Shallot?"

"Perhaps I am neither, or one or the other, or both. Since you are not Lancelot, I do not want to be the Lady of Shallot, but if you are Arthur and I am Morgan La Fey, then you are in danger. My druthers would be for me to be the Lady of Shallot, especially since I have found you or you have found me. My ending would possibly be a beginning due to your rescue."

"Correct me if I am wrong, but that would make you the Princess Elaine and your father King Pelinore. Dear Lady who truly are you? What is your name? Where do you live?"

"I am called Misty. I do live hidden away where I live in isolation."

"How is it you are here just now?"

"I have escaped for a little while."

"Where did you come from?"

"My grandmother was a MacNaughten. She is buried in the cemetery behind the little Church in the Glen at the mouth of the canyon to the right of the highway. If you go there, you will see her tombstone marked Cristabel MacNaughten. There are many McNaughtons buried there in the Rock Creek Cemetery, but she was not of a clan born here, nor did she marry. My grandmother came over from the old country. For my safety, I'm told to go by McNaughton," explained Misty.

"Are you in trouble? Do you truly want to be rescued?"

"I am and I will be if they find me here, if they find me with you."

"How can I help?" he said as he waded to her.

"Please kind Sir, carry me to the shore without allowing my gown to become wet."

He waded into the shallow water to take her in his arms and carry her safely to the creek bank. The tone of her soothing voice numbed his senses, and her fragrance quickly replaced the pleasant scent of roses, but her scent was more enthralling. It was only as he carried her through the water that he realized she was more a woman than a teen. She embraced him and clung to him not just for safety but also in search of genuine affection. As he placed her on the creek bank, she slid slowly down from his arms, but found his lips and lingered there. Stunned, John Mark's knees buckled and he fell backward into the water. Fortunately, his backpack remained on the creek bank where he had removed it from his shoulders.

"Alas," John Mark said, as Misty offered her hand to him, which he grasped and felt her flesh caress his own. "My Lady, tell me truly, how is it you are here?"

"If only you would continue to think of me as a lady, after you hear my story."

"Then do not tell me now, but come to the prayer meeting tonight six o'clock at the Church in the Glen, and all will be made right," he promised.

"I am trapped, but I will try. I really want to be rescued. I want your help, and if you are on a mission from the God of the people at the Church in the Glen, then you give me hope! Please...rescue me! Please do not be disappointed with me."

Caught in the breeze, her long tresses enveloped his arms, chest, neck, and face, while her scent wafted to his nostrils once again, "M'Lady, it is I who desires to please you...but where do you live?"

"I live at the Asherah House Bed and Breakfast. I have always lived there."

"Misty! Where are you?" someone called out.

"Will they hurt you?"

"Not physically. I serve too great a purpose for them, but please, you must stay hidden, until I have gone down the street," Misty said.

"As you wish," he said reluctantly.

"You will be at the prayer meeting...you won't leave me here. Will you, Farm Boy?"

"No, Misty, as God is my witness, I will be at the prayer meeting. That is where I am supposed to be tonight. By God's grace, I will help you," John Mark Cannikin promised.

"Till then, John Mark...you are very handsome!"

"Till then, my lady," he said, as once again the scent of her perfumed body lingered on his clothing and in the air around him, but then he thought oh, Lord what have I done, what just happened. Help me, Jesus!

Smitten, enthralled, captivated, plagued, bewitched, and enchanted, John Mark wondered if he had been both cursed and spellbound or blessed. Disoriented and distracted, he walked along the west side of the highway past an open field, which once had been a parking lot for football games at a former high school. Hardly noticing the dilapidated field, he passed by the school building, bus barn, post office, and stood waiting at the crossroads in the parking lot of a volunteer fire department. Directly across the street John Mark noticed a convenience store, while he waited for one automobile to turn left off the highway and onto County Road 403 toward Jericho Springs.

The lovely woman driver of a late model sedan waved at John Mark as she passed by, but he failed to respond. He crossed the street, passed by the convenience store, paused at the second of four houses, then walked across a driveway leading to Church in the

Glen, and nearly passed through a glen of trees before the mouth of the canyon. Stopping at a guard rail where the creek became part of the canyon, he turned to the right and entered the grove of white birch trees. On the other side of the creek, tendrils from red rose bushes climbed the mesa wall, and their fragrance further captivated and stimulated him to visualize Misty, smell her fragrance, and feel her embrace. Cool canyon breezes engulfed him. Mist from cold water rose from a stream, which emptied into the canyon from the mesa above it, cloaked and chilled him. Senses restored, John Mark sought a place to pitch his lightweight tent out of sight from both the highway and church parking lot. He needed a nap.

On the edge of the creek, John Mark found a suitable site near a foot bridge that provided shelter from the elements and passers-by. Promptly, he pitched his tent, unrolled his bedroll on the floor of the tent, but decided not to change his clothes and explore the graveyard. Instead, he removed his wet clothing and climbed into his dry bedroll. Before falling asleep, he thought about the day, the event at the Cozy Corner Café, his walk to Rock Creek including his stop at the bridge on CR 403 and the pond there, his trek along the creek to the confluence of two creeks and two roads, discovering the burned out trailer on highway 96, his discovery of the cowboys opening flood gates and herding cattle, and then he paused. John Mark knew he had been moonstruck, as he remembered he had walked boldly between the elongated mounds before entering the town of Rock Creek. Had it been a divine moment? A revelation about himself or his mission? Was it meant to remind him of whom he had been...to humble him? Was it an introduction to his mission, the nature of the battle? Mostly, he remembered Misty's whimpering, the sight of her, her embrace, and her kisses, especially her kisses, scent, and her touch. He breathed in, and all his strength left him, as his long walk from Denver had extracted its toll from him. As he slipped into sleep, John Mark wondered why Misty had been concerned that he would possibly be disappointed in her. Even more, he wondered about the coming prayer meeting and what God had in store for him, and then he heard the voice within his mind speak to him. He clearly heard he was to lead her into God's kingdom and into the righteousness found in Christ Jesus. There was no mistaking what he must do, John Mark thought, I must commit myself toward Misty's salvation and not act on desires of my flesh. He prayed for self-control to keep his lust in check. He confessed his weakness and asked for God to protect his witness. John Mark requested the Holy Spirit have pity and intercede for Misty, so she would gain her eternal reward.

***

Meanwhile, the woman driver, a lovely blue eyed blonde, who had waved at John Mark, drove west on County Road 403 toward Jericho Springs. At first she had been distracted by his wet clothing. She remembered the last person she had seen wearing wet clothes near the intersection of CR 403 and US 85/87 had turned out to be Izzy, the man now in charge of restoring Blair House. She remembered they had arrived in the valley on the same bus, that he immediately had waded into the creek with his clothes on, and then boarded the bus sopping wet. More important, his real name happened to be Ezra Freedom, Jr. His father, Ezra Sr., rightfully owned the Blair House and the mountain valley west of Jericho Springs, which included valuable mineral and water rights. Although Ezra Jr. had been raised by Paul and Lydia Blair, they were his guardians and not his parents. His father had gone to the Vietnam War, had not returned, and was believed to be dead. When Ezra Jr., nicknamed Izzy, found out he had been raised by the Blair's under an agreement with his father, Izzy had felt betrayed and ran away. Heartbroken the Blair's had spent a small fortune trying to locate Izzy to no avail and had died without finding him. Finally, the family lawyer, John Law, managed to unearth Izzy teaching at a university and persuaded him to return to the Rock Creek Valley and lead a group in the restoration of Blair House. Law had informed Izzy that he must arrive without detection, as oldtimers sought to have the Blair House estate declared public domain. A prominent clan had organized a corporation whereby all clan members would gain a share of the wealth. Meanwhile, part of the clan formed an informal group, unofficially titled the Night Riders, to run off all newcomers with hopes that a rightful owner of the property would not attempt to lay claim to the property, the house, water, and gold. The Jericho Springs City Council decided not

24

to declare the house and lands public domain when Izzy successfully organized a group to begin restoring the Blair House under the direction of lawyer John Law. They took possession of the property. As she drove her 1971 Chevy Nova toward the Blair House, she thought how remarkable all of this had happened in one short week.

Even more remarkable, thought the driver, Karen Gustafson, had been her role in what had happened. She had arrived there at the intersection on a bus from Quail Point, a neighboring town south of the canyon. She had come to town early to interview for a teaching position, and because she was a newcomer, she endured considerable harassment primarily at the Stage Stop Hotel where she stayed. At a school board meeting, she had received a one year contract to teach physical science and social studies at the local high school pending the return of another teacher, Jill Lowenstein. How strange, she thought, that she had been delighted when Jill returned. The contract provided for that circumstance. With Jill's return Karen's assignment changed for her to be a substitute teacher at regular teacher salary and to manage a special project for the school district and the city of Jericho Springs. Her assignment included her interviewing community leadership to find out whom they identified as leaders and what they believed were community problems and resources to solve those problems. Perhaps more significant, Karen speculated, had been that she had met another man immediately after disembarking the bus in Rock Creek. He became Karen's hero, when he rescued her from the Night Riders.

Local pastor, chair of the school district accountability committee, rancher, and all around good-guy, Adam Claymore, Karen thought, reminded her of both the man in the Marlboro cigarette commercial and Clayton Moore, the actor who played the Lone Ranger in the popular television show. Like the Lone Ranger, Adam had sought to make right that which was wrong, to use his might for what was right, and to protect women and insure their proper treatment. Adam had the reputation of being a stickler for proper behavior and for above board action by those in leadership roles. In a word, Adam was dependable. His yes meant yes and his no meant no. Although nearly bald on top, Karen thought, he had lived up to his reputation as the best of the eligible men in the valley despite his age, for he was a widower and at least ten years older than she. Besides, she remembered as her hand touched her lips, the memory of his lips upon her own lingered, and frankly, she wanted more of his lips upon hers. Karen longed to see Adam, before she continued her trip to Denver. She would pack her possessions stored at her parent's home in the Colorado Springs area, specifically Fountain, and then attend a workshop on the Leadership Identification Process that she was going to implement in the Rock Creek Valley when not substitute teaching. How interesting, Karen thought, as she wondered how many would indentify Adam Claymore as an important leader in the valley.

"Whoa," said Karen, as she let her automobile glide to a stop, while she watched the horseman ride his mount from floodgate to floodgate. Setting the emergency brake, she put the automatic transmission in park and turned off the ignition switch. She watched him briefly and noted what she knew about Adam Claymore. Physically, he was muscular from hard work, handsome in a manly way and not at all a pretty boy. His kind eyes had searched her own to find her inner-self. Balding with a friar's ring around the crown of his head, a wisp of hair on top enhanced his charm. Spiritually, she thought, he's not at all mean but is compassionate. Although strong, he had revealed an inner need for healing of the heart.

She opened the door, climbed out, and walked around the rear to the barbwire fence, where she whistled as loudly as she could. Karen shouted, "Hey, Mister, do you know where a woman in distress can find a dependable man to give her a hand?"

At her whistle, Adam's horse neighed and reared on its hind legs, and then Adam turned the mare toward Karen, as the mare broke into a trot toward her. In moments, Adam had dismounted and stepped between the strands of barbwire, and hugged her. Eagerly, he said to Karen, "How good it is to see you. It seems like you have been gone for months instead of two weeks."

"And I you, Mr. Man," Karen replied softly, as she gently touched then took hold of his hands, "You are a handsome sight on horseback!"

"And you are like an angelic vision with your blond hair gently blowing across your face," Adam smiled and said, "My partner, Red, and I have been moving our Angus herd to the mesa, so we can move our mountain herd down here. Once on the mesa, we cull out the steers and corral them for market. Our bulls are already up there waiting for the ladies to arrive. The calves will have a year on the mesa...I love when the tone of your voice seems to caress me and now how the touch of your hands give way to mine and envelop mine with your soft skin."

"That must be quite a trip to drive them down to here," Karen added as her hands tightened on his and her pale skin flushed to a pinkish hew on her face, and she added, "Sometime I would like to help you..."

"I need your help...and I realize you are capable of hard work, but I'm quite certain I would not change the softness of your hands. You help me...inspire me a lot...actually, we drive the cattle down to the mountain valley above Blair House, where the young will be branded, tagged, and castrated. That will take several days, and we want them to feed on the hay in those fields before coming down here. My men will be able to pick up any stragglers, while we are branding," Adam said as his eyes focused on her lips.

"Just asking because I'm interested, why not brand before you drive them to the meadows above Blair House?"

"Normally, we would. Karen, there is trouble on the mountain. An unusual bear is killing off calves. He or she is mean, kills to kill, and leaves the dead without eating. I've never seen anything like it. I'm likely going to have to kill the bear, and it is a big one. Rabbit saw its tracks and he said it is bad medicine. We will need to be very careful with it," Adam said breaking the mood.

"Will it follow the herd?"

"That might happen."

"Adam, please be careful. Can't your men do it for you?'

Startled at the suggestion, Adam said, "It's kind of the law of the land. My herd, my job."

"What about Red? Is he going with you?"

"I asked, but he is not able."

"So...why are you flooding this pasture?"

"Well, the Angus herd has done a good job on the grass here, and the herd that I'm bringing here will need feed for awhile. We've been cutting and baling hay all summer on Ezra's pasture, my pastures on the mesa, and Red's on the ridge. It is a struggle to have enough every winter, which is why I stacked so many bales across the road near my orchard. So...each year, we flood this area after Labor Day to grow one last crop, then we bring the herd down here. We're early, so I had to flood today. I leave tomorrow."

"Tomorrow?"

"Yes, I'm so glad you happened to see me in the field and stopped. You are back and I wanted to talk with you before I go."

"Same here, Adam, but I leave for Denver tomorrow to attend a workshop on the community study, which will allow me to pack and bring my furniture here. My parents will pull a trailer filled with all I have."

"Will you call the ranch when you arrive? I would like to meet them, if it's all right with you."

"Absolutely, thank you for asking. I have told them some about you."

"Really?"

"Yes, that you are a combination of Boaz, the Lone Ranger, Don Quixote, and Mr. Wonderful."

"That being the case, it is time for me to properly court you. May I?"

"You may, kind Sir. I would be disappointed if you did not want to."

"Then may I kiss, you."

"Please," Karen said softly, as she moved closer to Adam, rose on her tip toes, and leaned into him with a kiss that weakened his knees. Both parted misty eyed.

"Will you meet me for dinner after tonight's prayer meeting? I have something to share with you," Adam nearly begged.

"Absolutely, Mr. Wonderful!" Karen said, as she walked toward her automobile, "I have much to share with you too. I have some great news! Besides I need to see Sarah at the hotel. I promised to meet with her when I got back. It is important for me to continue to encourage and pray for her."

"I like your ride. Where have you had this?" asked Adam.

"Quail Point, at the garage there. I had it serviced and put on new tires, while I was here interviewing. It's a four door 1971 Chevy Nova with a 140 horse power Turbo-Thrift 250 cubic inch straight six engine. It has a Powerglide two-speed automatic transmission."

"Power brakes and windows?"

"No, Sir, those are manual, but it has fine upholstery on a bench seat and rubber floor mats with hand crank windows and an AM radio."

"I like the powder blue," said Adam.

"Me, too! Other than that it is a plain Jane," smiled Karen, as she opened the door to leave, but rushed back to Adam and gave him a quick kiss. "See you later, Mr. Wonderful."

All Adam could do was grin! What he thought was something else, when he said thank you to the Lord.

Again, Karen paused before sitting down inside her Chevy Nova, "I don't know why, but something just came to mind that I think you should know."

"What's that, I could continue this all day!"

"I just remembered seeing someone I haven't seen before in town...as I was turning onto 403; a man was waiting for me to pass by. He was on foot heading south."

"Was he carrying a backpack?"

"Yes and his clothes were all wet, like Izzy when I first saw him enter the valley."

"Did you see where he went?"

"No, I waved and kept driving here...where I found you."

"Good timing, I just finished flooding south of 403 and opened up the gates further north. A couple of minutes later I would have been gone for awhile," Adam paused, and then said, "and you said he was crossing the street."

"Probably to go to the convenience store on the corner."

"Maybe, but if he is who I think he is, then he was headed for the church. I need to meet him there," Adam said as he opened the makeshift wire gate to the pasture.

"Then you better hurry. If he continued walking, he is either at the church or has walked into the canyon. If he has entered the canyon, he couldn't have gone too far. Who is he, Adam?"

"Reinforcements," Adam shouted, as he mounted his mare, "God has sent reinforcements. I'll tell you tonight."

***

Relishing opportunity to talk personally with the man God had used to cause the gospel to be share with the crowd at the Cozy Corner Café in Ridge View, Adam spurred his beloved mare. Cantering, they promptly covered the miles between his pasture bordering West Rock Creek and the hogbacks just west of the town of Rock Creek. Slowing to a trot before the bridge over the Rock Creek, Adam halted the mare, then descended the county road and walked his horse along a path west of the creek. He slapped his chaps with his Stetson to rid himself of dust collected from the ride. While the mare panted from the exertion, Adam's excitement doubled as he saw a man standing on the footbridge behind the church cemetery.

Hearing horse and rider approaching him, John Mark turned to face the rider, as Adam dismounted his mare and looped his reins around the top rail of the footbridge. John Mark spoke first, "I hope you are the pastor of the Church in the Glen. I have had a long walk to come here to meet you."

"And you are John Mark, I presume."

"Why yes, I am," said John Mark, "how…"

"I joined my friends at the Cozy Corner Café shortly after you left there this morning," informed Adam, "and you created quite a stir, by God's grace."

"Indeed, what happened?"

"People in the crowded parking lot had waited for you to leave before entering the café. They said two very large men blocked the door while you were inside."

"Really, if they were there, I didn't tell them to block the entrance," John Mark said with a smile.

"I'm not surprised," Adam said, "and the crowd asked me to interpret what had happened. I asked Timothy to explain and he told them that you had talked with him about God and had told him to read some scripture. He said you promised to return sometime and check to see what he thought about what he had read. Then he handed me a paper titled the Ambassador's Toolkit. I circled key phrases and had Tim read them to the crowd. At first he just read *John 3:16* and the next few phrases, but then, he paused and remembered years earlier when he had accepted Jesus as his Savior and Lord. Tim recited the rest from memory, as he smiled and began to beam."

"So he did share the paper I gave him. I wish I had been there!"

"John Mark, you planted the seed and Timothy shared the good news. I had the pleasure of the harvest. A couple of men accepted Christ."

Tears glistened in their eyes, and John Mark said, as his hazel eyes twinkled emerald green, "More are coming. God told me to walk here from Denver. I walked a path to the top of the mesa and sat on a bench up there and prayed."

"That's where my deceased wife went to pray..."

"I'm sorry she died...I am supposed to help you, the pastor of the Church in the Glen in the town of Rock Creek. I'm supposed to help someone else too. Pastor, revival is coming, and where God is active, there is already opposition. Am I right?"

"Yes, life here has often been like a circus, but this morning was a divine moment."

"So is this," said John Mark. "I am a simple carpenter, Pastor, what can I do for you?"

"I am a deacon and interim pastor. You are a carpenter?"

"Yes, it is my trade, I am also a cup bearer," John Mark said, while remembering he had dreamed about a circus coming to the valley.

"How long will you be here?"

"Until God tells me to move on, so let's see what God has in store for this valley."

Adam turned and pointed toward his Rock Creek house, "The third house up the highway is one of my houses. I need to get it ready for a permanent pastor to come here and live in it. The garage there is about to fall down. The house is out of date and needs repair. It needs a back porch, and I need to re-open the second bedroom. If you want to, I will pay you what you ask to fix up both garage and house for a new pastor to come and serve at the little Church in the Glen. You can live in the house, while you do the work."

"Well, the prospect of not having to sleep out of doors in my tent is certainly welcomed. I can do plumbing and electrical work, too."

"You have walked here from Denver and you've been sleeping in a tent along the way."

"Yes, as a matter of fact, I set it up in the glen beyond the parking lot. I took a nap there before I climbed to the top of the mesa to pray. I hope it is all right."

"If you will do the remodeling work, I will pay you an hourly wage, provide you sleeping quarters, and I'll stock the freezer and pantry for you to use. Deal?" Adam asked, as he reached his hand to John Mark, who grasped and shook it.

"Deal, and by God's grace I'll be able to finish according to God's plan and time," John Mark said. "There is more He has told me to do."

"I'm pretty certain, I know part of it. You can go to the mesa whenever you want. It is a good place to pray!"

"Really, what part do you think that is?"

"If you come to prayer meeting tonight, it will be clarified for you."

"That is part of why I am here, Adam. I'm supposed to come here and deliver a message to a woman named Elaine, perhaps it is Elizabeth. Could you introduce me to her tonight?"

"Elaine?" Adam said, as he sorted through his memory of the attendees, "I don't remember anyone named Elaine. Since the Lord told you to deliver a message to her, and I assume you mean tonight, then she will be here. Perhaps she will eventually show up, while you are working on the parsonage."

"Perhaps, but I believe it will be tonight," John Mark, paused, then continued, "and there's more. Adam, I've done my share of hunting, mostly for deer and elk, where I have come upon bear scat. Are their bears on the mesa?"

"Black bear, my wranglers keep track of the property pretty well."

"Is it your property?"

"Yes, the entire mesa is mine all the way to Wolf City, to the base and over the mountain to the outskirts of a ghost town called Pryor, then back to Jericho Springs, and the valley between Jericho Springs and the hogback around this little town."

"You are blessed. You may want to look along the trail to the top of the mesa. I sat on the bench on top to pray over the valley."

"Thank you," replied Adam, "you are fretting, John Mark, what's bothering you?"

"I've stood here for fifteen or more minutes watching the effect of decreased water flowing down stream."

32

"That's because I've opened the floodgates west of my pasture behind us," Adam said, as he pointed toward Jericho Springs to the west.

"While I was walking, I stopped and used my binoculars to look at the mountains and the valley. I saw you and a man with bright red hair, as you opened the floodgates earlier this afternoon," John Mark said, then asked, "Is he friend or foe?"

"Interesting you would ask...I'm related to the redhead by marriage. He is Red McNaughton, and he and I partner on some things, but not on others."

"Well, Adam, as I stood here on the bridge looking into the water, the force of the whirlpool south of us let something rise to the top. I couldn't tell for sure what's down there, but it looks like the body of an animal, I think, a good sized animal."

"Where?" Adam asked urgently, "Describe where you saw it."

John Mark pointed to the whirlpool where it was clear that the water still held a body, which had risen to the surface. When John Mark started for it, Adam held him back and said, "Stop, John, this is now a crime scene. The body is probably Sam Gelding, the local insurance agent. He has been missing for a couple of weeks. Keep your eye on the body, while I call the Sheriff," ordered Adam, who rushed to the church and opened the pastor's office where he called for Sheriff Bailey.

When Deputy Cotton Candy answered the telephone and identified herself, Adam said, "Cotton, this is Adam Claymore. A body just rose to the surface in the creek behind the Rock Creek church. Send an ambulance and have the coroner ready to examine the body. It may be Sam Gelding."

"Adam, you have prayer meeting tonight. Keep everyone off the footbridge and away from the creek. We will be there post haste," Candy said, and then she barked out orders and went to her cruiser in the parking lot, where she called the sheriff as she sped toward Rock Creek.

Adam returned to the footbridge, led his mare across the bridge, and walked with John Mark away from the crime scene. John Mark and Adam prayed for Sam and his family, while waiting for the deputies to arrive. As soon as deputies had arrived, they pulled the body from the creek and found Sam Gelding's wallet in the pants pocket. There was no other quick way to determine the identity of the body as it had been underwater for several weeks. After John Mark had been interviewed by Deputy Candy, Adam escorted him to Adam's Rock Creek house, so John could examine the work he would be doing.

Sam Gelding, insurance agent to both the school board and city council, husband of Mara the high school secretary, and murder suspect, had been found. Deputy Candy asked the corner to determine not only the cause of Sam's death, but also to declare whether or not his death was by accident, suicide, or foul play, if possible.

# Moving into Blair House

## CHAPTER 3

*"... everyone whose heart God* had moved – prepared to go up and build the house of the Lord in Jerusalem." Ezra 1:5b and c

Rounding the corner of County Road 403 where it intersected with two dirt roads, Karen paused to think about the two roads not taken. While CR 403 continued to the right and passed through town north to US 85/87, the dirt road to the left crossed over Claymore Flats to Wolf City. Like Jericho Springs, Wolf City sat where a creek flowed out of the mountains into a valley. While the north fork of Rock Creek flowed through Ridge View and the west fork through Jericho Springs, the south fork passed through Wolf City. The north fork of Rock Creek joined with the west fork just north of the town of Rock Creek, while the south fork continued east where it merged with the water from the north and west forks at Quail Point. Jericho Springs sat on the northeast side of the Spanish Peaks, while Wolf City sat at the base of Mt. Huajatolla, the south side of Spanish Peaks. The rivalry between the two towns had been bitter primarily due to high school athletics. At one time or another, both had to go through the other to gain the league championship in basketball or football for the boys' teams and basketball and volleyball for girls' teams. Wolf City dominated track and field competition, while Jericho Springs excelled regularly in baseball. Both competed against Quail Point High School, where Karen had taught physical science last year. Fortunately, Karen would no longer be concerned about any rumors following her, because she had been vindicated and offered another position, if she would return there.

Instead, Karen Gustafson had signed the contract to teach at Jericho Springs High School. Since Jill Lowenstein did in fact return to her position, Karen's one year contract assigned her to be a permanent substitute teacher and manager of a project to identify community leadership. She fully understood the tenure process and had been informed that a social studies teacher had notified the school district offices of her plan to retire at the end of the school year. Karen felt comfortable with the assignment, as it would provide her time to be courted by Adam Claymore, the man who owned Claymore Flats. The road to the left travelled over his land all the way to the outskirts of Wolf City.

Although Karen turned to the right and followed CR 403, she could have driven due west and followed a dirt road into the mountain valley. The road into the mountains already had been significant to her. It looped behind the Blair House as the road ascended the slope of the land beside where West Rock Creek exited the mountains. Earlier she had stopped at the hairpin turn above the Blair House with her friend Ruth Browning and Ruth's son Andrew. The three of them had made the trip up the mountain road to explore what remained of the Live Oak, which stood upon a volcanic butte. The tree had been planted next to an oddity. When the pressure that caused the lava flow halted and recessed, a plug was formed as the lava cooled. The plug recessed downward and created a circular indenture on top of the butte. Thermally heated water seeped into the indenture and formed a hot pool, which eventually had been enjoyed by many bathers. At one time the hot water had been piped below to the Blair House, where it had been used as part of an elaborate but inconsistent heating system. Unfortunately, a rock slide struck the butte and cracked its west side, which altered the flow of the thermally heated water. The pool dried, the water pipes removed, and the heating system dismantled. Although the climb down from the road had been difficult, Karen, Ruth, and Andy found it well worth the effort. While the three explored the volcanic butte named Little Huerfano, each of the three explorers had an encounter with God as they looked upon the scene Ezra Sr. had carved on the north side of the tree.

Ezra Freedom Sr. had been living in a cabin in the mountains. He made his living by cutting wood. Some wood he chopped and delivered as firewood, while other wood he carved and whittled, and then sold as local art. Ezra had a dream, and he transferred his dream onto the Live Oak's bark and outer layer of pulp. As he whittled and carved, Izzy's father created a scene of a naked man standing before a globe on a pedestal. Behind and right of the globe stood four figures dressed in black. Left of the figures stood a giant of a tree. The tree offered one apple that the naked man chose to reach for and pick from the tree. Directly above the tree was a large sunflower. While the sunflower stem extended below and into the earth, its roots disappeared under the earth's surface, perhaps to the bowels below. Behind the sunflower appeared a pair of scissors. At the top of the scene were scissor handles that became a hand as they came closer to the earth. Left of the scissors and sunflower was carved a choir of many figures, which apparently were singing.

At first the scene appeared disturbing to Karen, Ruth, and Andy, until its meaning became apparent to them like it had to others. The man was everyman, man and woman alike. Each had choices. Decisions were required, and the man risked making the wrong choice by taking the apple from the tree. Forces of good and evil awaited the man's decision, while the hand of God had control of the circumstances. When the hand of God became flesh and blood, the Son of God would forever dominate the scene. Independently, each of the three onlookers prayed about what they should do in response to the decision that they had already made to accept Jesus as their Lord and Savior. And God had chosen to reveal his plan to them at the base of the Live Oak tree.

Decades earlier, Ezra Sr.'s choice in response to his circumstances had been to trust the upbringing of his child to two kindly folk, who were to raise his son and benefit from his estate while he went off to war. When the son learned he was not the couple's child, he felt he had been deceived and abandoned by his mother and father. Ezra Jr. decided to run away. Much later he learned his real mother had died in an automobile accident before his father went to war. His father, held captive, could not return. The couple who had raised him had died looking for him. Now, the child had returned home to rebuild his family home, and so had his father. Restoration, redemption, and forgiveness had been accomplished through their reunion. They knew what they were to do. Blair House would be restored to its one-time greatness, both as a dwelling place and as a beacon shining into the darkness that prevailed in the valley.

Karen responded to her encounter with God at the tree by accepting the position in Jericho Springs. Although it eventually meant she would be a full time substitute teacher, the position also required her to manage a project that had the potential of mobilizing community leadership and resources in solving community problems. Additionally, she signed on at the Blair House with a team of other believers to help restore the building and lands in exchange for food and lodging. Also, she decided to work part time either making or delivering pizza at the local pizzeria, which was managed by Jerry Sunday, a fellow boarder at the Blair House.

The dirt road leading into the mountains had been significant to Karen for another reason. Foolishly, Karen had not listened to Adam Claymore's wise advice after an inspirational Wednesday night prayer meeting at the little Church in the Glen in Rock Creek. Adam had urged her to accept his offer to stay at his ranch, because both a murderer and a local thug plotted vengeance on newcomers to the valley. Instead Karen had stayed at Adam's house in Rock Creek and had walked up the trail to the grand mesa where she prayed over the city. On her way back to Adam's house on US 85/87, she was accosted by a horrible man on the footbridge by the cemetery behind the little Church in the Glen. Fortunately for her, Izzy's father had promised to watch over those who were returning to their homes from the prayer meeting. He caught her assailant on the foot bridge before he could assault her. In the midst of the battle between the two men, Karen's head struck a bridge rail which knocked her out. Her assailant had been vanquished and tossed over the side of the bridge and into the waters below. Neither Karen nor Ezra Sr. had seen what had become of the man. Her bleeding from a scalp wound and lying unconscious in a pool of blood on the ground, Ezra carried her to safety at his mountain cabin, which is located up the mountain road and into the valley above the Blair House. Although she later identified her assailant as Sam Gelding, the local insurance salesman and husband of the secretary of the high school principal, his whereabouts remained unknown to his wife, the sheriff, and the entire community. Karen would travel up the mountain road again, but for now her memories of her travels were limited to her rescue from the clutches of an evildoer and to her encounter with God at the base of Freedom's tree.

As Karen completed her turn, county road 403 also became Main Street in Jericho Springs. Karen stopped at the Jericho Springs Convenience Store primarily to greet Mike Crowfoot, the store clerk, but also she wanted a candy bar. At first she could not locate Mike, as he had been restocking the cooler, but when he came out, he shouted out her name and greeted her. He welcomed her choice to return to the valley and teach alongside his sister, Janine, at the local high school.

"Karen, it is so good to see you! Have you been to the house yet and have you seen Janine? Married life suits her well."

"Not yet, Mike," Karen said as she hugged him, "I'm headed there now. I packed up my things in Quail Point, and I'm moving them to the house now. I just had to stop and say hello."

"Well, the two lovebirds are the talk of the town. Izzy has taken well to the task of rebuilding Blair House, and my sister stands with him as his helpmate. Glory to God how He has worked in their lives," Mike elaborated.

"It brought me hope," Karen replied, as she purchased a Snicker's bar, "Janine's hope that Izzy would return and her faithfulness to that hope."

"Don't forget Izzy's following through with what he said he would do. He promised to return and marry my sister!"

"Yes, but have they had the wedding yet?"

"No, Adam made them go through his premarital counseling program before he would perform the ceremony despite their having had a civil ceremony at the courthouse."

"And rightly so," Karen replied.

"Absolutely, it is a reminder to all of us who love them that though they made the wrong choice in rushing to marry at the courthouse, the man of God provided them a way to make right that which was wrong."

"Truly, we will all be blessed. What is the wedding date?"

"Sunday after next in the afternoon, this will be when Adam returns with his herd from up between the two peaks of Mt. Huajatolla," Mike informed.

"I fear what might happen."

"You mean the bear. My people, the Ute tribe, say it is bad medicine."

"And what do you say?"

"God goes with Adam. I, too, worry, but Adam is Adam. He protects what is his, and he protects the likes of us who care about him. He goes to kill the bear, to make certain it does not come out of the mountains and into our homes."

"Will he be going alone?"

"No, my cousin Rabbit Pinebow says several of his wranglers will be with him to bring the herd down to the valley above the Blair House where Mr. Freedom has his cabin back in the woods. Pilgrim Wayne goes with Adam with his Sharps rifle and Mr. Ezra Sr."

"Is the old man a hunter?"

"My people say he is a warrior amongst warriors, and though he loves the forest and all its creatures, it will be him who brings down the bear."

"Do they say that because of a mystical vision they have had?" asked Karen.

"No, no, Miss Karen, they know he was quicker than the cougar he killed with his knife, and he is no stranger to killing what needs to be killed," Mike offered. "You should be proud of what they say about you."

"Okay, you hooked me into asking," Karen replied with a smile. "What do your people say about me?"

"They say you have already slain the torment that haunts their hero, Adam Claymore," Mike revealed in complete seriousness. "You are good for him and you are healing his wounded heart. They say you can be trusted to do goodness, for you could have killed Roy Sentry, and instead you shot him in his heel after he and Butch attacked Deputy Candy after the school board meeting. Roy has a second chance."

"I am humbled by what you have said, Mike."

"You can imagine what would be said if you break Adam's heart," Mike said and then he added a disclaimer, "I'm just kidding Miss Karen, just kidding about that."

"Gosh, I hope so, our courtship has just begun!"

"Then it is official! The two of you are an item. Wahoo!" Mike said as he began a dance around the floor. "Oops! No pressure, no pressure! I am just happy for you, Karen."

"And what of you, Mike, where has your heart led you?"

"I wait to see real happiness in others, before I venture to court a woman. Most of the people I see come through the door at the front of the store...they don't look or act very happy."

"With that said I'd best be making my exit through that door and unpack my things at the Blair House," Karen concluded.

"I may be joining you there," Mike said. "My sister, Janine, invited me to join with her and Izzy and the rest of the team in rebuilding Blair House. What really attracted me is what she said would follow. Ask her about that. Besides having room and board in return for helping my sister sounds pretty good for the bachelor! Anyway, I interviewed with Izzy and Janine, and I think I'll be accepted!"

\*\*\*

"Till then," Karen waved, as she left the store to drive just a half block down the street.

Karen paused again a few houses short of her destination. She saw Kat Bond and her two daughters leave the porch of Janine's house, which she had shared with Jill Lowenstein. Stopping, Karen got out of her car to greet them, as she yelled, "Katarina, Kristin and Krystal!"

The three turned and hurried to Karen, "You are just in time. We have a meeting with Izzy, which will be important for you to hear."

"Isn't Jill coming?" Karen asked as she looked back at the house the Bond women had just left.

"She's already moved into Blair House. Adam agreed to exchange our rent for his lease of the pasture land in the mountain valleys west of Blair House. I'm going to run the Christian bookstore when Kip is gone. I'll help with the cooking as well," said Katarina.

"And we get to eat there!" Krystal chimed in.

"And help with the cleaning and upkeep of the castle once we help get the house restored," added Kristin. "The newlyweds have moved down to the first floor apartment. You are still in the southwest room on the second floor and Jill is across the hall from you."

"Kip Powell is second floor front left and Morris Goodenough is front left on the third floor," added Krystal.

"Do you mean Morris the bus driver has joined us?" Karen asked.

"Yes, he still drives the Trailways bus, but he will be here on weekends, when he doesn't have an assignment," informed Kristin.

"The man you will be working for at the pizzeria is here too," Katarina said. "He is on the second floor behind Kip."

"Jerry Sunday is completely moved in too," Karen said. "I'd better get everything stored, before I miss out on all the fun."

"Fun it is, Karen. Miss Rachael comes over from across the street and plays the piano for us. Izzy got it tuned, so she could continue giving him piano lessons. She is going to teach me and Krystal too," said Kristin. "I think Krystal is old enough to learn to play."

"You bet," said Krystal, "and anything you can do I can do better!"

"No, you can't, you can't, can't, can't," proclaimed Kristin.

"Yes, I can; yes, I can," sang Krystal.

"Girls, girls, stop bickering," Katarina demanded.

"Oh, Mom, that's one of the songs Miss Rachael is teaching us. It's from some musical," Kristin clarified.

"Are there others who have moved in?" Karen asked.

"Well, the bookstore is first floor left front, behind it is the Blair library, Izzy and Janine's apartment, and the kitchen at the back of the house. Front right is the piano room, and behind it is the dining room, which will also be a meeting room," Kristin explained.

"And behind that is the bathroom, a breakfast nook, and space for two clothes washers and one dryer," said Kat's daughter Krystal. "The men installed lines to hang clothes on. There are clotheslines on both the second and third floor porches. They installed other things on each porch for Mr. Ezra. He said it was for defense of the castle."

"Are," corrected Kristin.

"Stop correcting me," Krystal told her, as she slugged Kristin at her shoulder.

"You two," Katarina said, "stop now or I will leave you at home to clean the toilets."

"Sorry, Mom! We really do have a home again," the girls exclaimed.

"Continue, what have you left out?" Karen asked.

"The room on the second floor opposite Jerry was vacant, but Izzy just told us Beatrice Jaramillo will move there and help with the cooking. The room behind hers will be a study for all of us to use as our office area," Kat continued the explanation. "There will be a room on the third floor above the library, which will be a television room and meeting area. On the third floor only the two front rooms are occupied. As I said, Morris is front left and Ezra Sr. will keep front right for when he is down in town."

"Is Ezra still living at the cabin?"

"Yes, Karen, he still needs to be away from people most of the time. I think it has to do with his having been a prisoner of war. He says it is for all of our good if he stays away some of the time."

"I hope God will heal him," said Karen.

"Me, too!" said Kristin.

"And me," added Krystal.

"We pray toward that end, don't we girls?" Kat joined in, as her daughters nodded in agreement.

Kat noted Rachael McNaughton was about to cross the street, and closed their conversation, when she said, "We had better hurry. Rachael is always late, so we need to get there right away. Karen, park your car alongside north of the house. The driveway to there has been improved, and we are using it for parking."

With that said, Karen followed Kat and the girls in her car, while they passed Rachael, who had difficulty climbing the stairs. Dutifully, Kristin stayed with her to make certain she did not fall, while Krystal held open the door for them. Karen parked near the rear entrance so she could carry in her belongings without having to climb the front steps.

43

Once inside, everyone shouted, "Welcome home, Karen!"

Karen blushed and joined them in a hugfest, and then she said, "Where do we meet?"

Izzy led the way to the dining room, and said, "Everyone, have a seat, and Ken, please open our meeting with prayer."

When Ken finished prayer, Izzy continued, "Karen, some of our meetings will be here on the main floor, but we also have a library we can meet in directly above us on the second floor and a study or television room on the third floor."

"Wow!" said Karen, "You guys have really made good progress in a short time"

"Absolutely, and I have to tell all of you how grateful Janine and I are with all of your commitment to fulfilling our goals," Izzy replied. "Our home, your home is clean, bug and rodent free. Windows and doors are weather stripped, rooms are mostly painted, some furniture delivered, hookups for washers and dryer..."

"Thank you all," added Janine.

"Kip, please share with the others what you will be doing," Izzy asked, then added, "Please start with work you do to make a living, and then cover your work in restoring the building, and finally, ministry in the valley."

"Sure, I have moved my business headquarters from South Pearl Street in Denver to Blair House, and I've set up a Christian bookstore on the first floor in the southeast corner. Since my room is directly above the store, we will build a passageway there for me to be able to move to and from the store without disturbing the rest of you. A wall will be added to the south end of the room with a door accessing it from the lobby of the house. I will maintain my routes, which means I'll be gone often to service them, which would be mostly during weekdays, unless I get to fill in on a Sunday, preaching for a pastor somewhere," said Kip Powell, a kind and gentle man. "Katarina will help at the store primarily when I am out of town, or when I am calling on local pastors or doing in home parties. She will help me recruit at least one person per town to become one of my dealers, so I can replicate myself wherever I can. And I'll pitch in here to do whatever is needed of me."

"Parties? How do they work?" asked Rachael, eldest member of the group.

"Like Tupperware, only I sell books, Bibles, music, novelties, and children's educational materials like coloring and sticker books. I tell how the materials impacted my life, and people will be able to order from my catalog or directly through the store," Kip explained. "In each town where I have placed materials, I will try to recruit a dealer, who will replicate what I do, which means they will do in home parties, call on pastors, and serve their Sunday schools and adult curriculum needs as well as music needs. Kat will receive a small wage and the Blair House a tithe on what is sold out of the bookstore. In addition, I'll participate with Ken to start or renew the effort to bring a Christian radio station to the valley!"

"Hooray!" said the team.

"I will host a party," said Rachael, "and I know my friends will come even if I am across from the bookstore. Maybe I should be the first party as part of your way of bringing attention to the bookstore. I want to be a dealer too!"

"Good idea!" said Katarina, and Kip nodded in agreement, then she continued, "I get to help Kip set up the bookstore, since he leaves Thursday to do his routes on the western slope and will be back sometime next week, we will have the grand opening the following Saturday."

"One thing more," said Kip with a smile, "I get to work with Jerry and Ken to organize a series of community prayer meetings based on *Second Chronicles* seven fourteen. We will pray for our government on every level as well as for our first responders."

"They will bring healing to the valley," said Jerry Sunday.

"They will be a part of a nation-wide movement for revival in our country," added Ken, a recent victim of the Night Riders effort to scare off newcomers.

"Ken, please share your vision for your work here and beyond," urged Izzy.

"My workaday job is delivering the *Denver Post* in the afternoon and the *Rocky Mountain News* mornings to homes and businesses in the valley weekdays and Saturdays. Early Sunday mornings, I deliver both papers before dawn. Also, I deliver *The Outcry*, the weekly newspaper, on Wednesdays. Just this week, *The Outcry* hired me to service the businesses that sell the newspapers directly or have a metal newspaper box outside their establishment. My girls help me deliver papers, and I have to make collections as well. We are now living where Janine and Jill used to live, just down the street. Thanks to Izzy we live there as part of our agreement here. It was Izzy who asked Adam Claymore to trade use of the mountain pastures in exchange for our rent," said Ken nearly crying. "I'll work with Jerry and Kip on the community prayer meetings, with Kip on bringing radio to the valley, and with Adam on the Pastor's prayer meetings. God has showered us with blessings, and thank all of you for befriending us."

"It means so much to us, Izzy and Janine, to have a house to live in where we can be a family, especially after all of you volunteered to pitch in to help clean and paint the house, and fix a few things," said Katarina, "and while I'm at it, the girls and I will help with the cleaning and cooking for Blair House. We won't always eat with you, but we will most of the time. As Kip said, I will also help with the bookstore and help schedule in home parties and make appointments for Kip with pastors and worship leaders here in the valley. Rachael, my understanding is you will be doing piano lessons here as well. Can I help you schedule them? I could help schedule your parties as well!"

"Bless your heart, dear, you would be a great help to me, and I will tell all my students to get their music through our bookstore. Maybe their parents will want to have an in-home party too. I hope I am not too old for all of you. Sometimes I have my days, but I think God still has a plan for me. I'm this side of the lawn and each day is a gift from God. Lord willing, it will be a long time before my old body is on the underside of the lawn fertilizing all the trees and other plant life."

"Oh, Miss Rachael, please don't say such things, you are such fun to be around," said Kristin, eldest of the Bond daughters.

"And my sister and I want to take piano lessons from you too!" echoed Krystal Bond.

"Oh, you children are sweet. I also have a ministry, other than praying for everyone, that I'm not going to tell anyone about. It will be my secret with the Lord. He told me to do it!"

"Then Rachael, you keep it a secret and I'm certain we will all be blessed by it," said Izzy. "Now, let me fill in for a couple of the people who are not here. Jerry Sunday manages the pizzeria, where Karen will be doing some part time work. Jerry will also be leading us in some small group training materials written by Lyman Coleman, a leader in the small group movement. This will be important not only in working to restore this building but also in restoring the Blair House as a light shining in darkness. On this citadel, we will reach out to our valley by presenting the gospel and by ministering to individuals. It is important that we are like minded. Jerry will also work with Kip and Ken on the community prayer meetings, and I believe he will be helping to lead some evangelism efforts. He will be primarily available weekends and parts of some evenings as he has to close the pizzeria most nights."

Jill Lowenstein spoke up next, "Although I teach science and social studies at the high school, I can help with the cooking and cleaning. Believe it or not, I enjoy washing dishes and doing the laundry, but I don't iron clothes. I might be valuable if you want for us to raise much of our own food."

"Good idea, Jill," said Janine, "would it work to have Jill schedule the cleaning and laundry? I already asked Izzy and he ordered two automatic clothes washers and one dryer. The men put large eye-hooks and clotheslines on the second and third floor balconies."

"Yes, go ahead and tell the rest, my dear," said Izzy.

"Izzy ordered a top of the line dishwasher too!"

"Janine, you go girl! You guys don't know how long we talked about getting one," Jill Said. "It's like a dream come true, a new dishwasher and clothes washer and dryer!"

"I have to have a two twenty line put into the house, and we may have to do some other electric work. I'll let you know," Izzy informed the group. "Kat, you can bring your wash over here when you are working in the store."

"All for one and one for all," a couple of the group members said before the others chimed in.

"Janine, tell them what else, will you?" asked Izzy.

"Well, I think we need to put Jill in charge of spring planting and crop cultivation here on site so we could do canning, if desired, and perhaps organize a farmer's market."

"It's a job I'd like to do. Wouldn't it be grand to grow our own fresh vegetables?" said Jill. "Raising some rabbits and chickens would take care of a lot of waste in the kitchen as well as providing eggs and meat."

"Now you're thinking!" Janine continued, "The office on the second floor will have a photocopier, and Izzy has researched computers and ordered an Apple IIE with a dot-matrix printer. We haven't decided where to put it," Janine stopped short of telling everyone she was trying to get Izzy to put the computer where everyone could use it.

"As most of you know, Morris Goodenough drives the Trailways bus during the week, at least usually. He will be living here, and fortunately, he will be able to connect with his assignments at the bus terminal in Ridge View. God is in charge of circumstances, and he worked out Morris' situation. He will help with all the carpentry work as well as outside work. Adam usually has Morris do pulpit supply for the Rock Creek church, which brings up a topic," said Izzy. "Many of us attend the church in Rock Creek. Don't feel pressured to attend there. As we get more into the ministry phase of our project here, we will want to work effectively with all the Christian churches in the valley. It is especially important for Kip to have the freedom to visit churches as he needs.

"I don't live here. I live across the street, and I want to help," asserted Rachael McNaughton.

"Rachael, I need you to teach piano here, which will help bring people to our door. I'm going to be one of those you teach, and the Bond girls said they want to learn as well. You already mentioned you have a ministry you want to keep secret, and we are all good with that. You mentioned you may want to be a dealer under Kip and conduct in home parties. Let's see if you can keep from overdoing it. I would like for you to prepare for us to host a hymn sing for our neighbors, where you will play the piano and all of us will sing."

"Oh, you dear child, it will be like old times when you were my star pupil, my shining light," Rachael said, "and I can cook now and then and make some special recipe."

"Now Gramma Mac, we won't be operating a blind-pig," Janine said.

"Oh, I know my dear, I'll not bring any moonshine over here, but if you would like a taste of my special recipe, you just venture across the street," Rachael said, as the others laughed.

"Janine's brother, Mike Crowfoot, will join us and take the second floor second room on the right. He works at the Jericho Springs Convenience Store. He will be a lot of help with maintenance work inside and designing our outdoor landscaping," informed Izzy. "Another McNaughton gramma is joining us as well. You know Beatrice Jaramillo stays at the hotel. Buddy Smith hit her in the head with a beer bottle. She talked with her daughter after the city council meeting and convinced her family to let her join with us. She will be super in the kitchen cooking dishes we will all enjoy."

"Oh happy day, Beatrice and I are like sisters. It will be like our childhood all over again, but I mean like in a good way," Rachael said, as she broke into tears, "Izzy, you folks are bringing such joy into the life of this old woman. God bless you all!"

"You are an inspiration, Rachael," said Izzy with a smile, as Kat and her daughters fussed over Rachael.

"My brother, Mike, is good with livestock as well," added Janine, "and I suspect we will be adding sheds and a barn to the north on our property as well as having the garden space."

"How about a small orchard and a vineyard?" said Jill.

"Good idea! We have enough land," acknowledged Janine.

"Yes, and there are others who have contacted me that we will want to be involved in our effort," informed Izzy.

"Have you included the Brownings?" Karen asked.

"Yes, Robert, Ruth, and Andy, as they can, some of Adam's wranglers will join us too, primarily Pilgrim Wayne, Rabbit Pinebow, and Barnabas..."

"Does he have a last name...Barnabas?" Kat asked.

"I've never heard one...Adam Claymore has said he wants to help as well, although rumor has it he might be distracted," Izzy continued, as he smiled at Karen. "We will depend on and partner with the Rock Creek church as we work with other churches to reach the community for Christ. My father will also be a great help by providing a constant supply of firewood and boards, right now for the balcony decks.

He will need some help at the mill on occasion with both cutting lumber and compacting wood pellets for us to use."

"It certainly makes a difference, since you got rid of the stench from all the old clothes and mattresses on the front balcony," said Rachael, as the others echoed, and "Speaking of odor, Adam and Red have a feedlot on the ridge east of Rock Creek. I'll bet we could get plenty of manure from them. I collect road apples for my garden whenever someone goes by my house on horseback. It seems the nags always take a dump near my house! I make tea with it in my backyard."

"Tea?" asked Kat and Karen in unison with both Krystal and Kristin.

Laughing Janine explained, "Rachael scoops up the road apples the horses drop with her coal shovel, then she carries the manure to her backyard where she has a fifty gallon barrel filled with water. She dumps the apples in the water, which becomes liquid fertilizer. After it sits awhile, she takes a bucket, scoops a pail of tea from the fifty gallon drum and pours it throughout her garden."

"Mom," said Krystal, "it sounds like what you always tell Kristin and me!"

"What's that, dear," Kat said expecting some long and drawn out explanation.

"Waste not, want not," both Kristin and Krystal said, as the rest of the group broke into laughter.

"It's a great idea! We will need at least two well positioned drums," added Jill.

Regaining their composure, Izzy continued, "For now we have three open rooms on the third floor, and while I'm in no hurry to fill them, it would be good to have them filled with whomever God sends us. Since Kip has been able to order small group development curriculum for Jerry to lead us with, it would be good for all of us to be here. We need to proceed as God reveals His plan for us. For certain, and what we really need is a carpenter, one who knows his business and can guide us in doing this restoration properly. All of you please be praying for God to send us a master carpenter. One other thing, we really need to be careful to make certain it is God who sends people to us to live here and to help rebuild Blair House. Remember in the book of *Ezra* and the other books about rebuilding the temple, neighboring peoples wanted to help for various reasons, some good and some not."

"You mean like Irv Moss," said Kip. "He said he wanted to help when he delivered the bunk beds. He must have been a mole somebody sent to spy on us."

"He is also the one who first gave the ducks to the Brownings and was probably involved in the theft and sacrifice of them at the bonfire where the Brownings live."

"Ruth said Irv got the ducks from someone who got them as ducklings but didn't want to look after them during the winter," said Karen. "He took them to the feed and lumber store and arranged to give them to Rob Browning for his boy, Andy."

"Then when the Night Riders started doing their devilment toward newcomers, Irv knew how to be mean to the Brownings," Krystal concluded.

"We don't want people like Irv helping rebuild Blair House," said Kristin, "but what if it leads to their salvation?"

"We will have to listen to the lead of the Holy Spirit," her father, Ken, instructed. "Amen!" said Janine, as everyone emptied the dining room to help unload Karen's automobile, except for Rachael, who pounded the piano keys to everyone's delight.

***

By late afternoon, Deputy Cotton Candy arrived at the Blair House, parked on the street, and approached the front door. She admired all the improvements to the fencing, sidewalk, and porches. While waiting, she looked through the front window and strained to read the titles of books, and then she noticed the figurines and framed pictures. Kip descended his second floor room and answered the door in hopes he had a bookstore customer. He flipped on the light to display the room, which gave Candy a better view of its contents. Noticing the deputy through the window, he smiled and waved at her.

Kip opened the door, greeted Candy, and asked, "Welcome, Deputy Candy, are you here to see anyone specific, or would you like to tour our bookstore?"

"The tour will need to wait. Perhaps I can combine it with when I attend one of Rachael McNaughton's in-home book parties," Candy replied, "as you could see, I was admiring your wares. Actually, I'm here to visit with Jill Lowenstein and Karen Gustafson. Perhaps there is somewhere I can meet with them privately."

"Hang on, I'll get them for you...better yet why don't you follow me. You could meet with them in our second floor office area."

They ascended the staircase to the second floor where Kip escorted the deputy into the office midway down the hallway. "Make yourself comfortable, while I get them," he told the deputy after flipping the light switch. "I'll be right back." As Kip walked toward the back of the hallway, he called for Jill and Karen. Both had been talking in Jill's room and appeared in the hallway together. As they walked to the office, Kip reminded them about tonight's prayer meeting.

The deputy greeted them as they sat down at a wooden table in the center of the room, shook their hands, and said, "Ladies, this won't take long. Although we have already talked before, I wanted to review what you had said, and I wanted to tell you that Sam Gelding's body was found earlier today."

"His body was found? Where? How?" asked Jill.

"You mean Sam Gelding is dead?" said Karen.

"In Rock Creek...his body was found in the creek just south of the footbridge before the mouth of the canyon. It was badly decomposed, but his wallet was still in his pocket. I thought you might be relieved to know."

"Yes, thank you," Karen replied, "poor Mara, I'm sure you have already talked with her..."

"Yes, Karen, I think she was somewhat relieved the body had been found."

"Deputy, Karen and I work with Mara, and we will check on her," Jill vowed, "but who or how was the body found?"

"Someone saw the body late this morning from the footbridge over the creek. Another newcomer, named John Mark Cannikin. He was there to meet with Adam Claymore. He saw the body from the footbridge. When Adam irrigated his pastures, the water flow through the creek decreased and altered the force of the whirlpool there. The body just kind of bobbed to the surface and spun around," the deputy said, "and now that I have a dead body, I need to wrap up the investigation into Gelding's death."

"How can we help?" asked Jill.

"Karen's incident was the more recent. Earlier, I talked with you about how you were attacked on the bridge," the deputy said, and then asked, "Do you have any additional recollection?"

"No, I don't. After the prayer meeting, I walked the path to the top of the mesa and sat there awhile. When I came down and started to cross the bridge, I got an eerie feeling someone was waiting for me to cross, so I became more cautious," Karen explained, "Gelding rushed me from the other side of the footbridge, and I fell when I turned to run. I knocked myself out when I hit my head on one of the posts."

"Were you in the center of the footbridge or to one side?"

"Clearly, I had a hold on the top rail and stayed to the south side of the footbridge. I hadn't made it to the center."

"How did you know it was Sam Gelding?"

"I remembered the look on his face when he charged at me," Karen said. "Later, I identified his picture from one of your mug-shots. I had never seen him before."

"We know you are good with a gun," said the deputy, who then asked, "What about other means of self defense? Judo? Kung Fu? Are you certain you didn't scuffle with him and toss him over the bridge?"

Karen started to chuckle at the thought, thought better of it, and replied, "Is that how Sam died? Did someone throw him over the bridge? Did he hit his head on the rocks below? Frankly, I would find it hard to believe. He was a big man, or at least he appeared to be pretty heavy."

"Did you see anyone else?"

"No, not at all, and I don't know how I got to Ezra Freedom's cabin where I met Jill for the first time."

"So you had no prior contact with Gelding, never saw him before, never spoke to him, neither here or in Quail Point? Did you ever see him at any ball games or hanging around the high school in Quail Point? Do you have any idea as to why Sam attacked you?"

"No, he was a total stranger. I hadn't thought about that possibility...Is he connected with the murder of the high school girl in Quail Point too...he is, I'll bet. The only reason I can think of for Sam's attack on me is because I'm a newcomer and I arrived on the bus with Izzy Freedom and Ruth Browning...and because I was a confidant of the girl in Quail Point!" concluded Karen.

"All of it sounds plausible to me," said Jill, who added, "just like how I was a witness to what happened to Gloria Jones and Ezra came to my rescue. I saw Sam Gelding stuffing the body of Gloria Jones into the crawl space under the county road over Rock Creek. I had been to church and was walking the path to County Road 403 from the footbridge. Not realizing what was happening, I shouted at Sam. Called him by name, when..."Jill paused, "someone struck me from behind...I had heard the cough, cough, sputter, cough, sputter, boom of Ezra's old pickup, the Gray Whiz coming down 403 from Jericho Springs, before I shouted."

"Then Ezra must have seen you along the path. He may have seen who struck you," Karen added.

"Interesting Ezra showed up to help both of you and you both safely recuperated at his cabin. Minimally, he was in the right place at the right time, or does he have a reason to have been around at the time of both incidents. I wonder if Ezra knows something more, but I'll never find out. He can't talk, doesn't communicate, and won't write a statement."

"He has a knack or a nose for trouble...and I'm eternally grateful for it," confessed Jill.

"Ezra certainly rescued both of you. I don't see how Ezra could toss Gelding over the bridge, but if he did, it clearly would have been an act of self defense or acts defending each of you. Either way Gelding didn't drown in the whirlpool, nor did he die from cracking his head on the rocks below. He was dead before he hit the water. There was no water in his lungs. Somehow he died of a broken neck," said Deputy Candy, "and Ezra is a hero!"

"One question, Cotton," asked Jill, "Why is it the strange deaths in the valley...how is it they happened in Rock Creek?"

"Good question..." commented the deputy.

"Vestibule," said Karen, thinking out loud.

"What did you say?" asked the deputy.

"Oh nothing, I was just remembering a crossword puzzle I was doing on the bus when I first arrived here. One question asked for the name of the large space behind the entrance to Canaanite cities," Karen replied, "and vestibule was the answer. It was where defenders of the city engaged their enemies."

"And the town of Rock Creek is the vestibule..." concluded Jill.

# Wednesday Night Prayer Meeting

## CHAPTER 4

> "Make every effort to confirm your calling *and elec-*
> *tion.*"
> *2 Peter 1:10b*

Anticipation for the Wednesday night prayer meeting at Rock Creek's church had steadily increased over the last week and a half. Deacon Adam Claymore, interim pastor, had admonished all members and attendees to follow the instruction of *2 Chronicles 7:14* by confessing and repenting of their sin, and then committing to help build God's kingdom on earth, specifically right here in the Rock Creek Valley. Pastor had urged them to make themselves available to do what God wanted them to do. Adam instructed his flock to ask God for specific direction and to tell God they were willing vessels for His work.

While the flock sought direction, Adam listened as well. Feeling compelled, he contacted local pastors in the valley. He shared with many what members of the Rock Creek church had been doing. He asked the pastors to meet with him at Bustos Family Mexican Restaurant for a luncheon meeting. Although not all pastors responded positively to Adam's plea, most confessed they also had been stirred to take action!

Excitement had surged as Adam's flock prayed and listened. Most had never heard God call them by name. When it happened, they wept. Teeming with excitement, most had taken to heart that God really did have a plan for them and that their previous sin neither disqualified nor excused them from helping to build God's kingdom. Adam had instructed them to read the last of *Matthew* to understand that God would be with them as they went out on his behalf. Tonight, Wednesday night, members of Church in the Glen congregation were to report what God had told them.

\*\*\*

Excitement had flourished as well from the spread of two tales. First, news circulated about what had happened at the Cozy Corner Café. Although naturally engaging, Timothy McNaughton spent the day unusually buoyant. Joyfully, he welcomed his customers often at the café entrance, sang as they came into the café, and nearly hugged them by the time they left. Noting the difference in Tim, both the cook and dish washer couldn't help but be infected with Tim's joy. They whistled the tune Tim sang. Most but not all customers left feeling good and glad that they had eaten at the cafe. Some left singing, humming, or whistling "Oh, happy day." Additionally, customers, who heard Tim share about his encounter with John Mark, told co-workers and family members about the serendipitous event. Uplifted and encouraged, they told how Timothy had become radiant when he had shared the gospel. The second tale was hearsay about the removal of another body from Rock Creek near CR403. Although the sheriff's department had kept the information under wraps, speculation soon became rampant. Having kept a candle burning on her front room windowsill for her husband, Mara Gelding's fear overcame her. Acting on a hunch, she drove to her husband's office and found his automobile in the garage behind his Rock Creek insurance agency. She searched both his desk and files, and then hid boxed items from his office in the trunk of her automobile. Next, she parked her vehicle down the block on Indiana Avenue. Experiencing chest pains, she called the sheriff's office. A deputy dispatched an ambulance to rush Mara to the hospital emergency room in Ridge View. News of her ambulance ride spread throughout the valley. Rising speculation connected her with the body that had been found. When Deputy Candy visited Mara at the hospital, more people connected the dots. Warrant in hand, Deputy Candy gently informed Mara that

Candy had been authorized to not only search her husband's office, garage, and automobile, but also the warrant included a search of Mara's home.

Presuming Mara's innocence and lack of knowledge about her husband's activities, the deputy had said, "I'll wait until you are at home before I execute the search of your house, unless I'm compelled not to wait by what is found at the agency."

"Go right ahead," Mara replied coldly, "I'm certain you will find nothing at either place, but please put things back where you found them."

\*\*\*

Other than the pastor, Priscilla and Aquila had been the first to arrive at the Rock Creek church, also known as the little Church in the Glen. They watched over the church, as if they were its guardians. Before entering the church, they stood watching an unusual flow of traffic into and out of the canyon. Drivers had to pause before turning left onto the county road or left into the hotel parking lot, which began to fill with cars and trucks. People stood talking on the busy hotel porch, while others entered and exited the doorway. Once inside the church, the ladies began the first of their two duties. They not only cleaned the church regularly, but also they functioned as the official hostesses. There was a place for everything and everything had a place. Whenever chairs, tables, or other items had been used or borrowed, the ladies made certain every item had been returned properly. As they cleaned the church, the ladies prayed together to bind Satan's attacks against the church and the people who attended Sunday services and the Wednesday night prayer meetings. Next, they arranged the coffee service on one table and the hospitality center on another table where fliers and pamphlets had been mixed with Bible tracts. They nodded at one another, and then they stood ready at the entrance to greet the arrivals.

Both ladies were highly regarded throughout the valley. When Aquila and her husband, Randolph, tied the knot long ago, all acclaimed they had married well. While Randolph served as a local judge, Aquila served on the local school board. Priscilla King had also married well, as her husband now served as the elementary school principal. Both had been disturbed when their son, Robert, had begun having marital problems, which led to his being divorced by his wife, Dorothy. Robert, a realtor, shared office space with Sam Gelding, the local insurance agent. Robert's former wife, Dorothy, supported their children by making pizzas at the local pizzeria in Jericho Springs. The Kings remained supportive grandparents. Together, Priscilla and Aquila's circles of influence crosscut most sectors of societal life in the valley. God had a plan for them, which they were eager to reveal tonight.

Next to arrive in their pale blue, 1972 Chevrolet Impala station-wagon, the Brownings entered Rock Creek from the north. New attendees, Ruth and Robert with their son, Andy, had recently moved to a rural property located near the bridge outside of Ridge View on CR 403. Quickly, Andy had emerged as a congregational favorite. He could either be quite charming or decisively aggravating. If he were naughty or acting maturely, his parents called him Andrew. The tone his parents used when addressing him told the difference. If he had been acting his age or if he were being comical or silly, his parents called him Andy. Either way, he had begun to gain a delightful reputation as a source of humor. Robert removed his foot from the gas pedal, which decelerated his automobile, as it passed through the narrows of the hogbacks. The Impala slowed when cars turned suddenly to park off both sides of the highway. Watching erratic pedestrian traffic, Rob continued to let his station wagon coast through town to the intersection of CR 403 and US 85/87, the Valley Highway. As he guided his Chevy toward church, it entered the lane to the church parking lot, and Andy noticed the beautiful young woman crossing the highway at the mouth of the canyon.

"Daddy, I just saw the lady we didn't stop to talk to after prayer meeting a couple of weeks ago. Mom, 'member Dad, I said shouldn't we stop and pray for the lady, and Daddy, you didn't see her, but I did, I really did. I hope she comes to see us at prayer meeting. Can we sit next to her, so she knows she has a friend here? Can we, can we?" Andy said excitedly, "I bet she chews bubble gum, because she has a peaches and cream 'plexion! She's pretty like Miss Karen and Kristin and Krystal and you too, Mom!"

"Andy, it's not bubble gum that causes the complexion, although too much sugar can be bad," Ruth instructed, as Rob parked their station wagon, so it pointed toward the white birch grove, which surrounded the church parking lot.

Bounding from his place in the automobile, Andrew raced into the grove, then reappeared shortly thereafter with his treasure by the hand. Alluring, a young maiden emerged from the trees with her escort, Andy. Dressed in dark, blue jeans, she covered a pink blouse with a blue jean jacket, and she walked toward the Brownings in white tennis shoes without stockings. The young woman had not resisted Andrew's insistence to follow him to the church. Immediately, she had looked toward Rob, as she nodded her head and batted her eyes like the young doe had in the movie *Bambi*. While Rob tingled at her attention, an alarm went off in Ruth's mind as she surmised a spirit of seduction had accompanied the girl. Ruth looked at Rob, as she said, "Trouble," to Rob quietly, so neither the woman nor Andy could hear her.

"I am Misty McNaughton," the young woman said to Ruth, as she crossed the distance between them, "and you must be Andy's mother," Misty continued as she extended her soft hand with perfectly manicured nails.

With caution, Ruth responded defensively, "I am, and where does Misty live?"

"I am supposed to meet John Mark here somewhere. Someone pitched a tent in the glen, probably John Mark, so he must be somewhere hereabouts," Misty said, ignoring Ruth's question.

Having greeted Ruth, and not waiting for a response, Misty turned toward Robert and asked, "Could you direct me to where I should sit for the prayer meeting? I believe I will be more comfortable inside."

"Who is John Mark?" asked Rob.

"He's the man who invited me to attend the prayer meeting. A group came by where I live more than a week ago. I think they had been walking and praying around town, and I tried to catch up with them. Andy told me he had seen me, when you were leaving town."

"Then it's true. He said he had seen a beautiful young woman by the side of the road. He said we should have stopped to speak to you," said Ruth, as she stepped beside her husband and grasped his arm.

"Andy told me he was going to make sure someone here would tell me about Jesus, and that is why I am here," Misty said. "I have never heard," she paused, "I don't get out much. I don't get out at all."

"Son, let loose of her hand. She is safe, and we will make certain she finds a good seat inside," said Andy's father.

"Can I sit by her, Dad? She shouldn't have to sit alone," Andrew responded, "and she doesn't know anyone here, she doesn't know Jesus, and I think she needs a friend...that reminds me of a song."

Andrew's request brought tears to Misty's eyes, and she knelt before the boy and sincerely said, "You are a very kind young man, but your parents may not want you to sit by me, and that's okay. I don't deserve their kindness."

"Say no more, Misty," Ruth countered, "if you want to hear about Jesus, you are one of us. That is why we are here. By God's grace, you will soon become a friend of Jesus. Come, let's you and I go inside, while the men stay out here and greet people as they arrive."

Andy began singing, as did those gathered around the entrance of the little Church in the Glen. They sang or hummed a familiar hymn, which most had heard first in Sunday school class or during vacation Bible school. Andy next sang about God having the whole world in his hands.

Within minutes the church parking lot filled with automobiles and trucks from Ridge View, Jericho Springs, and small settlements scattered on the plains. Overflow parking lined perpendicularly in front of the four houses between the church and the convenience store. Next, late arrivals began parking in the hotel lot across the highway, which had already begun to fill with out-of-towners apparently involved with something at the hotel. Adam and John Mark watched as the parking lot became congested with cars and trucks and with people walking helter-skelter amongst the vehicles. Adam did not recognize the new arrivals, as he and John Mark walked back to the church from Adam's Rock Creek house.

Sealing their arrangement with a handshake, Adam had given John Mark a tour of his old house with its dilapidated garage. Completing the tour Adam handed John Mark a set of keys to the house. Adam marveled as the crowd gathered at the doorway to the church, but paused to contemplate. Were they here because of the incident at the Cozy Corner Café or were they here because of the discovery of Sam Gelding's corpse?

"Greetings, Adam," Randolph Parsons said as he waited for Adam and the stranger to arrive, "Is this the man from the Cozy Corner Café?"

"Yes, Judge Parsons, he is the one you heard about," said Adam, as he then introduced John Mark to the judge.

"You made quite a stir this morning. I must say I haven't heard so many people talking like they are about you, Timothy, and Adam!" the Judge said to John Mark, but then he turned to Adam, and continued, "Finding Sam's body has also brought a lot of speculation."

"Then it's confirmed?" asked Adam. When the judge nodded affirmatively, Adam added "I'll address both tonight. Come, let us go inside."

Once Adam maneuvered through the crowd inside to the front of the chapel, he stood at the pulpit to make announcements and started the prayer meeting. He said, "Welcome to all of you. It has been a long time since the pews have been filled, and we have standing room only. Many of you are here, I would guess, to learn more about two incidents that happened today. I'll clarify both, and our main purpose tonight is prayer. We had both sorrow and joy. This afternoon, my partner, Red McNaughton, and I began our annual flooding of our pasture this side of Jericho Springs. As most of you know, it always causes decreases in the flow of water into the canyon. As a result the two whirlpools, before and after the bridge over County Road 403... they disappear and whatever had been sucked into them often rises to the surface. It's been confirmed the body of Sam Gelding rose from the whirlpool just south of the footbridge. We discovered the body and called the sheriff, who came with an ambulance and pulled the body from the creek. Meanwhile, hearing the news, Mara Gelding came to town and discovered Sam's car parked in the garage behind his office. Mara was rushed to the hospital with chest pains..." Adam paused, then asked,... "Aquila and Priscilla, will you coordinate efforts to minister to Mara?"

The ladies nodded affirmatively, and then Adam asked the congregation, "Please, all of you silently pray right now for Mara."

Once the praying subsided and after a few questions were answered, Adam continued, "Since a criminal investigation is underway, the area before and behind the footbridge is a crime scene, so do not venture there. Let the sheriff do his work. You need to know bear scat has been discovered along the trail leading to the mesa. Take precautions. My wranglers will be riding the mesa at sunrise tomorrow morning to search for a bear."

"Pastor, we've had bear come to town before. They eat the berries and raid trash cans and get into the dumpsters by the restaurant. What's the concern?" asked Judge Parsons.

"The size of the scat..." John Mark said.

"What did he say?" asked Aquila.

"The size of the scat suggests it's a brown bear," Adam clarified. "In the past we have had bear come down and eat the berries along the trail and fruit off my orchard west of the bridge to deer fence along the hogback. Occasionally, a bear will make its way to the north end of Rock Creek and follow antelope up to the top of the ridge."

"A brown bear? Do you mean a grizz?" asked one of the visitors from Ridge View.

Adam's cook and wrangler, Rabbit, entered the conversation, "My people say there is bad medicine in this bear. There may be more than one. No one has seen it, but we think it is a grizzly bear."

"Let me explain," Adam said. "We flooded the pasture about two weeks early, because we have had trouble with bear in the high country. I'm leaving tomorrow with several of my men to bring our herd down from the mountains. After branding, we'll move most of them into the pasture we just flooded. Some will be moved to the range on the ridge north of Ridge View and east of Rock Creek, some to the mesa, and the rest will winter outside of Jericho Springs."

"Will the bear follow the herd?" asked Judge Parsons.

"Not if we find and scare off the bear?" said one of Adam's wranglers.

"Or kill it!" added one of Red's cowpunchers.

"Yes," Adam replied, "we don't want to, but we may have to kill the bear."

"Or try," said Beatrice Jaramillo prophetically.

"Please pray now about this—the bear, the safety of the town, the people in the valley," asked Adam, and then he waited while those gathered bowed their heads and prayed again.

Adam continued, "I have an announcement you will all want to hear...John Mark, please come forward, so I can introduce you," and as John Mark made his way to the front, "this afternoon I met John Mark Cannikin, a carpenter, whom I have hired to fix the garage and completely remodel my Rock Creek house, so we can recruit a pastor."

Murmuring rose within the crowd, "Mr. Claymore, aren't you the pastor?" "Why don't you want to be the pastor?" "Who would come here to a little church?" asked a man who had been at the Cozy Corner Café this morning.

Hearing the crowd, Adam said, "You need to remember I am a deacon of our church and an interim pastor. I've got a ranch to take care of and a personal life to tend, too."

Many of those gathered turned and smiled at Karen Gustafson, who earlier had taken a seat beside Ruth Browning and the young woman named Misty. Karen smiled, looked at Ruth, and then at Adam who flashed a broad grin before continuing his introduction of John Mark. "Many of you are here in response to God's work this morning at the Cozy Corner Café and you heard about a young man named John Mark. We know he is all about sharing the gospel and he is a carpenter. Here he is to share at least part of his story."

John Mark stepped forward and said, "What a blessed time this is for me to be able to share prayer time with all of you. What a blessing it has been to hear several accepted Christ as their Savior this morning. Revival is in the land...I believe it is why I am here... Adam asked me to share with you. A few days ago, while traveling with friends from Great Britain, I was in Denver where I once lived. I was visiting my mother, and I had prayer with her. We inquired of the Lord about our future and together we confirmed I was to walk to this church in this valley to this town. I was to come here and find someone, who would be here. God had given me a message to deliver."

"You were given a message to deliver to a person here. Do you mean tonight?" asked Adam.

"Yes, here and tonight. Pastor, all I know is I am to find her and speak privately to her."

"So, you are to speak to a woman here. I assume a specific woman. Do you know her name?" Adam said and chuckled.

"All I know is her name is Elaine or Elizabeth McClaren. I don't know much of anything about her, but I have an urgent message for her."

"Well, we know God was active with you this morning and many were blessed where you have been."

"Who is she?" asked Priscilla.

"I don't know anything else about her, just the message I get to share with her."

Beatrice Jaramillo spoke up and offered information, "I remember the McClaren name. Once a woman came to the valley, her married name was MacNaughten. It was not McNaughton like so many of us. She was from the old country, a wealthy family I was told, aristocracy I believe, and her maiden name was McClaren. She is buried in the church cemetery. Yes, I remember her now. Her name was Cristabel. I wonder if the woman you are looking for is related to Cristabel."

The crowd became quiet and looked around for a woman named Elaine whose middle name may be Elizabeth. No one could remember anyone in the valley named Elaine. John Mark scanned the crowd, and seeing that no one responded, he added, "Elaine, if you are shy and don't want to talk with me now, then meet me after the prayer meeting."

Hearing clearly for the first time, Misty leaned near to Ruth Browning, and asked her, "Did John Mark say he was looking for someone named Elaine?"

Ruth said, "Yes, all he said was he had a message for someone named Elaine. I didn't hear the last name. Do you know someone named Elaine?"

As Misty rose from her seat, she said, "I haven't been called Elaine since I was five years old when I first came here. It's been years since I have been called Elaine."

She moved down the row from where she had been sitting in the center of a pew. Up the center aisle she slowly crept fearfully approaching the pulpit where John Mark stood beside Pastor Adam Claymore. Tears began streaming from her eyes at the thought of God having a message for her, and then she shook and wept aloud. Priscilla and Aquila left where they had been sitting and joined her.

Priscilla put her arm around Misty, and whispered to her, "You are with child, aren't you, dear?"

"Yes'em, I am," Misty replied.

When Misty, who is Elaine, reached the front, it was Adam who first spoke, "Elaine, who has been living in Rock Creek for years...Have you been here or anywhere else for church services?"

In response, Elaine fell to her knees and lowered her head in shame. She said, "I have never stepped inside a church, never attended a service, never spoke to a Christian before this afternoon when I just happened to meet John Mark when he walked into Rock Creek."

"Then you know, John Mark?'

"No Sir, I do not know him, but I met him and he rescued me from a log in the creek," Elaine said to Adam.

"She must be the one I am here for," John Mark said, as he reached down and gently raised her to her feet, but Adam continued.

From the crowd Andy spoke up, "She tried to! My dad and mom and I saw her when we were doing the prayer walk. She tried to come to church, and we didn't stop for her. She would have come if we had asked!"

Adam looked first at Misty, who had been revealed as Elaine, and then at John Mark, before saying, "Elaine, I believe God has been working on your heart to become one of his own." Adam told her about Jesus and shared the Ambassador's Tool Kit just like Tim had done earlier in the morning at the Cozy Corner Café.

Softly Elaine responded, "I am not worthy, my sin is too great. I have been used here in Baal worship. I am with child, and it will be sacrificed." Her crying turned to sobs, and she nearly collapsed again, but John Mark held her.

"If you accept Jesus as your savior, you will be safe eternally. Misty, I helped you when I did not know you were the one I came here to find. That was no accident, no coincidence. God has a specific plan for you. Now, I understand the meaning of what I am to say to you and here it is," John Mark paused to let her take in what he and Adam had said to her.

Straining to hear and leaning forward in the pews, the enthralled crowd had not noticed two very large men who had entered the room and stood at the back of the sanctuary. Each held a sheathed long sword. They blocked the small entrance to the church and kept a group of men from entering the chapel. When men opened the lobby doors, the men saw what looked like giants to them. The group scattered like rats fleeing cats or like cockroaches fleeing light that instantly shined in the dark.

John Mark continued, "Misty, who is now Elaine, do you accept Jesus Christ as Lord and Savior?"

"Please Jesus, come into my heart and be my Lord and Savior. Please save me and rescue me and my child."

"Elaine, that is the message I've been told to tell you," John Mark said softly, "God asks you not to allow your child to die, not to be sacrificed, not to be killed. I am to help protect you and I will!"

"It is by faith in the completed work of Jesus," Adam said to Elaine, "that you are saved. Elaine...God has a plan for you and your child," and then Adam watched the two large men at the rear of the sanctuary open the entry door and disappear into the night. Next, Adam turned to John Mark, and told him to escort Elaine into the pastor's study. Pastor called Ruth Browning out of the congregation to join them there.

"Folks, God is at work. Elaine McClaren just accepted Jesus as her Lord and Savior. As you understand the Holy Spirit now resides inside her, just as he resides in you if you have accepted Jesus as your Savior. She is now your sister. Revival is coming!"

The people clapped their hands and shouted, "All praise to the Lord!"

One of those seated on the front pew asked a friend who sat next to her, "What did she say about Baal worship?"

"I don't know what that is...I thought she said she felt a little pale... that she's having to make a lot of sacrifices because she's pregnant."

"A couple of weeks ago, I asked the members of this congregation to go home and ask the Lord to tell them what He would have them do. I encouraged everyone to present themselves ready to serve in helping to build God's kingdom and report back tonight. I must say someone named Penelope Quick, and she may be here tonight... she sent me the kindest letter. Obviously, she knows me and spoke directly to my heart. I needed encouragement, so I know God has told someone to encourage me."

Priscilla raised her hand and said, "Adam, I received a letter from Penelope Quick too. It was written on a beautiful note card with a scripture that met me right where I was."

Aquila spoke up and said, "I got one, too. I thought it was from you, Priscilla, until I noticed how it was signed. I checked the address of who had written it. It was Penelope Quick at a postal box with no number listed. It mentioned concerns of mine I have only prayed about. It was precious."

Ezra Freedom Jr. stood and said, "I got a letter too. It supported our work at the Blair House and encouraged me to understand restoring Blair House meant more than bringing the house back to its former glory physically. The writer reminded me that the Blair House had been like a citadel on a hill, a place like an oasis, where people would go and visit the Blairs and be refreshed, because my parents, the people who raised me genuinely cared for their friends and neighbors...Who is Penelope Quick?"

"I didn't receive a letter," said Barnabas, "but look how telling someone or writing someone with kind words is sort of life giving. What a nice reminder!"

"It could be someone using a fictitious name, an alias," Karen said. "We have a mystery!"

"If it is someone using a pen name, I hope we never know who she is," Adam said, "and if she is here tonight, please continue to write your letters of encouragement!"

"I bet it is someone using a pen name, get it...Penelope Quick or Quick Pen. She's writing with a quick pen," said Janine Freedom, high school teacher of American and British literature.

"What a neat ministry!" said Izzy.

And those gathered together responded with a long round of applause. The woman who wrote the letters wept, but she was not distinguishable, because so many others also wept with joy.

"Let us hear from more of you. What has God told you to do? Tell us so we can join with you, if needed, or so we can pray for you in your efforts to be obedient," urged Adam.

Priscilla and Aquila stood together, "We are to work with others to do a periodic street corner ministry in all three towns. We need at least two more helpers and preferably two more per town."

"What will you do?"

"We will make signs that say 'Got Problems, Let's Pray,' 'Stop Here for Prayer,' and 'Honk, if you love Jesus!' and then we will set up on prominent street corners and hold our signs and pray for people who stop."

"How often are you going to do this?"

"Once a month in each town, as long as the weather holds," explained Aquila, "and let us know if you would like to help."

Next, Rachael McNaughton stood up, and said, "I'm old, but God reminded me Moses was eighty when he got his big assignment. I'm going to teach piano at the Blair House and my students are going to learn to play hymns."

"That's great, Miss Rachael," Adam said.

"Hold on Pastor," Rachael said, "We are going to have Singspirations, nights of singing hymns, prayer meetings, and songfests of praise both across the street from me at the Blair House and other places too. Adam, I am to get ready to pound the piano keys once again for the Lord! I get to and I'm not to let anyone stop me from playing! That's what an old widow lady can do."

A visitor from another congregation stood next, and said, "Pastor, I'm here tonight because of what I heard happened at the Cozy Corner Café in Ridge View. I'm the Sunday School Superintendent at the Ridge View Southern Baptist Church. I met with my staff this afternoon and we were inspired to initiate a project we call 'Trash to Treasure.' We are going to work with the leader of our men's ministry to have fathers learn to share the Gospel of Jesus Christ with their children, which we will reinforce through our Sunday school classes. Then the children, working with their fathers, will go to their neighbors and ask their neighbors to save their aluminum cans for the children to collect for a church project. The children then finish their presentation by telling their neighbors that what they will do in collecting the cans is like what Jesus does with us. He takes us as trash and turns us into treasure, His treasure!"

"The Trash to Treasure project could work in Jericho Springs as well," said another visitor. "Would you mind if we did it too?"

"Heavens, no, wouldn't it be great if fathers throughout the valley shared the Gospel with their kids, and then worked with their children to do ministry."

Andy Browning shouted out, "You mean I don't have to wait until I'm old to share Jesus?"

Andy's father, Robert Browning, said, "My little man, we will do it together! Our neighbors are not close by, but we will do it."

"Cool beans, Pop!" exclaimed Andrew, and then he asked, "But, why couldn't moms do it too?"

"Great question!" said the Sunday school superintendent, as the congregation murmured, "We just decided we needed to start with the fathers."

"I know something I'm to do," Karen Gustafson offered, "and it is something anyone can do."

"Does it have to do with teaching firearm safety?" asked Pilgrim Wayne, one of Adam's wranglers, "Seriously, we know you are skillful with firearms."

Although most thought Pilgrim was kidding, Karen understood the possibilities and said instead, "No, but what I'm going to do and have done hits the bulls-eye. Whenever I eat out at a restaurant, I'm asking the waitress or waiter how I can pray for him or her. I'll do it each time, so I develop a relationship with them. Eventually, I'll be able to share the Gospel, but every time I'll be able to minister to the wait staff."

"Good idea, Miss Gustafson," Pilgrim said, "I bet I could do the same thing with the clerks at a drugstore, grocery store, or at a gas station."

Others chimed in and shared what God had told them. All were blessed. All were inspired to present themselves to God to work at helping to build His kingdom. Those who attended out of curiosity left no longer as skeptics. Those not yet Christians left considering their need to accept Christ as their savior. Seeds had been planted. Harvest had begun. Revival took root.

\*\*\*

After closing the prayer meeting, Adam met with Janine Freedom and Ruth Browning. He asked Elaine and John Mark to join them again in the pastor's study. He had already arranged for Karen Gustafson to meet him for dinner at the Stage Stop Hotel. Adam began the meeting by informing them about what had happened at the back of the sanctuary. He said, "Two very large men came inside during the meeting. I didn't recognize them, and frankly, I'd have a hard time describing them accurately, except that they wore cowls. Some other men attempted to come inside, but they literally fled at the sight of the first two men."

Janine asked, "What is a cowl, Adam?"

It was John Mark, who answered, "A cowl is a hooded garment, and it extends below the waste and often to the feet. It is made of rather drab material and is often gray or brown in color. Monks or brothers at a monastery wear them as primary outer clothing."

The women looked at one another and then at Adam, then all three at John Mark. Adam asked John Mark, "Then my eyes did not deceive me. Did they, John?"

"No sir, each matches the other in size and appearance. They are twins and brothers to me. Adam, ladies, if you will please, keep them a secret for as long as possible."

"I didn't see them at all," said each of the women.

"I'll explain later, and Adam, if you permit me, I'd like to have them stay at the house with me and help me remodel the parsonage and restore the garage. There would not be need for additional salary beyond what you and I have discussed. Let's just say they are here on a ministerial assignment, a pilgrimage," John Mark said. "Try not to speak to them and expect a verbal answer. Theirs is a vow of silence at least to the end of their pilgrimage. From there I do not know, nor do they. They are carpenters by trade, but both are trained in the arts of war. They are superior hunters, and obviously, they can be very intimidating..."

"Three for the price of one is a bargain I cannot refuse. And as the saying goes, I won't look a gift horse in the mouth," Adam replied, "I have a hunch it is best we keep them a secret as long as possible, but the men they kept at bay are likely to tell others that they kept them from coming inside the church."

"They came to interfere with what we are doing here, Pastor," explained John Mark, "Where God is at work, slew-foot comes to rob the joy."

"Did they walk here from Denver, like people say you did?" asked Ruth.

"No, they rode here in a yellow jeep."

"Where are they?" asked Janine.

"They drove into the canyon and found a road, or rather a path to the top of the ridge."

"That would be toward Coyote Springs, where the eagles nest," added Adam.

"Rather mysterious," said Misty.

"Yes, and we don't mean to bring attention to us. Each of us is on a mission. Mine involves Elaine or Misty. What name will you be using?" said John Mark.

"I have a new beginning, please call me Elaine McClaren," Misty smiled as she responded.

"Aye, yes, you will be in trouble unless you leave here tonight, Elaine," urged John Mark, "Now, while all the others are leaving."

"Probably, they will come looking for me," agreed Misty, who then asked, "You will protect me, won't you John Mark?"

"Yes, my yes is yes," he said taking her hand in his, "I am to protect you. I will be working here at the house in Rock Creek at least for awhile, and I will not abandon you. You will be surprised how quickly I can come to you."

"Adam," Ruth said, "I'm certain Rob would agree to take her home with us tonight like we did before with Janine and Izzy."

"That would be good for tonight or the next several days, but you may want to consider staying at Blair House. We have some vacant rooms," suggested Janine, "but we will need to talk with you about what we are doing. It may be like jumping out of the frying pan and into the fire."

"My guess is we are being watched by those who were at the doorway," Adam concluded, "or perhaps by those parked in the hotel parking lot. It is unusual for so many people to be in Rock Creek."

"You are probably right, but my hunch is we are also being protected," said John Mark, "by forces gathered here tonight."

"Rob and I parked just outside your door, Adam," Ruth said. "Suppose Elaine and I slip out the back door and into our station wagon, while Janine and Karen go to Izzy's car. We leave in opposite directions, and we may be driving through unfamiliar people."

"Good plan, then Janine could swing back by and drop Karen off at the hotel where I will wait for her."

"I have a suitcase by your tent in the glen," Elaine said.

"I will get it and somehow get it to you," John Mark volunteered.

"Time is of the essence," said Adam, "but let's pray for your safety now, and then execute your escape."

Promptly, all the pieces fit together, and Elaine went home with the Brownings, while the Freedoms dropped Karen off at the hotel after making a circuitous trip to Jericho Springs and back. John Mark packed his tent in his backpack and took it with Elaine's suitcase to Adam's house three doors up the highway.

While Adam waited for everyone to leave not only the church parking lot but also from the congested lot across the highway, he thought about tomorrow, but mostly he thought about Karen. Finally, night prevailed as the sun reclined completely behind Mt. Huajatolla. Remembering John Mark's discovery of bear scat, Adam did not turn off the yard light in hopes that the light would prevent animals of any nature from entering the crime scene. Before leaving he made a note on his calendar to visit Mara Gelding early in the morning at the hospital in Ridge View. Next, he would meet with the pastor's group, and finally, ride out by noon to catch up with his wranglers. He was tired from a long day of irrigating his orchard and the pasture land, driving the Angus herd to the mesa, and then riding to Rock Creek after talking with Karen. Her enthusiasm toward him reminded him of what he missed being married. His Mary had been the center of his life, and he continued to attend the little Church in the Glen because he continued Mary's commitment to the little town. Now, Karen was moving to the valley and actually wanted him to court her. He didn't know how that would work as he managed his ranch and participated in so many community functions. Karen would be teaching at the high school, conducting the community leadership study for the school district, and delivering or making pizza at the local pizzeria. This afternoon she had moved some of her belongings into the Blair House where she had committed to work eight hours weekly in exchange for room and board. She had promised him to keep Wednesday nights and Sunday open for church activities. He had no idea how their schedules would mesh, but he was determined to build a lasting relationship with her. Karen had lifted his spirits and he looked forward to dining with her.

Instead of walking past his Rock Creek house, Mary's original residence, Adam made a beeline toward the front porch of the Stage Stop Hotel. He crossed the Valley Highway, US 85/87, and into the lot, which had accommodated overflow parking for the prayer meeting as well as an unusually large Wednesday night crowd at the hotel. He recognized several vehicles and determined some of those belonged to people who had attended the prayer meeting. They would be dining at the restaurant, or so he thought.

Adam remembered intruders had attempted to enter the church during prayer meeting. He realized they possibly had intended to force Elaine to leave with them. Wondering what they might be capable of, he paused and scanned the area behind him beginning at the mouth of the canyon. Moistened by water flowing from the small stream on his mesa, a cool breeze touched his face refreshingly. The breeze had gathered fragrance from the climbing rose bushes, which his Mary had planted at the mouth of the canyon. It mingled a wilder fragrance from wild roses, which grew not only along the mesa wall but also in the sides of the ridge to his left. He watched as eerie shadows seemed to dance amongst the trees in the forest, which spanned the length of the parking lot from the canyon mouth toward the rear of the hotel. Intermittent cloud cover blocked moonbeams temporarily, and then opened to create more optical illusions, or so he thought.

Adam turned back around to face the hotel and heard loud music coming from the jukebox in the bar. It resonated as laughter mixed with it. Many of the patrons left the rear exit by the bar but did not appear in the front parking lot, nor did any automobiles or light trucks leave the rear parking lot. To his left six men exited the Tobacco Store as well and walked behind the hotel. Suddenly, the merriment stopped and lights in the bar were extinguished. Adam's pace quickened toward the stairs to the porch, which extended the width of the building. He scanned both upper floors and noted no one had turned out lights in the hotel rooms that he could see. The restaurant itself remained illuminated. Others left both the restaurant and bar, followed by more from the Tobacco Store.

Once on the porch, Adam found and climbed the fire escape ladder to the third floor where he crept along the east edge of the building to the third floor landing of the external stairwell. He arrived there in time to watch a parade of people leaving the Asherah House Bed and Breakfast with lanterns to light their way. He watched as the parade became a single file of people climbing a game trail to the ridge above the valley. No laughter followed with them. Once they were all above the valley on the ridge, a fireball erupted skyward followed by a steady display of flames. Singing and shouting followed.

Adam continued to watch as the hotel parking lot began to fill again with new arrivals. Emerging out of the canyon south toward Quail Point, cars and trucks entered the parking lot. Exhaust from the tailpipes mixed with and eliminated the pleasant fragrance of roses and destroyed the refreshingly moist air from the canyon. Hurriedly traveling the county road west from Jericho Springs and Wolf City, more vehicles stirred pungent dust into the night air. Not only could he smell the fouled air, but also he could taste it. Wiping his mouth, Adam looked north and witnessed the passage of more vehicles between the hogbacks. He saw motorist parked their cars and trucks in the old school parking lot because the east side of the highway had already reached capacity. Passengers from the north walked a trail behind the backyards of houses facing toward the hotel, while those from the south and west followed one another directly below him through the causeway between the hotel and its offices. They passed through the backyard of the Asherah House Bed and Breakfast building before climbing the trail to the ridge.

Having seen enough, Adam climbed down the ladder to the porch below just before moonbeams from the full moon would reveal the stairwell steps. Briefly, the moon shone brightly on the scene, and then it was pitch dark. Only the fire on the ridge, the church yard light above the crime scene, and the few street lights illuminated the town of Rock Creek. He remembered an axiom that Satan tries to follow where God has been active, so as to steal away the believers' joy. Determined to keep his joy growing, Adam marched the length of the hotel porch to dine with his friend, Karen Gustafson.

Loudly, he spoke from *James,*
*"Every good and perfect gift is from above"*
*(James 1:17a).*

# Revelations

## CHAPTER 5

*"You are the salt of the earth."*        *Matthew 5:13a*

S ome rave participants had arrived in time for breakfast or lunch and later. Often they rented lodging at either the hotel or the Asherah House Bed and Breakfast. Wisely, local residents moved their vehicles out of their garages and driveways to use street-side parking spaces. Residents commuting to and from their workplaces had to navigate their congested street to exit and re-enter their driveways to park safely. This had been a strategy to discourage what had happened previously during a rave on the ridge. Previously, shenanigans on the ridge spilled onto Indiana Avenue. As a result, early arrivals had limited space available to park their cars and trucks on Indiana Avenue. Most early arrivals had eaten at the Stage Stop Hotel, which thrived all day long. Not only had all rooms been rented, but also the kitchen and wait staff kept busy from breakfast through late lunch. Waitresses marveled at how well the rave participants tipped. Some early arrivals toured the valley and drove over Claymore Flats or into the mountains west of town. Others went to Jericho Springs, walked around downtown, and stopped to eat at restaurants like Bustos Family Mexican Restaurant or the Jericho Springs Pizzeria. Many drove to Ridge View to eat at the Cozy Corner Café and other venues. They shopped at the hardware store, gift shops, jewelers, and clothiers. Even the cashiers at all the convenience stores in all three towns sold nearly all their sandwiches, chips, ice cream, soda pop, candy, and beer. Gasoline prices and sales soared. Grateful merchants wrung their hands with delight. No matter what might happen tonight, they thought, today had been a banner day!

More rave participants arrived later and first filled what little vacant land remained just south of where the two hogbacks nearly joined together from each side of the Valley Highway, US85/87. Once the area filled completely, new arrivals parked vehicles across the highway in school district parking lots and on the football field. From the south and west, more arrived and parked amongst those attending the Wednesday night prayer meeting. They had traveled US 85/87 from Quail Point, or they drove County Road 403 from Wolf City and Jericho Springs. Once they entered the town of Rock Creek, they competed for parking spots with arrivals from as far away as Denver and Walsenburg, who had travelled Interstate 25 to enter the Rock Creek Valley. The visitors came and went by the rave site throughout the day, but they all returned to Rock Creek by dusk. The "No Vacancy" sign for the Asherah House at the end of Indiana Avenue and the one for the Stage Stop Hotel announced the success of the venture. All filled up! All had felt the impact of an invasion of rave participants!

Fascinated by seeing what had been unfolding before his eyes, Adam correctly guessed the rave was about to happen on the ridge above Rock Creek. While climbing to and from the third floor ledge from the front porch of the hotel, he watched both youth and adults gather at the base of the game trail behind the houses on the north side of Indiana Avenue. He watched as they followed one by one like sheep going to slaughter. They turned neither left nor right, but all fixated on one direction. Single file they ascended the game trail like antelope, which would gather north of town to drink cool refreshing water from the creek and then return to the ridge by ascending the game trail one by one.

Once back on the porch, Adam stopped short of the hotel entrance and looked into the hotel lobby from a window. Karen stood before the reservation desk, intensely involved in a conversation with Lila Longdon, the night desk clerk. So as not to interrupt, he silently slipped inside, and then closed the entry door. He listened to the noise from the dining room and marveled at the silence in the bar across the lobby. No loud conversation or boisterous activity erupted from the bar. Adam wondered if the customers had totally emptied the bar but not the dining room. Had they climbed the game trail to the ridge east of the hotel?

Waiting for Karen to finish her conversation, Adam sat on the couch along the lobby's east wall. He peered across the wooden floor toward the enclosed telephone booth. No one stood inside, yet the inside light glowed. Not only was there no activity in the bar, but also, the lights had been switched off recently. No one climbed the lone interior stairwell between the bar and the desk clerk counter to the floors above the lobby. He shifted his gaze, faced the window to the front porch, and looked south down the highway in time to see a jeep with three passengers travel south into the canyon. Then he noticed the church yard light still illuminating the parking lot across the highway. "It's a good thing I left it on," Adam said aloud.

Meanwhile at the desk clerk counter, Karen concluded her conversation with the night clerk. "Well, I just wanted to keep my promise to your daughter. She wanted to have coffee with me sometime."

"Please do, she will need a friend when she gets back in town," Lila gratefully said.

"I'll be gone until after this weekend. I have a conference in Denver."

"That's where she's having the...I mean that's where her doctor is."

"Is Sarah all right?" Karen asked.

Lila's emotion broke through her rough exterior, and she said, "Oh, Karen, why is it we get into trouble, why don't we use good sense and protect ourselves?"

Stammering, Karen replied, "Is she having an abortion?" When Lila nodded, Karen continued and asserted, "Lila, I hope she doesn't. I mean I know you may have different feelings about this, but Lila..."

"I know what you are going to say and I agree with you. It's life and would be my grandchild we are talking about, but there is more to the story. Watch what happens tonight, and do not tell anyone about Sarah. She could face some real trouble! And that includes the fella sittin' on the bench waiting for you."

Karen turned and looked in Adam's direction. Though frowning, she relaxed and smiled at him before turning back toward Lila. Karen waved and held one finger before her, a gesture asking for just a few more moments with Lila. Karen asked, "Do you mean she would be in trouble with Adam?"

"I'm not sure what I mean...It's what I hear...He's like the only one who doesn't just go along with things," Lila asserted.

"He's the good-guy, long on compassion, I hope..."

"Sometimes I think he's the only one around here."

"I'm glad to hear you think well of him," Karen said with relief. "Where can I reach Sarah when I get back?"

"Right across the street. You know where Adam's house is...Sarah and I share the house between Adam's old house and the convenience store on the corner. Stop by, and if a light is on at any time, one of us is at home. We'll have a cup of tea," Lila replied, as her facial features softened. "My daughter needs a real friend, Karen, and so do I."

"Doesn't everyone?" Karen nodded as she turned to join Adam on the bench, but Adam rose up to greet her with a warm hug before she could sit down.

"Sit with me a minute, Karen, before we go inside to eat," Adam said, as she consented and sat down beside him while he held her hand. "Do you hear the Lord at work inside while evil seeks to distract on the outside?"

"I hear the ruckus outside," Karen confessed.

"Nothing from the bar, nothing in the lobby, only one person's voice inside the dining room. Look at Lila paying attention to what's being said," Adam said softly. "Let's move closer to the entrance, but don't go inside yet. I don't want to interfere or disrupt what's being said. Tim McNaughton's going to speak."

"From this morning at the café?" Karen asked, as she smiled, captivated by Adam's radiance, while they listened to Tim's oration.

"Yes, I think someone asked him to tell about what happened," Adam said, as a wide grin crossed his face.

Humbly, Tim rose from his seat, and began to speak, "Most of you know of me, or perhaps I served you at the Cozy Corner Café where I wait tables. This morning something wonderful happened to me, something I didn't understand at first, but I do now. We've come tonight from a prayer meeting at the Church in the Glen. You all know it and perhaps you have worshipped there at one time or another. That's where Adam Claymore is the interim pastor."

"What happened this morning, Tim?" someone interrupted.

"It was a God thing," Timothy said, then paused, "a man sat at the counter where I work and said exactly what I needed to hear at the moment I was thinking about my future with my girl friend."

"That would be Heather Ross, wouldn't it, Tim?" said one long time resident.

When Tim nodded affirmatively, many in the crowd said, "Oh... the Ross girl!"

"Let him tell his story. No more interruptions," said an eager listener.

"It was like he knew what I was thinking. He told me about men and women in the Bible and how the women had the power to bring out the best in a man or the worst. Then he pointed me to scripture I should read to help me make a decision that I think will influence my future with or without Heather. He pulled a Bible out of his backpack and gave it to me. I read all he said for me to read and more."

"Is that it? Is that all?" said the long time resident.

"No, the guy left, and a whole lot of customers came inside when he was gone. You see it was like they weren't supposed to be there until after the guy spoke to me. But there's more. Red came in and everyone began discussing what happened, then when Adam Claymore arrived, we all asked him what it meant."

"What did it mean?" said the eager listener.

"Well, you know how Adam is," said another long time resident.

"He's got an answer for everything," said someone in the know.

In the lobby both Karen and Lila began to bristle, but Adam smiled and touched Karen's shoulder with his hand, "Don't miss this," he said with a smile.

"Yeah, he does and he is almost always spot on target," added a member of the McNaughton Corporation.

"What did Adam say?" asked a newcomer.

Tim continued, "Adam said I was treated to a divine appointment, and then he said all of us in the restaurant had the same. The guy at the counter had given me a paper to read. I showed it to Adam, he circled some words, and he told me to read what he circled. So I did!"

The crowd in the dining room chuckled, and then Tim continued, "I began reading from the paper and all of a sudden it was like I wasn't speaking myself... I'm kinda timid. I mean everyone heard me and I spoke clear as a bell...and what I was taught in VBS and church camp took over. I said God sent his son to save everyone who would believe in him, Jesus. He said all of us fall short of God's glory. All have sinned and the wages of sin is death; that's what we deserve, but God provided a way out for us. He gave us the gift of his son to pay the price for our sin, so we can live forever with God. All of it! He said it's a free gift, there is nothing we can do to earn it, but we must be born again. We must believe in our hearts and confess with our mouths that Jesus is Lord. We must ask for forgiveness of our sins and ask God to save us. We must take Jesus as our Savior and invite him into our hearts! If we do, we will have life eternal with Jesus and it begins immediately. And do you know what? Several people accepted Christ as their Savior, and then everybody ate. Some people helped me take breakfast orders and some helped serve all the customers. It was the strangest thing I've ever seen, I mean it was wonderful."

As the crowd murmured, Tim continued, "Listen up! I'm supposed to say something more. Perhaps someone here would like to accept Jesus as your Savior. I'm no expert, but I'd like to pray right now for everyone who would like to pray."

"You're doing fine, Tim, I'll help you. Rabbit and Pilgrim will help too. Everyone bow your head and let Tim pray for us. With heads bowed, raise your hand if you would like to accept Jesus as your Savior. If you would like to have your sins forgiven, now, bow your heads. Close your eyes. Go, Tim," said Barnabas, one of Adam's wranglers.

As heads were bowed and Tim prayed, Karen and Adam quietly entered the dining room and took seats at an empty window table without making a sound. Outside on the ridge above town the noise increased as wild behavior became more obnoxious. Tim concluded his prayer and Adam's wranglers each met with one patron of the diner. With their anonymity intact, Karen and Adam watched as people left the dining room chatting about what had just happened. Some were scoffers and others believers, but all had been treated to one man's witness of God's impact on his life. Timothy had been obedient to share his testimony and proved reliable to spread the Gospel.

While the dining room nearly emptied, Karen and Adam began what promised to be a revealing conversation about current status, recent happenings, and future plans. Both intended to test the waters in their conversation earlier at the pasture, but any hopes at being aloof dissipated when they met. Game playing would not be a characteristic of their relationship, and instead, honesty tempered by grace and mercy would prevail.

Adam began their dialogue by asking, "You are here now, but what is next for you?'

"Bright and early tomorrow, I head for Denver for my conference on the Leadership Identification Process, and then I will spend most of the weekend with my parents in Fountain, where we will load the last of my belongings in a trailer. My parents will follow me back to the Blair House and help me unload on Monday."

"Then I will make a point of being available to meet them," said Adam, and next he asked, "Could we have dinner at Bustos for some Mexican food?"

"Great, let's plan on it."

"Are you free of obligations in Quail Point?"

"Yes, and it will be fun to see some of my friends when football and volleyball schedules bring Quail Point and Jericho Springs together," said Karen, "but it will be weird not to root for Quail Point."

"By then you will know many of the kids here," concluded Adam, "and they will watch how you respond to your former students."

"That will be a challenge; I have a lot of friends in Quail Point."

"And it was difficult to leave them behind?" he asked.

"Yes, but I gained some satisfaction over the last two weeks."

"How so?"

"I was exonerated," Karen said, as she started to choke up with relief, "and the superintendent of schools offered me a job, if I would come back this school year."

"Really?"

"Yes, my former student didn't commit suicide. She was murdered. She certainly had considered taking her life, but apparently she was killed," Karen said holding back her tears. "I talked with her mother, who told me that she was having sex with someone she met at what the mother said was a rave or concert her daughter had attended.

Her mother also said she thought her daughter was involved with a prostitution ring at school."

"Human trafficking of high school girls? Were you surprised?" asked Adam.

"I knew some of the girls were very promiscuous, but I thought it was with boys at school, not men in town and elsewhere. I suspect more information will become known about that."

"So, you were cleared of any blame."

"Yes, but that doesn't change the fact that one of my students, one of my friends, died and I wasn't of much help despite my efforts."

"You may still have a chance to help," reflected Adam.

"How do you mean?" Karen asked with interest.

"The study you are going to be trained on Friday includes identifying community problems doesn't it?" asked Adam, who then said, "My guess is that you will uncover a host of perceived community problems."

"There's more you haven't said, isn't there?" Karen asked.

"Yes, you heard the story about how Mara Gelding kept a candle burning on her windowsill in hopes her husband Sam would come home?"

"She seemed to maintain hope to the end."

"Not quite. Remember that she went looking for Sam's car in the garage behind the insurance agency," Adam said as Karen nodded affirmatively. "Well, apparently she found some incriminating evidence that suggests Sam not only killed Gloria Jones, but also, that he had gotten someone pregnant in Quail Point and whoever that was made Sam very angry when she said she was going to get an abortion."

"I would think he would have supported the abortion."

"So did I, but there's more to the story than what's been revealed," Adam suspected. "The sheriff is tight lipped about this, and I think we are going to see more of Detective Jones."

"Officially or unofficially?"

"Gloria was his sister, but he shared he requested to be transferred to the Human Trafficking Task Force. Karen, I fear what might have been going on right under my nose not only as former school board president and local pastor, but as an involved community leader."

"What do you think about Misty?" questioned Karen.

"She is pregnant and has lived at the Asherah House for a long time. According to her, she didn't leave the house much, if at all. Sounds to me like she may have been born and prostituted there. It is strange that John Mark comes out of nowhere with a message for her."

"Do you question his sincerity?"

"Not at all, God is using him to directly intervene and rescue her. Who knows what will be revealed before all of this is resolved..." Adam said, and paused, "Karen, you have a role in this, too, through the study you will be conducting. I confess I'm a little afraid for you."

"Me too! But I know I'm to be here and to do the project," asserted Karen.

"Agreed! I think you have been called to be here..." Adam said, as he searched her eyes with his.

"Do you have some pleasant news, something positive?"

"I do, a few things as a matter of fact," Adam said with enthusiasm. "Izzy and Janine have completed their marriage counseling, and the wedding is planned for Sunday, September 14. Andy Browning will be baptized then too. Also, John Mark is a carpenter and I hired him to completely restore my house here in Rock Creek."

"Wow! It will be quite a project."

"He may have a couple of helpers he can bring in on the job. He will be staying at the house as he works to fix it and bring it up to date."

"You have plans for it?"

"I believe God does," Adam said with a smile, "and I think that means a pastor for the church and probably a family as well."

"Which will allow you to be the deacon instead of the interim pastor."

"Yes, I plan to spend time in pursuit of a certain maiden."

Karen smiled and blushed at the same time revealing she fully understood his intent, and then she said, "You mentioned a third."

"I did and I told you and the congregation about the nice note I received by mail from someone named Penelope Quick. It's true, you know, how words impact us. A kind word turns away wrath. But also words either bring life or death. Effectively used, they bring out the best in people, and unkind words often bring out the worst," Adam mused, and then he continued, "I wasn't the only one to get a card from Penelope Quick. Priscilla and Aquila also received a note of encouragement. Someone has a neat ministry that is uplifting and encouraging to others."

"I have a piece of good news, Adam, about Blair House. The bookstore will soon be open and an open house is being planned. Rachael McNaughton will not only be giving piano lessons, she will also be helping to sell books by conducting in home parties somewhat like that plastic-ware company does. She will be sharing her testimony and how Christian books and music have not only encouraged her but have taught her. And she is preparing to lead a Singspiration for the neighborhood!"

Both paused in reflection and smiled at one another, and then Adam confessed, "Karen, I hate to say this but I need to hit the hay and go to bed before too long. Tomorrow after a lunch meeting at Bustos Family Restaurant with pastors in the valley, I ride out to start bringing my herd down from the mountains first to the meadows by Ezra's cabin and then down to the pasture in the valley."

"That's why you were flooding the area?"

"Yes, Red and I flood the pasture before bringing down the herd with hopes we will get another good cutting before winter."

"Then let's order. We can talk more over dinner," replied Karen, as she reached across the table and laid her hand on his, then whispered, "This right now, right here will be one of my favorite memories."

Adam signaled the cook, who had been anxious to get rid of them, so he could satisfy his curiosity about the rave. They ordered Morris Goodenough's favorite, The Rocky Mountain Cheeseburger Deluxe with fries. While waiting, Adam went to the jukebox in the corner of the dining room, found slow songs that they could dance to, placed some quarters in the slots, and pressed the correct buttons.

Adam turned from the jukebox, looked sheepishly at Karen, and said, "I've been dying to hold you in my arms. May I have this dance?"

Smiling and with haste, Karen danced and twirled toward him where he caught her in his arms and both embraced and kissed her. Imitating an old song, she said, "Now that's what I like."

They danced and swayed around the floor. At first they looked into one another's eyes, and then she nestled her head against his chest, as he tilted his above her hair. Her fragrance proved intoxicating, as both closed their eyes and visualized what could but wouldn't happen before they married.

Before serving the couple, the cook watched them from the kitchen. Although he enjoyed their dancing, he knew the hamburgers would soon lose their heat. Instead he walked toward their table and said, "Sorry to disrupt you two, but your food will soon cool off. Enjoy your dinner!"

"Thank you," Adam said, as they hurried to their seats, "you're not the usual cook. Didn't I see you this morning?"

"I'm subbing for Butch, while the whole gang except Lila went to the rave. I'm the day cook at the Cozy Corner Café. I was there in the kitchen when John Mark spoke to Tim and then when you and Tim spoke to all who gathered there. It was amazing! Wonderful to see God at work!"

"You were there and you witnessed it all?" asked Karen.

"Yes, and I was here again when Tim boldly proclaimed the Gospel message!" the cook proclaimed, and then he said, "Revival has come to the valley."

"You are a believer?" Adam asked.

"Without a doubt I am and for quite some time."

"I don't recognize you," Adam said, then asked, "What is your name?"

"I'm rather new to the valley. Chauncey Brown hired me to cook at the Cozy Corner," the cook said. "My name is Luke, and my friends often call me Doc."

"Well, it is good to meet you, Doc," said Karen, "I'm new too."

"And to you as well Miss Karen and you too, Adam," Doc said, "and now if you'll excuse me, I'm going to go up the trail and observe what happens at the rave...there will be need for healing after this event."

As Luke took off his apron and left through the back door, the couple began to eat their Rocky Mountain Cheese Burgers Deluxe with a basket of fries. "Interesting," Adam said, "he didn't say his last name."

"I wonder how he got his nickname..."

"Me too, Karen," Adam paused, "Tonight, after the prayer meeting and before coming in here, I retraced your steps as you surveyed Rock Creek."

"You did!" she said, as he nodded, "Where did you go and what did you see?"

"I climbed the fire escape ladder to the third floor ledge, like you did when you first explored the town, and I crept around to where I could see the Asherah House, the hogbacks where the highway cuts between them. I watched cars park on the vacant land, and then I turned around and watched as cars from the west brought a dust cloud with them and I felt dirty watching them...like they were invaders, and I could feel the dirt cloud cover over me and even got in my eyes."

"Invaders?" Karen responded, "Interesting...what else?"

"The people looked robotic as they filed through the causeway between the two halves of the hotel below the external stairwell. They gathered at the base of the game trail waiting to climb to the top of the ridge in single file," answered Adam, "but what was most repulsive was what happened when they arrived out of the canyon."

"It's like Glenwood Canyon before the interstate was built."

"You're right," acknowledged Adam, "and what I saw and felt disturbed me. The exhaust dried the moisture from the water my stream puts into the air...I felt a difference on my face...the air no longer naturally moistened the town..."

"From the waterfall off the edge of your mesa like the west end of Grand Mesa..." Karen restated, "tell me more..."

"I could no longer smell the roses..."

"Adam, this reminds me of the crossword puzzle I was working on when I first arrived in Rock Creek. I rode the bus here..."

"Really? How does the puzzle fit in?"

"Well...Joshua led God's people into the Promised Land, not Moses, and he led them into battle to defeat enemies of the Lord. The enemies were Canaanites, who built their cities with a vestibule behind the main gate, not always, but you get the picture..."

"And if the enemy broke through the main gate, they were met by defenders of the city in the vestibule. The defenders tried to kill the invaders in the narrows of the gate, and if the enemy began to win the battle, reinforcements could drop down from the ledge and catch the invaders as the enemy came through the narrows," Adam added. "Did you finish the puzzle?"

"No, I am sorry to say," Karen said. "I do know we had prayer support my first week here from each direction for seven days…and after seven days or nights, the resistance broke down."

"Most of the Night Riders were in jail," Adam said as he laughed, "and it's too bad you didn't finish the puzzle. I'd like to know the rest of the questions."

"So we could sort out the answers?" Karen said, as Adam nodded, "So, am I one of the invaders, a newcomer, an enemy? Is Rock Creek the vestibule for the valley?"

"You are a blessing!" Adam asserted, and then questioned, "And how would what happens tonight fit into the puzzle?"

"Good point! First, when revival begins with God telling individuals His plan for them…"

"And they say yes…report it at church, and they get to work…"

"At God's direction on the street corners, in cafés, door to door!"

"And now the enemy tries to steal away the joy, attempts to intimidate us with the rave tonight," concluded Adam. "You need to get to Blair House and me to my ranch, but I'll need to be alert and ready to take action, if necessary."

"What will you do?"

"I don't know for certain, but God will tell me. I've discussed a plan with Barnabas, Rabbit, and Pilgrim," Adam reported, as he thought God's word tells us to confront evil where we find it.

After a tender kiss, each found their vehicle and drove away from Rock Creek toward Jericho Springs. Adam followed Karen protectively, until he branched off the road toward Claymore Flats, while Karen continued to the Blair House where all the team was in the piano room singing hymns in preparation for their first Singspiration. Karen greeted them all, and then climbed the stairs to her room accompanied by the group singing, "We are…climbing…Jacob's ladder…soldiers of the cross!"

Quickly to bed, the thought of being salt and light came to mind, before Karen drifted off to sweet dreams. "Definitely defender…I'm a defender of the city."

\*\*\*

Activities on the ridge opposite the hotel were about to attract unwanted attention. Participants had climbed the game trail in single file, presented their event tickets or paid twenty dollars cash, and feasted at the barbecue table. All trash burned in fifty gallon drums at the north edge of the clearing. Regular festive participants had maintained and enjoyed anonymity, which covered their unwholesome, if not irreverent, practices. First time participants prepared for a shock that some would enjoy, others repulse, and several would be bound in secret evermore. None would be the same afterward.

Once darkness disguised his assent like a spy penetrating enemy lines to gather information, John Mark trailed after intoxicated followers, who like sheep had ascended the game trail while entranced. Boom boxes provided rhythmic music from the back of a pick-up truck. Kegs of beer waited for all from the back of a second truck. Three twin sized mattresses had been unloaded from a third truck and placed on the edges of the clearing. Each truck bore a rifle on a rack in the cab. Covered license plates hid the identity of each truck's owner. All consumed the barbecue, most drank too much beer, and many gave in to more decadence in preparation for the ceremony around the Asher pole.

Simultaneously, residents at the Blair House experienced a quickening to pray for safety of the innocent in the valley, while ranch hands on Claymore Flats reacted with alarm to the plume of smoke they witnessed across the valley. Earlier, several of Adam's wranglers had helped drive Red McNaughton's herd out of the valley pasture to the ridge. Once they had crossed through the creek beneath the highway bridge, these cowpunchers drove the herd to the top of the ridge by way of the highway east of town and left nearly two hundred head of cattle to roam sparse pastures both north and south of Colorado Highway 96. Watching the plume of smoke rise from the ridge, Adam's men guessed some of Red's wranglers were settling in for a long night of tending to the doggies, which they had escorted to the pasture on the ridge.

As the sun reclined fully behind the twin peaks of Huajatolla, a sudden wind from the south brought cloud cover over the mesa.

Soon it enveloped the entire river valley and hid the moon from sight. Thunder clapped! Were it not for a few street lights, more light from inside the convenience store on the corner where the county road meets the highway, the church's yard light, and light from inside the hotel, Rock Creek would have been frightfully dark. When shots rang out from the ridge, street light bulbs and lenses shattered and extinguished what light did shine as sentries for townsfolk.

On cue, lights in the convenience store and at the hotel were switched off. Only the bonfire and the church yard light remained. Seemingly from out of the bonfire, one man with a large red mustache stepped forward to the edge of the ridge. He drew bead on the yard light and fired his weapon. He was heard to say, "I've wanted to put out the light of that church for years."

John Mark took cover under a gray pick-up truck where the shooters had placed their weapons. He watched and waited, as he let the air out of the truck tires. Next, wind, like a Wyoming "howlee," blew forcefully and noisily through the canyon south of Rock Creek. Dense mist and bone chilling cold followed the wind. As the cloud cover seemed to dance in the sky, more thunder clapped. The lack of restraint in the sky matched what had begun on the ridge, as pagan ritual ensued. Crawling out from under the truck, John Mark gathered the rifles from the bed of the pick-up and dropped them over the edge of the ridge. The rifles landed on the path behind the grove of trees. John Mark returned under the truck undetected, as all were distracted by the gathering storm.

Without fanfare, Adam Claymore dispatched three riders-Barnabas to the Blair House in Jericho Springs and Rabbit Pinebow and Pilgrim Wayne to the east end of the grand mesa. Pilgrim took his Sharps rifle to set up on the mesa's edge where he would survey the town of Rock Creek and the ridge to the east where the bonfire grew. Rabbit was to climb down the trail from the mesa to Adam's orchard west of the foot bridge, which led to the little Church in the Glen. He would wait there guarding the building and the widows who lived one house north of the church. Adam hoped John Mark would join their effort along the highway.

Next, before driving his F-250 Ford truck to Rock Creek, Adam placed three telephone calls. He called the sheriff's switchboard to first talk with Deputy Cotton Candy and then to Sheriff Bailey. Adam had no doubt where Candy stood on issues, but he was less certain how easily Bailey might succumb to influence and pressure. That call preceded Adam's call to Attorney John Law, who had worked to organize the effort to restore Blair House and often acted with him, as a tag team partner, when they wrestled for what was right, true, and just.

"John, it has started again," Adam said. "Please call Detective Jones and tell him we think there is going to be a repeat of circumstances like those that got his sister, Gloria, entrapped at the Asherah House. If events unfold like before, he needs to get to Rock Creek now!"

"Adam," John replied, "Caleb Jones is already here. He has already made some alliances and will be staying at the Blair House. My guess is he is either in Rock Creek or with the folks at Blair House."

"Please check with Izzy and make certain all are safe."

"I will. I'll check on Jill, Karen, Kat, and Janine," John Law paused. "Where is Misty? She would be a target, especially tonight."

"She went home from church with the Brownings. Rob will keep her safe."

"Both her and his wife, Ruth! Adam, where will you be?"

"I sent Barnabas to Blair House, Rabbit to the church, and Pilgrim to the east end of the mesa. I'm driving into town."

"You'll be a target," said John Law.

"Just like usual."

"Take your sidearm and keep your rifle handy. It is hard to tell what is about to unravel."

"After we beat them at city council and most of the Night Riders were booked at the sheriff's office, we knew there would be more trouble," Adam reminded his friend.

"I think the fact of Misty escaping their clutches has probably done the most damage. That and our discovering what Sam Gelding had been doing. Besides it's a full moon tonight. You'd better get to where you are going."

"You, too, keep them safe, John."

"God is with us!"

Finally, Adam placed his third call to his partner, Red McNaughton, but no one answered.

\*\*\*

Meanwhile, the unexpected was about to happen on the ridge above Rock Creek. Earlier in the evening, music from boom-boxes scattered cattle away from the ruckus. Townspeople resigned themselves to endure the spectacle without help from law enforcement. All twenty-one houses were now occupied in Rock Creek, and all residents lowered window shades and switched off porch and yard lights. This included the Asherah House Bed and Breakfast, which would end up being the focus of the night's activity after the bonfire and ritual on the ridge. Also, the hotel would prosper. The bar would reopen as well as the kitchen until early in the morning when the partying ended. Perhaps there would be a different outcome for the rave tonight!

South where the ridge became part of the canyon, a trail led from highway pavement east nearly halfway through the canyon between Quail Point and Rock Creek. A highway sign pointed brave travelers east toward Coyote Springs. A jeep with three occupants left the highway and slowly followed little more than a game trial. Through the narrows surrounding the trail, eagles nested in the crags of rock walls. Wind, rain, and drainage damaged the trail, yet the driver of one solitary vehicle successfully navigated the trail to the top of the canyon. Once there, the three planned their escapade to prevent a ritual about to be performed with a few consenting women as well as an unsuspecting woman and two teenage girls from surrounding communities. The assault team in the jeep waited for heavy drinking to disorient men and women, so the team's illusion would be successful. They waited in a ravine down slope from the level plain where the Asher pole stood planted in the soil, as if it had grown there. Before the pole stood a long rectangular table with a white linen tablecloth on it. A pitcher of water and wash basin accompanied a bar of soap, several towels, and bottles of scented lotion.

Out of the darkness at midnight a procession of six men dressed in black bear suits approached the Asher pole. Assistants escorted four pre-selected women and two teenage girls from the crowd to the table, two forcibly. Though many were shocked, the crowd drew closer around the scene. From the south two of the assault team rose up from the ravine and stood positioned on its edge. Suddenly, thunder clapped, clouds opened and released a heavy rain, as distant sirens announced the approach of a deputy sheriff's cruiser. Wind howled from out of the canyon. One man-bear roared loudly and lifted a laughing woman on the table, as she laughed frantically.

Meanwhile, Rabbit completed his descent from the mesa, across the highway from the ridge. Crossing the footbridge in the rain, he hurried through the cemetery behind the church. He rounded the front corner of the building in time to witness a massive brown bear standing on its hind legs and clawing at the front door to escape the mayhem in the night. Startled the bear dropped to all fours, and then rose again to face Rabbit. Just as the man-bear on the ridge completed his roar, the brown bear let out a blood curdling roar at Rabbit, which echoed back and forth between the walls of the mesa to the ridge. From the mesa Pilgrim discharged his Sharps and landed a thunderous bullet ten feet up the Asher pole with a resounding thud. Charging from the south, the assault team's jeep lurched upward from the ravine with two large men running alongside it. The driver switched on headlights and sounded the jeep's wailing horn. Rabbit fled narrowly escaping the rushing bear. Rabbit darted toward the woodshed behind the church. The bear passed him, as it fled across the footbridge and into the orchard. Not stopping, it ran until well beyond the road, which lead to Wolf City from Jericho Springs, and it climbed up the mountain.

Intoxicated and rain soaked, much of the crowd fled in a drunken stupor. Young and old, men and women stampeded toward the slippery game trail like the cattle had fled earlier away from the ruckus. When amassed at the head of the narrow footpath, two of the man-bears shoved two women and a man, who lost their footing and pummeled over the edge to the valley floor. Landing below, they lay unconscious. Others stumbled when pushed aside, and then lay bruised on the ground along the game trail. Still others fled into the pasture toward the herd. Three in bear costumes each took one willing woman and fled with them. In costume two drove their trucks through the pasture on a rarely used trail to highway 96. Though hobbled, another followed, as the driver drove his truck on deflated tires. The assault team arrived in time to rescue two teens, which were being forced to participate in the ritual. One woman accompanied the three remaining men dressed in the bear suits down the trail and through the backyard of one house where they entered the Asherah House at the end of Indiana Avenue. Most of the crowd fled in the rain to their vehicles on both sides of the highway and in the hotel parking lot. Some drove north toward Ridge View or to the junction of highway 96 where they turned east away from the valley. Others hurried south through Rock Creek into the canyon toward Quail Point and beyond, while some turned at the county road to travel to Jericho Springs or across Claymore Flats to Wolf City.

Although many vehicles passed Adam at the CR403 intersection, he walked to the former high school as Deputy Candy entered Rock Creek in her cruiser with siren blaring. While most participants fled to their trucks and automobiles to escape in the downpour, others re-entered the hotel through the back door of the restaurant. Some hotel patrons climbed the exterior rear staircase to their rooms, which they had rented for the night. Temporarily, many occupants of the second and third floor rooms of the hotel switched on the lights to their rooms. Suddenly, someone switched on the convenience store and the hotel dining room lights. No one from the fleeing crowd tended to those who had fallen from the ridge or who lay beside the game trail. At the Tobacco Store west of the hotel, card players peered out the backdoor and laughed at the crowd, but they quickly became bored and returned to their game. When no one crossed the highway to go to the store or to buy gasoline, lights were switched off there.

Candy parked her cruiser in front of the old high school at the end of Indiana Ave. and left its flashing lights on, while she called for back-up. She asked for a deputy to park just south of Ridge View to collect license plate numbers. Also, she asked for help on site to record plate numbers from vehicles that remained in the parking lot. A yellow jeep arrived from out of the canyon and stopped at the hotel hitching posts. Two girls and Detective Caleb Jones climbed out of the open topped jeep, while two other occupants promptly made a u-turn and disappeared.

After Candy moved her cruiser to the county road intersection, John Mark arrived from the ridge and said, "Officer, I think we will need ambulances. At least two people fell over the edge of the ridge when the crowd stampeded. Also, I managed to recover the rifles used to shootout the street lights. They're in the grove of trees against the cliff. Hopefully, you'll be able to find out who owns the rifles and who discharged them tonight."

"Adam, please call the hospital and request two ambulances, if they are available, and check on the injured," Cotton Candy asked, then speaking to John Mark, "and who are you that you know so much about what happened?"

"John Mark Cannikin, I live in Adam's house," he said, as he pointed down the highway.

Candy looked at Adam, who nodded, and said, as he walked toward his house, "He moved in today. This is some introduction to Rock Creek!"

"When will it quit?" Candy said.

To which John Mark replied, "When the Lord comes!"

"Huh? Oh, yah, I'll want to interview you, John Mark," Candy said, and then asked, "and you were the one at the Cozy Corner Café this morning I suppose?"

"He's the one," Detective Caleb Jones said, as he approached Candy with two frightened teens in tow. "I'd like you to meet April and May Osteen, the sixteen year old daughters of..."

"August Osteen, Mayor of Quail Point," completed the deputy. "Please, put them in my squad car, detective, and thank you for your help." Turning to the girls, Candy said, "We will call your mother, January, and father to pick you up. It is obvious you've been smoking pot."

"I don't think you understand that all of this was just a dramatic production!" said April.

"Yeah, there was certainly a lot of drama tonight," said the detective.

"Couldn't you just take us to jail, so we don't have to face our father?" objected May.

"Not on your life, missy, you have earned what's coming!" said Candy, who then turned to John Mark and asked, "Will you bring me the rifles? And can you be certain not to touch anything but the barrels. Put them in my trunk."

"Will do," said John Mark as he sprinted to the approximate location of the rifles and retrieved three, a 30-30, an M1, and a Winchester. He secured them as requested.

Rabbit, though visibly shaken, joined the conversation, "There's a grizzly running through the orchard..."

"What? I can't do anything about...a grizzly bear? Are you serious? There aren't any grizzly bears in Colorado! I can't do anything about... have you been drinking too? I need you to help Adam check on the injured at the base of the cliff, Rabbit," said the deputy.

"Got it," said Rabbit, as he dodged vehicles leaving the parking lots and yelled, "It was a huge grizzly bear!"

"I'll help him," offered John Mark, "but what about zoos or circuses?"

"Deputy, some sort of ritual was about to take place up there," Detective Jones said, after escorting the twins to the deputies cruiser, "but the girls said it was a dramatic reproduction of some play loosely based upon Canaanite religious practices. Something about Baal worship, area history of Asher poles, and the Asherah House name as well as the fact that one of the towns in the valley is named Jericho Springs."

"Save your thought, Caleb, I need you to help me contain the people and gather names and information," Deputy Candy told the detective. "I've a good idea who might be involved. It is McNaughton land up there. Please be around where we can talk later in private. See if Adam will open the church."

"Of course, I'll help, but if the girls are correct, you will want this flyer as part of your evidence," the detective said as he handed her the flyer. As she briefly examined the paper, he added, "I'll want a copy of it for the case I'm working on."

Candy handed the flyer back to Detective Jones, and said, "Rock Creek Rave, a musical dramatization of Canaanite worship practices in the Rock Creek Valley. Baal worship...whatever that is...you hold on to it for now, Caleb. This is really bizarre. I thought a rave was only about music."

"Deputy, when the parents arrive to pick up the girls, can I release them to their parents or do you want to hold them?"

"No, just keep them safe until the parents get here and send them home. Tell them I will call later. There is so much commotion going on and who knows what was really intended for them here."

John Mark added another detail to the commotion, "One more detail, Officer."

"What is it?' barked Candy angrily.

"I disabled a gray pick-up when I let all the air out of its tires. There were three trucks involved in transporting food and tables to the site above. None were plated. It may still be in the field. Or it could be riding on rims by now. After they shot out the street lights, the shooters put the rifles in the bed of the gray truck. Everyone was drinking and most were smoking pot."

When the ambulances arrived, Candy moved to the location of the injured in time to witness Adam covering a teenage girl with a blanket. "She's dead," Adam announced, "and two others are seriously injured."

"I should have been over here tending to the injured instead of other things," said Deputy Candy,...as she momentarily broke down.

"It's not your fault, Cotton," counseled Adam. "What happened to your back-up? Where is the Sheriff?"

"I don't know...I just don't know..." Candy echoed.

Rabbit added, "Candy, you managed all of us well. We may not be law enforcement, except for Caleb, but the community came to bat for you. You did a good job."

"Thanks...do we know the injured and the dead girl?" Cotton asked.

"She is Ute, Betty Strong Bull, and one of my clan in Wolf City," answered Rabbit Pinebow, "but the other two, the ones who are injured, are from Denver, Mr. and Mrs. Walter Anderson. I don't think they have any connection here."

"You mean they may have just been passing through and maybe stopped to eat, but got caught up in the excitement?"

"Something like that, or else word of this event was far reaching. And Deputy, Betty is a Strong Bull, the Chief's family."

"Adam, it would be best if you made the phone call. Could we meet at the church in about a half hour? You, Rabbit, John-boy, Caleb, and me...I'm going to the Asherah House."

"Yes, and Pilgrim. He's somewhere around here. Do you want some back up?"

"Thanks, Adam, I'll be okay. I doubt they will mess with me. Not tonight. I also doubt they'll show me their guest register without a warrant, but I'll try to see it."

Detective Jones joined the conversation and informed Candy, "The parents picked up the girls. The mayor was very indignant that his girls were held in the cruiser, but they're safe."

Pilgrim joined the group and said, "Well, I tracked the grizzly through the muddy orchard. He has a lair in the side of the mesa where he has slept, but for now he is headed for the mountain and may just follow the road depending on which side of the creek he chooses."

"Rabbit said he saw the bear!" said Adam.

"I'll meet you at the church in less than a half hour," said Candy.

\*\*\*

While Deputy Cotton Candy went to the Asherah House to check the register, the men who helped her prayed at the little Church in the Glen. They prayed for her safety and they asked for wisdom and understanding about what had happened tonight. They prayed to see where God was at work. Despite the circumstances, they felt encouraged knowing God was in charge and He knew exactly what had happened.

When Cotton arrived from her effort to gain information at the Asherah House, she stopped before entering and gasped at the great bear's signature carved on the face of the front doors. Holding onto the frame, Candy pulled the damaged door open to enter the sanctuary where the men inside waited for her.

"Rabbit, you weren't kidding about that bear! Was it really a grizzly?" Candy asked.

"There's not supposed to be any more in Colorado, but it was huge. Did you notice the width between its toes?" said Rabbit.

"Wait till you see the tracks it made through the orchard," Pilgrim asserted.

"Hopefully, it won't circle back around or stop in the meadow where we are going to move the cattle," added Rabbit.

"We'll start hunting it tomorrow when we go to move the herd," Adam paused, "and we'll have to depend on John Mark to watch out for the people here."

"It may be a personification of the evil ritual they were going to perform on the ridge," theorized John Mark, but at first, no one listened.

"Well, John Mark, you were the only one of us who saw things close up. Perhaps the bear was the embodiment of what is to come," added Adam.

"Its circling back is a possibility. I found a lair it has been sleeping in," Pilgrim added, "when I tracked it through the orchard about midway between here and the road to the mesa."

"We'll count on you men to track it and either kill it or scare it out of the area," Candy said as encouragement.

"Adam, let me take my Sharps and follow the road on the Flats to Wolf City then on to Pryor, so I come up south of the herd, while others follow it up the road," Pilgrim offered.

"If it didn't follow the road and went left of the West Creek and over the mountain, where would it likely come out?" asked Candy.

"Settlements around Pryor," explained Rabbit, as Candy nodded.

"I hate for us to hunt this thing separated, but it makes sense to cover the area. Since it has been hunting the herd from multiple locations, it's a good plan. You could leave in the morning, while I have my luncheon meeting with the pastors. Barnabas will run the line crew, while we are gone, and Rabbit will be with me," Adam concluded.

"And I'll cover Rock Creek," added John Mark.

"Keep us posted at the sheriff's office," Candy stated, and then said, "Gentlemen, it's getting late, and I want to confer with you, while details are fresh. Thanks for hanging around."

"We're with you, Cotton."

"Here's what I'm thinking, obviously, it was on Red McNaughton's land again, but that doesn't prove he is responsible for it. None of the participants at the rave actually live in Rock Creek, except for women from the Asherah House. The others are all from surrounding communities on the eastern slope. Somehow employees at the convenience store, the hotel, the Asherah House knew what was going on. Most, if not all, took orders to turn out their lights."

"Add those at the Tobacco Store."

"The hotel, convenience store, and Asherah House profited," the Deputy said, "and the locals were terrorized, while their town was used. All of you came to their defense and you don't even live here."

"Didn't most businesses in the valley benefit financially?" asked John Mark.

"Yes," said Adam, "a lot of money was spent before the actual event, and my guess more will be spent tonight and tomorrow."

"Look what happened at the last rave," said Detective Caleb Jones.

"What happened?" asked John Mark.

"About the same thing, but apparently Sam Gelding killed my little sister and stuffed her body in the crawl space under the county bridge."

"This time Betty Strong Bull died," said John Mark.

"They wrecked havoc, malicious mischief, John-boy, but let me continue," Candy said, "and follow the money trail. Who owns and manages the hotel and restaurant? The convenience store? Who is responsible for the Asherah House?"

"Red runs the hotel, but I don't know who owns it. It's kind of a mystery as to who runs and owns the Asherah House, and Van Allen owns the convenience store," said Adam, "but who organized the rave and how did the word get out?"

"Whose trucks were used to transport the food and equipment?" added Rabbit.

"Whose rifles were used to shoot out the street lights?" asked Pilgrim.

"At least you have them," said John Mark.

"Yes, and they should be registered and hopefully, we got plenty of license plate numbers, so we can track who was here," said the deputy.

"We certainly have a lot of unanswered questions," John Mark stated and then suggested, "I would check on the truck with the flat tires. If the truck went far on them, they were repaired or someone had to replace them."

"I want to know who wore the bear costumes," said Gloria's brother, Caleb Jones. "The lights were shot out, so no one would see what was happening to the women who were going to be the victims. There were six."

"A man with a thick red mustache shot out the church light. He shouted out he had wanted to put out the light at the church for a long time," reported John Mark.

"Well, we know who that was. Don't we? Was he wearing a bear costume?" said Adam angrily.

"Sounds like Red McNaughton...who owns the land, runs cattle on it, and at least shot out the yard light at the church," said the deputy.

"But he wasn't wearing a bear costume...at least not then. Under the cloak of darkness, their evil was to be done, but praise be to God, the innocent were rescued," announced John Mark while he understood the Baal worshippers believed they were thwarted by their own storm god.

"No matter how snotty the innocent were," said Candy.

"Or how their parents were unappreciative!" added Caleb, "My prediction is we are going to find human trafficking, prostitution along with what else is discovered, and I want to know if Gelding operated by himself or if there were accomplices."

"Question!" stated John Mark, "When was the trailer burned? Is there a connection between the fire and the rave?"

"Good question!" Caleb answered, "The fire eliminated possible witnesses, near the scene of the rave, witnesses who could identify who was involved. And what about the trailer across the road from the burnout..."

"Deputy, you said a rave happened before. Where was it held and who owns the location?" asked John Mark.

"It was held north of Ridge View in the foothills..." answered Deputy Candy.

"Three raves on Red's land," interrupted Adam, "two here and one north."

"Who would be powerful enough to organize something designed to bring people and money into the valley?" John Mark continued.

"Obviously, Red is part of it, but not big enough to pull it off without help," Adam said.

"More to check out deputy," said Pilgrim. "So what happens to the townspeople while you find answers to all those questions?"

"The church is active here building community and ministering to the people. Good things are happening!" asserted Adam.

"Yet only one of you now lives here and I need his help," said Candy.

"Me?" answered John Mark, newcomer carpenter.

"Yes, will you organize the people as a neighborhood watch?" asked Candy.

"I know the concept, and I've experienced it. I'll do it, if our meetings can be at the church at least to start with, then we will switch locations possibly. We will need window stickers, a telephone tree, and a highway sign at each entrance to the community."

Candy replied, "We will need a neutral location like the senior center."

Rabbit raised a clenched fist and proclaimed, "Power to the people."

# Separate Paths

## CHAPTER 6

*"Do not conform to the pattern of this world, but be transformed by the renewing of your mind."*
*Romans 12: 2a*

Early Friday morning much of the valley awakened without knowledge of the disaster that had happened the night before. Other than in Rock Creek, last night's storm had gently soaked lawns, fields, and forest. Rainfall seemed to wash away, if only temporarily, both depression and anxiety. Clean, moist air invigorated those living in Jericho Springs, Ridge View, and on the plains to the east. Generally, both residents and the business community had felt encouraged by the temporary influx of visitors who had spent the last several days and nights spending money at restaurants, gasoline stations, gift shops, grocery stores, motels, bars, and liquor stores. In Rock Creek the storm had been violent!

Of course the whole valley realized how the rave event had brought people, money, and traffic, if only briefly. It reminded older folks of the good old days before school reorganization had torn the heart out of their enclaves by closing schools and centralizing attendance areas around bigger and better school buildings. Oldtimers remembered what life had been like before the interstate construction. Although often complaining about the hustle and bustle of traffic and people, those in the valley had profited from the construction workers, until their efforts resulted in Rock Creek Valley just being designated as a highway exit with gas, food, and lodging.

Like an earlier rave, the musical event brought with it a false sense of well being for most. Previously, it had been easy to disbelieve rumor about the death of a young woman from the Asherah House and the allegation that Red McNaughton's son was the guilty party. After all... folks knew Red had hosted the rave... boys will be boys...and what happens at the Asherah House stays at the Asherah House.

The euphoric, if not manic, sense of well-being elsewhere had not been shared by those living in Rock Creek. Those meant to participate in the rave ritual had a split decision about the rave's failure. Those willing to participate had been paid well, while one other had fled and two others had been embarrassed when held in a sheriff's cruiser until their parents arrived to take them home. Across the valley from the event were those who had witnessed the smoke plumes lifting to the sky before the sudden storm entered the valley and drenched both participants and defenders of Rock Creek. Rain had drenched good and evil equally in the town of Rock Creek.

Living along a flood plain, long time residents of the valley knew well the possible consequences of a violent storm. West and North Rock Creek remained swollen, and where once merged, the creek had spilled over its banks and flooded Adam's pasture land between the creek and the hogback surrounding the little town. East of the highway, the wetlands and land surrounding the other hogback became one large pond. Water had invaded the backyards of houses on the north side of Indiana Avenue, and it extended south beside the cliff behind the grove of trees to the mouth of the canyon. Where flat, the path to the game trail had been washed out. Above, the town's cistern perched on the hogback like a castle surrounded by a moat. On top the ridge only the Asher pole stood, as the ceremonial table had been knocked over by fleeing spectators and drums of trash had been hauled away in the beds of the fleeing trucks. Water pooled the length of tire made ruts to highway 96 where the un-plated trucks had escaped the scene through open fence next to the burned out trailer. Heavy rain destroyed the crime scene both above and below the cliff. Those who had watched the smoke plumes from a distance had slept peacefully believing the rain would quench the fires.

The rave event violated the safety of local residents. Participants and spectators alike, who had escaped without being interrogated by Deputy Candy, felt relief and hoped not to be connected with the event. But...Rock Creek residents seethed with anger that someone's daughter had either been murdered or accidently killed when pushed off the cliff to the rocky ground below. They seethed when learning two others had been injured from the fall. Residents seethed at the sight of their cars and trucks, which they had parked along Indiana Avenue. All had been bumped or side-swiped by stupefied rave participants fleeing in the darkness. They seethed when cast into darkness by someone who had shot out their street lights. Since most of the residents had secured car and homeowner insurance through the local insurance agent, they seethed! They bore animosity toward the hotel and the convenience store, as both had cooperated by switching off their lights, which darkened the town. Several Indiana Avenue neighbors took action against the Asherah House, which still housed some participants. Some men and women came out of their houses armed with rocks and pelted the bed and breakfast. Thrown rocks smashed windows, broke clay pots, and pounded against walls, porches, and doors. With glee the residents hastily retreated to the safety of their homes, as porch and balcony lights of Asherah House switched on. A clear message had been delivered, and when someone from the house called the sheriff's office and asked for help, a deputy on the other end of the line muffled her phone, as she laughed out loud.

Were it possible to vacuum together the questions and prayers from the valley, the assortment would have included: Was Thursday night's rave a dramatization like the Osteen girls had asserted, or was it blatantly of evil intent? Was the bear the personification of what was to come as it attempted to shred the entrance to the church and enter in? Would all participants and spectators be shamefully impacted by what had happened? Who had organized the event? What had caused the stampede to the game trail resulting in the death of one and the serious injury of two others? Was it the sudden storm and lightening, the thunderous clap of the clouds? Was it the bullet from the Sharps rifle shattering the Asher pole or the assault team in the jeep with horn blaring? Or was it because the spectators like sheep had followed one another up and then down the game trail made perilous by the darkness? Was it the sky made dark by the sudden storm that caused the stampede?

Others would include: What had happened to those attending? Some injured and frightened, rain soaked and mud laden, one having to replace four tires, three losing their rifles? What had happened to the woman who entered the Asherah Bed and Breakfast with the three men wearing bear skins? What had become of the three who fled in the pick-up trucks? What had happened to the one teenager who fled from the scene into the night amongst the cattle? Were the raves nothing more than a venue to practice a variation of Canaanite Baal worship or were they just as advertised – a dramatic performance to compliment the music?

Most attending the evil performance had scattered the night before, but not all, for a remnant remained at the Asherah House and the Stage Stop Hotel. Though impacted by the raucous event, defenders of the innocent had obligations to tend to Friday morning. One man remained at the Blair House to defend what was to become a bastion of Christ centered activity. The others followed separate pathways away from their own refuge.

***

4:00 a.m.—Friday morning Ken Bond had prepared to work alone. His girls, Kristin and Krystal, would help their mother, Katarina, as she created breakfast at the Blair House. Ken Bond left the house on Main Street and drove on CR403 through Jericho Springs to Ridge View to meet the *Rocky Mountain News* delivery truck at the interstate exit. From there he not only delivered papers door to door in Ridge View, Jericho Springs, Rock Creek, and surrounding areas, but he also placed papers in boxes at restaurants, grocery stores, truck stops, and gas stations. When finished, Ken distributed the day's *Rocky Mountain News* to an additional fifty households in Jericho Springs that had not subscribed to either the News or the *Denver Post*. Earlier he had completed the same process with free sample copies of the *Denver Post* and of the weekly newspaper, *The Out Cry*. With each sample, he inserted a flyer inviting each resident to subscribe to the newspaper. Motivated to maximize his subscriber list, Ken planned next to call on each non-subscribing household to invite every resident to enroll to receive door to door delivery of at least one newspaper.

However, today Ken promised to complete his deliveries, return home promptly, and take his family shopping for school clothes. Earlier, the Bond family had lost their possessions when the trailer they rented had been set on fire. Since the trailer had been a total loss, owner Adam Claymore had taken the family to his ranch house on Claymore Flats, where the Bonds stayed until Izzy and team occupied the Blair House. Arson had been added to the Night Riders' list of charges, which included terrorizing newcomers who may have had a legal claim to the Blair House and its mineral and water rights. Adam Claymore arranged for the Bonds to use his rental in exchange for Adam's use of Ezra Freedom Sr's. mountain pasture. When Jill Lowenstein and Janine Freedom moved into Ezra's Blair House, the Bonds moved into Adam's house on Main Street. Though the Bonds had lost everything, they gained not only a home to live in but also work where all of them contributed to the restoration of Blair House.

* * *

5:00 a.m.—Pilgrim Wayne had tracked the bear through Adam's orchards the night of the rave. At early breakfast he shared with fellow wranglers that he blamed himself for the death of Betty Strong Bull, the granddaughter of a long time friend. He figured it had been his rifle shot that had caused people to flee the rave. He believed the wounded grizzly may have headed over the mountain or south beside the Claymore Flats Creek instead of going directly up the valley road beside West Rock Creek. If he were the wounded bear, Pilgrim figured that the grizzly would have avoided the climb over the mountain initially, but then wondered if it would go into the valley despite the irritating sounds of the saw mill, wranglers, and automobiles in favor of the quiet and gentler terrain on Claymore Flats. Though the rain had disguised the grizz's route, Pilgrim visualized the bear hesitating left of the west fork of Rock Creek where joined by the lesser tributary, which drained much of Claymore Flats. Pilgrim thought the grizz would eventually climb over the south peak of Huajatolla and head toward Pryor, Colorado. Once convinced, Pilgrim Wayne saddled his favorite mount, an appaloosa named Spirit, and he rode out from the ranch onto Claymore Flats, a land mass nearly equal to Grand Mesa by Grand Junction. He welcomed the long ride and the challenge of killing the bear after what had happened the night before. While sadness gripped him, he smiled when joined by a cinnamon growler named Bruin, which had run to accompany Pilgrim on his redemptive quest. Such was the state of Pilgrim's mind and bruised emotions.

Had Pilgrim followed the road in the opposite direction, he would have been encouraged by Katarina Bond and daughters Kristin and Krystal, who walked down the street past a few houses to Blair House. Briskly, they walked around back of the house and entered the kitchen through the porch. They arrived in time to prepare a sumptuous breakfast, especially for Janine and Jill, who would be reporting for their first day of school where both taught. Though duty called, what occupied their minds with excitement was that later in the morning Kat and her daughters would meet husband/father Ken to go shopping for school clothes.

***

5:30 a.m.—Notably, Karen skipped breakfast, briefly greeted those in the dining room, and left the Blair House to attend a school related conference in Denver. Her mission became more complex. Hurrying, Karen's plan had been to stop at her parent's home near Colorado Springs where she would rent a trailer to haul her possessions back to Jericho Springs. Perhaps it was her haste that led Karen Gustafson mistakenly to turn right out of the Blair House driveway instead of left. A left turn would have led her through Jericho Springs on Main Street, north on County Road 403 past the Browning's house, and on to Ridge View from which she could directly head northeast and intersect the interstate highway. Perhaps it was because she dwelt, euphorically, on thoughts of dancing with Adam last night that led her back to the Stage Stop Hotel! Realizing her error, she decided to follow CR 403 to Rock Creek and to turn north toward Colorado highway 96, which would lead her east to the interstate.

Along the way Karen picked up a bedraggled hitchhiker, a young woman who was her former student in Quail Point. Mutual recognition and warmth from the car heater quickly led to revealing conversation. The girl, June Osteen, reminded Karen that she was a niece of the Quail Point mayor and his daughters were her cousins. Her family had moved away two years ago. Karen asked why she was out in the middle of nowhere hitchhiking. June began sobbing and revealed she had spent the night safely sleeping amongst the ruins of the burnt out trailer. She apologized about her appearance, damp clothing, and circumstances. The young woman revealed she had received a flyer about the rave by mail from her younger cousins, who later told her she could make one hundred dollars by participating in a dramatic Canaanite ritual. They had convinced her it was only a dramatization of Baal worship, a play conducted during the musical event. As a result, June agreed to participate. The sisters then had said she should come back to the valley and if she stayed, she could make a lot of money working at the Asherah House. June confessed she had been naïve about what she agreed to do, but learned quickly as the event unfolded. When the shot rang out and the thunder clapped as the lights illuminated the group, she fled when rain fell as if it were poured from buckets.

"Miss Karen, I saw them push the Indian girl over the cliff. I saw them push the old couple over too..."

"Do you mean to say they were deliberately pushed...pushed over the cliff...on purpose?"

"Yes, without a doubt...two men in bear skins pushed the girl, and I think the old couple may have been what you would say...collateral damage. I doubt many saw or realized what had happened...it was a mindless stampede...so much drinking and pot...Are they okay?"

"The girl died from the fall, but the old couple was taken to the hospital."

Genuine remorse gripped the young woman, now more like a little girl, who wound herself up in a ball against the door next to her, and said, "Please let me sleep now...there's more to tell about another girl murdered in Quail Point and about a girls' club at the high school."

Karen reached over, patted June on her shoulder, and said, "You are safe now, I'll take you to your home in Colorado Springs. We'll talk later."

"Thank you, Miss Karen," June said, "I can't believe they left me and never came looking for me."

As Karen drove her light blue Chevy Nova up the interstate, she thought that this had not been pleasant to hear, but it was a divine moment, which shed light on the rave event and on what was happening at Quail Point. She took her former student to the girl's home in Colorado Springs, stopped briefly at her parents' home, then went on to her workshop without renting a trailer

\*\*\*

7:00 a.m.—Five of Red McNaughton's ranch hands had arrived earlier and unloaded horses from Red's trailers. Leaving vehicles aside they saddled their mounts, as Adam's wranglers appeared from the Claymore stables and joined them. Rabbit, the lead wrangler, leisurely led twelve others from the ranch to the junction where Claymore Flats Road intersected County Road 403 and the dirt road leading west into the mountains. Travelling parallel to the West Fork of Rock Creek, the wranglers began to follow the mountain road toward open range where they would round up cattle and bring both herds down to Ezra Freedom's pastureland. At the hairpin turn immediately west of the Blair House and the Live Oak tree, the horses spooked and broke into a spirited cantor which culminated at Freedom's saw mill.

Reining his mount to a halt, Rabbit turned to face his fellow wranglers and asked, "Did anyone see or hear anything back there?"

"At the hairpin?"

"Yeah?"

"Not a thing, but I saw scat."

"I saw it too, but it looked dry, old."

"Pilgrim tracked the bear to the road, but he thought it might have crossed the creek and headed up the mountain toward Pryor," said Rabbit, "or it might have followed this road or the one on the Flats."

"Either way it could circle back."

"Did anyone smell anything?"

"Just Tiny's stinky feet!"

"Yeah, it must have been Tiny."

"Tiny, you ride drag. We'll need your stink to ward off any bear."

With that said, Tiny spurred his robust mount and the race was on again, until the horses tired from the uphill climb.

\*\*\*

7:30 a.m.—Two incidents happened at the same time, one at the hospital in Ridge View and the other at the Jericho Springs high school.

In Ridge View, Deputy Cotton Candy visited the Andersons, just before they were released from the hospital. They told Candy their involvement happened by accident. Walter explained they were on their way to Denver from Walsenburg when they had turned off the interstate at the Quail Point exit, so they could drive through the canyon before stopping in Rock Creek for dinner. While waiting to order, they heard conversation between folks seated at a neighboring table about a worship service to be held up on the ridge. For twenty dollars, they could attend and enjoy plenty of food and drink. When the others suddenly got up from their seats and walked out the back door, the Andersons followed them up the hill.

"They were very orderly. They walked up the path in single file and each paid ten dollars to eat and see the service," said Mrs. Anderson.

"We got something to eat and just stood around watching folks pass by us," Walter added, "but soon the atmosphere changed."

"It got scary," Mrs. Anderson said. "Everyone was drinking beer and many smoked, what Walter said was pot, and I knew this was not the outdoor service we had ever experienced. I wanted to leave and I started for the trail back down, when Walter grabbed my arm to protect me..."

"At first I thought the bears were real, but then I realized they were men wearing black bear suits. They wore real bear hide, or so I think, and they ran up the trail to what were ceremonial tables," Walter explained.

"Walter, you forgot to tell how some man with a red mustache pulled out a gun and said something before shooting out the yard light at a church across the way."

"Yes dear, then three others lined up and shot the street lights…"

"Lights at the gas station and hotel were darkened too!" the deputy said with surprise.

"Clouds rolled over the sky and blocked the moon," said Walter.

"Walter doesn't see too good, and I couldn't see a thing until they fired up the bonfire with a boom."

"I watched another feller crawl out from under a pick-up truck where the three men had placed their rifles after shooting out the street lights. He came near us and dropped the rifles over the cliff without much clatter. He laughed and put his finger to his mouth… and you know he was asking us to be quiet."

"I really enjoyed what he did with those rifles…"said Mrs. Anderson, "Lord knows what those fools might have done!"

"Next thing we knew the clouds clapped with thunder, lights appeared to the south, and two huge men approached from out of the dark just as six women were being led to the table by men in the bear costumes…"

"I suppose the huge men were part of the celebration…" the deputy concluded.

"I don't think so…but a rather large but young woman came up next to the Misses and began shouting something," said Walter, "and when the rifle shot split the large pole by the memorial table and lightening struck the top of the pole, the heavens opened up and poured on all of us."

"How did you and the young woman next to you end up falling from the cliff?" Deputy Candy asked.

"Well, then the stampede began…and when two of the men in bear suits came near, the Indian woman grabbed one, swore at him, pounded her fist on his head, and called them fakers," said Walter.

"They pushed her toward the edge of the cliff, and Walter yelled for them to stop!"

"One said something about a chance and how they would at least complete part of the ceremony."

"We didn't fall! We were pushed over the edge. First the young woman went over…then we were…only I hung on and I tore off the cuff of his costume," Mrs. Anderson said with a smile, "I 'spect you might want this for evidence."

Candy tucked the evidence into a plastic baggie, wrote down the Anderson's contact information, and drove them to the Stage Stop parking lot where they were observed leaving in their automobile by several inside the hotel dining room.

\*\*\*

At the other end of the valley at 7:30 in the morning, several more residents of the Blair House prepared to address their duties. School teachers, Janine Crowfoot Freedom and Jill Lowenstein ate a hearty breakfast with the Bond girls, Jerry Sunday, Izzy and Kip Powell. After breakfast Janine and Jill began the new school year by walking a few blocks to the high school for the annual school district teacher orientation. Were it not for her conference in Denver, Karen Gustafson also would have walked to school with Jill and Janine.

Mara Gelding served as secretary to John Alden, high school principal. It was her job to greet all district staff at the front desk in the school office, which meant all had been immediately confronted with the tragedy befallen the community. Mara Gelding's plight evoked sympathy from all her co-workers despite rumors that DNA and other evidence pointed toward her dead husband as the murderer of Gloria Jones. Only news of Janine's marriage to a childhood friend sparked life in the conversations of staff, but questions remained as to whether or not they were really married or just living together at the Blair House.

During the district level meeting, Clarence Moss, superintendent of schools, invited Janine to resolve the issue. Whereupon, Janine announced she and her husband, Ezra Freedom Jr., had mistakenly rushed into a civil marriage but were going to have a formal Christian ceremony in two weeks to which all were invited to attend the ceremony and/or the reception here at the high school. Janine explained many might recognize her husband by another name, Izzy Blair, which heightened the excitement as most realized Janine had married into great wealth, Colorado gold and water rights.

Janine promptly brought levity and compassion to those gathered as she said, "You know I teach Shakespeare's great play *Romeo and Juliet*. Remember the key line by Friar Laurence in Act 2 Scene 3

114

when he says of the young couple, 'They stumble who run too fast'. That's what I did. What can I say?"

While Janine's announcement elevated the staff's mood, Principal John Alden made another that alarmed most of the staff and dampened the spirits of many. "I'm sorry to end on a sad note, but you need to be aware and watch for students struggling with the loss of a friend or relative from Wolf City. Betty Strong Bull, granddaughter of Chief Strong Bull and cousin of Janine Crowfoot...Freedom, died last night of a broken neck when she fell off the ridge in Rock Creek at the end of another rave," Alden said. "You will need to be alert for how students respond to the death of one as young as they are... and be confident our counseling department is well equipped to help grieving students. Our condolences to Janine and her extended family here and in Wolf City. Also, if you have not heard, it is confirmed our school secretary, Mara Gelding, received news that her husband is deceased. Please extend your condolences to her in this difficult time....People, we are like a family, you and I together with our kids and one another, and remember we teach children first, state test is important but secondary to our watchful care for our students and one another."

***

Meanwhile, Jerry and Izzy helped Kip finish installing a stairwell banister from the bookstore to Kip's room on the second floor. The stairwell project had required more remodeling than expected. Doorways at the bottom had been added not only to the bookstore, but also to the library behind the store. On the second floor the stairwell opened into a walk-in closet, which would be accessed by Kip through the sliding closet door. Lights had been added to the second floor closet and at the bottom of the stairwell. The team had not removed the original south window to the first floor porch, which now helped illuminate the stairwell. A sheetrock wall was added to enclose the stairwell, which had been taped, textured, and painted. Hanging the doors required more time than thought. With installation of the stairwell banister, the bookstore project had now been completed. Kip Powell, proprietor of the Blair House Bookstore announced, "It is finished and ready for our open house!"

*** 

8:45 a.m.—A yellow jeep left the garage at Adam's Rock Creek house and headed north on 85/87 then west CR 403 into Jericho Springs. With little fanfare, the driver parked next to the Bustos Family Mexican Restaurant on the side street below John Law's offices. Two men wearing cowls climbed out of the jeep and carried two large pots and bags of soil and mulch upstairs to the offices of John Law, Attorney.

When entering the office lobby, they startled Amanda Sentry, secretary and receptionist for John Law. Both their size and appearance in the cowls had startled her, as each more than filled the doorway. She had become even more startled when they didn't speak, but offered Amanda two large pots and bags of soil and mulch plus two acorns. Next, they pointed toward a file storage room where she had been nurturing a Live Oak sapling. In an attempt to call the sheriff, she reached for the telephone on her desk, but one gently touched her hand on the phone and removed the hood of his cowl from his head. As he smiled, his countenance relaxed Amanda, and she could not stop looking at his face and red, shoulder-length hair. Dwarfed by both she set down the telephone, graciously moved around her desk, and reached upward to touch the red headed giant's face. Amanda touched his locks and stroked his red beard, while he closed his eyes, simpered with a silly self-conscious smile and a prolonged blink, and then he exhaled.

Next, Amanda startled them when she reached for the red head's hand and held it in both of hers. Grasping his hand she counted his fingers touching them one by one, and then she looked searchingly into his blue eyes. Were he a draft horse, he would have neighed, as his eyes dilated and he bowed his head in respectful submission. She smiled and motioned for the other to bend close to her, whereupon she reached up and removed the head covering and revealed his flowing blond hair.

Tears moistened Amanda's eyes, and she said looking first at the blond and then at the red head, "I dreamed of you," she paused and blushed, "and you also. I don't know if you are angels or not, but I know I am to help you. You have come for the Live Oak sapling I have in the file room."

When they nodded, Amanda continued, "I see you have brought me an exchange. Two pots, bigger than I imagined, soil, and mulch that I suspect will bring surprising results."

Both nodded, as Amanda escorted them into the file room where the morning and noon day sun would shine directly on them. Carrying the pots, soil, and mulch, these gentle giants turned sideways, entered the room, bowed to pray, and invited Amanda to do the same. She watched as they made an inaudible prayer. Which one will it be? Amanda wondered.

After planting the acorns, the red head took a vial of liquid from his cowl pocket and poured exactly one quarter of its contents on the soil mixture above the first acorn, then another quarter above the other acorn. Amanda grinned with delight and thought, now I know, as she said, "I know you have a vow of silence, and I cannot know what you will do with the sapling, but I am to give a message to you both before you leave." Both the redhead and the blonde looked at one another and smiled with delight.

Amanda walked with the men, or angels, to the door of the office exit and asked them to wait. She hugged each of them, and then pulled the redhead to her, whereas he lowered his head and received a kiss on his lips from Amanda's blushing face. The blonde smiled from ear to ear watching how stunned his twin brother appeared at the maiden's kiss.

"I know I will see you again," Amanda said as the gentle giants descended the stairwell to their yellow jeep.

\*\*\*

9:00 a.m.—Denver Detective Caleb Jones met with off duty Deputy Sheriff Cotton Candy at the museum in the school district administration office building in Rock Creek.

In the quiet of the museum, Caleb and Cotton discussed details of the two raves, the one last night and the other Cotton believed eventually resulted in the death of Caleb's sister Gloria Jones. After learning his sister had been the only dark skinned woman residing at the Asherah House, Caleb confessed he had thought his sister's death had been the result of a racial crime. When he found out the 'Bed and Breakfast' was a moniker, an alias and a ruse, for a prostitution ring, he realized his sister had worked as a call girl. Cotton advocated it had nothing to do with Gloria's skin color or even that she had worked part time at the Asherah House. Cotton stated she became convinced it had more to do with the ritual that Gloria possibly had been forced to endure during a rave. Cotton asserted Caleb's sister became a part time call girl after a rave.

Caleb questioned whether or not other women had been involved in the ritual, and if there were, what had happened to them. Cotton informed him that apparently a total of six females participated in each ritual, willingly or not. Also, the only other known participant or victim from the first rave was Hannah Rahab, who became a desk clerk at the Stage Stop Hotel after the previous rave. Cotton reminded Caleb that Hannah had disappeared with Harper McNaughton after Harper had shot former deputy Butch McNaughton in the back a few weeks ago. Caleb remembered Hannah had been the daytime desk clerk at the hotel and she, like his sister, had no relatives in the area. Both were newcomers to the valley.

"You said known participant and you said females not women. You suspect...what?" asked Detective Jones.

"Well, we know Hannah was one, and it's safe to say your sister was another, and I do suspect the dead girl from Quail Point may have been one more."

"And that's why you said females not women," Caleb added, "because she was a teenager, a high school student, and a minor...at a party, albeit a large one, where booze flowed freely."

"As did the pot smoking..." Cotton answered, "And probably one more."

"Continue..." Caleb invited.

"Earlier this morning I interrogated the Andersons before they were released from the hospital," said Cotton, "and they provided the name of one more, at least I think so."

"The Andersons must be the old couple who fell off the cliff with Betty..."

"Strong Bull, the granddaughter of Chief Strong Bull, which makes her a cousin to Janine Freedom, Janine's brother Mike Crowfoot, and Rabbit Pinebow, one of Adam's wranglers."

"Janine of the Blair House fortune, where I live, and Mike who works at the Jericho Springs Convenience Store and has a room where I stay, plus Rabbit, who confronted the bear last night at the church?"

"The same..." Candy replied, "And the Andersons said they were pushed over the cliff by two of those wearing the bear skins. They went on to say that Betty was pushed after she called them fakers and grabbed at one of those wearing a costume."

"And would you conclude she may have been in a ritual...?"

"Yes, previously, and Walter Anderson said one of the men said something about a chance and how they might at least fulfill part of the ceremony."

"I wonder what that meant..." Caleb paused, then added, "let's see...we have my sister Gloria, Hannah the desk clerk, the girl from Quail Point, and now Betty Strong Bull. That's four...we need to identify two more...Are there common denominators?"

"Two...your sister and the girl in Quail Point were said to have been pregnant and rumor has it that Betty was too. Also, your sister and Hannah just showed up in town after the last rave and they stayed."

"Which means some women or girls are locals and some come from towns nearby, and at least one from as far away as Denver..." Caleb paused again, "Have any other women just showed up? Is anyone else pregnant?"

"I think Heather Ross, who is Tim McNaughton's girlfriend and has little or no visible means of support. Also, obviously Misty, who apparently has spent her life at the Asherah House. She is definitely pregnant."

"I've heard men talk about Heather. They say she's very provocative..."

"Your thinking about something else," Cotton said as she studied his wearied face. "This has got to be difficult for you. Have you had enough for now?"

"No, no, I'm okay, just a little tired...I'll be all right. Thanks for your concern," Caleb replied, "I just realized we've made two assumptions, and they may not be accurate."

"They are..."

"Well, one is that we assume each rave included six women or girls for the ritual and we don't know what was going to happen, if the rain hadn't thwarted the event. There could have been more or less women involved. We do know there were six wearing a bear costume and we assume each was a man."

"Let me guess the other..." said Cotton, "just because we know about two raves doesn't mean there haven't been others. Others may not have been so public. We know there have been two raves, the one in Rock Creek and a previous one on Red's land north of Ridge View."

"Interesting..." Caleb said pensively, "my sister Gloria, Sam Gelding, and Betty Strong Bull—all died in Rock Creek...all may have been murdered in Rock Creek. What does your crime data say about that?"

"Those deaths are the only ones that were not of natural causes or vehicular or other types of accidents in Rock Creek Valley."

Candy and Jones finished developing their plan. Since Sheriff Bailey could not be found the night before and since he had not responded to her calls for help, they decided to keep him out of the loop for now. Caleb informed Candy that he had been assigned to the valley at the request of the Colorado Bureau of Investigation, Human Trafficking Unit, which had a cooperative arrangement with the Denver Police Department.

Candy clarified she would be working on the case mostly when off duty. Caleb suggested they start meeting in the offices of John Law to which Candy concurred. Both would be researching who had done what to whom. Who had organized each known rave? How had the raves been advertised? Who owned the Tobacco Store, operated the Stage Stop Hotel, owned and operated the Asherah House Bed and Breakfast? Who wore the bear costumes and what was going to happen during the ritual? Who were the women marked for the second rave? Caleb wanted to know one more answer. Had Sam Gelding acted alone or was he carrying out someone else's orders to murder Gloria Jones?

Deputy Candy put her hand on Detective Jones' forearm and asked, "Is it true that your sister was pregnant?"

Jones responded, "Unfortunately, she was, which compounds the murder."

"Pardon me for this, but we know Sam Gelding had relations with Gloria, but have you considered the child wasn't his?"

"How would that play out?"

"I think we need to order an autopsy of the dead girl in Quail Point," Candy said, and continued, "and then compare the DNA of both fetuses. What if the DNA of the fetuses does not match up with Gelding's? I believe Mara Gelding had said her husband could not sire a child, which is why they never had any."

"I'll take care of the autopsy request today. Do you bet the fetuses have been destroyed?"

"Yes, I do, which would tell us something else...Let me know what you find out," Candy said to Caleb Jones, whose eyes had become fiery.

"Candy, can you contact Hannah Rahab and Heather Ross?"

"I'm on it!" Candy replied, "And I picked up a key from Mara Gelding this morning to do another search of Gelding's home and office."

"You have a warrant for both?"

"I do and I have the cuff from the bearskin suit that Mrs. Walter Anderson managed to tear from one of those who pushed her over the edge of the cliff in Rock Creek!"

"Well done, Deputy, well done! We need to talk with someone who knows more about Baal worship and the Canaanite culture."

"Usually, I would say Adam or another one of the pastors in the valley..." Cotton thought, "But I've got some related concerns or questions about the Tunnicliffes, who just showed up with long swords. My guess is we should ask John Mark Cannikin about Baal worship and the Canaanite culture."

"He was up on the ridge hiding under a truck, he gathered the rifles and tossed them over the cliff...and he helped afterwards."

"Yes, and I think we can count on all those we talked with at the church. We may need their help," Cotton added. "Did you hear many, if not all of the Night Riders, have been released from jail?"

"Yep...they plead guilty, and only paid a hundred dollar fine each," said Caleb, who continued with, "They were assigned community service, and credited with time served...and a couple of other deals were made."

"Who was the judge?"

"Parsons, and you should know Adam Claymore was in on it or at least he influenced a plea bargain concerning his nephew Butch McNaughton," Caleb answered with disgust. "I find it hard to believe that Claymore would help them...they torched his trailer."

"Caleb, it might not happen in Denver, but here it is different. Boys will be boys and sometimes even the judges buy into that mentality." Candy explained. "The community often enables young boys and young men..."

"They don't want to ruin a kid's life, nor do they want the boys to experience the consequences of their behavior," said Caleb. "I just hope Adam's deal will straighten out Butch!"

"I think we can trust Adam on that one," Cotton replied, "and now that I think about it...I don't think I should interview the Osteen parents. The mayor would call Sheriff Bailey and Bailey would be alerted to what we are doing. Let's establish more probable cause. What would the opposition do in response to our investigation?"

"I've got your back, and you've got mine..."

"Then since I've got Mara's keys let's go to Gelding's office again and take a look."

They exited the museum, walked across the highway to the insurance agency, entered in, and discovered it had been partially trashed, but not all of the office area. Deputy Candy called Mara Gelding at school to alert her about what they had just discovered, and Mara asked if the realtor happened to be in his office. While still on the telephone, the realtor, Robert King, entered from the rear door and asked them what they were looking for. Caleb showed him Candy's search warrant, and then asked King when he had arrived. King confirmed the condition of Sam's office. He said it was a mess when he had arrived around eight this morning. Candy had King report the same to Mara Gelding, who thanked Robert King and promptly hung up the telephone.

King smirked and said, "Let me know when you are finished."

\*\*\*

11:00 a.m.—Ezra Freedom Sr.—woodcutter and whittler, father of Izzy Freedom, rightful owner of the Blair House and its water and mineral rights extending into and through the mountain valley west of the Blair House and more—passed through town down to Adam's Rock Creek house with a load of wood. Although he had considerable wealth, he maintained his service to the Rock Creek Valley by cutting wood and delivering it personally to customers. In his spare time, he attended city council and school board meetings and managed to attend events at all the churches. Many alleged he had been the one who had placed gold nuggets in collection plates and other places to the benefit of nearly all agencies and organizations in the valley. Although he could not speak, he had demonstrated a lot of concern for the community. While a prisoner of war in Cambodia during the Vietnam War, his tongue had been cut off. He had returned from the war to find his child was missing, so he had hired his attorney John Law to find Izzy. John got the job done, and Izzy had returned home. Somehow both Jill Lowenstein and Karen Gustafson had stayed at his cabin in the woods above town after he had rescued them from life threatening circumstances. Since then Ezra was considered a hero by all the women's organizations, and he was well on his way toward becoming a dandy.

After unloading and stacking wood at Adam's Rock Creek house, Ezra entered the Stage Stop Hotel restaurant and ordered a Rocky Mountain Cheese Burger Deluxe with fries and a cola soft drink. Ezra savored what he could taste, while watching and listening.

\*\*\*

Meanwhile, Adam left Claymore Flats and drove his red F-250 long bed Ford truck to Jericho Springs. On his way he had picked up Kip Powell to go with him, so Adam could introduce Kip and show his

123

support for the new Christian book store at the Blair House, which would soon hold an open house. They stopped at Bustos Family Mexican Restaurant on Main Street. Directly below John Law's offices, Adam and Kip waited for pastors to arrive from all around Rock Creek Valley.

Adam's formal agenda included discussing the idea of a monthly get together where the pastors could pray for one another and for their community. Additionally, Adam hoped the pastors would want to talk about the prayer walks his congregation had been doing as well as the activities of Priscilla and Aquila on street corners. He hoped their conversation would produce prayer walks in each of the towns. He wanted to share Rock Creek church plans and hopes for revival in the valley. He wanted to tell about Ezra Freedom's restoration of Blair House and about Rachael McNaughton's in-home party where she would give a testimony about the influence of Christian books and music on her life. He wanted to stifle gossip about Janine and Izzy Freedom by his explaining that they had a courthouse wedding, he had completed counseling with the couple and would soon be performing a marriage ceremony. Adam had his agenda, and he knew his fellow pastors would have agendas of their own. Adam relaxed and prayed for God's will to be done.

Twelve pastors arrived and the wait staff joined tables forming a rectangle. Adam had each pastor make an introduction, then he introduced Kip Powel and had Kip share about the bookstore, the grand opening, services for pastors and churches, Kip's book fair at Canon City on Saturday, about Rachael, and Kat Bond would be operating the book store when he was out of town. All expressed genuine interest and invited Kip to call upon them, and then the conversation opened up.

Letting the conversation take a life of its own, individual pastors asked, "Did you know some people had walked in Jericho Springs as a prayer walk, encountering people and sharing the gospel? Did you know it happened also in Rock Creek?" "Did you see Aquila and Priscilla working the street corner in Ridge View with signs saying 'Got Problems, Let's Pray,' 'Honk if You Love Jesus', and 'Jesus Loves You, Do You Know Him?'" Others asked about Sam Gelding's body being found and whether or not Izzy and Janine were living together or married, but no one asked about what had happened the night before. Also, a pastor asked if anyone at the meeting had received a card of encouragement from Penelope Quick. Delightfully, this ended the meeting on a positive note and a regular meeting schedule was struck for noon every Thursday. The lunch meetings would rotate to every community. The next meeting had been scheduled for the Cozy Corner Café in Ridge View...

\*\*\*

2:00 p.m.—Encouraged by the pastor's reception, Kip Powell left town traveling south to Quail Point to set up outlets wherever he could establish them. He met with a potential dealer there, who was willing to conduct in home parties and learn to call on local pastors. Next, Kip traveled on to Canon City, the Royal Gorge, Loma Linda, and Howard. He stopped in Canon City at the Methodist Church to finalize details for a book fair, followed by his preaching assignment on Sunday at a community church.

\*\*\*

By 2:15 p.m. Izzy had been left alone and had just completed the final cleaning of the third floor bedroom in the northwest corner. He heard a reverberating crack and an explosive crash from on top of little Huerfano where Freedom's tree stood and where his father had carved a picture meant to be seen by all in the valley. Izzy heard another crack and crash, as he climbed through the third floor window and stood on the balcony. He watched as the grizzly gathered itself after tumbling to the ground. It had climbed on the south limb of the tree, and the bear's weight broke the limb just like it had broken the one on the west side of the Live Oak. The great bear had snapped the dead apart from what had regained life, at least in part by the efforts of Izzy's father, who had been faithfully watering the tree nightly.

Next, the mighty bear stood on its hind legs and began clawing the south face of the tree like it had on the church door in Rock Creek the night before. All alone and without a firearm, Izzy stood

125

on the third floor balcony and shouted at the bear, which understood Izzy's shout as the challenge he had intended. The bear stopped and intently sized up Izzy, while Izzy climbed the balcony rail and roared at the bear.

Was it just a bear, Izzy thought, or was it the personification of evil? There are no grizzly bears in Colorado. They had been killed or moved to Wyoming, he remembered, yet here it was damaging something of great value to Izzy. The tree stood on top of little Huerfano like a beacon on a hill, the citadel on a hill. In the center of the top was a dry pool which once had been filled with water so hot it had been used to heat the Blair House. It was believed early members of the local Ute tribe had planted the tree long ago. Beatrice Jaramillo had confirmed this legend, and said that her people revered the tree. Mike Crowfoot, Janine's brother, said the same thing as had Rabbit Pinebow, one of Adam's wranglers and cook.

The standoff ended when Izzy's father arrived in the pick-up truck that he was using as a temporary replacement for the Gray Wiz. Izzy watched as his father leaped from the cab of his truck with his shotgun and charged up the hill toward the bear. With two blasts, he hit the bear from a distance. Ezra Sr. dropped his shotgun and ran uphill with his Bowie knife in hand. To Ezra's disappointment, the bear had high-tailed it to the hairpin turn in the road above Freedom's tree and crossed the creek where it began an ascent of the mountain toward the ghost town of Pryor.

Izzy watched as his father roared mightily at the bear, which ran away from him. Certainly, there would be a rematch, Izzy feared, then scripture came to mind and Izzy spoke it aloud, *"And we know that in all things God works for the good of those who love him, who have been called according to his purpose" (Romans 8:28).*

Father waved at son with fist lifted toward heaven and son roared mightily and waved at his father, while both had admired the other's steadfast repulse of evil. They had experienced a reminder that in rebuilding Blair House, they would need to have a spear in one hand, while placing a brick on the wall with the other.

Izzy climbed down from the third floor porch to the ground below, and then joined his father on top of Huerfano. They examined the broken limbs, large as tree trunks, and placed their hands on the claw marks for good measure. All had been occupied elsewhere except for Izzy when the bear sought to destroy the tree and leave its signature. Ezra Jr. and Sr. prevailed, as the grizzly fled and traveled over the mountain toward Pryor. The Freedoms knew it would be back!

# Arrivals

## CHAPTER 7

*"... our God will fight for us!"*     *Nehemiah 4:20b*

B eing routed before completing the pagan ritual on the ridge east of the Stage Stop Hotel had been one of several recent failures for the McNaughton Corporation. The Jericho Springs City Council refused to condemn the Blair House property and make it public domain. Council stood against the corporation's effort to gain the mineral and water rights held by the true owners of the Blair House. In defiance of the city council, Red McNaughton and other corporate leaders had sought to have the courts reverse the city council's decision. They had been humiliated in court when the judge refused to honor their claims to gain the Blair House. Their sense of entitlement had been dashed with the revelation that the true owners of the house were not newcomers. They lost public support as well as support from their own membership when long time residents learned the rightful owner of Blair House was a veteran who had generously given gold nuggets to churches and other organizations in the valley. Even the corporate leadership had been charmed by how the owner's son, Izzy, had returned home to claim his childhood sweetheart, Janine Crowfoot, a revered teacher at Jericho Springs High School.

Despite the negative press that Night Riders had earned for the corporation through their recent reign of terror, Red McNaughton and the rest of its leadership had been delighted when the Night Riders had been released from jail. The corporation had paid their fines, while the group's members had fulfilled sentences of time served at the local jail. Each had been assigned probation with an overworked probation officer. Also, each had been assigned one hundred hours of community service. As expected, Butch McNaughton had gained his own special deal. All Night Riders committed to stop harassing newcomers and locals who got in their way.

The Night Riders and others had been angered by the results of the recent rave. Only travelers and other outsiders died or were injured during the stampede. The pagan worshippers failed to complete their Baal fertility ritual. None could understand how the puny church in Rock Creek had prevailed against them, especially after Red symbolically destroyed the yard light and the uninvited grizzly bear shredded much of the entrance to the church. Corporate leaders hoped for a different outcome to their next effort, and those who had resisted them would be in for more trouble. Dark forces gathered for more direct assaults upon newcomers to the Rock Creek Valley.

Led by Red, corporate leadership had gathered around tables at the Tobacco Store to discuss the resistance. Primarily, it had come from the little Church in the Glen led by Adam Claymore, interim pastor and Red's partner, and a handful of faithful followers, who may have been Blair House residents. Joining the resistance, three men had invaded the rave just as the ceremonial ritual commenced. One drove a jeep from somewhere south of the Asher pole with lights flashing and horn blaring. Two large men ran before the lights waving long swords, which frightened many loyal followers as well as curious onlookers. Oldtimers figured they had to be part of the group restoring the Blair House. Even the dark clouds seemed to have worked against those who planned the rave, when lightening lit up the sky and thunder clapped when the clouds opened and dumped torrential rain. Leaders of the event escaped without detection by local authorities. Three fled down the trail from the ridge to the Asherah House Bed and Breakfast where they enjoyed the fruit of two ceremonial participants, while three other leaders escaped in their trucks with each taking another willing woman. No one knew what had happened to the sixth woman, nor did they really care. The corporate leaders had been delighted to hear it had been a mighty grizzly bear that had roared the night before and that it had marred the entrance door to the little church in Rock Creek. They marveled at how the bear's sudden appearance had coincided with their planned ritual. What really angered them was that one woman, named Misty, who had participated in a previous ceremony, had escaped to the little Church in the Glen. Although their followers had attempted to rescue Misty from the little Church in the Glen, their effort had been repelled by what was reported as being two angels or at least giant men. What followed had stirred their followers to flee from the ridge, when a shot rang out from across the mouth of the canyon and a slug nearly split the Asher pole. Seemingly, the shot had followed the mighty roar of the fearsome beast from the town below, before the clouds opened and all had been drenched.

"Red!" his son Butch said loudly as the corporate leaders had been stunned by his intrusion, "We all are pretty clear about what happened...at least how we see things..."

"What do you mean...how we see things?" growled Red, who raised his voice and scraped the table with his Bowie knife.

"Red, you sound like that old bear," laughed Butch's friend, Roy Sentry, as he rocked back in his chair, "and you're clawing the table like it too."

As Red kicked Roy's chair and Roy fell backward, Red replied, "What's with you two? Who brainwashed you when you were in jail?"

In an unusual act of kindness, Buddy Smith helped Roy off the floor and he said, "Red, we spent a lot of time sitting on the wrong side of the bars...we all had time to think about things...like how I hurt nice old Beatrice, one of your family's grammas. I can't believe I actually hit her in the head with a beer bottle, and I feel bad about hassling Mrs. King and Mrs. Parson on the corner where they invited people to stop and pray..."

"My sister, Amanda, went door to door with a bunch of people in Jericho Springs. They left gifts at every house," Roy added, while refusing to return to his seat at the table.

"Dad," Butch said, as Red flinched at the tone of the endearment, "the people Roy and Buddy mentioned are not newcomers. Each is one of us...they're friends and family...and I was surprised at what you said when you shot out the church yard light...I wonder what Adam thinks about all we've done..."

"We torched his trailer…" Buddy added, "I'm glad the little girls weren't home…"

"You remember we had you do that, so they wouldn't be witnesses to the rave," Red growled, as he stabbed the table with his knife.

"We didn't do anything to the trailer directly opposite Bond's on the other side of the highway!" said Butch.

"Their daughter was one of the girls chosen for the night!" added Roy.

"You told us to do a lot of things, and we did them," Buddy said, as both Butch and Roy nodded agreement, "but it was us who were behind bars…and Sheriff Bailey would come by our cell and act like he didn't know us."

"You'll be paid well when we get the gold and water rights! You three just don't understand what's at stake," Red said without growling, "You just don't understand…"

"I wonder about Hannah…I have nightmares about Gloria Jones and now Betty Strong Bull…I wonder what happened to the girl who walked away from the crowd and into the herd," Butch said with moist eyes, "and what I was trying to say…"

Chauncey the banker, Ralph from Wolf City, Van Allen from Jericho Springs, Robert the insurance agent, Dr. Wood the assistant superintendent of schools, and Night Riders watched Red grow furious with his son. Red interrupted Butch once more, "What are you crying about…at least now everyone knows you didn't kill Gloria Jones…"

"Red," Chauncey said as he grabbed him at the shoulder, "I think we all need to hear what Butch has to say," and pausing to look around, he continued, "Am I right, boys?"

As the crowd nodded agreement, Red said sarcastically, "Go ahead, Boy, say your piece."

"Look at who we have harmed…Ken Bond and his family. He's a nice man who came here to recover from a heart attack. I hope you have noticed how members of his family take care of one another," Butch looked around, "and Beatrice Jaramillo, she's a McNaughton gramma. Gloria Jones, who worked out of the Asherah after one of our raves. She's someone's daughter, Detective Jones' sister…Betty Strong Bull, she's a granddaughter of the Chief…"

"We didn't do anything to her!" proclaimed Ralph.

"Didn't we?" Butch responded, and then continued, "My Uncle Adam…isn't he the best of us? And Priscilla King and Aquila Parsons… Izzy Freedom…I really identify with him…Like me he didn't know his mother."

"I don't want to hear anymore!" Red said nearly shouting.

"I'm almost done, Red," Butch continued, "Just read *The Out Cry*, you know the weekly newspaper Ken Bond delivers throughout the valley."

"Yes, Butch," Red responded with a snarl, "he delivers it to the house."

"The ads have changed. So have the postings on the bulletin board at the convenience store. Someone convinced the manager to clean up the language…Mrs. King and Mrs. Parsons aren't the only ones working the street corners and praying with people. At least three groups are doing the same, one in each town. The paper has stories about churches holding community prayer meetings. Something about *Chronicles* and chapter fourteen seven or maybe it's seven fourteen," said Van Allen.

"I saw an announcement about Rachael McNaughton hosting a Christian book party…" added Robert King.

"I overheard my pastor say he's meeting together with other pastors about what we've been doing…" said Dr. Wood.

"And I read about a new bookstore opening at the Blair House…" Ralph said enthusiastically.

"And someone's trying to get a Christian radio station…" added Chauncey.

"Yes, and what I'm saying is what we've been doing isn't working. It is wrong!" Butch said forcefully as he stood up and backed away from the table…"Red, you may have broken the church's yard light, but the light isn't out of the church or the Blair House. We all understand we are trying to overcome what was lost with school reorganization and construction of the highway away from the valley, but neither the raves nor harassment of newcomers have gained the water and mineral rights."

"Neither have the Asherah House and Baal worship," said Chauncey the banker.

"A lot of money has come into the valley that we wouldn't have had," Red said defensively, as Butch, Buddy, and Roy moved to stand against the wall by the rear door, "and we have some unfinished business with Misty."

"She wasn't at the rave, and no one has seen her..." said Dr. Wood.

"They had her at the church," said Van Allen. "We tried to go inside, but we couldn't get past two really big men. They blocked the doorway and came toward us with hands on really big swords."

"Van's right...I was one of those with him. They had these big smiles on their faces...like they were looking forward to take us on," said one Night Rider.

"We watched for Misty from the glen beside the driveway, but we don't know what happened to her...We didn't see her leave the church," continued Van Allen.

"Perhaps she was kidnapped by someone from the church. She's probably at the Blair House," said Sheriff Bailey, who had just entered the back door of the Tobacco Store.

"She's not there!" said Van Allen, "We've been watching night and day."

All became silent as they awaited the arrival of more of their comrades at the Tobacco Store in Rock Creek. As others arrived, side conversations started about who had opposed them the night before. They had heard the bear, saw Adam standing defiantly at the crossroads, wondered who were the three men in the jeep and the two at the back door to the church. No one doubted the sound of the rifle shot. It had to be from a Sharps rifle and that meant Pilgrim Wayne had been the shooter.

Jerry Sunday arrived and delivered multiple boxes of pizza from the Jericho Springs Pizzeria, while Lila made several trips from the hotel bar, carrying beer to wash down their feast. Both made mental notes of what they had seen and heard, as they left together. Butch, Buddy, and Roy followed them out the Tobacco Store exit.

Jerry and Lila overheard Roy say, "So what are we, chopped liver?"

***

Others in the valley anticipated the arrival of both friend and foe. First, Adam left Claymore Flats in his F-250 Ford truck pulling a two horse trailer behind it. He had honked at Ezra Sr. and his son Izzy as they stood on the volcanic butte, little Huerfano, while examining indistinguishable marks on the Live Oak tree. Both waved toward Adam encouraging him to stop, but he did not as he had made a late start for the wranglers' camp up canyon. He continued to ascend the valley road first passing Ezra's saw mill and onward to where he followed the road between the two Huajatolla peaks. Much to her delight, Misty's arrival with the Brownings at Blair House had been next, while coinciding with the honking of Adam's truck horn. Expecting to see John Mark and other men, Misty primped in the rear view mirror before leaving the Browning's station wagon.

Although Misty relished her time with the Brownings, Ruth welcomed the end of Misty's short visit. Ruth had tolerated Misty's need to monopolize their conversations and became irritated as both her husband and son seemed enthralled by Misty's every statement, or so Ruth thought. Every request for help had been preceded with a syrupy please and followed by an even sweeter thank you. Ruth felt sickened as she had watched Rob or Andy cater to Misty's whims. Ruth tolerated Misty's self-centeredness knowing she would soon be gone, and Ruth knew her pastor would remind her that Misty was a new creation. Ruth believed her pastor would scold her with words to remind her that a battle raged within Misty between her old and new selves. But Pastor, Ruth thought, I understand she had been a captive at the Asherah House, but with her new found freedom, Misty has occasional lapses. Ruth would tell the pastor to take notice of how Misty brushes by Rob so seductively. How competitively Misty vied with me for the attention of both my husband and son. Despite Ruth's insecurities she had proven to be a welcomed and positive role model for Misty, but Ruth's initial experience with Misty had proven to be a stretch for Ruth. Misty had been stretched as well. Later, Misty would dwell upon their time together, as she remembered her walking and talking with Ruth the most.

Misty ran up the hill to where Izzy and Ezra stood examining the Live Oak. She hugged both men, and then gasped as she found she could put her entire finger in each mark of every toe claw. She shuddered and sought Ruth's embrace as fear altered her countenance, and a flashback stirred forth a memory of her participation in the bear ritual one night under the full moon. Ruth held on to her and whispered you are safe now in Misty's ear. Misty wept.

"Could we go down to the Blair House?" Misty asked Izzy. "More trouble is coming. I can feel it. I remember it. Will John Mark be here tonight?"

"I believe he said he would check in on you as soon as you got here," Ruth offered.

"I hope so. He knows what's coming."

"I'm sorry you don't feel safe here, Misty. We will watch out for you," said Izzy.

In response Ezra Sr. let out a low moan from deep within himself, and he put his arm around Misty. She wept and hung on to the old man, and then touched his lips with her finger, "You know...you see..." Misty said as Ezra nodded his head. Rob and Ruth exchanged glances, and then with Izzy, who looked bewildered.

"Misty, tonight you will be safe! Look who else has arrived," Izzy said as he pointed toward the base of the mound, and then shouted to the two new arrivals, "Welcome, Detective Jones! Who is with you?"

Rather than answer, the detective motioned for the group to come down from the hill, which they did, then the group entered the Blair House where they would talk more privately. Once inside, Izzy asked Ruth and Rob to escort Misty to a larger second floor bedroom in the middle of the hallway. The detective with Hannah, who had arrived with him, stepped into the first floor library with Izzy and Ezra where they could talk in private.

"What's happening, Detective?" asked Izzy.

"Izzy, I got a call from John Law telling me the Night Riders had all been fined and assigned to do community service," said Caleb.

"Inconceivable!" replied Izzy.

"Sheriff Bailey contacted John Law and asked him to let us all know what was happening. I guess they were assigned to a probation officer."

"I wonder if Adam knows. Red didn't go with Adam on roundup because he had other business to take care of. This is probably part of what kept Red here," Izzy surmised.

"That's my guess."

"What holds you here, Caleb?"

"An autopsy."

"An autopsy? You do know who killed your sister, don't you?"

"Yes, there is no doubt that Sam Gelding is the killer as well as the one who assaulted Karen Gustafson and Jill Lowenstein," Caleb asserted, as Ezra put his hand on his son's shoulder.

"But...?" Izzy asked.

"I asked for and got an autopsy of my sister and also one for the girl Gelding killed in Quail Point. My sister told our mother she was pregnant and she was afraid the baby would be killed if born."

"Really?"

"I also met with Mara Gelding, who told me her husband may have been with both girls, but he couldn't have fathered their babies. He was incapable of fathering a child and that's why they never had any children."

"That's what I heard too!" said Hannah.

"Hannah, what is your role in all of this?"

"I am sorry to say I willingly participated in the bear ritual...like what had been planned for the other night," Hannah said before glancing at Detective Caleb Jones.

"Go on and tell them, Hannah," said Caleb.

"I really don't know a whole lot about it. It has to do with some kind of variation of a pagan worship....Baal and an Asher pole. I was told I should consider myself to be honored to be found acceptable for the ceremony," Hannah explained.

"Who made that judgment?" asked Izzy.

"Well, Butch talked me into it. He told me he was the one I would be with...and well...I liked his attention...at least at first."

"What changed your mind?" asked Caleb.

"When I didn't get pregnant and when they learned I couldn't get pregnant, I wasn't so special. Just like how Sam wasn't special anymore."

"When someone learned he couldn't make a baby?" said Izzy.

"Exactly!" said Caleb.

"So Sam..." said Hannah.

"Was involved with younger women..." interrupted Caleb.

"A girl in high school?" asked Izzy.

"Mr. Freedom, it is happening at the high schools," Hannah asserted.

"Is she correct, Detective?" Izzy asked.

"We don't have enough proof yet, but that is why I'm here. I'm assigned to the Human Trafficking Task Force, and we believe high school girls are targeted and recruited for the bear ritual. Once they go through the ritual, some are recruited to do other things."

"So why would Sam kill your sister and the girl in Quail Point?"

"Near as we can figure, the girl in Quail Point is said to have wanted to commit suicide after she had an abortion. The autopsy proved my little sister was no longer pregnant and must have miscarried or had an abortion."

"And Sam must have been assigned by someone to tie up loose ends?" guessed Izzy.

"I think so," said the detective. "My guess is the assignment would be the proof of his manhood."

"That is sick!" said Hannah.

"Even worse, which brings us back to Misty," said the detective.

"How so?" asked Izzy.

"Unconfirmed, but Hannah testified that Misty was in the same group with her. She was one of the women, who willingly participated in one of the rituals with Hannah," Caleb explained.

"Who are the men dressed as bears?" asked Izzy.

"All we know about for certain is Butch McNaughton, and Hannah is here to help us, in order to help her boyfriend Harper McNaughton," Caleb continued as Hannah nodded in agreement.

"The one who shot Butch twice in the back with Karen Gustafson's twenty-two pistol?"

Hannah nodded affirmatively, and then said, "I'm here to help Misty as well. In fact, would you mind if I join Rob and Ruth to get Misty situated?"

After Hannah excused herself, Izzy continued, "I assume now that Gelding is no longer doing the dirty work...someone else will be assigned to deal with Misty."

"She's more complicated."

"Really? She's a prostitute from the Asherah House Bed and Breakfast, isn't she?" asked Izzy.

"Yes, but we're not certain who she really is, or where she comes from, then all of a sudden, John Mark comes to town and he has a message for her to keep the baby," said Caleb, as he raised his hands in frustration.

"Keep the baby?"

"Yes, and I don't know who he is or whether or not he is acting alone," said the detective. "I hear some remarkable things have happened since he has come around."

"I don't know anything other than he showed up to a prayer meeting and called her out. I also heard he had a remarkable incident at the Cozy Corner Café, and Adam is having him restore the house of his late wife in Rock Creek, so the church there can hire a pastor."

"I think he had a hand in disrupting the ritual on the ridge. Apparently, three men in a jeep came on the scene and helped start the panic," the detective said, while concealing his own involvement.

"I know Adam Claymore has referred to John Mark as a reinforcement. So...why are you telling me all this?"

"Izzy, your trouble isn't over just because the city council ruled in your behalf. Too much is at stake. And it looks like you intend to do more than rebuild this house to what it used to be...physically."

"True, like Adam shared at the pastor's luncheon, this house was a citadel on the hill, a beacon in darkness bringing the light of Christ to the valley."

"Izzy, you can expect Satan is going to be active where God is active. There will be a counterfeit, an opposition to battle you. Like the book of *Ezra*, you will need to rebuild the house with a brick in one hand and a spear in the other. You will have to have people willing to stand in the gap. You will need to be careful about who you let help rebuild. Some helpers may be moles, seeking to devour and destroy. Already you have Hannah as well as Misty here, and frankly, I'd like to stay here for a few months, while I'm investigating, which could bring you more trouble."

"You've been reading the Bible...You could be a reinforcement like John Mark."

"I'd like to think so, but people may not take kindly to you having a black man here."

"Caleb, I use to know how this small town works. Right now I'm viewed as a newcomer, and you are one too, and that would be worse than being black! You won't be the only black either, Morris Goodenough will be joining us as well."

"The Trailways' bus driver?"

"Exactly!"

"Great, if you guys get to be too much to take, Morris and I can hang out together."

"Both of you are well respected by a lot of townspeople," said Izzy after chuckling with Caleb and Ezra. "You may have heard Morris sometimes substitutes for Adam at the church. I'll depend on both of you to keep your eyes and ears well tuned to what is going on."

"Another thing, Izzy."

"I'm listening…"

"The bear! The whole thing with the bear is unusual. It doesn't just kill to eat, and it made a direct assault on the church building"

"And on the tree. It tore into the south side of the tree after it broke two major trunks off the west and south sides. They were both dead and brittle," added Izzy, as Ezra moaned.

"Well, I'll be…"

"It would have done more damage, if I hadn't distracted it, and then my dad arrived in his truck and charged the bear with both barrels of his shotgun blazing," Izzy clarified, as Ezra nodded affirmatively.

"What happened?" Caleb asked.

"The bear ran away… crossed the river, and headed toward the mountain top."

"What's on the other side of the mountain?" asked Caleb.

"Pryor, mostly a ghost town now, but once it was a coal town," Izzy explained.

"Well, what do you think about me staying here for awhile?"

"Caleb, I really do believe you are a reinforcement. I know you have a job to do, and I appreciate the assignment you have, but I welcome what time and help you can give us. How about rooming on the second floor west of Hannah and Misty? I put them in a bedroom directly above this library in the center of the floor. You'll be between them and Karen Gustafson."

"Sounds good, Karen and I will protect the south wall."

"Literally, the south wall and the southwest corner, and you can help watch out for the girls," added Izzy, before his father Ezra nudged him, "and my dad is on the third floor, northeast corner, Morris-third floor southeast corner, Kip Powell-second floor southeast corner, Beatrice Jaramillo-on the watch, second floor northeast corner, with Mike Crowfoot, my wife's brother, in the room next to hers."

"What about the northwest corner?" Caleb asked.

"Jill Lowenstein is second floor, northwest corner, directly across from Karen Gustafson. There is only one bathroom on each floor. On the first floor, it is below the stairwell, but on the second and third floors, they are located at the west end beside a door to the porch, which wraps around the whole house. Contrary to modern code in most places, there is no outside stairwell that leads to the ground outside of the house, except in the back where we have a narrow one that leads to each porch," explained Izzy, "and I don't plan to change that...at least for now, unless I'm forced to do it."

"What about the third floor northwest corner?"

"It will be the last to be filled," said Izzy, "which means we have one vacant room between Mike and Jill on the second floor and six rooms vacant on the third floor. We'll see whom God sends to fill them."

Caleb looked first at Izzy and then at Ezra, who nodded in agreement, and then Caleb asked, "Do you have laundry facilities?"

"Yes," Izzy replied, "down the hall, right of the kitchen, there are two clothes washers and a dryer. Lines are being strung outside on each porch, where you can hang clothes out to dry. But...you may want to use the coin operated laundry by the convenience store or the laundry and dry cleaners downtown."

"How do you heat such a big house, and do you have plenty of hot water?"

"Don't know, it remains to be seen," Izzy laughed, and said, "but we ran butane to a fifty gallon hot water tank in the basement. My dad and the rest of the men cut and deliver firewood all around the valley. The back porch is almost filled, but heating this big of a house will be a problem. The cook stove generates plenty of heat for the kitchen and laundry room. It is vented to the floors above it, which works for the two corner rooms above it. We have fireplaces on the north and south walls, which means we have to haul a lot of wood up the stairs and ash down the stairs."

"I can see why you need more help," mused Caleb. "Has it always been so labor intensive?"

"I'm working on another plan to include butane and/or electric wall heaters, but in the old days, before the rock slide hit the butte where the tree is located, thermal energy heated water that steadily seeped into the dry pool by the tree," Izzy explained. "There's the remains of a pipe system the Blair's used to provide water for an old radiator heat system which served each room adequately."

"How unique!" said the detective, as Ezra nodded enthusiastically.

"Yes," replied Izzy, "and I often slept with the window opened in the third floor northwest corner room in the dead of winter, January. Now, we have a hot springs pond that stays warm all year long."

Ezra grabbed Izzy's shoulder, before the other two heard the pick-up truck enter the driveway with more wood. Izzy said, "Caleb, here comes the last load for the day. Our goal is to fill the back porch, floor to ceiling, before more snowfall, which is predicted to be sooner than later. Why don't you get your things and set up your room... Sorry, but you'll find we only have a twin bed, a chest of drawers, and a lamp and lamp stand in most rooms. Dinner will be later."

As a community with common purpose, members of the Blair House clan gathered together. Rachael came over from across the street and began playing hymns on the piano. Katarina and her daughters arrived from their home down the street to help Beatrice start dinner, while Janine, Ezra, and Izzy helped Morris and Jerry unload the truck. Jill came down to help after mapping area for a garden and vineyard, sheds, and a pole barn. Caleb unloaded his automobile, but stayed in his room briefly unpacking both his and his sister's possessions, as if he were casting an anchor to the room. He stored what he had in the chest of drawers, and then with tears swelling in his eyes, he sorted through his little sister's belongings for the third time. He looked for more clues in what he had gathered from the sheriff's office and from the Asherah House. Only then was he ready to join the others.

"I've mapped the garden and vineyard and where the buildings will go, but I need your help," said Jill.

"What's the plan?" asked Janine, as the rest joined her making a human chain to move the wood quickly to the back porch.

"We ordered grape vines, which will need planting, and I want more manure and sawdust to scatter, and then turn over into the garden plot," explained Jill, "but only after we clear more rock once the porch is filled."

"Ezra, Kip, Jerry, Morris, Mike, and I have been building the wall around Huerfano with rock you have gleaned from the garden area, but we will need to get fertilizer for the slopes," said Izzy.

"Izzy, Ezra, and I have been watering the tree with bucket loads from the pond," added Janine.

"What can I do?" asked Caleb, as he arrived from his room, followed by Misty and Hannah from their second floor room.

"Don't forget us! We want to help!" Misty declared.

"Take our place here," said Janine, "while Izzy and I water Freedom's tree. Jill, show the others the garden site, then meet us on top by the tree."

As the Blair House crew went about their chores, John Mark drove Adam's old Chevy on to the property. Alert to John Mark's arrival, Misty ran to the old car and embraced him as he opened the driver's side door and attempted to exit. Grabbing his arm, Misty led him to the stand of pines, where the others could not see her forcing herself on him.

John Mark laughed and nervously said, "Misty, I've missed you too, but you've got to stop doing this."

Not use to a man resisting her charms only increased her attraction, and Misty said, "Okay for now, but sometime soon, you'll be wanting me as bad as I want you. You'll see!"

Misty frowned, crossed her arms, walked out of the trees without John Mark, and then caught up with the others who were exploring Jill's plan for the garden and outbuildings. As John Mark recovered from the encounter with Misty, he walked toward Little Huerfano and saw Misty's coquettish glance back toward him. You are indeed a vixen, he thought, how long can I resist her? It was then John Mark noticed two men watched from above on the west ridge behind the tree. They must have been watching as the Blair house group walked the grounds, but they had not seen those hauling water from the pond to the tree. John Mark continued to watch them as he climbed the butte, while keeping them in sight. In an instant the two men, Night Riders, knew trouble, as Ezra Sr. attacked them unmercifully knocking them to the ground. While they were unconscious, Ezra rolled their bodies to and over the side of the ridge where a sandy slope allowed them a gentle yet unseen descent to the bottom.

\*\*\*

John Mark stood above the crowd and watched as all climbed the butte to gather on top of it. Izzy guided them around the dry pool, showed them the land bridge created by the rock slide, pointed to where hot water seeped from below, and explained how a culvert under the road carried high water from the creek to the pond, if desired. He showed them the two giant limbs that had died when the rock slide apparently destroyed the root system which fed them. Next, he escorted the crowd around the north side where John Mark sat gazing at Ezra's carving on the Live Oak tree. One by one members of the Blair House clan gathered around John Mark to see the sight from his perspective, and then the artist appeared before them from the backside of his tree.

Ezra invited them to inch forward to where they could clearly see his carving. It was different from before, thought Izzy, and then he recognized his father recently had painted the objects. First, Ezra framed the scene as his hands framed a portrait rather than a land-scape scene. Next, the whittler pointed at the naked man, to himself, and then to each one gathered before him. Every man, John Mark thought. Then Ezra demonstrated a podium by first outlining its shape with his hands, followed by his grasping its corners. With his hands on the podium, he circled an object and peered at it intensely, as if it were a crystal ball that he looked into to find answers. He then pointed at the tree in the center of the carving, and then at the tree before them, as he widened his arms to take in the breadth of it. Next, he pointed to the top left of his carving where figures dressed with hooded red gowns appeared to be waiting. Ezra pointed skyward and let out a long melodious yet throaty song that one in the crowd identified as an angelic throng singing. Ezra nodded, while smiling joyfully, as he scanned every face before him.

Ezra stepped toward the crowd, turned around, bent over to look at the carving from where most sat, and then stepped toward his carving. He rolled up the long shirt sleeve of his right arm and pointed his arm downward and squeezed his right hand multiple times, as if it held something his hand had been manipulating. He stood erect, turned to his side, extended both arms apart and then together with a cutting motion like scissors. Pointing at the open hand in the carving, he followed the hand to the length of the arm and stopped at the top where the arm became handles. Ezra paused and motioned to encourage a guess from the crowd.

"The hand and arm are like mine and yours..." offered Jerry.

"But the handles are not..." countered Morris.

"The hand points toward the ground, whereas the handles are further away from the ground..." concluded Jill, as Ezra looked toward her and beamed forth a smile, while he pumped his fist skyward.

Ezra pointed to a sunflower top center in the carving above the tree, and he traced the length of the stem from flower to root and root into the ground where it became entangled with the tree's roots.

Janine asked, "Do we spell the flower with o u or with an o? Is it sun or son?"

Catching on, Hannah added, "And are the roots of the tree and of the flower connected by a purpose as well as a function?"

"Hmmm...the sunflower seems to bring light...from above," Caleb surmised.

"It is yellow in color..." said Morris.

"Like the sun..." added Katarina, who had arrived from the kitchen.

"The scissor handles become flesh like a hand...and this represents one's right hand...perhaps the son," concluded John Mark, "but notice what the man, you and I, is doing. He searches the crystal ball for answers and reaches for the succulent apple on the tree... perhaps for truth and knowledge, but he seems to miss what is on or in the center of the tree."

"What do you see, John Mark?" asked Izzy, as the crowd inched closer to the wood carving on the Live Oak tree.

"I see man missing the mark by looking for answers where he shouldn't, where he was told not to seek, while missing the source of truth and knowledge," John Mark shared. "I see in the center of the tree...a man on wood, in the shape of a cross, the man's arms are spread out nearly the length of the cross piece, which is horizontal..."

"Is it Jesus?" asked Misty, who answered her own question with, "It is Jesus! I am to seek truth...knowledge not through pagan worship or rituals...I am not to chose the apple...I am to choose to seek knowledge and truth in Jesus who was hung on the cross for even me!"

Ezra clapped his hands and the group joined hands and all said, "Wow!"

"But wait," said Misty, "There is more...Isn't there?..Show them Ezra!"

Ezra nodded agreement and pointed at four figures standing around the podium where man stood searching and then he moaned, "Arrr..."

"Hey Father," said Izzy, "this hits close to home, right here, right now...and you carved this long before the arrival of..."

"Angels?" someone said from the crowd.

Ezra stepped before John Mark, reached behind his neck, and pulled the drab hood over John's head. John Mark stood up, the whole length of himself, taller, broader, and more muscular than the rest, even more so than Caleb Jones.

John Mark's eyes flashed emerald green with emotion, before he spoke, "I am but a carpenter on assignment from the Lord. I am here to help build your church in Rock Creek and to help those who live in Rock Creek. Adam asked me to remodel his house there, so that a pastor and his family may live in it. My brothers are helping me."

"Were they at our church the night of the rave?" asked Janine.

"Yes, they were in the back of your sanctuary Wednesday night when men tried to enter and kidnap Misty. My brothers eliminated the threat."

"You said at church you were there to deliver a message to Elaine. Was it true?" asked Hannah.

"Yes, I was also on assignment to find and now protect Misty, who is Elaine McClaren," said John Mark, who then spoke directly to Misty, "My Lady, it is important for you to understand and accept that mine is a holy mission, a quest if you will. It calls forth fealty, which means faithfulness by the knight to our Lord, who is the Christ. The knight is to receive nothing from the Lady in exchange for my loyal protection."

"Altruistic..." Jill commented, then asked, "Does your quest mean no romance?"

"That's what I'm hearing," Misty said with disappointment, but then the memories of her conversations with Ruth Browning flooded her mind.

"Yes, my lady," said John Mark, as he bowed before her to his knee and touched the handle of his sword to his head.

"And I am to prove myself by helping to bring out the best in you," said Misty, who is becoming Elaine, wept tears but only briefly.

"Then are you Sir John Mark," asked Janine, "a real knight?"

"Sir John Mark Cannikin of Northumberland," he replied.

"We heard you helped Deputy Candy after the rave. Were your brothers there?" asked Izzy.

"Two of my brothers made an appearance at the rave in a successful effort to end a pagan ritual that would have resulted in the deaths of one or more women during the ceremony. Unfortunately, one other woman died when she was pushed over the cliff. My brothers commandeered Caleb Jones to help them. He drove our jeep, while my brothers ran in front of it. It was no accident...my brothers appeared before the crowd with swords drawn like this one I pull now from a sheath sewed into my cowl," explained John Mark, "I want you to understand that had the rains not dispersed the crowd, there would have been mortal combat between my brothers and men there who were armed with rifles as well as pistols."

"That sounds ominous," said Janine.

"You would have to understand the strength of the enemy's conviction. This is not new to us," explained John Mark.

"How tall are you, Sir John Mark Cannikin?" Kat asked.

"Barefoot, except for one of the brothers, I am the shortest. I stand six feet and eight inches," replied John Mark.

"Where are your brothers John Mark?" asked Jill.

"Meet Drostan and Coinneach, translated Tristan and Kenneth. They stand two inches taller than me, right behind you. I must inform you that they have vowed not to speak until they have secured their assignment...but dear people, one and all, let us ask you to not speak of this and allow us now to pray over you and for your cause, for it is not just against flesh and blood you do battle. You also battle against powers and principalities of darkness," pled John Mark.

"Yes, Sir," said Misty coyly, before she like the others turned around to see his brothers.

Before anyone saw their faces, the Brothers fled in response to two sounds. The first made by Rachael from the backdoor when she hollered trouble in the parking lot. The other came as an intruder accidently struck a horn on the steering wheel of one of the automobiles, as he fled detection. He raced toward the street, as a pick-up truck arrived to rescue two invaders. The driver sped away toward the convenience store on the south edge of town, but not before the Brothers memorized the license plate number.

Meanwhile, John Mark continued his oration, "Perhaps the two causing trouble in the parking lot were the ones you accosted earlier, Mr. Freedom, if not, we had at least four enemies spying on you... Don't be alarmed...but you do have to be alert and recognize people are curious about what is happening here. Izzy, this is your project, but I encourage you to allow me to pray over you and the ones yet to come."

"We welcome your prayers, John Mark," replied Izzy.

"Let us come sit one by one in a straight line where we can see north and east of here," invited John Mark. "As I pray over you, I ask you stretch out your hands, so both directions and the space between them are covered."

"As you wish, Farm Boy," answered Misty.

John Mark prayed, "Father, thank you for the lesson taught in Ezra's carving in the Live Oak tree. While his voice was taken from him in captivity, you have restored it through his art. You had called these good people to be here to do what you have in mind for them to do, and that includes my brothers and me. Though bruised and flawed, you have given them another chance. They have obeyed your call. Many here and in the towns below have prayed the instruction of your word to seek your face, to confess their sin and turn from their wicked ways...they have humbled themselves admitting their need for your forgiveness of their sin. Father, these people, a band of men and women, who seek to restore the house below to what it was not so long ago...they have committed to make this house a building where the light of Christ will shine over this valley. Father you have been honoring their work and that of loyal followers in the communities below. Like the Canaanites who practiced Baal worship, they have enemies that seek to block their efforts. The actions of the enemies are evil like those of the Canaanites. Innocent people have been injured, others even died, and we ask you will forgive our sin and keep us safe from the enemies. We ask you to thwart the evil in the land, that you rescue those who will respond to your call to them, and that you bring revival to this valley. We know you hear this prayer, and we ask you will heal this land where we point our hands. In Jesus name! Amen."

# Two on Missions

## CHAPTER 8

*"Be on your guard, stand firm in the faith; be coura-
geous; be strong."*                    *I Corinthians 16:13*

Two people searching for what is right and good
became conflicted by circumstances leading to their next mission. One searcher, a flawed woman bruised by her previous
experiences. She had resigned from her former teaching position
at the request of her administrator not because what she said was
wrong, but because it was believed what she said had led to a student's suicide. The irony was the student had intended to kill herself
after having an abortion, but she had changed her mind. A murderer
had sought to punish her and succeeded. Exonerated, the teacher
gained a second chance to choose again to do what was right and
good not just for herself but also for her new school and community. The other searcher, a good man, noted for his skill and courage,
had done what was right. He believed he had caused the death
of Betty Strong Bull, a relative of his friend and co-worker Rabbit
Pinebow. Betty had attended the rave on the ridge and died upon
impact when the mob bolted away from the ceremony and knocked
a teenage girl and two others over the edge of the ridge. The teen
landed below head first and then cushioned the fall of Mr. and Mrs.
Walter Anderson, travelers from Denver. This good man had shot the
rifle bullet that split the Asher pole, before the mob stampeded like
a herd of buffalo, and pushed Betty over the edge of the cliff or so
he thought. It had appeared to be an unfortunate accident, but the

truth was two wearing bear skins had deliberately shoved Betty to her death. Enthusiastically, the woman arrived ready to confront her new opportunity, while the man's sadness, his bruising, intensified by what he discovered along the path, which led to the roundup in the mountains.

After the recent rave, Dr. Maurice Wood, assistant superintendent of schools, opposed Karen's project. He attempted to block her attendance at the Denver based conference as well as her actual implementation of the Community Leadership Identification Project. Dr. Wood lobbied each school board member insisting the negative impact of the rave would skew the results of the study. Wood's effort failed when each board member supported the project by declaring that the rave demonstrated need for the project. New teacher and project manager, Karen Gustafson successfully attended the conference and ended it with a one-on-one appointment with the primary consultant, Kenneth Lippincott, author of *Community Leadership: How to Find It and Make It Work for You*. He had concluded his part of the workshop by offering to meet individually with those who had been hired to implement the leadership identification process. As promised he met with Karen for thirty minutes discussing details of conducting the interview process and data interpretation. She shared that Dr. Wood seemed to be opposed to the project unless he had direct control of the interviews. Lippincott warned Karen about some of the pitfalls when handling the data and of the need to keep the results confidential. When she shared that a former student had informed her about human trafficking at the local high schools, Lippincott's last words to her were she had a real opportunity to make a difference. Before leaving, she had become convinced one result of her study could be the school district would make better use of its resources.

Karen said, "I really believe bringing diverse people together to solve problems would result in our gaining public support for solutions."

Lippincott replied, "And the committee members, the community leaders, would be the advocates for the solutions."

"It would be like they owned the solution..." she concluded.

"Exactly, and Karen...since you have opposition by way of an assistant superintendent and since you are a newcomer in a small town... it would be wise for you to keep a copy of every survey...keep them where they would be safely tucked away. And don't tell anyone you have copies."

\*\*\*

Karen's enthusiasm included more than getting back to Jericho Springs to start her work. Soon she would see her parents, who would help her move her furniture and clothing to the Blair House. Her father had guided her in her decision making by helping her to decide what was important to her. He had advised her to take her ten most valued possessions with her on the trip to interview for a teaching position, which caused her to clarify what she valued. Looking forward to setting up her room, she had visualized what it would look like. She also looked forward to meeting with Sarah, the waitress at the restaurant in the Stage Stop Hotel. Karen felt certain Sarah would soon accept Christ as her personal savior and would be willing to let Karen disciple her. Last but certainly not least significant, Karen wanted to return to Jericho Springs because in just a few short weeks, Adam Claymore had made a commitment to court her. Adam was prominent, wealthy, kind, sensitive, and more. He looked like the Marlboro Man in the cigarette commercial, who rode tall in the saddle. Like the Lone Ranger in the popular television program, Adam sought to make right that which was wrong, he fought for what was right and good, and as a widower, he knew how to treat a woman. Even Adam's name was similar to the television star Clayton Moore, who played the Lone Ranger. Karen concluded Adam also compared well with a biblical character. He was a kinsman redeemer like Boaz in the book of Ruth, and Karen longed for when she could properly lay down beside him or like Ruth, who had lain down at the feet of Boaz. While enthusiasm marked Karen's return to the Blair House, the same was not true for Pilgrim Wayne.

\*\*\*

Pilgrim had met with the rest of Adam Claymore's wranglers at five that morning before most departed for cow camp. While the others would travel the mountain road outside Jericho Springs, Pilgrim was to travel the long way across Claymore Flats, through Wolf City, by the cliff dwellings, and into the ghost town of Pryor. The morning conversation revealed a few of the cowpokes had been at the rave. Some had been curiosity seekers, and others, like Pilgrim, helped disrupt the rave. No one had counted on the injuries and fatality that followed, which weighed heavily on Pilgrim. While John Mark had attested to what he had seen during the rave, neither Rabbit Pinebow nor Adam Claymore had witnessed the actual ceremony. Both had heard what had happened, during the debriefing at the church. At the time Rabbit had been visibly shaken, but had not shared the dead girl was his cousin Betty Strong Bull from Wolf City. "Betty had no business being there," Rabbit later exclaimed. "She had no business..."

I'm so sorry, Rabbit," Pilgrim explained, "I took the shot thinking it would stop what they were doing, but I didn't think the people would panic and run." "It wasn't just you firing the Sharps..." said Adam, "It was the combination of things." "Like the deputy said, many were drunk and some smoked pot..." reminded Barnabas.

"The howling wind from the canyon and the roar of the bear shook me up," countered Rabbit.

"Lightening and the cloud burst...then all of a sudden the deluge of water...the field must have become mud..." said another wrangler.

"Who was driving the truck that just appeared with its lights on?" asked Barnabas. "Who were the men who cast the long shadow?"

"And what was with the bear?" asked Pilgrim.

"You mean the men cloaked in the bear skins or the bear that practically clawed through the front door of the church?" Rabbit asked. "I thought I was a gonner. It's a good thing the church yard light was not on. The grizz ran right past me when I circled around back of the church."

Adam had thought for awhile, and then entered the conversation, "Rabbit, we are all sorry for your loss and we hope your family will blame no one for what happened. The lightening and deluge were enough to make people scatter. If the streetlights had not been shot out, everyone would have seen the edge of the ridge...and besides there should have been barriers safely marking the game trail and cliff."

"That's right," they all concurred.

"Pilgrim, I always send one wrangler out the Flats to Wolf City and on to Pryor to find stragglers and to determine how far south the herd has wandered. The bear may have caused more scattering than usual. You've drawn the short straw. Take your rifle and side arm. We know the bear went over the mountain and will probably pass through Pryor. It's probably the one that's killed so many calves. Do me a favor and kill it, if you can!"

"Thanks boss, I appreciate the quiet time to deal with this," said Pilgrim.

"Gentlemen," Adam said to his wranglers, "this may just be a bear, a grizzly at that, but I've got a feeling more is at stake. You and I know what was billed as a rave was a deception, a fraud to cover what was really going to happen. It wasn't about free speech or freedom of religion. We know it happened at least once before. God's people are on the move and the little church in Rock Creek is spearheading God's revival in the valley. We have stood against evil, we prevented what was going to happen on the ridge, and we were not alone. Yes, there were consequences, but what we witnessed with the bear may have been the personification of the evil that was about to happen. Pilgrim, I know you will ride with your Sharps in your lap. I know you will be reading your Bible along the way. Be certain to read from Psalms."

It was Barnabas who gathered the wranglers in a circle and offered a prayer of both thanksgiving and safety for all. He led a group to ride line and fix fence on the mesa, while Rabbit led the roundup.

Alone by the barn except for his horse and dog, Pilgrim remained behind watching both groups ride out to work. He paused, distracted by what had happened the night before at the rave, and he said, "By God's grace, I will kill the bear, and if it is not me who kills it, I pray its death will result in something good."

*** 

Meanwhile, Karen had risen early at the home of her parents on the outskirts of Colorado Springs in Fountain, Colorado. Her parents resided up on Fountain Mesa in a bi-level on Roaring Spring Avenue. It was like the good old days the night before. Her family stayed up late soaking in the hot tub on the deck, followed by some late night television provided by a massive satellite dish on the hill in the backyard. Finally, Karen retreated to her downstairs back bedroom, where she slept soundly thanks to the swamp cooler on the roof top. In the morning her mom and dad helped her pack her belongings, both the back bedroom furniture and all of her remaining clothes from the downstairs front bedroom.

Before breakfast, Karen helped her mother in the kitchen, where Karen found her mom looking out the window over her sink. "You're gazing at your bird feeder aren't you, Mom?" Karen said, "A penny for your thoughts."

"Yes, Daughter Dear, I was dreaming about your new adventure. A teaching position and you are a project manager to help identify and mobilize community leadership to solve problems and build a better community. I'm very proud of you," said Karen's mother.

"Anything else?" Karen knew to ask. "Yes, Mother, I'm glad I attended the conference."

"Yes, my little girl, when your bedroom set and your things in the front bedroom are gone, then you are gone officially. My little girl will be completely out of the nest."

"Is there more!"

"Yes, you imp! I look forward to meeting your gentleman friend. From all you have said, he must be wonderful despite being ten years older than you."

"Is that bad?"

"No, certainly not in your case...It will probably take an older man to rein you in," said Mom Gustafson, while laughing with enthusiasm.

"We aren't married...yet...we just formalized the fact of his courting me."

"And if he proposed to you now, you would say yes, wouldn't you?"

Smiling like the cat that ate the canary, Karen replied, "It's too early to tell, but I do know he is absolutely wonderful...I do have a career and so many things I want to do."

"Then remember this...he will be fifty ten years before you, and 60 and 70."

"I get the picture."

"What about children?"

"He has none that lived, and he lost a precious woman, his wife, at an early age. Mom, he is a precious man who is surrounded by and revered by so many, but his heart aches and I want to bring healing to him. I believe God has given me permission to minister to and respect him."

"Well said, Daughter Dear, you give me credit. You will have our blessing," said Mom Gustafson.

"You will see I've already hung my bird feeder outside my window on the south side of my room."

"It is good to know you have your priorities rightly aligned!" Mom concluded.

Mom and Dad and Daughter Dear enjoyed a sumptuous breakfast of blueberry pancakes, sweet cream butter, and pure blueberry syrup with eggs over easy, hash brown potatoes, and a pound of hickory smoked bacon. All washed down by a combination of freshly squeezed orange juice, mountain roast decaffeinated coffee, and filtered water taken fresh from the refrigerator.

While Mom cleaned the kitchen, Dad and Daughter Dear began loading her furniture in a rented trailer hitched to Dad's new 1980 Ford 150 truck. Although Karen already had many of her things moved into her room at the Blair House, the last of her belongings filled the trailer and much of the truck bed.

All loaded, Karen led the procession, followed by her mom and dad in the new candy apple red Ford truck.

***

Pilgrim departed the ranch on Spirit, his tall appaloosa with red and brown spots on its white rump. With her reddish tail swishing behind her, the mare had been followed closely by Pilgrim's cinnamon coated growler named Bruin. The three had walked to the official entrance of the Claymore Flats Ranch with its moniker spread above them from beam to beam across the driveway. Pausing, rider, horse, and dog looked longingly right and then left before entering the dirt road where one group had left for roundup and the other to repair fence bordering the edge of the grand mesa from point to crooked point. Like Adam, Pilgrim rode tall in the saddle at the beginning of his ride, but once he opened his Bible to the twenty-third psalm and read aloud, he relaxed his reigns and himself, while paying little attention to the road ahead of him. Sensing their master's somber mood, Spirit lifted her tail and dropped road apples, while Bruin growled as he stepped around them.

Placing his Bible in his saddlebag, Pilgrim took heart and began watching the mountain side of Claymore Flats and sought sign of bear scat along the way. He saw plenty of fewmet along game trails and wondered if the bear lacked interest in the deer which had defecated along the beaten paths. The bear itself was entirely an oddity because no grizzles were known to be at large in Colorado, especially on the eastern slope. With his Sharps rifle still in his lap, Pilgrim tied it loosely to his saddle with leather straps on each side near the saddle horn. Secured, he gently spurred the appaloosa, which loved to cantor. Knowing what was about to happen, Bruin broke into a run immediately down the dirt road. First, Pilgrim engaged the mighty beast in a trot that quickly became a gallop and evolved into an outright cantor. Spirit caught Bruin with the gallop, then within seconds, flew passed him when the cantor kicked in. On curves or bends in the road, Bruin left the roadway and ran cross country until a straight away brought him back to the road. Near the end of Claymore Flats, Pilgrim reined Spirit to return to the gallop and then the trot and into brush for a cool drink from a spring which emptied into the barrow pit beside the road. Catching up, Bruin lapped the water as well and lay down briefly. Pilgrim dismounted and drank crystal clear water from the source of the spring. A snap of a branch gained his attention and Pilgrim drew his colt revolver. He looked up slope in time to watch small stones trickle down slope having been disturbed by a sizeable animal which had scurried away out of sight. All refreshed Pilgrim climbed somewhat gingerly onto his mount so as not to indicate another race was to be started. He watched where the rock had been dislodged, tightened Spirit's reins, and ordered Bruin to stay, as both horse and canine had lifted their noses to collect scent. Tempted to ride upslope, Pilgrim thought better about riding uphill and breaking horizon not knowing what might greet them.

"Stay Bruin, not now…" he said as his companions responded with a growl and whinny.

Instead, Pilgrim trotted on toward the town of Wolf City. Once there followed by Bruin, Pilgrim and Spirit promptly took over the center line of the highway as they paraded down Main Street. Fully expecting both praise and jeers, he was well known in Wolf City. This was classic Pilgrim Wayne riding Main Street, as if he owned it, with his Sharps rifle still strapped to his saddle. The renowned Wayne, bull rider and all around cowboy, often compared well with historic Casey Tibbs of the Pro-rodeo Hall of Fame. Tibbs was famous, but in this county Pilgrim Wayne reigned as champion. Here in Wolf City, Pilgrim not only ruled the rodeo, but also he championed all shooting contests be it with a rifle or a side arm. If bare knuckle boxing were allowed, he would win those contests as well, but another would rule over the wrestling competition. In a word Wayne was the archetype cowboy.

"Who's the cowboy?" a young woman asked of her beau.

"Honey, he's the legendary Pilgrim Wayne. I wish I could ride and shoot half as good as he does."

"You are kidding me! Surely, you are as good as him."

"No, and I don't mind saying so."

"Humph," the girl responded as she took a lingering look at Wayne, as he tipped his hat toward her. "Well, I'll be."

Another man said, "That's Wayne. See his rifle. He had to be the one who split the Asher Pole."

"Hmm…Ralph said Red thought it was him. Said Red knew it when he heard the shot and nearly jumped out of his bear skin," said one of the Night Riders.

"We're gonna get even with him. Aren't we?" said a friend of the McNaughton Corporation.

"Not me, I'm not going to mess with him," said the Night Rider.

"Funny…I never thought about who would be against us…" said another Night Rider.

"The church, of course, and the Pastor, but Pilgrim Wayne…" said the first man.

Listening as he could, Pilgrim caught what had been said about Ralph and knew the Night Riders and those at the Tobacco Store in

Rock Creek had somehow been involved with the rave. Having heard what he sought, Pilgrim stopped early for lunch at the Wolf City Café, tied Spirit to a porch rail, told Bruin to stay next to his partner Spirit, and took his rifle into the café. With his back to the wall and his eye on his horse and dog, Pilgrim ordered the day's special in a to-go box, two beef enchiladas covered with cheese and onions, swimming in pork green chili, and accompanied with refried beans, a scoop of rice and a flour tortilla. He added a crispy beef taco and a dry avocado pork burrito, which he would dip in the pork green chili smothering his enchiladas. Also, he asked for a cold glass of water and a cola soft drink. When served, he tucked paper onto the front of his red and black checkered shirt. He lingered over his meal by slowly eating and savoring every bite. When finished, he followed by his using the flour tortilla to scrape every morsel of chili gravy from the bottom and around the sides of the to-go box. Removing the paper towel from the neck of his shirt, he finished by thoroughly wiping his mustache. Pilgrim looked for but could not locate the proprietor, his friend Chief Strong Bull, grandfather of Betty. Pilgrim knew the Chief might challenge him to enter the ring by the bar, but Pilgrim was not in the mood to be beaten again in a wrestling match, not today.

Both horse and dog stood at attention as Pilgrim left the restaurant with his rifle. He patted and spoke words of encouragement to both before untying the reins from the porch rail and climbed back onto Spirit. Expecting to run again, Bruin stood ready and waited for the signal to get a head-start, which was not given. Instead, Pilgrim started out again with a slow walk and then a trot. Once nearly a mile out of town, they veered off the dirt road to a fence Pilgrim loosened to let horse and dog enter into a pine forest. On Claymore land, they would travel off road until they arrived at a road that led to Pryor.

An hour later, Pilgrim and team paused before entering into a small gorge, and surveyed the landscape. He watched both horse and dog lift their noses in the air and said, as he patted his chaps, "I smell it too...slowly...stay by my side."

Spirit snorted and Bruin whined! The team passed into the gorge, which opened to a modest basin bordered by pinion and ponderosa pine trees along the slopes to the walls of its ridges. Scrub Oak dotted most of the area not covered with trees, which left only a soft dry creek bed to traverse. He watched as clouds passed overhead and looked for damage caused by night rain. After several minutes Pilgrim arrived at what he had traveled out of his way to see. The gorge divided into two lesser ones with steeper sides, yet with small sections of flat ground above dry creek bed. He followed sandy loam into the gorge to the left and located cliff dwellings. They had been built high enough on the northwest wall of the canyon slope to catch early morning sunlight, while well protected from casual sight-seers and enemies. Both ponderosa and pinion pines encircled the ground below the cliff dwellings like sentries, while scrub oak restricted easy passage from lower levels.

With Bruin, Pilgrim climbed to the dwellings where man and dog entered what they could without a ladder. Stone walls with mortar lined most of the span of the dwellings, and he could only reach one lower part of the structure. Bruin ran directly into the room and promptly traversed the lower level. Pilgrim climbed into the first room, which featured an oven carved into a corner with ample room for both heating and baking. Mortar covered the front of the oven and a lip had been added to the base to keep ashes from escaping. One continuous stone made the north and west wall, while the outer south wall had been built of flat stones piled one upon another with mortar pressed in the crevices. Part of the east wall featured a half wall connected to the side frame of a low doorway. Like the cliff dwellings in Manitou Springs, at six feet, Pilgrim had to crouch to climb through entrance. Once into the adjoining room, Pilgrim discovered a larger space with air vents built into the outer wall just above the floor. A nearly square pit occupied the center of the room and appeared to have an open drain at its bottom.

Not able to climb further into the apartment like dwelling, Pilgrim responded quickly to the neighing of Spirit and the barking of Bruin by the east half-wall and looked over the short structure. Dirt and pebbles toppled down before him from somewhere above, and the grunt of a beast made him withdraw to the back of the room. At first he couldn't tell where the grunt originated. He wondered if the beast was on the ridge above the dwelling or if it was closer in one of the rooms, which he had not climbed into without a ladder. Either way Pilgrim knew he needed to reach his horse and dog pronto.

*** 

Exiting Interstate Highway 25 onto US Highway 85/87, Karen led her parents toward Ridge View, which was a small town almost the size of Jericho Springs and considerably larger than Rock Creek. Although the junior and senior high school had been constructed in Jericho Springs, unlike Rock Creek, Ridge View boasted a newer elementary school, while the old high school in Rock Creek had been repurposed as the administration building for the valley's one school district. It also housed the local museum and senior center with both as keepers of the lore, history, and folk tales of the valley, the one written and the other oral history.

Driving past the truck stop at the entrance to the town, Karen purposely turned left off the highway and down Main Street to reveal the sights. Compared to Rock Creek, Ridge View lacked the character of an old town. It wasn't old. Ridge View had been a small settlement that grew because construction of Interstate 25 bypassed the rest of the valley. Ridge View prospered thanks to the truck stop and highway department facilities. Next, a hospital had been added, as was the county sheriff's office building and jail. At the end of Main Street and its shops and stores, Karen drove past the feed and lumber yard and reconnected with US 85/87, as it circled the main part of town. At the intersection the name of the highway changed to the Valley Highway. The Gustafson family stopped for lunch at the Cozy Corner Café.

Exiting their truck, Mom Gustafson asked, "Karen is this Jericho Springs? Where is the Blair House with its big tree?"

Approaching her, Karen responded, "Come let's eat in this café. I want you to experience the flavor of the local culture. A lot of decisions impacting the valley are made inside and something wonderful recently happened here."

Dad Gustafson took his wife by the hand to escort her inside and said, "Come Mother, let's look and listen. Shall we sit in a booth or at the counter, Karen?"

"Today, let's sit at the counter."

"Why?"

"Come along, Mother."

Karen picked the stools directly opposite the opening to the kitchen where meals were placed under heat lamps before being picked up by the wait staff. A swinging door swung silently slightly to the left of the small opening. The lone waiter produced menus in an instant and asked them what they wanted to drink, where- upon, they asked for water and diet colas, cheese burgers, and fries all around. Back and forth the waiter worked, but as he worked, he softly hummed a familiar tune. Soon Mom, Dad, and Daughter Dear looked at each other and simultaneously sang, "This is the day..." as they nodded to one another.

When the waiter returned with three plates of burgers and fries, it was Mom who said, "This is the day that the Lord hath made."

And the waiter responded with, "Let us rejoice and be glad in it!" as he set each plate before them.

Karen touched his arm, as he placed her meal before her, and said, "Tim McNaughton, I'm Karen."

Goose bumps rose on both of their arms as Tim replied with a smile, "Karen, Karen Gustafson? Adam's friend?" and as Karen nodded, he continued, "I saw your truck and trailer. You must be moving in today. Depending on when I get off work, I'll be moving into the Blair House tonight or tomorrow."

"Great!" Karen said, "I'm looking forward for all of us to be there."

Tim smiled and continued his work now singing, "Oh, happy day, oh happy day..."

To which the Gustafson's replied, "When Jesus walked, when Jesus walked."

*** 

As the Gustafson's finished lunch, on the other side of the moun- tains, Pilgrim Wayne rode into the ghost town of Pryor, Colorado. Local inhabitants zero, or so he thought. After a harsh winter last year, all that remained standing was the semblance of an old Catholic church. Stone upon stone the front wall stood on a hillside with a gentle slope. In the middle of the wall, an opening marked where a wooden doorway once barred entrance. Across the top of the flat stone work above the doorway, lay a short Pinion Pine beam which had been strong enough to hold the wall together. Pine trees had grown where church pews once stood, and the gale of the wind played music through needles and cones, while a dust devil danced disruptively on the hillside.

Bruin spotted the boys at the edge of the forest and raced toward them without barking, but his growl broke the silence like how a spoon striking an half empty glass rings a sharp clear sound. Taken by surprise, Pilgrim followed the flight of his dog, and when his growler passed by the boys toward the stand of trees, he loosened the straps from the rifle on his lap. He swung the Sharps toward the trees, as he stood in his stirrups, took aim, and fired a shot toward the grizzly's massive chest. The bullet struck the bear where earlier a shotgun blast had torn into its flesh. Momentarily stunned, the giant of a bear had not reacted in time to escape Bruin's bite to the same area. Gaining its senses, the grizzly rose on its hind legs and swatted Bruin from his grip on the bear's chest. Distracted by the growler, the bear had not seen Pilgrim's charge toward it. Spirit cantered through the brush free rein, while Pilgrim opened the breach, reloaded his single shot rifle, and raised the Sharps' long barrel to discharge another bullet into the bear's chest. The rifle rose when fired and Pilgrim missed his mark, but he made a painful entrance through the tip of the bear's black nose. Reeling in pain with blood spurting from its nose, the bear ignored Bruin lying on the forest floor and hastily fled the scene.

Pilgrim pursued the bear to a clearing in the forest and discovered a cabin in the woods with smoke rising lazily from the chimney. To the left stood a modest pole barn with a corral connected to one side. When Spirit neighed, a black and chestnut mule entered the clearing from the forest. It wore a hackamore with a broken strap and had scrapes on its forelegs and side from when it broke through the corral to escape the bear. To the right of the cabin, a large garden had prospered until the bear had rummaged through it. At the edge of the garden, Pilgrim gasped when he saw the bear had slain a man first, and then a woman had fallen dead on him. She still held the butcher knife she had used to protect her husband from the bear without success.

162

The words of the marriage vow quickly came to mind, as Pilgrim said aloud, "Till death do us part. Side by side to a bitter end."

Slender and frail, the boys entered the clearing with hopes that gunfire and the resultant chase had ended with the death of the bear. Happy to see them, their mule greeted the boys with a joyful neigh. Though clawed and bleeding, Bruin joined the boys and licked the hand of them. The boys walked to the garden where Pilgrim stood shocked by the sight of the carnage the bear had done. Hearing Bruin's growl, he turned to the boys.

"Don't come closer. You won't want to see this."

Dazed, the older and taller of the two said in a monotone, "We've seen it. Dad came to rescue us when the bear treed us. It wouldn't leave, it hates us, and when my father struck it with the head of the garden hoe, it turned on him. My father scampered toward the garden, while he shouted at the bear, so we could climb out of the tree. Then he told us to run for the road, to go to town."

The younger boy added, nervously clinging to his older brother, "When the bear knocked down my daddy, Mama ran out of the cabin with the butcher knife in her hand. She stabbed the bear in its front part, before it just broke her in half with one swipe of its paw."

"It's all my fault," the older boy said, as tears swelled in his eyes, "if I had done my chores when my father told me to, we wouldn't have been out back choppin' wood. It's all my fault..."

"Me too," the younger boy said, as he hit his brother's arm with his fist, "I picked a fight with my brother and we was in trouble. That's why we hadn't done our chores." Both began to cry, which promptly became sobbing.

Pilgrim knelt in front of the boys and placed an arm around each of them. He said, "That's not what I see."

"What do you see?"

"I see a man who saw his children in real danger. Your dad risked his life to save you, and that's what it cost him. He loved you very much. You must be good boys. And I see what kind of wife your mother was. She risked her life to save your father from the bear. She was a woman of great courage."

"She was! She fought off coyotes and a skunk too. They were after our chickens."

"But Mama chased them off with the garden hoe, and then she had to soak her clothes in tomato juice."

"We moved here, because my father had a problem drinking. He couldn't hold a job."

"Mama found this place to live, so my daddy could escape the bottle. He did too. And you know what, my daddy said it was because my mama loved him. He stopped drinking because my mama loved my daddy, but now they're dead," said the older son.

"Boys, it will start getting dark soon. We need to bury your mom and dad, but we must leave before the bear comes back. It does that. I have been tracking it for days. It is a mean one, and now it is wounded, which makes it worse."

"We have shovels in the barn. I'll go get them," said the older brother.

Pilgrim asked the younger brother, "Can you get your mule and bring it here?"

"Yes, should we get some clothes to take with us?"

"Listen now. Really, the bear will come back here. He will likely follow us. I'm headed for a cow camp where I work. I will get you to the cow camp and then to Jericho Springs. I'm certain you will be able to stay at the ranch where I work until we can come back and get the rest of your things and see to it your parents are properly buried."

"We don't have much," the older boy said, then asked, "What's going to happened to me and my brother?"

"You'll be safe with me and Bruin. Isn't he a great dog?"

"Yes, but he's always growling..."

"It's like he's purring, as if he were a cat," Pilgrim replied.

"Don't you have a truck we can ride in?"

"No, it's just me, my horse Spirit, and my dog Bruin, and as you know, he is a growler..."

"So, you're a real cowboy with a big rifle and a six gun!" the little boy said, as Pilgrim nodded.

\*\*\*

The Gustafson's left the Cozy Corner Café and headed south down the Valley Highway until they reached the intersection of the highway and County Road 403 where it leads to Jericho Springs. Instead of making the turn onto CR403, Karen pulled off to the side and parked her 1971 Chevy Nova. Exiting her car, she waved at her mom and dad to join her.

There on the corner, four ladies held signs. Each sign displayed a message. Karen recognized two of the ladies, Aquila Parsons and Priscilla King. On the closest corner Aquila held a sign with a message, "Got Problems? Let's pray?" Across the street Priscilla held a sign proclaiming "Jesus loves you! Do you know him?" Across the highway, stood two other women that Karen had not recognized. Each held a sign displaying the same message held by Priscilla or Aquila.

The Gustafson's approached Aquila and Karen introduced her mom and dad to her. Karen's father said, "Great message on your poster. What are you doing?"

"What God would have us do?" replied Aquila.

"Explain please."

"Well, we are to minister to the needs of people and we are to share the Gospel of Jesus Christ. We hold the signs up and wave as cars go by. Sometimes they stop; sometimes they don't. When they stop, we ask them how we can pray for them…and then we pray. Once we finish our prayer, we ask them if they have heard about the four spiritual laws. If they say no then we take out this pamphlet and have them read it with us. By the end of the pamphlet they have read the Gospel message and are offered an opportunity to accept Jesus as their savior," explained Aquila.

"What if they are already believers?" asked Mom Gustafson.

"Well, if that's the situation, I pull out this other pamphlet about spiritual breathing. I help them read it, and I help them discover how to increase the Lordship of Christ in their lives."

"Do people respond?" Mom questioned.

"Almost everyone responds. You might notice the sign leaning on the fence that says 'Honk if you love Jesus.' We get a lot of honks or thumbs up. Sometimes people show us another finger, but not often."

"Do people stop for prayer?" Dad asked.

"Not a whole lot, but when they do stop, we know God is at work."

"Nifty!" he said, while stroking his chin with his hand.

"Yes, and the only financial cost is for five hand made posters and a marking pen. No church budget item."

"What I like about it," Karen said, "is that it reminds people to pray and these ladies have made themselves available for God to use. Everyone in the valley travels through this intersection."

"Do you only work here?" asked Dad. "What about the other towns in the valley?"

"Two of us started this, and two joined us. When two more join us, Priscilla and I will move to another location. We keep inviting others to come along side us, but God has to convict them to take a chance to do this."

"We could do this where we live!" said Mom and Dad Gustafson.

"Perfect!" replied Aquila.

*** 

The Gustafsons returned to their caravan and continued toward Jericho Springs down CR403. As Karen drove her Chevy over a Rock Creek bridge, she motioned for her parents to look to their left at the idyllic scene in the meadow. The creek emptied into a pond before spilling over a waterfall and continuing into the valley beyond. Further up the road, the Gustafson's noticed a small farm house and barn, where a boy played with his white boxer pup. As she passed, Karen honked her car horn, which drew a wave from the little boy and his mother. Dad decelerated his truck, coasted by the mother and son, and also waved. Mom and Dad Gustafson wondered who they might be and commented about the Eden like setting.

"Doesn't this bring back memories?" asked Mom.

"As if it was yesterday, and I played outside with our little girl, while you were most likely fixing dinner," said Dad.

"Or she and I were out there waiting for you to get off work and come home."

"Both would be true Mother, and between the creek that flows into the pond...the waterfall, the grassy knoll, and the forest around it...I'm reminded of the Garden of Eden."

"I too think it would have been the perfect spot to raise our little girl..." said Mom.

"And now we follow our only child to a house she is helping to restore..."

"To a town where some cowboy has already stolen her heart..."

"Both adequate and competent...already out of the nest, and confidently flying!"

"Like a paycheck to us, isn't it?" Mom asked wistfully."

"Yes, Dear," he replied as he reached across the bench seat and took her hand in his, "God has blessed us, indubitably!"

"Indeed, Father, without a doubt, He has blessed us!" she smiled and said.

Karen stopped again just outside Jericho Springs before passing through the hogback, which surrounds the town. Mom and Dad gazed at the formation with its slopes topped with a wall of uplifted sedimentary rock extending more than eight feet above the mounds below it. Their gaze shifted to another scene exposed before them. At first their gaze followed the path of the county road, which was about to become Main Street for Jericho Springs. And then they saw it perched atop a butte where the foothills begin before giving way to rugged mountains.

"That must be the tree where Karen had the encounter with God," Dad said.

"Where do you see it?"

"Look where the foothills begin near the end of this road and to the right. There is a butte, which must be where a fissure had opened and now heats a hot spring beside it."

"She said there is a dry pool on top of the mound that once held water so hot that former tenants used it to help heat the house."

"Mom, the origin of that tree is a mystery. How did it get there?"

"Who planted it?" asked Mom.

"She said we will want to see the carving on the north side of the tree. She said it is fascinating, and that the owner of the house and the mountains and valley behind it did the carving."

"Ezra Blair?"

"No, Mother, it is the Blair House after the name of the people who raised Izzy, while his father had gone to the Vietnam War and was captured then held prisoner in Cambodia. Izzy's father is Ezra Freedom."

As the Gustafson's chatted, Karen left her Chevy Nova and walked back to her dad's truck, whereupon he rolled down his window. Karen asked, "Do you see it? You can see it from here as it stands like a sentry on top of the hill."

"Yes, Daughter Dear, what kind of tree is it?" asked Mom.

"It's not native to the area and how it grew so well on top of a volcanic butte is amazing. Mom, I think it is a Live Oak tree the way the branches spread out almost as if it had four trunks," said Daughter Dear.

"Do the trunks mark the directions?" Dad asked.

"Almost perfectly..."

"What's the lore about how it got there?"

"Mom, Beatrice Jaramillo, whom you might meet at the house, asserts her people planted it hundreds of years ago."

"Her people?" asked Mom.

"Yes, Ute Indians is what she says. They believed it was a sacred place and she says her people planted the tree there. Sometime I'm going to see what history I can find about it at the museum in Rock Creek."

"Karen, your mom and I saw you wave at a little boy and his mother just after we stopped on the bridge. Was she your friend who you were with on the hill with the tree?"

"Yes, Dad, she is Ruth Browning. Her son is really funny at times, full of 'spit and vinegar,' as they say. To the left of the pond, where you can still see some charred ground, is where some of the Night Riders tossed Andy's ducks onto a bonfire."

"That's horrible, Dear. You need to watch out for those men," said Mom with concern.

"We've had some encounters."

"Was the young man you shot in the heel one of them?" asked Dad.

"Yes, as was the deputy sheriff he was with."

"Foreboding," said Dad.

"Who were the ladies that are sharing Jesus on the street corner?" asked Mom.

"I attend church with them in Rock Creek. The one named Aquila Parsons... Her husband is one of the local judges. The other is Priscilla King."

"And her husband?" inquired Dad.

"Arthur King, her husband is the elementary school principal here in Jericho Springs. I heard his staff calls him King Arthur...but in addition to sharing Jesus on street corners, both those ladies clean the church in Rock Creek."

"They are neither ashamed to share the Gospel, nor to be bond servants for Jesus."

"Yes, Father, they are real servants of the Lord, and they are also the hostesses for most functions at church."

"My guess is they will show up in your community study," guessed Dad.

"Interesting," concluded Mom.

The caravan to Blair House continued into Jericho Springs and down Main Street. As Karen drove her car, she pointed toward the pizzeria where she would be working part time. Next, she directed their attention toward the courthouse, where city council decided not to condemn Blair House, and Bustos' Family Mexican Restaurant with Attorney John Law's Offices above it. She stopped at the sign where one would turn to go to the high school where Karen would be substitute teaching. At the beginning of the last block on Main Street, Karen pointed again toward Ezra Freedom's tree and the Blair House. Karen turned her car at the driveway and climbed the incline to the makeshift parking lot then slowed to a stop, while her father followed closely behind her.

Karen's parents quickly scanned the scene. While Mom Gustafson looked somewhat horrified in response to the condition of the house's exterior, Karen's father made immediate note of what could be tools to defend the house. He noted a zip line cable led from outside the northeast corner bedroom to a massive Ponderosa pine tree in a grove between the parking lot and Main Street. His eyes shifted to the back columns of the first and second floors, which had metal brackets attached to them. He speculated they were hand and foot holds for some very skillful climber. Dad surmised neither the cable nor the hand holds would be seen by the casual observer during the daylight and unseen by everyone at night, unless viewed by the person who had installed them. Good tools! He thought.

When Dad Gustafson backed the trailer toward the front entrance, several of the new residents came bounding out the front door of Blair House to greet Karen and her parents. Katarina Bond and her two daughters also joined in and were the first to greet them. Newlyweds Izzy and Janine Freedom followed Jill Lowenstein, Jerry Sunday, and Morris Goodenough out the door and down the stairs, while Hannah Rahab and Misty McClaren peered out the front window and Ezra Freedom Sr. watched from the third floor balcony.

Izzy announced, "Take all of Karen's things to the back room on the left of the second floor."

Kat followed Izzy, and said, "Hey everybody, I've got a great announcement...Pastor Borden stopped by and told me his church has finished making the prayer walk through all of Jericho Springs! He placed an order for them to go door-to-door with outreach materials!"

Everyone cheered, including Mom and Dad Gustafson, as Jill whispered to Kat, "Please order the Bible on cassette. I want to give it to Ezra as a thank you gift."

As everyone pitched in to help Karen get situated, Hannah and Misty met the women carrying boxes or clothing once inside the door and carried them up the stairs and down the hall to the back bedroom. The men did the heavy lifting and moved Karen's furniture to her room. Mom and Dad joined Karen where she took her mom by the hand and guided her out the back door and left around the balcony to where their shared treasure had been hung.

"There it is, Mom, right outside my window where I can look at it when I want to fly away."

"It looks brand new. I thought you had broken it when some fella tripped over it and landed on the table outside the hotel restaurant."

"I also dropped it on the head of the deputy sheriff, who had been chasing Hannah and me."

"Did the deputy ever catch you?"

"No, but he did keep my bird feeder for awhile, until he tired of it and tossed it onto Ruth Browning's yard. She gave it back to me."

"I hope you get a chance to hit him or one his friends in the head again!"

"That might happen, but till then I'll just put feed in it and watch the birds enjoy the little cabin you gave me."

"It truly is one of your ten favorite possessions, isn't it?"

"Yes, Mom, and I considered its importance to me when I was deciding whether or not to come here. It is one of my favorite things, and when I look at it, I am reminded of you."

"Thank you, Daughter Dear," Mom said with tears glistening in her eyes, "it is hard to let go of your children no matter how old and competent they become. You know, I really look forward to what happens here. I believe God is at work and you figure prominently in bringing revival to His people in this valley."

\*\*\*

While Karen settled into Blair House with the help of her parents and all those who had already moved there, Pilgrim Wayne worked with the boys to bury their parents by the garden, at least temporarily. He worked quickly, so they could make haste to cow camp where the boys would be relatively safe. Certainly, if the bear invaded the camp, it would be met with a hail of gunfire.

Pilgrim told the boys to gather what they considered essential, while he saddled their mule. Already he heard the bear rumbling in the stand of trees behind the house, and he watched both Spirit and Bruin react nervously. He calmed his horse and told his dog to stay, which complied. With no time to spare, Pilgrim and the boys climbed their mounts as the grizzly broke for the cabin from the stand of trees. At first the bear looked longingly after the trio, but then entered the cabin and shredded bedding and clothing before shattering a dresser and the kitchen table. It lapped beef stew from the pot that the boy's mother had left cooking in the firebox. Sitting on its haunches, the bear licked its chops and wiped its mouth with its paw, then belched, before it made pursuit of those who fled from it.

Guessing the bear would soon follow, Pilgrim led the boys quickly toward where he thought cow camp would be located. He told Bruin to find Adam, which the canine understood and growled. The dog lit out on a dead run northeast of the cabin and up a game trail through the forest and out of it, up a slope and over a ridge before stopping to let horse, mule, and riders catch up with him. Giving them no time to rest, he descended the ridge, crossed a creek, and steadily climbed a mountain where Bruin slowed his pace.

No bear could keep Bruin's pace. The grizzly gave up its pursuit of the quarry at the creek when it saw trout swimming in the cold water. It paused, looked at the fish in the water, and then looked where horse and mule had carried the man and boys. Still hurting from Pilgrim's bullet, which took the end of its nose, the bear put its bloodied snout in the clear, cold water before sitting down in the stream. It reclined and let the cold liquid wash over the knife wound the woman had inflicted, the bite the dog had made, the entry point of Pilgrim's bullet, and the little punctures from Ezra Sr.'s shotgun blasts. None of its wounds hurt more than its sensitive snout.

While the bear gave up its pursuit, Pilgrim continued to press the boys, mule, Spirit, and Bruin to make haste. At twilight they discovered cow camp and slowed mule and horse to a walk, while Bruin entered camp growling. Barnabas met the dog on his knees and the pup's countenance changed, as he greeted a friend who would make a fuss over him. Joyfully, the dog greeted Adam and his other wranglers, but was standoffish toward Red McNaughton's men.

Pilgrim rode in with the two boys beside him. Adam first met them and said, "What have we here, Pilgrim?"

Before answering, Pilgrim told the boys to dismount and get something to eat from the camp cook. They promptly complied, while Pilgrim began his report, "Adam, these boys have had quite a time. This morning the bear we are looking for killed the boys' parents outside their cabin over near Pryor. Apparently, it had treed the two boys when the father came to their rescue. He didn't have a sidearm or a rifle. When the bear charged the man, the bear made quick work of him. The boys' mother tried to save her husband and attacked the bear with a butcher knife to no avail. The boys said the bear nearly broke her in half with a single blow. While the fight ensued, the boys ran toward Pryor where I intercepted them. We rode back to the cabin, and the bear followed us. It may have been tracking me earlier."

"How are the boys doing?"

"Pretty rough, they blame themselves. They hadn't done their chores when they were told to and as a result, the bear found them easy prey and treed 'em."

"How did you leave it?"

"I buried the parents and quickly saddled their mule, just before the bear charged their cabin. It was plenty mad. The woman had stabbed the critter in the chest, and I hit it in about the same area before I got to the cabin, while doing a cavalry charge toward it."

"You went full bore with guns blazing?"

"Yes, and it didn't back off. I hit it solid with my first shot, then I got off another round, while going down slope and on the rise the barrel went upward as I pulled the trigger. This part is humorous."

"How so?"

"I hit the beast in the black tip of its nose, and my shot, hitting such a tender spot, made him react. Boy was he angry!"

"I'll bet."

"But Adam, this isn't over. I covered ground quickly. I told Bruin to find you and he ran pell-mell in your direction, but the bear followed us. He may not have continued right then, but he is headed our way."

"Is it the bear that clawed the church door?" asked Adam.

"I don't know, but I think so. Remember, while Rabbit was at the church, I was on the mesa. I tracked it, but I never saw it. The one I shot is no ordinary bear and certainly not a black bear. I've never seen a grizz up close and personal, but I've seen this one and I know enough to not want to face him alone again. Adam, I hit him with my Sharps, and a fifty caliber bullet should have put the bear down," Pilgrim replied.

"Certainly, the Lord was with you. You arrived in time to save the boys' lives and get them to safety."

"By God's grace two boys and this one man made it to safety," Pilgrim said humbly.

"By God's grace, your sharp shooting, a quick horse, and a faithful dog."

"What do you want to do about the boys?"

"I'm heading for Jericho Springs to meet Karen's parents. I'll take the boys to the ranch before going to the Blair House, and I'll have someone take care of them there. Too bad the bear has already been to Blair House. He marked the tree there, or so I heard, otherwise, I'd see if the boys could stay there. Besides I wouldn't want to attract social services to them. Worse case is for me to get them to Barnabas and the line crew for a few days. I'll stay at the ranch tonight and make certain they feel safe, and then I'll return here in the morning. I'll call John Law and ask him what to do to keep social services at bay for as long as possible. Maybe John can locate their kinfolk, who can come get the boys. I'd hate to just put them on a bus to somewhere."

"What about the boys' parents?" asked Pilgrim, who then said, "I buried them in a shallow grave by their garden, but you and I know what can happen to the bodies with coyotes around."

"We will need to get their remains to Wolf City or maybe Quail Point soon. I'll work on a plan. Meanwhile, say your goodbyes to the boys and help them feel good about going with me. I can only imagine what they are experiencing right now. I lost my wife, and they have lost both parents. They probably feel all alone, except for you."

"Adam, I think you do understand their feelings...one other thing, Boss, I think the bear tailed after me from just south of the ranch, and then again after I left Wolf City and went to the cliff dwellings. I'm pretty sure it was there, but it went ahead of me and killed those folks in Pryor. I can feel it in my bones. The critter will follow me and the boys to cow camp."

"That's covering a lot of ground in a short amount of time. Interesting that it left you and got to the folks in Pryor before you could get there. It sounds..."

"Methodical?" Pilgrim said and completed Adam's thought.

"Sounds like they were the target...but the whole thing with the bear is just plain odd..."

"Like the raves," Pilgrim added.

***

The boys said their goodbyes to Pilgrim, Bruin, Spirit, and their mule, and then climbed into the cab of Adam's Ford F250. They marveled at the size of the vehicle. With full stomachs both boys soon slept, but nightmares invaded their sleep. Adam kept the speed of his truck just below thirty, as he crept down the mountain road, while watching for deer along the way. At dusk he slowed his truck, as he watched a white tail buck join several does in the meadows to eat their fill, while also lapping cold water from the stream. His thoughts switched from the boys to Karen as he continued his descent. He knew she would understand his late arrival once she heard his tale about the boys. As a result he stopped at the Blair House before taking them to his ranch on Claymore Flats. He had an uninspiring introduction to Karen's parents, or so he thought, as his clothes were more than dusty from a day's work at cow camp. He quickly told his tale to Karen and the Gustafsons about how Pilgrim had rescued the boys, how he was taking the boys to his ranch, arranging a burial party for the boys' parents, and intervening for them with social services.

Upon hearing his plans, Karen put her arms up and around his shoulders and gave him a long kiss in front of her parents. Dazed, she looked at her mom and dad, and sheepishly said, "Isn't he wonderful? I told you he is like Boaz, the kinsman redeemer."

"Yes, Daughter Dear," Karen's dad said, "I think we have seen and heard enough to believe you are in good hands." Then shaking Adam's hand, her father looked Adam straight in the eyes, and said, "We will be back for a more formal introduction. Meanwhile, we trust you will watch out for our daughter, especially as she gets into the leadership identification project."

"I do, I mean will, Sir," Adam replied.

"A Freudian slip, I hear, Mother," said Karen's father as he chuckled, and hugged his daughter and whispered in her ear, "We will have to come back here soon, I trust!"

After embracing her daughter, Karen's mother hugged Adam, said her goodbyes, and then left with her husband for a pleasant ride back home to Fountain, Colorado.

Adam suggested he take the boys home, put them to bed, and then come back tomorrow morning to take her out for breakfast at the restaurant in Rock Creek. Saddened, Karen consented and kissed him again. This time it was he, who was dazed, but he said, "Make it a double, and I'll be back for more in the morning. Is six o'clock too early?"

"Yes, Sir, I have to bathe and perfume myself before I see you again. Please...be here at eight."

Karen watched Adam climb into his truck and drive down the slope from the parking area, turn right on CR403, and head for Claymore Flats. Karen breathed, "What a man..." and realized she could have said the same about Pilgrim Wayne, but without the affectionate tone.

# Warfare

## CHAPTER 9

*"Tear down your father's alter to Baal and cut down
the Asherah pole beside it. Then build a proper kind of
alter to the Lord your God on the top of this height."
Judges 6:25b-26a*

From his room on the middle of the south-side second
floor, Detective Jones climbed out his bedroom window to do
some investigating. Caleb wondered how different his sister's
path might have been, if she had managed to connect with people like
Paul and Lydia Blair instead of those operating the Asherah House or
organizing the raves. Studying the history of the valley, he understood
how school reorganization, followed by construction of Interstate 25,
had altered the valley's culture and economy. He understood how
longtime residents had felt entitled to gold and water rights, which
had supposedly become available. Understanding escaped him when
it related to his little sister. Why and how he thought, had Gloria
become a prostitute at the Asherah House after attending one of the
raves conducted on the ridge above the town of Rock Creek?

Sauntering toward the front of the house, Caleb realized he had
been seen by Katarina Bond, as she walked purposefully to the Blair
House from home. No longer able to move about unnoticed, he gave
up his effort and re-entered the house through the second floor front
door. He hurried down the stairwell, opened the front door, and
eased Katarina's load by taking her grocery bags. Greeting her, he
followed her lead to the kitchen and set the bags on the kitchen table.

"Busted," Kat said, "and you thought you could have some early morning privacy!"

"No kidding," the detective said, "I thought I could do some snooping around, but now I have to make a guilt payment by helping in the kitchen."

"Just set the bags down...and if you would, please fill the wood storage box. If you hurry, you'll be able to climb the butte and see the sun come up," Kat said.

While Katarina loaded the stove's firebox and lit both paper and wood, Caleb gathered an armload of firewood from the back porch and added it to the supply stored inside near the kitchen stove. Caleb left the kitchen, walked through the back porch, and up the slope to explore the volcanic mound, dry pool, and damage that the grizzly bear had inflicted on the Live Oak. In studying the dry pool, he found a man made hole, where a pipe had been inserted to channel temperate water to a heating chamber inside the house below. His gaze followed to the south side of the tree, where two large limbs had been broken from the main trunk of it. Each limb was large enough to have been a trunk of a separate tree. He examined how cleanly the bear had snapped the two limbs from the west and south sides of the tree. With one hand on each scar, he felt both wounds at the same time. Warm to the touch, he thought, despite the early morning hour. Finally, with his own large hands, he partially covered the claw imprints crafted by the grizzly.

"Had the bear been marking territory with its signature or was this a threat?" Caleb questioned, as the sun broke the horizon the dawn gave way to the morning light.

Caleb circled the massive tree to view its more fabled side where Ezra Freedom Sr. had carved a scene of a man facing an alter surrounded by four hooded characters. Were they good or bad, he wondered, as he sat upon either a large knuckle of a tree root, some kind of a stone, or something entirely different. Reaching for a folded knife from his pants pocket, he opened its primary blade and perched on one knee. Scraping the top of the object, he made a series of predictions. If it were part of a root, it would be moist and fibrous. If it were a rock, it would likely be basalt rather than sedimentary, and he would not be able to break basalt easily. Continuing to scrape the surface, he dug the tip of the blade into the object. It proved dry, fibrous, and hard to break. It might be petrified, he thought as he dug further, and concluded indeed it was not a rock or part of Freedom's tree at all, but it was wood. Out of the corner of his eye, Caleb saw something or someone run the top board of the third floor balcony railing. At first he couldn't believe his eyes, so he stood to see if he could detect what it was and where it went. Caleb had not looked quickly enough, as the morning sun fully appeared as a golden red ball and the sunlight became unbearable to see.

Inside Karen's room on the southwest corner of the second floor, she had watched Detective Caleb Jones climb the butte from her west window. Watching as he made his observations, she savored his examination of Ezra Sr.'s carving on the tree. She hoped God had chosen to meet Caleb like He had met her and her friend Ruth earlier. Karen relished Caleb's careful examination of the root knuckle and wondered what he had discovered. When he quickly rose to his feet and hastily looked toward the house, she wondered what had caught his eye, but gained no answer. She enjoyed the people watching event and looked forward to knowing the detective better. After all, Karen thought, Detective Jones is a professional seeker of truth.

After watching the detective's descent from little Huerfano, Karen shifted her chair to look out the window on the south wall. Watching the road from Claymore Flats, she read the latest edition of the local weekly newspaper, *The Out Cry*, and waited for Adam to take her out to breakfast. The lead article featured the rave and how the sheriff's office had been investigating the death of Betty Strong Bull, a longtime resident of Wolf City. It hardly mentioned injuries to two others, who happened to be sightseeing in the area. According to the travelers, they had accidently happened upon the town by mistake. Karen thought how interesting that the article had not identified the organizers of the event, nor had it given other details of how those injured and the deceased had fallen over the side of the ridge. The article also mentioned that Strong Bull's accidental death had been the third fatality in Rock Creek Valley, which had not been of natural causes. Interestingly, all three deaths had occurred in the small town of Rock Creek, which stood like a fortress where the creek left the valley and entered a spectacularly rugged canyon. Also, Rock Creek was like a vestibule where northbound traffic exited the canyon and entered the town before it passed into the river valley.

Karen became aware of other local events by reading more announcements and news. Today, all school personnel were to report to their building assignments, and she knew that she was to go to the high school to meet with Principal John Alden at 10 a.m. She noted that this Saturday Kip Powell and Katarina Bond were to host a grand opening of the Christian bookstore at the Blair House. Also on Saturday, Rachael McNaughton would be hosting a book party, which would feature books for personal growth, Bibles, gifts, and Christian music, both recordings and sheet music, and more. Great! Karen thought I'll attend, unless I have to work at the pizzeria. Next to the book party announcement, she read an advertisement inviting residents to enroll for piano lessons with Rachael McNaughton. The ad informed readers the lessons would be conducted at the Blair House in Lydia Blair's old piano room. Rachael also invited residents to attend a hymn sing at the Blair House. When Karen read the next article about an annual shooting contest next spring, she thought her father may want to join the competition. Last, Karen read a letter to the editor from Beatrice Jaramillo, former long time resident at the Stage Stop Hotel. Beatrice complained about the indecent magazines featured next to children's material on display at the Rock Creek Convenience Store. Ending her letter she demanded the store management or owner clean up the community announcement board at the store. She insisted it include the wholesome offerings in the valley. Beatrice wrote both the current announcements and magazines were not only bad for business, but also, they promoted an impression of the community she opposed. Until both issues were resolved, she wrote she would no longer make purchases at the store or any other in the valley that had the audacity to display such perverse and degrading material. Further, Beatrice gave notice she would encourage her family, friends, and neighbors to boycott! Wow! Karen thought, one McNaughton matriarch had spoken and the other was doing great things! Alone each was influential; together they were formidable! "Praise the Lord!" shouted Karen.

Realizing someone had been fixing breakfast directly below her room, Karen decided to join the team effort. Hurrying down the hallway to the stairwell and into the kitchen, she joined Katarina and Jill Lowenstein, who were cooking and discussing preparations for Janine's wedding reception. Kat promptly assigned the scrambled eggs to Karen and handed her a whisk, while Jill set the dining room table. Meanwhile, Kat turned bacon on one end of a grill on the wood stove, while she added several pats of salted butter on hash browns at the other end. Preparing toast would be last, as she would use a cookie sheet to heat white bread, which she had baked the day before. Karen finished the eggs and placed them on top the cook stove to stay warm. Kat asked Karen to prepare two pitchers of orange juice from concentrate. As Kat reached for the cowbell to announce breakfast time, Adam knocked on the front door.

When Karen opened the door for Adam, he presented her with fresh cut, red roses from one of his own flower gardens. Karen took the roses in one hand, smelled them with a long breath, rose on her tip toes, placed her free arm around his neck, and pulled him to her, as she leaned into and kissed him.

"Hello, Mr. Wonderful, I've been waiting for you!"

"Not long, I hope. You smell better than the roses, my dear!"

"How is it you still have freshly picked roses?"

"Ah, my dear, I have not yet shown you all the secrets of buildings and the land on Claymore Flats!"

From the stairwell came a chorus of retorts from fellow boarders, beginning with Jerry Sunday, who said, "All my life, I've been waiting handsome!"

"Since the daylight kissed the mountains," added Morris Goodenough.

"I've pined away the morning since sunrise," said Caleb Jones, which was accurate.

From the kitchen, Katarina rescued the couple by demanding the men stop their teasing, by saying, "Hey, you guys, give a girl a break. She's been helping me in the kitchen, while you've been lounging around! Come and get it!"

While these and others bounded down the stairs, Adam questioned, "Does this mean we eat breakfast here instead of going to the Stage Stop?"

"Do you mind? I have a meeting with the principal at ten o'clock, and I'd like to show you what the bear did to the tree. You can see Ezra's addition to his carving, and we can sit a spell. We can pray together on Huerfano."

All Adam could do was smile.

As the crew assembled, Izzy and Janine joined them from their first floor apartment by the kitchen. Ezra Sr. escorted Beatrice Jaramillo from her second floor room. Hannah Rahab and Misty McNaughton made their way down from the second floor room, while Kip Powell entered the kitchen through the back porch door.

Hannah asked quietly, "Who are you today?"

Misty replied, "It's a struggle. I want to be Elaine McClaren, but right now I'm Misty McNaughton."

"We ought to have our devotion and pray for one another before we leave our room," said Hannah.

"Welcome home world traveler," Kat greeted Kip.

"It is good to be here with you all, and I hope I'm on time for what's planned."

"You are," Izzy replied, as Ken Bond entered from the back porch with his daughters, Kristin and Krystal.

"Do you have room and food enough for three more?" he asked his wife.

"We have enough room and good food for all assembled," Kat said.

Izzy added, "Adam, this is our first meal where this many of us have come to break bread together, and I'm glad you are here to bless not only our food, but also the physical and spiritual efforts we will be making to restore Blair House! Pastor, please pray for us."

"Thank you, Izzy. I am honored and frankly, the Lord just gave me scripture to quote for you from *Philippians*," Adam said, as he pulled a small print Bible from his shirt pocket. "Father you are good all the time, all the time you are good. Thank you for what you are doing through us. All are bruised, all flawed, all with secrets. We are imperfect people you have plans for and we get to be about your work. Thank you for this food we are about to eat." He paused and read *"Rejoice in the Lord always. I will say it again: Rejoice! Let your gentleness be evident to all. The Lord is near. Do not be anxious about anything, but in every situation, by prayer and petition, with thanksgiving, present your requests to God. And the peace of God, which transcends all understanding, will guard your hearts and your minds in Christ Jesus. Finally, brothers and sisters, whatever is true, whatever is noble, whatever is right, whatever is pure, whatever is lovely, whatever is admirable—if anything is excellent or praiseworthy—think about such things. Whatever you have learned or received or heard from me, or seen in me—put it into practice. And the God of peace will be with you" (Philippians 4:4-9).* Amen! Let's eat!"

"O'Mama, that's my favorite scripture," said Kristin.

"I know, and you have been encouraged just now to follow it," Katarina stated.

More laughter ensued. John Mark Cannikin arrived to check in on Misty. Adam offered John his seat across from Misty, who flashed her doe like eyes and captivating smile, which produced a stunning effect on John.

"I don't mean to break the mood, folks, but I need to ask all of you to follow a common procedure that Janine and I don't have to follow! We are married to one another! Yahoo!"

"Is this going to be a birds and the bees talk," laughed Jill.

"Yes, it is," Izzy said as he became serious, "it occurs to me that ours is a special fellowship where we will be working not only to build an effective small group here, but we will be watched by the community at large in how we love one another."

"He's right," Morris said, Caleb nodded, and Misty's look focused on John Mark's lips.

"The individual privacy you have when you are in your individual rooms will need to be respected by everyone. Dead bolt locks will be keyed and installed on all bedrooms. Security locks will be installed on all windows, all three floors. Of course, Janine and I will have an extra key for each room in our office. We have a reputation to develop and maintain if this really is to be restored as a Christ centered home. We aren't the Stage Stop Hotel and we are not the Asherah House Bed and Breakfast, but we are the Blair House. My father and I knew them well, so did Rachael across the street. Janine as well, as she was a frequent visitor. Let us set a standard that, hopefully, will encourage other people to follow. It applies to all of us, but especially to how women are treated. Some will remember what we said in John Law's office," said Izzy.

"I remember, right for right!"

"Might for right!"

"Yes is yes, and no is no!"

"Making right that which is wrong!"

"Equal justice for all!"

"And," said Izzy, "the proper treatment of women!"

"That's from the Arthurian Legend, the code of chivalry, I remember," said Jerry.

"It's good, solid biblical principle," added Morris, "and how will it play out here?"

"Two ground rules," informed Janine. "One is that no mixed company is allowed in bedrooms. There are common gathering areas on each floor—first floor piano room where we added new couches, an office area on the second floor with a computer, copier, and more, which should be delivered today. We will have a TV lounge area on the third floor. At least we'll have good reception up there! Essentially, outside guests need to be met in the first floor piano room, unless of course, Rachael is giving lessons there."

Kat added, "Hopefully, we will have a lot of customers for the bookstore."

"Good point, we will want to limit access to the rest of the house, although a customer may need to use the bathroom on the first floor," added Kip.

"Good point, I'll work on that," said Izzy.

"We will need some sort of barrier to the upper two floors," added Janine.

"Perhaps a chain or fancy rope across the front of the stairwell," said Kip.

"What's the other rule?" asked Jill.

"Speaking of bathrooms and access, we have one bathroom on each floor and each has a shower stall. Admittedly, bathrooms are going to be a point of congestion and a scheduling problem," began Janine.

"Some will need to bathe at night," concluded Hannah.

"Ladies, we are going to need to put on our make-up in our rooms," said Janine.

"I'll bathe during the day, after most of you have gone to work," offered Misty.

"Like in *To Kill a Mockingbird*, the ladies glisten late morning and afternoon," joked Janine.

"Could we have long mirrors in our rooms?" asked Misty.

"Good idea," said Izzy. "The point is everyone must use a long bathrobe and cover up. There will be enough temptation as it is."

Janine emphasized, "Cover up, don't linger in the bathroom, clean up after you finish showering, take your towel with you, and don't leave underwear hanging around. Use your perfume and after-shave in your rooms."

It was Ken Bond who made the culminating suggestion, "Idea! Kat and I don't sleep here but we will be here a lot. Could one of the gathering rooms be divided and partitioned so we have a small room to use for prayer?"

"Like a prayer closet!" said Morris.

"Yes, something without distractions!" added Jerry.

"Where we could leave prayer requests with or without identifying ourselves..." said Kip.

"Let's record answered prayers too!" added Karen.

"Have an in use sign on the door," suggested Adam.

"Great...absolutely...indubitably...without a doubt!" said Izzy.

Jill led the chorus refrain, "All for one and one for all," which was repeated multiple times for effect and laughter. The good mood had not been broken. Sometimes it would be, but not today.

\*\*\*

In the midst of a discussion about wedding arrangements at the Blair House, Adam and Karen excused themselves to ascend Huerfano, the volcanic butte behind the house. Once they neared the top of the butte, a furniture truck arrived and was directed to park up the driveway in the parking lot to unload its contents—bunk beds, double beds, mattresses, end tables, rocking chairs, office furniture, and more. Briefly they watched Janine take over as she marked off the items she and Izzy had ordered through the local department store in Ridge View.

Too late for breakfast both Tim McNaughton, the waiter from the Cozy Corner Café, and Janine's brother, Mike Crowfoot, the clerk at the Jericho Springs Convenience Store, arrived with their possessions in time to help carry furniture to second and third floor bedrooms. Having previously interviewed both of them to join the team, Izzy welcomed them, and introduced them to the rest. Next, he assigned them bedrooms. Tim's was on the third floor, while Mike's was on the second floor by his Gramma Bea.

New arrivals, Tim and Mike, had been assigned to completely clean their rooms, which meant washing walls, ceiling, windows, doors and hardwood floors. They were to hang curtains and select bedding from a shipment Janine had received earlier. Each was to submit a list of repair and other needs for their rooms. A team would be scheduled to complete all repairs, and Janine announced she and Izzy had committed to buy everything either directly at a local store or through one. She reported Ezra Sr. had written his son a note asking Izzy to buy locally. His note read that what we have came to us out of the mountain, so let us use and spend it in the valley whenever possible.

Since Janine had to report to school, Katarina would have to sign for afternoon deliveries. One delivery included additional goods ordered through the home town catalog store. The shipment included a photo copier and scanner, desktop computer and printer, fax machine and paper shredder. Another order of office supplies would be delivered from a store in Pueblo, Colorado.

Marveling how the team below worked well together, Karen took Adam by the hand and finished leading him to the dry pool where she was to escort him around the top of the butte.

"Come, Mr. Wonderful, checkout what the bear did when it was rousted out of town in Rock Creek."

"I wish I had actually seen it," Adam said, which he would regret later.

"Rabbit certainly did—up close and personal," Karen said. "It is a wonder it didn't kill him."

"Rabbit said he was properly named, but he never wants to face the bear again," Adam explained. "He says his people call it the embodiment of the evil in the valley."

"My guess is the bear was frightened by all the noise and storm like all the people were," Karen surmised.

"Rabbit says his people have a warning about this bear. He was totally serious, when he said it, or so I thought," Adam again explained, "because Rabbit said they claimed it was not just the white man who ushered evil into the valley, with their vile and corrupt ways, nor was it due to the Indians leaving the ways of old."

"What did they say it was?" asked Karen.

"They said a war party is coming and it may bring death and destruction to some."

"Death?"

"Karen, that's all he said, but then he placed his hand on my arm, and with his black eyes, he looked me in my eyes. He told me I am in danger."

"Why?"

"He said I will not be the one who kills the beast, but someone close to me will."

"Fortune telling?" Karen asked.

"Well, next Rabbit laughed out loud and struck my shoulder with his fist. He said Adam, my people love you. You are a man of great courage to them, but you are only one man... who can be depended upon to do what is right. You be careful!"

"They are right. That is what I love about you..."

"Love, did you say you love me?" Adam smiled, as he repeated her meaning.

Exposed by her own words, Karen recovered by adding, "Everybody does! You do what is right, you make right that which is wrong—proper treatment of women, equal justice for all. Adam you are the Lone Ranger, even your horse is named Silver and your dog should be named Bullet instead of Big Foot. How could anyone not love you?"

"You and I both know there are many in the valley who don't," replied Adam, who paused, then said, "My dog before Footers was named Bullet. He was a great dog. Actually, he belonged to Mary first."

"See what I mean? It will be interesting to learn what the survey I'll be doing will say about you," Karen paused and led him to the back of the tree. "Look here at the claw marks! They must be six feet above ground level."

Adam spread his hands over as much of the marks as he could cover and held them there. "It's the same as what's on the front door of the church," he said and looked at her. "Bears mark their territory with their claws like this. It's a statement, a warning to other bears, I think."

"Perhaps it is a challenge," Karen replied, "and it is interesting the marks are on both the church door and this tree."

"What do you make of it?"

"Well, if the bear is the embodiment of evil, it arrived, at least publicly, during the rave," Karen declared. "Weren't there six men dressed in bear costumes during the so called drama they were performing?"

"Yes, I hear that," Adam concluded, "but you've learned more, haven't you?"

"Yes, and I'll reveal that in a moment, but look at what else the bear did," Karen said as she pointed at the two broken branches. "Izzy said he watched the beast climb on each branch, one at a time, and break them both. He said it was like the bear purposefully snapped them off."

Adam placed his hand on both scars, and said, "They are both warm to the touch."

"Izzy said he stood on the rail of the porch outside a room on the third floor and yelled at the bear."

"What did the bear do?"

"It rose on its hind legs and roared back at him, and then went down on all fours in what appeared to be a charge. Then Ezra Sr. drove up, climbed out of the cab of his truck with his shotgun, and started charging up the hill."

"He would too! Did he hit the bear?"

"He got off two rounds before the bear high tailed it. My guess is Ezra hit it."

"It must not have been the time..."

"Adam, suppose Rabbit was not kidding with you. Suppose the bear is the embodiment of evil in the valley..."

"It would mean battle for the valley had stepped up a notch and the efforts of the people and the churches are gaining ground," Adam prophesied. "You and I both know God is at work here and we get to be a part of it."

"And I get to be part of it..." Karen pondered

"One thing for certain...," Adam said with a grin, "Ezra will either have a lot of oak for his carvings, or someone will be able to use it to smoke some meats, or Katarina will have long lasting fuel for the kitchen stove!"

"Winter's coming, you can tell it by the trees. Some are already losing their leaves."

"Yes, winter's coming and soon the bear will either be dead or hibernating."

"I fear what it will take to kill it."

"God knows..."

"Adam, come see Ezra's carving," Karen said, while embracing his left arm with both of hers. They walked to the north side as she continued, "I'll show you where Ruth Browning and I had our epiphany, and I knew I was to accept the teaching position and come live at the Blair House."

"Some said you had a come to Jesus meeting..."

"Yes, it was as if God, through the Holy Spirit, I believe, chose to meet the two of us at that time at this location to reveal his plan for each of us and for the two of us working together."

"Some say it was the tree..."

"The tree may have a role in what happened, but it wasn't a pagan experience."

"Not God in nature?" Adam asked.

"God is reflected in what he created for sure. If it had anything to do with the tree specifically, it was what was carved into the wood by Ezra...the message he was given to present to those who will gaze on the carving," Karen emphasized.

"Certainly, it was for his son."

"According to Janine and Izzy, that was precious to learn, especially when Izzy realized his father had returned home from war looking for his son...and then when John Law arranged for them to meet for the first time here before the picture carved on the tree."

"Could the tree be a spiritual symbol?" asked Adam.

"It is...I think...it goes with the house. The way Izzy tells it and both Rachael McNaughton and Beatrice Jaramillo confirmed it. And you know it. In its glory the tree provided shade for much of the town, a covering if you will, and it stood upon this citadel, a high point, where the Blair House shined like a beacon of goodness, because of who lived here and how they functioned."

"Paul and Lydia Blair were a blessing for the valley. They were not only good people, they were not at all ashamed of the Gospel, and they were faithful to share the message of Jesus, anywhere, anytime. Both of them had a profound influence on me," Adam shared.

"Did they lead you to the Lord?"

"Yes, and they inspired me to not be afraid to live for Jesus. Mary was a McNaughton, but her mother was a Blair."

"Oh, Adam, I wish I could have met her."

"Me, too, you would have liked her, and I know she would have been good friends with you."

"How will I ever..."

"You are in no competition with her. She would have wanted me to find another."

"Not to take her place..."

"No...to fill the void, to come along side me and to be my partner..." Adam said, as the hair on Karen's arms stood on end and tingled.

"Back to the house and tree, Adam, what I heard was that the house with the tree on the high point... it stood out symbolically for the valley as a spiritual high point, a center for Christian activity," Karen added. "It's not a church, but it is a place where people once lived and really practiced biblical instruction."

"And Paul and Lydia hosted Bible studies, and Lydia taught piano lessons, and they had hymn sings, and after school Bible clubs, and more, Karen."

"And it was the center of Izzy's life. He was surrounded by all of that growing up."

"Yes, when he ran away after learning the Blairs were not his parents, things kind of collapsed for Paul and Lydia."

"So, Izzy really is on a redemptive mission in restoring Blair House, like a quest," Karen concluded.

"To bring it back to what it once was?"

"At least in part, but I think there is going to be a different twist to things."

"How so?" quizzed Adam

"Izzy is working at the direction of both his heavenly father and his earthly father."

"Both Izzy and his father returned home. As John Law said, right for right, making right that which is wrong."

"John quotes often from the Arthurian legend."

"I like it. It's how you function as well," said Adam, "integrity. In just a short time you can be depended on to function honorably."

"Thank you. Did you know the Lone Ranger story has its origin there?"

"Really? In the Arthurian legend?"

"Yes, the legend begins with a hero arriving out of nowhere bringing justice and a legal system."

"Hmmm…" Adam grinned and said, "That's a stretch…look closer at the carving."

"Okay, but you look like the Marlboro man, tall in the saddle, handsome, and you seek truth and justice not just for yourself but also for others…like at the rave…taking in the Bonds and now the little boys from Pryor," Karen asserted, as she watched him closely examining the carving, "Adam, what do you see?"

"I guess the obvious is apparent… the man before the alter has choices and like the first Adam, he's reaching for the apple from what would be the tree of life."

"And what of the rest of it?"

"I think all the heavens and the earth are waiting to witness Adam's response. The heavens are ready to sing and the underworld is ready to explode forth."

"Anything else?"

"The hand of God becoming flesh as it gets close to the ground, I think, represents the fact of God having control of circumstances and God is operating in the world regardless of whether or not man makes the wrong decision."

"Hmmm…"

"Karen, my first impression of the four hooded figures around an alter in front of the man was that they represented something evil. I'm not so certain now."

"That's what I thought," agreed Karen.

"I just got a flash across my mind. They are tall figures, four of them, cloaked in long dark cowls," Adam said.

"Now, check out the root knuckle, Adam. Earlier this morning I watched Caleb Jones climb Huerfano. Like the detective he is, he investigated the dry pool, the broken branches and like you, he felt the warmth coming from the tree where the branches had been broken. Next, he moved to the other side like we just did, examined the picture in the tree, then he took out his pocket knife and investigated the root knuckle."

Adam did the same. Like Caleb, Adam removed a Swiss knife from its holster on his belt, bent down on one knee, but first examined what Caleb had discovered before inflicting the object with his own knife. "Karen, he not only scraped the top, but also, he penetrated the wood with his blade. Here, I can cut out a portion of wood."

When Adam handed the small portion of wood to Karen, she said, "It's not alive. It's been dead for a long time. I don't think it is from Freedom's tree at all. It is different."

"Well, you are the science teacher..."

"Yes, physical science, but I do have a life science background to go with that."

"Beatrice said her people, the ancient ones, planted Freedom's tree..."

"A Live Oak..."

"Long ago, but I wonder what this was," Adam said, as he cut deeper into the wooden stump and broke a larger piece from it.

"This, Dr. Watson, adds to our mystery. Come sit on the hill beside me and let me share more with you," Karen said enthusiastically.

Enthralled by Karen's alluring glance, Adam rose, brushed off the knee of his pants, and sat down beside her on the hillside. Karen said, "I'm sorry you missed having time with my parents, but I'm glad you took care of the two boys. They must have been devastated by losing their parents."

"I think they were in shock. It hadn't hit them yet…what had happened to them. I called and asked John Law to intercede for the boys to prevent social services from getting their hands on them. John will contact their relatives and let them know the boys are safely accounted for. The family will have time to show up and bury the boys' parents, and then they can take the boys with them. But today may be pretty rough for them."

"No doubt, it was devastating. Let's be certain to pray for the boys before we go down from here."

"Back to the reality we will be facing."

"Yes, I told you about my conference. I meet with my principal at ten."

"You will like him. He is one of the good guys."

"I certainly hope so. Since he is relatively new to the valley, the study I will be doing will benefit him the most. At least I hope so," Karen relayed to Adam, "but I've got some alarming news for you. Frankly, I was shocked to hear it."

"What is it, Karen? What has disturbed you so much?" he asked.

"When I left for the conference, I took a wrong turn. It was providential. Instead of heading north on 403, I went south."

"You turned right out of the driveway on Main Street and followed 403 to Rock Creek?"

"Yes, and when I got to Rock Creek, I turned left on 85/87 and headed toward Ridge View, but instead of meeting the interstate through Ridge View, I turned right onto Colorado Highway 96 with the intent of merging onto the interstate.".

"Karen, all of that makes sense." Adam nodded supportively.

"A couple of miles beyond the burnt out trailer the Bonds rented from you, I came upon a young woman, who was walking along the highway toward the interstate."

"She was in for a long walk! What was she doing there and why wasn't she headed back to Rock Creek where she could get help?"

"Adam, she just wanted to get away from the valley, from what had happened the night before."

"Was she at the rave?"

"She was to be one of the women who had been recruited to participate in the so called dramatic presentation of temple prostitution."

"Temple prostitution?" said Adam, shocked by the suggestion.

"Yes, the rave invitation advertised a dramatic re-enactment of a Canaanite religious practice to go along with the concert, and she had been recruited to participate in the drama."

"So the play was going to be an R rated production."

"She seemed to think it would be more than a dramatic production," Karen added.

"Are you saying she knowingly had consented..."

"Adam, she said directly to me that she was recruited to participate and was to be well paid as well, because she had belonged to a group of girls, who had done similar things while in high school."

"While in high school? Where?" Adam reluctantly asked.

"Where I use to teach!"

"You mean in Quail Point?"

"Yes!" Karen said in tears. "I suspected it was going on. I shared my fears with the high school counselors. They in turn reported my suspicions to the school administration. The girl I counseled, the one who ended up dead...and I was accused of putting too much pressure on her. The one Sam Gelding apparently killed. She belonged to the group."

"Then you know the girl you picked up. Did you have her in class?"

"I never had her as a student, but I knew of her. She graduated a couple of years ago and moved to Denver. She knew me and wanted to tell me what had happened. What she saw," Karen shared. "She said she and others in the group would receive messages from someone in the office during one of their classes to be somewhere at a certain time, and they would leave school between classes or at lunch. If it were an urgent appointment, they would get a pass from their teacher to go to the bathroom and never return."

"Then it is happening here too. Usually, it is girls, but not always. They cut classes and are out and about town," Adam said, while remembering his time as a school board member.

"Exactly what she said, and it's not just at Quail Point and Jericho Springs. It is also happening at Wolf City."

"Karen, this is human trafficking we are talking about. It appears to be well organized as well."

"There's more, Adam, I've researched my Bible handbook and dictionary. I looked at my concordance and researched all related scripture, especially *Judges, Chronicles,* and *Kings.*"

"I'm not sure I want to hear more…".

"But you've got to Adam. We can't be blind about this," Karen emphasized. "I didn't just happen to meet this girl on the road. She fled from what she witnessed, and she feared for her life. She shared with me, because she knew me and because she knew I was a Christian. She asked me for help. God is in charge of circumstances, and I made a couple of wrong turns and just happened to pick her up along the road."

"As if this weren't enough to frighten her…" Adam reflected, "What happened that made her flee from everyone else?"

"She said both Gloria Jones and my former student were supposed to be in the dramatization. She said they disqualified themselves, and then she said some girl named Misty was also supposed to be in the play, but she had run away and was being harbored by the church in Rock Creek."

"And Gloria Jones and your former student are dead, killed by Sam Gelding."

"They were very angry toward all three girls, but what she saw may have been an effort to fix what was missing."

"What do you mean? Wait a minute…I think I can guess," Adam thought and said, "The Canaanites practiced Baal worship, which means temple prostitution and child sacrifice. It also included Asherah and the Asher Pole. Parents often required their older children to serve in the temple. It was part of their duty. Is that what you mean?"

"That's more than what she said, but I think you have called it what it is."

"So what else did she say?"

"To be direct, she said she saw three dressed as bears commit murder or attempted to commit murder."

"Three meaning men or women…I guess we don't know for certain," said Adam, who then asked, "Do you mean the slaughter of innocents on an alter?"

"Not quite, she said when the crowd fled down the game trail, the three dressed in bear costumes literally pushed three people over the edge of the cliff."

"Not an accident, but a definite effort, as you said, to fix what was missing?"

"Indubitably...without a doubt...she said."

"One was Betty Strong Bull," Adam concluded."

"What's the point?"

"If it truly were to enact or practice Baal worship with fertility, it may also have been intended to include more."

"Misty is pregnant."

"And she fled the Asherah House before the rave."

"Because an outsider showed interest in her and rescued her from the waters of the creek."

"A divine moment?"

"Yes, but no one will want to hear this, especially the church," Karen predicted, and then confessed, "I hear it and I don't want to believe it."

"Nor I, it is too insidious," said Adam, "and Gloria Jones and your former student in Quail Point aborted their babies...and then they were murdered."

"Which meant the babies could have been used for the ceremonies, like what is documented about Canaanite religion," Karen synthesized, "and that's too evil to be believable?"

"Or, too evil not to be believable."

"Adam, how many raves have happened in the valley?" Karen probed.

"Two we know about...those were public, which is quite surprising...Karen, I'm afraid, literally afraid that this might explain some other things that have happened, if I were to think and connect some dots..."

"What do we do?" asked Karen as they embraced and held onto one another.

"The most important strategy? We pray, and I need to pray God will place a hedge of protection around you as you work in the schools and as you do the community survey," urged Adam, as he realized the real and present danger she might face.

"And I need to pray for you as pastor of the church in Rock Creek and your work with the community pastors group."

"For the work being done in the house below us and their plans to impact the community for Christ.

"To keep you safe from the bear," said Karen, as she climbed down the butte to keep her appointment with Principal Alden.

"For truth and justice, grace and mercy to prevail," ended Adam. As he left for cow camp, Adam wondered about what might have been planned for the Osteen girls, and he began connecting historical dots.

\*\*\*

Meanwhile, fresh out of jail and returning from court appearances, more angry Night Riders gathered at the Tobacco Store in Rock Creek. Staff worked the numbers board and a bookie logged horse racing results. In the corner an ongoing poker game continued with chips moving from player to player, while the house managed to keep ever increasing stacks of red, white, blue, and black chips. Some played twenty-one in another corner, and a small group of men watched the major league baseball game, as they bet on balls and strikes and the type of pitch the left hander would throw. Since the NFL season had started, a group of football fanatics used an official NFL schedule card to record the outcome and scores for each week's games. Usually only one player would win the football pot. Winners were determined by number of correctly selected wins plus the total points per game. Of course, most said that no one ever got hurt when playing at the Tobacco Store. Each week the numbers grew of those who knew differently.

Receiving a hero's welcome, more members of the unofficial Night Riders arrived at the Tobacco Store. Though conflicted after the previous meeting with his father, Butch McNaughton led the others inside. Brothers Irv and Ellis Moss tailed after Butch followed by Roy Sentry, and then Buddy Smith. Buddy received the most acclaim for having been accused of murdering Karen Gustafson, who had later re-appeared alive and well. No matter, everyone thought, Buddy had given the sheriff's deputies a good chase after attempting to harass those occupying the Blair House south on Main Street in Jericho Springs.

"Thanks, fellas, I've had quite a ride the last few weeks, but you know Gustafson's just a new teacher here, but she was in Quail Point for several years," Buddy said.

"But remember, Bud, she's the one who shot me in the heel of my foot…" Roy reminded everyone.

"Yes, and if the stories about her are true, she could have shot you in the small of your back or at the bottom of your brain stem," Butch added.

"No matter, Buddy, you gave the law a good chase…"

"True story…" Buddy responded, "but I wish I hadn't hit Gramma Bee with the beer bottle…"

"Enough!" growled Red McNaughton, "Sit down and shut-up!"

*** 

Ezra arrived at the Stage Stop Hotel in time to watch Butch and crew stroll across the driveway from the front of the hotel to the backdoor of the Tobacco Store. He made note of each of them on a pocket sized note pad, which he carried in the pocket of his western cut shirt. He had been able to park on the street side of the hotel where he stayed awhile to see if anything else transpired. A few weeks ago everyone in the hotel, Tobacco Store, and the convenience store across the highway would have known he had just arrived. Now, he drove a loaner truck because his old truck, a 1953 Chevrolet named the Gray Whiz, had been towed to the dealership in Ridge View for much more than an oil change. Previously, the Gray Whiz would announce the arrival of the old man, as the engine sounded out cough, cough, sputter, cough, sputter, boom in methodical progression. Tonight, Ezra arrived without a warning.

Predicting trouble for someone, Ezra left the truck and bounded up the stairs toward the front door of the hotel. Instead of entering, he made his way to the east end of the porch. Reaching around the side of the building, he grasped the fire escape ladder and swung himself onto the second step. Ascending the ladder to the second floor, he next walked a two foot ledge across the east end of the building, turned left, and continued toward the back of the Tobacco Store. He watched as a Lincoln Continental turned east from the highway at Indiana Avenue where the driver parked it. The driver switched off headlights, but not before revealing someone had walked down the game trail path from the ridge. Ezra laid flat on the ledge and watched as the driver of the Lincoln met the man who descended from the ridge. In the shadows Ezra recognized the two—Chauncey Brown, banker and chairman of city council, had arrived in the Lincoln, while Sheriff Bailey had descended the ridge on the game trail. Ezra guessed Bailey's truck or department cruiser could be found on the ridge…But why? Ezra made notes, as the banker and sheriff entered the back door of the real estate/insurance building. He had not recognized a third man, who rounded the corner of the building and entered through the back door. No vehicles had passed by on the highway, no one had left the hotel or bar, and no one else had walked along Indiana Avenue.

While Butch called the hotel bar to order beer and pizza, Buddy Jones took his place in leading the rest of the Night Riders in a bear growl. The gamblers joined in, as the sound became uproarious. Noise from the Tobacco Store echoed so loudly, it disturbed surrounding residents as well as patrons in the bar. Sarah the waitress refused to carry pitchers of beer to the store. Finally, she consented to make the delivery, when her mother, Lila Longdon, revealed her pistol, which she carried in her desk clerk jacket.

"Come on daughter, we are not going to be intimidated by those hooligans any longer, even if Butch runs this place," Lila asserted. "Besides you're still pregnant and you know what they want."

"Okay, Mom," Sarah said, "but sometime soon we are going to need help to deal with all this."

"And you know we will either have to stay and testify, or run and escape the coming fury."

"Hopefully, Karen will stop by soon, and we can talk with her."

Carrying pitchers of beer and plastic drink cups out the back door of the bar and walking the short distance across the parking lot to the Tobacco Store had been easy. Working their way across the Tobacco Store floor, while being groped, was not. Previously, they put up with the attention, but now they found it increasingly repulsive.

Almost across the floor, Sarah handed two pitchers of beer to one of the patrons and wielded a strong slap across the face of Butch's friend Ellis Moss. Sarah's mother set two pitchers down on a table and grabbed the handle of the pistol in her pocket. As Ellis raised his hand to backhand Sarah, Buddy Jones restrained him.

Ellis' brother Irv said, "Ellis, check out Lila," and then, "Lila, what's in your pocket? Hey, fellas, I think Lila's packing."

The men backed up and gave the two women ample room to complete their delivery. A chorus of bear growls followed mother and daughter across the Tobacco Store floor to the back door. Some of the men watched the two women leave and return to the hotel. Others returned to their gambling and testy conversation.

"Butch, what do you make of Lila packing a pistol?"

Someone said, "Don't pay any attention to 'em. How would you like to be groped as you attempted to pass through a room?"

Another replied, "I'd shout, 'more, more, more!'"

"I'll bet you would!"

"I'll talk with them tomorrow and find out what's up," Butch said. "We've got more important things to do."

His father, Whitney "Red" McNaughton took over and said, "Butch, Seamus, Van Allen, and Ralph, let's go to the real estate office. Lead the way Robert, it's your place now that Sam is gone."

"God rest his soul," someone said, then laughed aloud.

Another said, "There's no rest where he has gone."

"'Fraid, so," replied Irv Moss.

As Red's men made their way up US 85/87 past the antique shop to the real estate and insurance offices, Ezra tailed after them like a spy as he noted their names as they spoke.

"Robert, has anyone been named to take Sam's place," asked Seamus.

"No, nothings been said so far. His wife cleared out most of his things, and Deputy Candy and Detective Jones were here rummaging through everything."

"Open the door, Robert," said Red, "I trust you left the back door unlocked, so the others could join us."

"I did. They should be in the back room. Can you see your way back there? I prefer not to turn on a light."

"Understood, walk through the dark."

Once in the room, lights switched on revealing all who had gathered around a conference table. Peering through a window, Ezra recorded more notes. The third man to enter through the back door had been from the school district offices. Ezra slipped away back to the hotel where he went inside, ordered a slice of apple pie, waited and listened, while Red provided the greetings.

"Chauncey, Maurice, Sheriff,—I'm glad you were able to meet. Chauncey, Maurice, I think you know my son Butch and Van Allen, Seamus, and Ralph from Wolf City. Robert you know Maurice, the assistant superintendent. We all know Bailey."

"Yes," said Butch and the others, "we've all met the Sheriff, one way or the other. You'd think you would cut us a break now and then."

"When you stop doing stupid things, that could happen," Bailey said.

"Cut the banter, we need to work together, if we can ever get through this," ordered Chauncey, banker and city council member.

"What's tonight's agenda, Red?" asked Maurice, assistant superintendent of schools and step-father of Irv and Ellis Moss.

"Just like how you do your planning, Maurice. We know we want two things. One to get the water and mineral rights from the Blair House estate, and the other to conduct our raves without interference, especially like what recently happened."

"Let's cover the raves first," Bailey said, "because right now that is attracting the most attention."

"Okay," said Red, "no one knows who organized our event. I'm the only one who can identify names of the six bears and the temple priest."

"Bailey, do you know what Caleb Jones is doing here?"

"No, CBI won't tell me anything. Has anyone seen Jones lately?"

"I saw him at the restaurant, but he was eating by himself," said Butch.

"Hopefully, he went home to Denver," added the Sheriff, "but I don't think so. He arranged for autopsies of his sister Gloria and the girl Sam killed in Quail Point plus Betty Strong Bull."

"What's important about the autopsies, Sheriff?" asked Chauncey.

"One common denominator," informed Red.

"Come on, Dad, which was what?" asked Butch.

"They were or had been pregnant."

"Then Jones is on our track," Chauncey concluded.

"You mean how we recruit the women for the raves? What we want to happen?" Van Allen questioned.

"Yes, and if he makes the connections, he will find out about our other business," said Chauncey.

"Which leads back to the Asherah House," Maurice added.

"What women do we have left?" asked Seamus.

"Sarah and Misty," reported Red, "plus the ones from the other night."

"They're worth twenty to seventy thousand," said Chauncey the banker.

"Misty is missing," Butch paused, "Have you noticed a difference in how Sarah is acting? You know she made a trip to Denver?"

"Do you suppose she got an abortion?" asked Robert.

"Don't know," said Bailey. "Are you sure the ones from the rave are accounted for?"

"We don't know what happened to the one from Denver," said Van Allen. "The last anyone saw of her, she was headed east into the pasture."

"I'll send some wranglers out to track her," said Red. "She probably hitched her way home."

"Red, then you must tie up some loose ends," said Maurice.

"Red, we need to know if Sarah is still pregnant. Find Misty and get her back. Bailey, investigate Detective Jones. See if he is now part of the CBI Human Trafficking Task Force. Butch, find out if he is staying at the hotel," ordered Chauncey.

"Here's one for you! We need to find out what Adam Claymore knows and if John Law has a role in what Jones is doing," growled Red.

"What about Candy, Sheriff?"

"What about her?" barked Bailey.

"She will be trouble!"

"So will the rest of the deputies," added Butch.

"Do you really want them to do differently?" asked Bailey. "Look, I'm watching Candy, keeping her busy...if she's investigating, it's on her own time."

"What's with the bear?" asked Ralph from Wolf City, "Is it true that it marked a challenge on the front door of Adam's church? Did it do the same on the Live Oak tree at the Blair House?"

"Yes, it did and Adam has his wranglers and some of mine at cow camp. He has promised to kill the bear."

"So Adam is temporarily out of the picture," said Ralph, "and I saw Pilgrim Wayne ride through Wolf City like he owned it. He carried his Sharps fifty caliber in his lap, ate lunch at the diner, and sat like he was Wild Bill Hickok with his back against the wall. My guess is he is hunting the bear too."

Robert King piped up, "I've been wondering something."

"What?"

"Like the rest of you, I was there at the rave. I put the rifle I used to shoot out street lights in the back of my truck with two others. When I went to drive away, when the downpour shut us down, the rifles were gone and my tires were flat."

"What did you do?"

"With the sirens blaring and a deputy entering Rock Creek, I drove on those flat tires all the way to the highway, and then I limped home on them," added Robert. "My ex-wife really questioned me, and she is still up in arms about it."

"Dummy, you just identified yourself as a vandal and as one of the bears. Only the bears had trucks on the ridge. The girl who lives with her parents across from Adam's burned-out trailer must have ridden with you," analyzed Maurice, "and that was too easy to figure out."

"Wow! Am I in trouble or what? At least I wasn't one of those who pushed the three people over the ridge. I didn't kill anyone," Robert the dummy said, as the others looked at one another. "I wonder who took the rifles and where are they? Sheriff, have they shown up?"

Sheriff Bailey took the floor and said, "No, they haven't, and that is a problem, but I have another, more important question. What made everybody panic and run? The storm clouds gathered and blocked the moon, so all the light we had to see by was the fire we built. Thunder and lightning were horrific, as was the howlee blowing through the canyon."

"What about the terrible sound of the bear's growl?" said Van Allen.

"How about when lightening nearly split the Asher Pole?" added Bailey.

"Lightening did not split the pole. It was a bullet, and it sounded like a fifty caliber from a Sharps rifle," said Bailey. "Pilgrim had to have been the shooter."

"Agreed, but who were the three giants to the south? In the light, it looked like two of them were flashing metal, long pieces of metal," said Robert, who added, "and Bailey and Van, thanks for the company, because you two proved you were there. You, Sheriff Bailey, wouldn't have heard the shot or seen it splinter the Asher pole and you, Van, wouldn't have known about the girl fleeing into the herd. So now, who is the dummy?"

"Metal like long swords..." Butch reflected, while the others laughed at Bailey and Van.

"Kind of, but what do you make of it?" said Chauncey.

"Just folk lore," Maurice noted, "and you make six, Chance."

"Shut up, Dr. Wood," Red growled, "you forget I know you were there, too, I know all who were there! The rest of you guessed right. Only two of us know who the temple priest was, and I'm not saying."

"Loose lips, ruins the bliss!" commented Butch, who added, "Red, Bailey, Robert, Chauncey, Van Allen, Dr. Wood, and me. Two, maybe three of us pushed the Strong Bull girl to her death," he paused to contemplate, and then concluded, "I think it was the sudden drenching. The earth turned to mud, and I had trouble walking, let alone running. That's what caused the panic, but the giants with their swords in the light were awesome...spooky!"

Improving on his son's conclusion, Red discounted the idea of giants in the south with their long swords and the mystic of the bear, and said, "What's with you Butch...It was an eerie night. It all worked together. Like buffalo, we all ran for cover in the midst of a downpour. The people in the jeep were probably from the Blair House. Izzy was probably one of them."

The rest agreed, but they looked toward Ralph, realizing he was the only one not at the rave.

"So, Robert, are you back with your wife?" asked Ralph to divert attention from the rest.

Robert shot back with Butch's comment, "Yes, she and I are talking! You be careful of your loose lips!"

"I'll tell you where we messed up..." Butch paused hoping for a response, "there should have been barriers marking the trail!"

"Okay, next topic: we are at war with those who occupy the Blair House. In order to get the water and mineral rights, what are we going to do?" asked Red.

"This is where I leave you. I have no part of what you plan, so don't say anything until I'm gone. If you break the law, I'll have to arrest you, unless I don't catch you," said Bailey, as he smiled. "Butch, don't do anything stupid. What I don't know, I can't get caught lying about."

"One thing all of us need to remember is appearances are important, and our success as a corporation will depend on how we function in secret," emphasized Red.

"The longer it takes to get rid of those at the Blair House, the harder it will be..." said Chauncey.

"We all have family and family interest to protect. No one, and I mean no one, talks about my being here or what we have discussed. Got it?" Bailey said, as he looked each man in the eyes before walking out of the room, down Indiana Avenue to the end of the street, and up the game trail to where he had parked his private automobile. Without turning on the headlights, he drove along the path through Red's pasture back to Colorado Highway 96.

"Does anyone not understand Bailey's message?" Red growled, "No one talks!"

"Get on with the plan, all of us need to be somewhere else," declared Chauncey. "If we are correct about the opposition, we better do something about Adam, Pilgrim, and Izzy."

"Okay, we start this weekend with the football game. There will be plenty of revelry," said Van.

"One more question," asked Robert. "What about the churches?"

"What about them?" countered Butch.

"Aren't we likely to make them angry? Won't they do something to oppose us?"

"What are they going to do, pray?" Red said.

"Have you ever got your prayers answered?" asked Seamus.

"You mean you pray," Van Allen said then laughed.

"What are you worrying about? If Chauncey wasn't on city council, we would need to worry about the council's reaction. But churches... how long will their effort last? Have you ever known a church to have a sustained effort about anything?" Red asserted.

"Unless it has to do with money, do you know of anyone sustaining an effort on anything?" said Ralph.

"Let's see how the churches respond. Priscilla and Aquila have been working the street corners in Ridge View inviting people to pray with them. A lot of people stop and pray. I've got a hunch they're not going to be intimidated," said Chauncey.

"You know you are talking about my mother," Robert King said, "and she is not a quitter. She is more like a bulldog than my father is and he's a school principal."

"Robert might be right. When we had the city council meeting to get the council to condemn the Blair House property, the Rock Creek church worked with the Baptist church and another church, and they walked through Jericho Springs praying up and down every street. Now they've been going to every door leaving a plastic bag with a Bible, a children's storybook, some tracts, and a couple of flyers about the churches," said Van Allen.

"We know how fired up the Church in the Glen is in Rock Creek, but did you know Adam is having the newcomer named John Mark restore his old house down the highway from the church," added Maurice Wood, "and the rumor I heard is it's being fixed up for a fulltime pastor to move his family into."

"I use to attend church there. I was baptized there too, and for the longest time Adam worked with me. He said he was making a disciple of me. When I was a kid, Adam led me in a prayer that worked," said Butch. "He stuck with me until my prayers were answered. He sought me out no matter where I was. He checked on me to see how I was doing. Adam never gave up on me all the way through high school."

"Really," said both Seamus and Van Allen. "What happened to you?"

"I graduated from high school, and I became a deputy sheriff. I walked away from the church."

"You prayed with Adam," said Butch's father, Red McNaughton. "What did you pray about?"

"Home..."

# Internal Battles

## CHAPTER 10

"The path of the righteous is like the morning sun,
shining ever brighter till the full light of day."
Proverbs 4:18

Two opposing forces made themselves ready to clash in open battles and behind the scenes with skirmishes in Rock Creek Valley. While one sought only what benefited themselves and their family alliances, the other sought to usher in revival for believers and salvation for the lost souls residing in the towns of Jericho Springs, Ridge View, Rock Creek, and on the plains and on the eastern slope of the Rocky Mountains. One sought water and mineral rights that belonged to another, while the other brought living water and hope to the valley.

Both forces gained reinforcements. Night Riders had been charged with felony and misdemeanor crimes then released from the county jail in time to participate in the rave held on the ridge in Rock Creek. Another ally appeared in the form of a bear, a demonic beast bent on killing both man and cattle. It had defaced two symbols of God's work in the valley, the Live Oak tree above Blair House and the entrance door to the little Church in the Glen in Rock Creek. Adam Claymore, interim pastor of the little Church in the Glen, opposed the other side. He gained support first from the congregation of his church, and then from a local pastoral organization he initiated. Often perceived like the Lone Ranger movie and television hero, he battled for what was right and made right that which was wrong. Reinforcements arrived through unusual means – earlier a lovely woman and a prodigal son had arrived on a Trailways bus, more recently a man walked into town from Denver, and two others followed after him. Additionally, members of the pastor's flock put shoe leather to their promises and took to the streets to encounter the opposition with the Gospel of Jesus Christ. Although the rave was just a façade for an evil ritual, Christ followers thwarted the event by using their might to rescue innocents. One life had been lost and two injured, while two had been rescued – Hannah Rahab and Misty MacNaughten. Others had been set free.

A rematch was certain. Both sides had met and developed plans to engage the enemy. Night Riders met to orchestrate battles and skirmishes openly in the valley, while also working behind the scenes to steal through the legal system. Unknown to them a giant of a bear wrecked havoc first in the mountains and then in the river valley. On the other side, Izzy Freedom and his team at the Blair House set the bulwarks of the building by first repairing the structure then by staffing it with the likes of Detective Caleb Jones, bus driver Morris Goodenough, convenience store clerk Mike Crowfoot, Christian book salesman Kip Powell, and more. Their plan was to first structure an oasis where the citizens of the valley would come to Blair House. They would visit the Christian bookstore, sit awhile in the piano room, and listen to hymns played by piano students. Upon invitation, many would bathe in the hot springs pool, climb the hill behind the house to view the artwork of Ezra Freedom Sr., and encounter God wherever and whenever He saw fit. Also, the members of the household began instigating efforts to take the good news to the people through prayer walks, street corner ministry, hymn sings, and more. The outcomes promised to have both external and internal consequences. Battles and skirmishes involved individuals and groups.

\*\*\*

Just because Misty MacNaughten, now Elaine McClaren, had accepted Jesus Christ as her savior did not mean that he had become Lord of her life. Within Misty a battle raged. As a new believer, Misty's transformation was not just a war in her flesh, but also it was a battle for her mind. The battle began during her trip with the Brownings to their home from the little Church in the Glen. Whenever around men, Misty had been trained at the Asherah House Bed and Breakfast to gain their undivided attention. She had experienced no other basis for a relationship. The Holy Spirit began to work in her immediately upon her conversion. Ruth's role was significant, as she prayed for Misty and spent time reading the *Bible* with her.

Changes began to be made. At Misty's request they had started reading the short book of *Ruth*, and Misty marveled at how Ruth had chosen to go with her mother-in-law instead of back to her people when her husband died. When Misty read and listened about Boaz, she told Ruth that John Mark would be her Boaz despite his youth. After reading the *Gospel of John*, Ruth invited Misty to help her wash and dry the dishes after each meal. Next, Ruth led Misty in reading *Proverbs 31:10-31*. Misty confessed she would have to think about being such a woman. Ruth asked her if she thought the *Proverbs 31* woman would be attractive to John Mark. Misty had been stung by the possibilities.

Ruth engaged Misty in serious conversation. They walked the grounds of the Browning's home to where the North Fork of Rock Creek flowed under a County Road 403 bridge. Ruth had Misty watch how the water emptied into then lingered awhile in a pool before flowing over a water fall. Watching there, Ruth attempted to guide Misty about her gender, the role of women, and women's influence on men. Misty knew well about how to gain and maintain a man's attention, at least for a little while, but anything beyond the superficial proved foreign to her. At first the concept of being a partner with a man frightened her, until she realized a partner meant some sort of interdependence beyond the physical. When she realized being a partner also carried responsibilities, she became threatened and insecure. She knew she would dominate in a physical relationship, but she figured being a partner would mean she would be looked to for input. Uncomfortable, Misty decided what Ruth talked about would require her to take a deeper look beyond what she had experienced. Misty recalled and spoke aloud to herself the conversation she had with Ruth and Rob Browning.

"I think I have spent my life in the pool. Perhaps I've been trapped there...no...I'm quite certain that has been my situation, especially with men. They would rush to the house, stay awhile, and then hurry away. Some were about to fall off or jump off a cliff..."

During the short drive from the Browning's home to the Blair House, Ruth had said to me, "This really is a good opportunity for you."

"Sure, I guess, I mean I know... people will be watching out for me," I had replied, "but my hope is you mean something more...that I can get out of the pond and into the stream of real life."

"Yes, the people at the Blair House have a sense of purpose, one well above their personal needs. They seek to become a team where each one of them has a purpose, a role, and function with the others, but also each has a ministry beyond the team," Ruth had said.

"Huh?" I said.

"Take a look at them. You'll see people who are bruised and flawed, people who have secrets, and now they have a second chance," Ruth told me.

"A second chance for what?" I asked.

"One is to follow Jesus not just as their Savior, but also as their Lord. Each has decided to put much of their life on hold, while they fulfill their commitment to help build God's kingdom in Rock Creek Valley," Ruth had explained.

"That might be a bit much for right now, Ruth," had said her husband Rob, as her son Andy had been all ears listening to what his mother had been saying.

Taking my hand in both of his, Andy had looked dreamily into my dark blue eyes, and had said, "Miss Misty, it's like if you and I was married, and we made some mistakes that made each other mad, it would be like having a second chance to get things right."

"A second chance? I haven't even had a first chance," I had said soberly, "I've never really been important like what your mother is saying."

"You do now, Misty, praise the Lord! You have a chance to be important to the team at Blair House," Rob had encouraged.

"Watch the other women, Misty. Most have been Christians for quite some time. Janine just married her husband Ezra or Izzy as we call him. They were childhood friends. He promised to come back and marry her. She resolved to wait for him and she did for more than a decade," had said Ruth.

"You mean she didn't have…" I started to say until Ruth interrupted me I guess because of Andy.

"Exactly, she kept herself for marriage, just as she had vowed," Ruth had said.

"And it paid off," I concluded.

"Janine is a school teacher and she is a partner with her husband in restoring Blair House," Ruth had emphasized.

"Jill and Karen will be helping as well and both are school teachers. Both help with the cleaning and repair of Blair House. I think Jill is supposed to take the lead with the garden and crops," Rob had said. "She's a science teacher."

"And Miss Karen will be working at the pizzeria too. Miss Misty, would you go there and have pizza with me when I am older?" Andy had asked.

I told Andy that, "I would go have pizza with you any ol' time. We are buds!"

"Mom, Dad, going out for pizza with Miss Misty would really give me something to crow about," Andy had said as he began to sing a song he had already sung to me.

"Andy, shhh, I want to hear more," Rob had said.

"Katarina and her daughters live down the block, and while Mr. Bond is delivering papers each morning, they work in the Blair House kitchen preparing breakfast for everyone. When Mrs. Bond, Katarina, finishes cooking and cleaning the kitchen, often she runs the bookstore for Mr. Powell," Ruth had added, "so she manages her home, helps at the Blair House, and works at the Christian bookstore," Ruth had added.

"Everybody has a job to do and the others depend on them to do it," I had concluded, and then asked, "What about Hannah and old Mrs. Jaramillo?"

"Mrs. Jaramillo, Beatrice, will help with the mealtimes. Everyone loves Mexican food and she has promised to fill that need as well as helping with the cleaning and laundry," Ruth had explained.

"And Hannah?" I had asked.

"I'm not sure. My guess is she like you will have to find her place in the group. I know it won't be to sit around and look pretty," Rob had joked.

"No, Hannah's not too pretty, but I could do it," I had replied.

"I think you'll see real beauty as the women grow in Christ, like you will too, Misty," Rob had said.

Ruth had concluded the conversation as we arrived at the Blair House, when she said, "Misty, my prayer for you is for the beauty of Jesus to radiate through you and that the Holy Spirit will grow wisdom, knowledge, and understanding in you. Perhaps he will give you the gift of discernment!"

"Ruth," I said, "you are a good friend. I think you just identified the job I'm to have—that the beauty of Jesus be seen in me!" I had said eagerly, "And I really want it to happen!"

"Amen," we had said together, while beaming toward one another, and I stored up all of what had been said to me during my time at the Browning's home and in their car.

\*\*\*

As Misty walked down the front stairwell, she called forth her memories of time spent with the Browning family. Vividly, she remembered the details. "This morning," she said with resolve, "I'm going to start leaving the pond."

When John Mark had arrived for breakfast and sat down across from her, Misty had beamed toward him, and then tilted her head to one side and looked at him with doe like eyes. She gently thrust her foot under the table, and when she found his, she barely touched his shoe enough for him to know her presence. She gathered the plates of food around the area where he sat, and got up to fetch him a glass of water when his became empty. Although Misty made him nervous, John Mark found himself helpless to pull his foot away, and as a servant's servant, he enjoyed her attentiveness. When Adam and Karen had been excused from the table to climb the hill, Misty boldly asked if she and John Mark could be excused from the table. John Marked appeared dismayed not really knowing what to do with Misty, other than to insure her safety. Her response caused him inner turmoil he had never experienced before.

"Yes, but please come help if we get a delivery soon. Oh, and Misty, remember, no mixed company in your room," Janine emphasized.

"Yes, Miss Janine, I understand," Misty said sincerely.

Out the backdoor Misty promptly led John Mark across the driveway and into the stand of trees. In the dense foliage, she promptly stopped, turned around, raised onto her tiptoes, leaned into him, place her arms around his shoulders, then relaxed in his arms, and kissed him like she had when he rescued her from the log in the creek. At first he tried to resist but was helpless to her advances. His head spun and he nearly blacked out, and then he returned her kiss with equal fervor. Pleased with his response and feeling in control, Misty kissed John Mark again gently with equal results. Their passion subsided some to where both gained balance and comfort. Into her mind came thoughts of how Janine had controlled herself for a decade waiting for the one she loved to return to claim her. For the first time, she had wanted to learn to function appropriately and to have this man want her to be his partner and helpmate. She wanted a real relationship with John Mark where he would seek her point of view and input. Also, Misty desired for John Mark to want to understand her despite her own lack of knowledge about herself.

Both looked upward at the canopy provided by the deciduous trees. John Mark noticed the zip line extending from the third floor balcony to the tallest and thickest Ponderosa pine in the grove, while Misty motioned for him to look around the canopy. Nets of rope lay ready to be triggered to drop and entangle whoever or whatever they would fall upon. While they marveled at the intricacies of the defense in the glen, they had not seen all the devices Ezra Sr. had deployed to defend Blair House from invaders. Predator enemies could soon become prey in the glen.

When Karen and Adam descended the hill from Freedom's tree, Misty and John Mark had already circled behind the glen and had traversed the grassland to an outcropping by the foothills just north of the butte. On the west side of the outcropping, John Mark found a metal handle partially covered by undergrowth. He tugged on the handle, which displayed a small door. While Misty wanted to explore it further, John Mark resisted by telling her the doorway may become important to the defense of the Blair House. We should not go further without telling Izzy, in private, what we have found. To his surprise Misty agreed, who thought exploration of the door could be for another more intimate time with John Mark. Instead, she wanted to climb the west side of the butte to see what Karen and Adam had climbed Huerfano to discover.

This time John Mark pulled Misty by the hand and they began singing, "Jack and Jill went up the hill…" until they reached the top of the volcanic mound.

"Beautiful," Misty said, as she gazed toward the plains, "I've never been this high before. I've been on top of the ridge during the ceremony, but I've never been in the mountains before now, nor have I seen this much of the valley."

John Mark realized how thoroughly imprisoned Misty had been. He stood to her side, slipped just behind her, put his arms around her, and said in ancient Gaelic, "Elaine McClaren, God has a plan for you and it is good. The baby inside you must be born, for you are to return with him to our homeland, once Blair House is fully restored and all that was wrong is made right. God will tell us when to go. Others may leave before us Misty, and I am to escort you there. My guardians will protect us. Meanwhile we have a mission to complete here, and I am to remain chaste throughout my assignment. It is a discipline I must adhere to in order to honor both Christ and the vow I pledged."

"I love your language," Misty spoke nestled in his arms, "I really do not understand all you said, but I love being held by you."

"It is that of your ancestors. Dear Elaine," John Mark said, "it is for your benefit I am required to remain chaste while completing my mission, which is to keep you safe. I need you to help me be true to my word."

"Oh, John, why?"

"It is for you," John said, "and for the boy who grows within you."

"Boy? How do you know?" Misty asked.

"It is foretold," he replied, as he turned to face the carving on the tree, "and this carving helps explain our circumstance."

Misty moved closer to the tree, nearly stumbled over the wooden stump in the ground, touched the tree, and then followed the lines of the carving with her hand. "Is this you?" she asked as she touched the man in the picture, and then focused on the four figures standing opposite the podium where the man stood.

"Yes, I believe we can say so. The question for you to answer is whether or not it is you standing this side of the podium."

"You silly, I don't look that way," she smiled coquettishly at him, then said, "And are those your traveling companions?"

"Two of them...so far."

"Will I meet them?"

"Not before you leave with me...at least I think. One person has met two of them, a kind woman who gave them something she had been entrusted to preserve."

"Kind of mysterious..."

"Not really, I just don't know her name or what she gave them. If I don't know, I can't tell and reveal a secret. Shouldn't we go down from here and help with the furniture?"

"Yes, thank you. I need to be helpful here and do my part, and I'm to learn to be a Proverbs lady," Misty said, as he smiled in approval of her decision.

"I hope for that too!"

\*\*\*

When Attorney John Law scheduled a meeting with Deputy Sheriff Cotton Candy and Denver Detective Caleb Jones, his reactions proved ambivalent. Originally, he had organized the effort to involve the Colorado Bureau of Investigation and the Denver Police Department in both solving the murder of Gloria Jones and in forming a task force to investigate human trafficking in the Rock Creek Valley. Barely out of high school, Gloria had come to Rock Creek one weekend and stayed to work at the Asherah House Bed and Breakfast. Somehow Law thought it was no coincidence that Jill Lowenstein and Karen Gustafson ended up at Ezra Freedom's cabin after being attacked on the bridge behind the Rock Creek church. Jill had witnessed the death

215

of Gloria Jones, Caleb's sister. Karen had survived an attack by a new suspect in Gloria's murder.

Previously, former Deputy Sheriff Butch McNaughton had been the chief suspect in the murder of Gloria Jones. Due to his position and family connections, the investigation had remained open, while some had clamored intensely for his indictment. Instead, Butch remained free until Night Riders were arrested and charged with the assault of Beatrice Jaramillo during a spree of vandalism, harassment, and intimidation of newcomers to the area. While Butch was jailed, a high school student was similarly murdered in Quail Point, a town south of Rock Creek at the opposite end of a rugged canyon similar to Glenwood Canyon near Glenwood Springs. The bodies of both girls had been stuffed in a crevice underneath bridges covering Rock Creek in their separate towns. As a result Butch had been released from jail, as he could not have murdered the girl in Quail Point.

At first Night Rider Buddy Jones had been accused of assaulting and perhaps murdering Karen Gustafson. When pursued by sheriff's deputies following one of the Night Rider's escapades, Buddy had fled from the Stage Stop Hotel parking lot down a driveway that lead to the Church in the Glen. He ran behind the church to cross the footbridge over Rock Creek, tripped and fell headlong at the end of the bridge, bounced off a post, and landed in blood soaked mud where Karen had bled profusely when previously attacked. Deputies snickered at the sight of the bloody mess on Buddy's head, face, and jacket. They decided to do the community a favor by adding charges to Buddy's arrest, which made him a suspect in Karen's disappearance. Buddy remained in jail, but later gained release based on information provided by both Karen and Jill Lowenstein. The women had met with John Law, and Jill revealed she had seen Sam Gelding murder Gloria Jones, while Karen identified Sam Gelding as her attacker. As a result those charges against Buddy Smith were dropped, yet he had been kept off the streets for a short amount of time.

Three questions remained unanswered. How had both women ended up at Ezra Freedom's cabin? Was the death of Sam Gelding an accident, foul play, or the result of someone rescuing Karen? What role did Ezra have with the women? No one witnessed Jill's arrival and Ezra offered no answers. Somehow Jill and Karen had appeared at Ezra's cabin in the mountains west of Jericho Springs. Neither knew exactly how or why, but Jill saw Ezra carry Karen into his cabin where both she and Ezra had tended to Karen's wounds. Later Ezra transported both women to John Law's office where they revealed their stories. Since Ezra's tongue had been cut out during his captivity in Cambodia, he was unable to testify orally to what he had seen or done. He could, however, put his testimony in writing, if necessary, if required. Very likely, John Law had thought, Ezra truly was heroic and for certain would have known how to kill the likes of Sam Gelding. No evidence placed Ezra at the scene of the assault on Karen, nor were there any signs of a scuffle on or near the footbridge. His finger prints had not matched those found on the bridge handrails. Since Gelding's body had been in water several weeks, the only discernible signs of damage to his body were a broken neck and blunt trauma to his head. Investigators assumed Gelding either fell or jumped from the bridge into the creek where he landed head first on the rocks below.

At first all three, Attorney John Law, Deputy Cotton Candy, and Detective Caleb Jones- preferred not to pursue Sam Gelding's death. Each believed somehow Ezra was a hero, yet Sam Gelding's widow deserved to know the cause of her husband's death, no matter what he had done. As a result they committed to find out how Gelding died. This was complicated for John Law. He had been permanently retained by Ezra to find his son and to establish his claim as the lawful owner of the Blair House and its water and mineral rights. John located Ezra's son, gained Izzy's return, and protected Ezra's interests against the efforts of the McNaughton Corporation to take the water and mineral rights from him. Caleb Jones believed if Ezra had been responsible for Gelding's death, it was probable Ezra had rescued someone who had witnessed the death of Caleb's sister. Jones believed Ezra probably had protected Jill from being killed before she could testify against Gelding. Additionally, Law held a natural desire to protect others against bullies as well as a spiritual need to support those who were trying to advance God's kingdom in the river valley.

Cotton Candy had an affinity for Ezra from the beginning. He brought her a truck load of wood each winter without letting her know he was the deliveryman. Cotton's neighbors informed her of Ezra's good deeds, but Ezra refused her attempts to pay him. The probability that Ezra had rescued Karen from Sam's attack also endeared Ezra to Candy. She had spoken for Karen when Karen had been recommended for a teaching position at the high school. Candy provided an additional reason for Karen to be hired. Candy asserted Karen would not only be a good role model for young women but also she could be a real asset to the school and community if she were to teach gun safety. Candy said she looked forward to competing against Karen in the community's annual rifle and pistol tournaments. Most of all Candy appreciated that someone had stood for the proper treatment of women and appeared to have been victorious in bringing justice to one who had not been a respecter of women. Each concluded Ezra was the real deal, a stand-up guy!

The actual meeting had been brief. They had limited evidence girls from local high schools in Wolf City, Quail Point, and Jericho Springs belonged to a prostitution ring. Somehow the Asherah House Bed and Breakfast was involved as was the Stage Stop Hotel and the Rock Creek Tobacco Store. They suspected the raves had a role in the recruitment of girls. The team vowed to uncover Sam Gelding's connection to the human trafficking, if any. Reluctantly, they also committed to find out how Sam died. As a result, Caleb Jones agreed to stay in the Rock Creek Valley to help crack the case in league with Deputy Candy and Attorney John Law. Since they suspected Sheriff Bailey's involvement, he had not been contacted or involved in their investigation. Since both Hannah Rahab and Misty McClaren had allegedly participated in previous raves and now resided at the Blair House, Caleb explained how he had joined with the group there. Candy committed to interview both Karen and Jill, while John would deal directly with Ezra Sr. Reluctantly, John Law, Caleb Jones, and Cotton Candy vowed to find out Ezra's role in Gelding's death and hoped they would not be stumbling blocks to the good work started at the Blair House.

"One other thing I know both of you will be tuned into, I'm certain..." John began to say.

"Which would be...?"

"I can guess," Deputy Cotton Candy offered. "You are concerned about the wedding ceremony in a few weeks."

"Yes, my friend Adam has alerted me to expect trouble. Izzy and Janine have asked to have the ceremony moved to the Blair House. They hope to have the house totally cleaned at least, and the book store is opening." John elaborated, "I fear what the Night Riders and others might attempt to do...and what the Blair House team might do in response."

"I heard a piano student playing for Rachael McNaughton in the front room one night as I drove past the Blair House," said Candy. "Rachael could be collateral damage like what Beatrice suffered from the hands of Buddy Smith."

"Really? Her music is a delight to hear. She starts early, and sometimes she accompanies breakfast with really fine tunes," Caleb added. "Everything seems peaceful, but Ezra Sr. has already set snares."

"He is no one to mess with. We really don't know what he went through as a prisoner and as a soldier," responded Candy...

"Have you ever heard of him acting inappropriately?" asked John.

"No," she said, "but this is about his son and daughter-in-law and their wedding."

"And this is about his house...his land...and Ezra defending what is his," concluded Caleb...

"And this is really about our question of what happened, if anything, to Sam Gelding," ended John Law. "This I have from a reliable source that the Night Riders will try to destroy the Blair House before the wedding."

"Well," Caleb said, "that sets a timeline for our investigation, which is good to know."

"John, you know Caleb and I found nothing when we executed the warrant I got from the judge to search both Gelding's office and home."

"How did Mara respond?"

"I arranged to pick up keys from her at school to search the offices, and I made an appointment with her to search her home," Candy explained.

"You went out of your way to be considerate, Deputy," John said, "but have you considered any school office could have photocopied flyers to advertise the rave's."

"And if girls turn tricks during school hours," Caleb added, "appointments could be arranged where?"

"From school offices, where they would receive a pass to leave school grounds..." Candy concluded, "I don't like the implication. It may explain the smug look on Mara's face when I picked up her keys."

"Don't feel bad, Candy," Caleb sympathized by saying, "I also got the autopsy reports confirming both my sister and the girl from Quail Point had been pregnant and did have abortions. Betty Strong Bull was pregnant when she died."

"Which brings us to the question of who were the women who were meant to participate in the ritual..." said John Law, "and who were the ones from the earlier one?"

"We should be able to get info from Hannah and Misty," concluded Caleb, "and could you quietly find out who owns the hotel, the convenience store, the Tobacco Store, and the Asherah House. I tried but I was kind of stonewalled."

"At county records, I suppose," John said, "I'll have Amanda do a search, and I'll have her make some calls to find out who has what kind of printing capabilities. Since I'm legal to both the school district and the city, I have reason to ask such a question."

"Also, gentlemen," Candy shared, "I ran the data base re the rifle registrations on the ones used to shoot out the lights in Rock Creek. Turns out, they are related to former cases, which means they had all been taken from the evidence room at the sheriff's office. And there is more...I checked on tire repair thanks to John Mark. I also shared descriptions of the three trucks on the ridge. One truck belonged to Robert King and the others may belong to Sheriff Bailey, Red McNaughton, or Van Allen."

"Belonged in the evidence room..." Caleb nearly whispered.

"Cotton, this runs deep into the heart of the valley!" John urged, "You watch your back and be careful what you say around town."

"On a positive note," Cotton chuckled and added, "I receive multiple calls from residents in Rock Creek and there's not many people living there. I'm meeting with John Mark to start a neighborhood watch there. We'll hold a meeting at the senior center, and John will help do some of the work to get it started."

"Great, let us know what happens," said Caleb.

"I read an announcement in *The Out Cry* that Rachael McNaughton would be playing for a hymn sing at Blair House and the community is invited to attend," said John.

"Ezra and the others will be ready is my guess, but I will encourage them to be on guard," added Caleb, "and it might be good to make certain to have some well placed guests to attend."

"Good meeting," Cotton concluded, "I have to leave, but I have one parting thought..."

"Which is?"

"I wonder what would have happened to the Osteen girls, if the ceremony had been completed?"

\*\*\*

Well after dinner one weekday night, Misty wrestled internally battling with herself. She relished her growing relationship with John Mark. Had she been working at the Asherah House, she would have known what to do with him, she thought, but reconsidered when she came to realize she had never really had a genuine relationship with anyone. At first she talked briefly with Janine, but learned Janine had waited for the love of her life for a decade in hopes he would return to claim her. Janine's story included that she had not dated despite being pursued by more than one of the eligible bachelors at school where she worked, at church where she worshiped, and around town where she fellowshipped with a wide-range of people. Misty figured the story about Janine meant she had remained chaste all that time while waiting. Janine wasn't the one to consult further, Misty concluded, but she knew to watch how Izzy and Janine worked together as partners.

Misty considered talking with her roommate Hannah, but figured advice from Hannah would not be much different from what Misty already knew. Since both Hannah and Misty had recently accepted Christ as their Savior, Misty figured it would be good to talk with Hannah about her progress in becoming a *Proverbs* woman. Together they read *Proverbs 31*, but decided to seek help from others to understand it. Remembering she and John Mark had watched Karen and Adam as they climbed the bluff behind the Blair House and spent time alone there, Misty concluded Karen would be one for her to seek for advice. As a result and without speaking with Hannah, Misty walked down the second floor hallway toward the bathroom, but stopped short and knocked on the door to Karen's room.

Karen welcomed Misty into her room where she had been talking with Jill about how Janine was going to need their help with the upcoming wedding. Jill started to leave and go to her room directly across the hall, but Misty asked her to stay in hopes that Jill may also have some good advice for her.

"Sure," Jill said, "what's up?"

"I gather both of you have been Christians for a long time."

"Yes?"

"And I know you both date and have boyfriends."

"Right?"

"I don't know how to say it politely, but here's the deal. I've been reading the Bible and all, and you know I accepted Jesus as my savior. I know all my sin has been forgiven and that includes the past, the present, and the future. Right?"

"Yes, where is this going?"asked Jill.

"And you know I'm pregnant with a child that's not John Mark's."

"Misty, that is obvious, and I was there in the pastor's study at church when John Mark said you were to have the baby, that you are to protect your pregnancy regardless of who is the father," said Karen.

"See, that's part of what I don't get. I love John Mark, and I hope he loves me. I hope he will marry me despite who I've been and what I've done. It's hard for me to understand and believe, but I also read the story, I mean the true account, of Joseph and Mary where she was pregnant and Joseph married her even though she was pregnant. I'm not saying that's my situation... and I'm not saying their circumstances are like mine. It was just so wonderful how Mary and Joseph listened to God and were obedient."

"You are learning," said Jill, "and what John Mark said to you is pretty wonderful too."

"About me keeping the baby alive," Misty said. "I know that means I am not to get an abortion, and I know that means I am to take care of myself, but does it mean I can't have John Mark."

"You mean you want him to..."

"Absolutely, I can't get him to, it's like he refuses no matter what I do, and I learned a lot at the Asherah House. One of the things he said was he made a vow to be chaste, so his mission with me would be successful."

Karen said, "You started the conversation recognizing your past, present, and future sins are forgiven because you accepted Jesus as your savior, so you know it would be a sin for you to have relations with John Mark out of wedlock"

"That is good!" added Jill.

"I guess that's right, but what difference would it make? I'm already pregnant, and my future sins are forgiven."

"I think you know," concluded Jill. "Having our sins forgiven doesn't mean we are free to keep on sinning. We are forgiven of our sins, but that doesn't mean there won't be consequences for our sin. We earnestly try not to sin because that is what he wants us to do. He died for us, and we are to live for him. He wants us to choose to be obedient. Dead to sin, alive in Christ."

"The promise is he will be with us in all circumstances, so don't take him into circumstances...like when you willfully sin," added Karen.

"Do you mean the baby could be hurt?" Misty asked.

"Yes, but probably not," Karen stated, "but there is more to it. You have an honorable man who has taken a vow to remain chaste, so the mission he is involved with concerning you will be successful. I'm sure he would want to do what you want to do. But Misty, if you really love him, don't make it hard for him to keep his vow."

"She needs to read *Colossians* and *Ephesians*," Jill said to Karen. "Misty, you have a man interested in you regardless of you being pregnant by another man, which is not what happened to Mary. But another man made you pregnant, and John Mark still wants you. Wow! Misty, John Mark has laid down his life for you, your baby, and your safety. He has put your interests before his own, which is what a husband is supposed to do for his wife."

"We aren't even married!" Misty exclaimed.

"There's something more, Misty. Past sin is a foothold Satan will try to use to get you to sin again, where he will try to tear you down and your witness. You have to be careful."

"And Jill don't forget to tell her why we don't keep on sinning."

"Right Karen, Misty, the Holy Spirit is in you. He is the teacher, as is the Bible. He will illuminate the scripture for you to learn what to do. The Bible tells us what we should do, and our choice is whether or not to follow what the Bible says."

"One other thing in reading the Bible, you will learn how precious God considers all of us. He made us...He is active in the construction of your child. All of us are precious in his sight. You need to read *Psalm 139*," added Karen.

"And *Hosea* about Gomer," added Jill.

"I think I understand why and how Janine kept herself for Izzy. I'm just amazed someone would persevere so long believing a man who said he would return for her would actually do it," Misty said.

"You'll hear us often use the phrase, 'Yes is yes and no is no,' Misty," Jill elaborated. "Janine teaches the Arthurian legend as part of her high school lit class, and we kind of adopted a modern version of the code of chivalry for ourselves."

"I watched the *Sword and the Stone* movie. The individual knights went on special assignments to earn their knighthood. I think it was called a quest," Misty mused. "Thanks for listening to me, goodnight."

While Misty turned to leave, Karen said, "Perhaps you should find out more about John Mark's mission, and you may want to talk with Katarina. Her husband gave up a good job to attend seminary, but he had a massive heart attack two days before becoming an assistant pastor at a church where they lived. Kat has been through a lot of heartache watching and helping her husband heal. They moved to this valley, and he delivers newspapers. They lost all they had when someone set fire to the trailer they rented from Adam Claymore. Now they live down the street and are helping here in exchange for their rent."

"I wonder what God has in store for them..." Misty said as she walked toward the door to go to her room, but stopped and said, "Thank you both...you are very kind to me...I'll read what you said."

Misty walked down the hall, entered the room she shared with Hannah, crossed over to her and covered her shoulders with her blanket, as Hannah slept. Whispering, Misty said, "This is the first time I've ever done this for anyone. I want to be your friend, but I really don't know how to be a friend. Jill and Karen make it seem so easy. I'll read what they told me and maybe I'll learn. Others have said the Bible has all the answers..."

***

"What's wrong?" Jill asked Karen, who sat before her frowning deep in thought.

"I must be telegraphing my thoughts..."

"Very hard to miss, Karen," said Jill. "You've barely started at school and already you're wearing a frown. Did you have your meeting with the principal?"

"Yes...he said something that got my attention."

"He's one of the good guys, Karen. It would be wise to listen to him. John hasn't been here long himself, and he will benefit the most from your survey project."

"I know...and I'm under the direct supervision of Dr. Wood for the project."

"Not good," Jill responded, "but what else?"

"Principal Alden asked me to give him a copy of every interview."

"Is that a problem?"

"Yes, Dr. Wood made a point of saying I should submit the interviews I complete every day to him as early as possible. He said for me to bring them to him the next morning before school starts. He specifically told me not to make copies."

"Even if you have a sub assignment..."

"Even then?"

"It's probably so the next set of interviews can be scheduled. Are you being paid for mileage?"

"Yes, but not for daily trips to the school district offices. The original arrangement was for me to make a weekly trip. Jill, you know Dr. Wood and John Alden. What would you do?"

"I would write a letter to Wood with a copy going to Alden. Summarize your understanding that you are to make a daily trip to the school district offices each morning before school starts instead of the agreed upon weekly trip and that you will not be paid mileage to do so. Include that this could cause a conflict at the high school as you may have morning duty dependent on the substitute assignment.

225

I would also write that your understanding is you are not to make copies of any interviews."

"Won't that make Alden angry?"

"I don't think so. You didn't say anything about Alden's request for a copy of the interviews. Since Wood's request could possibly create a hardship at the high school, it is reasonable for a copy of your memo to go to Alden. It informs the principal of what the assistant superintendent is doing, and it gives Alden a chance to deal with Wood."

"Good idea, Jill!"

"One more thing..."

"Which is..."

"Make a copy of each interview here in our office, and keep them in a secured location here at home. Don't tell anyone, even me, what you are doing."

"Hmmm...why do you say?"

"Regardless of how the data is supposed to be used, you and Alden may need the information for future battles...I mean purposes."

# Skirmishes

## CHAPTER 11

*"For though we live in the world, we do not wage war*
*as the world does."*                    *2 Corinthians 10:3*

After the new furniture had been situated, team members took care of their own business. Simultaneously, Hannah and Misty offered to clean up the dining room and kitchen, and then set up for both lunch and dinner. Welcoming the help, Kat relinquished her duties to them, so she could walk with Kristin and Krystal to elementary school. Kip opened the bookstore to prepare displays in connection with the night's hymn sing. Karen, Janine, and Jill were long gone to school, as were Mike to the convenience store and Tim to the Cozy Corner Café. Ezra Sr. and Jr. rode together to the saw mill where they unloaded a new press to make wood pellets for a new pellet burning stove delivered with the furniture. Having received a telephone call from Rabbit requesting help with Pilgrim and the Pryor boys, Beatrice solicited Caleb to drive her to the Claymore Flats Ranch house. Janine and Jill worked in their respective classrooms, while Karen studied maps in the school library to prepare herself for future travels throughout the valley to conduct her interviews and to deliver pizza.

Mara Gelding delivered a message to Karen that her first interview appointment with Adam Claymore had been postponed. From the school office, Karen called the ranch house on Claymore Flats to talk with Adam. Rabbit answered the telephone and told her that Adam had ridden out late this morning to hunt the bear which had

227

killed Pilgrim's dog Bruin. Rabbit reported he had brought Pilgrim down late last night from cow camp, after the bear had attacked him. Rabbit told her Pilgrim only had a broken ankle and Bruin had rescued him from certain death. Hastily, Rabbit told her that Adam wouldn't be back until the bear or he was dead and that he had asked Ken Bond to preach for him until he returned. Realizing what Rabbit had said to her, he said no more, and then asked her to pray with him. Since the doctor prepared to leave and needed to give him instructions, Rabbit said his goodbye and hung up the ranch telephone. Sudden fear gripped Karen. She immediately prayed for Adam's safety and hoped his good sense would prevail.

Karen shook her head from side to side and said aloud, "Why does he always have to be the hero?"

As Janine's classroom was next to the library, Karen rushed back there to tell her about her telephone call and ask for prayer for Pilgrim and Adam. What she discovered was a message written on the chalkboard. Janine's message indicated she had been called to the office. Not knowing what to think, Karen hurried back down a different stairwell and found Janine speaking on the school secretary's telephone. Mara Gelding stood close by listening to the one sided conversation.

"Thank you, Mara," Janine said and smiled pleasantly, but offered no explanation. When Mara sought information, Janine took Karen by the arm and went into the hallway.

"Listen, Karen, we don't have much time before meetings start. I just got off the phone with Izzy. He spoke with Tim before we left this morning, but couldn't relay the information. then Tim overheard plans that the Night Riders and others are planning an all out effort to cause trouble for newcomers and especially those at the Blair House."

"Then it's not over."

"Hardly, and get this, they are also targeting my wedding," Janine said as tears flowed when anger rose up her neck to her now red face.

"We are nearly ready for them," Karen replied. "The men are putting on the finishing touches of our defense today."

"I know, it hurts me to think this would be happening in my town. I have lived here all my life. The Crowfoots are originals and the McNaughtons are newcomers to us."

"We'll fight back!"

"We always have!"

"But listen to this. I was planning my interviews and my first was with Adam at the ranch."

"Cozy..."

"He cancelled this morning early. I called the ranch and spoke with Rabbit."

"What's happened?"

"Last night the bear attacked Pilgrim and his dog saved him."

"Must have been the Growler, Bruin."

"Apparently, Bruin paid the price for his courage with his life."

"Bruin's dead and Pilgrim's alive, but hurt. My guess is he's at the ranch..."

"Where the doctor just arrived..."

"What about Adam?"

"Rabbit said he rode out this morning and won't be back until either he or the bear is dead."

"That's Adam."

"I fear for him. This is no ordinary bear."

"We think it is evil," said Janine, "the embodiment of evil."

"Adam is no ordinary man..."

"No, and he is a hero to my people. It takes a man like Adam to confront the evil facing a community such as ours."

"But Janine, we are all called to withstand evil wherever we find it."

"Then let us go on the attack through prayer as our first line of defense, while we hurdle spears and arrows of prayer on the offense. Tonight, we will address this, probably at dinner."

"Meanwhile, I'll do my interviews..."

"And say nothing of this where eager ears listen to learn what we are doing."

"And you mean Mara Gelding."

"Especially Mara, but there are others here and many at the school offices in Rock Creek."

"Gotcha!"

\*\*\*

Karen's next appointment began right in the high school office with Principal John Alden. She figured she would soon learn if her memo to Dr. Wood had caused trouble for her or anyone else. Approaching Mara, the principal's secretary, seemed ominous. Karen had comforted Mara during a city council meeting when Mara had been looking for her deceased husband, and Karen had met her again during the summer when she and Ruth Browning had stopped for Karen to see Jill's classroom. My gosh! Karen thought, we talked this morning about Adam's cancellation. But here, now, Mara treated Karen as if she were an unknown quantity, a foreigner, an outsider, a newcomer. She surmised correctly that no matter how she handled the next few minutes with Mara, it would be reported to Principal Alden and to those at the administration in as poor a light as possible.

As a result, Karen shot an arrow of prayer, "Help me Jesus!" Karen said under her breath. She approached Gelding's desk and waited behind the counter. Karen thought Mara would make her wait as long as tolerable before the exact time of her interview with the principal; however, seeing her, Principal Alden came out from his office and by-passed his secretary.

"Miss Gustafson, so good to see you," Alden said, as he pulled open the barrier between them and asked Mara to bring coffee. Alden ushered Karen into his office, invited her to sit opposite his desk. Since he knew his office door would need to be closed, he passed behind her chair to secure the door and whispered for Karen to be certain the door was tightly closed after Mara delivered the coffee.

"Go ahead and practice saying to me what you would to someone not familiar with the survey."

Mara arrived with the coffee, and said syrupily, "Will there be anything else?"

"No, thank you, Mrs. Gelding."

Since Mara left without closing the door, Karen rose from her seat and closed it tightly. She sat down without missing a beat and began, "Thank you for meeting with me, Mr. Alden. I know you are a very busy man. I won't take more than twenty minutes of your time."

Karen shifted her weight and leaned forward slightly, "As you were informed when your survey was scheduled, this is a study to identify community leadership and to gain their perceptions about community problems or concerns, as well as resources available to address each. The information I collect is totally confidential. Your survey responses will be compiled with others for use in forming local advisory committees and task forces to address what our community perceives as problems, issues, and concerns."

"Good businesslike approach, a little chilly, but I like how you set the parameters," said John Alden.

"What do you suggest?" Karen asked.

"I had you scheduled first with Adam Claymore, because I believed you would be comfortable interviewing him first, which is part of my point. Almost everyone knows the two of you are an item. People also know about your episode defending Deputy Candy with your pistol. Butch may be a McNaughton, but people have tired of McNaughton influence and Butch's behavior. The time is right for positive change."

"What's my role?"

"You're like a breath of fresh air. As someone recently said, they haven't had anyone like you in the valley since Mary Claymore died, and she is missed by friend and foe."

"Adam's first wife, I wish I had known her."

"Me too, but aren't you part of the Blair House group? People have great hopes for what you will be doing."

"How do you mean?"

"I think that is part of what we will find out through the survey. Introduce yourself, that you are new to the school district and that part of your job assignment is to manage this project, then let them make the connections."

"Then let's take the first question," Karen said as John nodded affirmatively. "If you had a plan for improving your community, what five people would you go to for help, and how can they be contacted?"

"Adam Claymore, Chairman of the Accountability Committee and former school board member. Willa Sentry, Chairman of the School Board and former president of the parent-teachers organization. Beatrice Jaramillo, matriarch of the McNaughton clan and ties to the Ute tribe. Jill Lowenstein, head of the valley teacher association, and Superintendent Clarence Moss. I'd contact the Superintendent at his office in Rock Creek. All but Beatrice can be reached through the school district. Beatrice has a room at the Stage Stop Hotel."

"Had a room at the hotel, now she's at Blair House with Jill and me. Thank you, question two: What five people do you consider to be the most influential or successful people in the valley?"

"Interesting," Alden said as he leaned back in his chair, "A McNaughton grandmother lives at Blair House and another across the street and teaches piano at the Blair House... Let me see, influential: Adam Claymore, his partner Whitney 'Red' McNaughton-north of Ridge View. I don't know his address. John Law, a local attorney, whose office is in the same building as the Bustos, upstairs on the north side; Chauncey Brown, local banker and Chair of the Jericho Springs City Council, and I don't know his address; and last, Judge Randolph Parsons from Ridge View."

"Thank you, question three: If you wanted to know the thinking of the community and its segments, what five people would you go to and who do they represent? What segments of the community?" said Karen.

"This is an important question. Well, they all are, but this one helps identify the polarity, so we could pull together people from all interests, all points of view. I'd say Red McNaughton re the McNaughton clan and corporation; Izzy Blair or I mean Freedom re newcomers; Adam Claymore re pastors and churches; Rosa Jaramillo re teachers, McNaughtons, and the Ute's; and Deputy Cotton Candy re law enforcement and those without a voice, Neighborhood Watch."

"Thank you, and now question four: What do you consider to be the three most important problems facing our community, your specific community?"

"I've been thinking about this for some time, and as a father of young children I am greatly distressed about certain things in our community. Number one is the lack of community involvement in education, in the lives of their children. Not just in the decision making processes, but also in their own lives. So many are not lifelong learners. The results of this survey will help that. Number two is the breakdown of the family, which directly relates to number one. I mean serial marriages, divorce, single parent families, children born out of wedlock. Really, it all started with taking God out of the classroom in the late '50's. We are spiritually, morally bankrupt. Number three is an outgrowth of the first two problems. Teen pregnancy, abortion, and more pointedly, human trafficking. I believe we have a group of girls involved in prostitution, and I don't just mean after school. With an open campus at lunch, it is reported to me that some girls may be spending lunch hours prostituting themselves here in Jericho Springs, at the truck stop and bus depot in Ridge View. I'm not certain what's happening in Rock Creek, but I heard the raves may be used to recruit girls. Law enforcement doesn't seem to want to do something about it either."

"Although I'm not supposed to comment on what the interviewee says..."

"Then don't, Karen, resist the temptation no matter how valid or supportive your comments may be."

"Another time then, Mr. Alden," Karen said as John nodded affirmatively. "Question five: What do you see as resources available for each of these identified problems?"

"I have high hopes for this survey and its results regarding community leadership, and also for the position the school board and city council has taken to fund this project. It will provide the data we need to get started to involve those who know the thinking of people, who have influence, and who are perceived as helpers. The breakdown of the family is insidious. Fortunately, our churches are coming alive and the pastoral community is as well. I understand we have a new Christian bookstore at the Blair House, and I hear rumblings about the possibilities of a Christian radio station being made available to the valley. Surely, the Blair House will be an important asset. I'm at a loss about the human trafficking. I've had opposition to closing the campus during lunch hour from the Sheriff's Office, local business, the school board, and city council. Unless I get the right people involved, this one might cost me my job if I continue to pound the drums like a poor little drummer boy in a field of the dead bodies of my friends in arms. The enemy has over run us, and it is coming back to finish off the wounded without burying the dead. Others have tried to solve this problem and failed, including my predecessor and his counseling staff."

"Well, Mr. Alden, this completes my interview with you, and as I indicated at the start, your answers will be held in strictest confidence."

John Alden reached over the desk and laid his hand on Karen's arm, and said, "To whom will you be submitting my interview?"

"The superintendent's secretary, Beth Ellen McNaughton."

"If people find out she is the one receiving the surveys, then we are dead in the water."

"What about giving them directly to Dr. Wood?"

"Same answer different player."

"What do I do?" asked Karen.

"Mara's with them too, so I have to be careful. They know I will be your first completed interview. My suggestion is that you speak directly to Clarence Moss, the superintendent, who is your next interview. I have expressed my concerns to him. Didn't Lippincott emphasize the need to keep the individual surveys confidential at your workshop? Your training included how to compile the data. I presented the list of first round interviewees to the superintendent and board, so no other information is needed for them until round two at which point you can provide the information for round two scheduling."

"What do you fear about these people getting the information?" asked Karen.

"Useful information depends on the confidentiality of the surveys. Small towns often have a lot of small people trying to keep control of what they have. They fear outsiders, they fear change, and if you think about it, they have nowhere to go. You and I came here from somewhere else. Our ancestors didn't homestead the area, our blood, sweat, and tears have not combined with the soil. We haven't buried anyone here. A loss here would only be uncomfortable, an inconvenience. You and I can move on without much loss of face. I really want to make a positive change here for, by, and with the people. I believe God has called me here to do so."

"What you've said includes Adam Claymore."

"With one exception..." Alden said, "he's not behind anything criminal or immoral. He is pro-family and Adam Claymore has confronted evil over a lifetime, while attempting to serve our Lord. Even after he lost his beloved Mary."

"I get it. Adam is not a self centered egomaniac out for what is good for him at the expense of others, and especially those who have no voice," Karen synthesized.

"Exactly..."

"I'll do it. I'll raise the issue with the superintendent!"

Karen left the high school and drove directly to the superintendent's office where she would interview Clarence Moss. Beth Ellen McNaughton greeted her coldly like Mara Gelding had, and after getting a soda for Karen and Clarence, she left the superintendent's office door open for her to eavesdrop. Clarence noticed what she had done and was quite use to correcting her directly for being nosey. As a result it was easy for Karen to persuade the superintendent to allow her to compile the list for second round interviews and to report out that list at a school board meeting. Besides, she concluded, the daily drive to the administration offices added unnecessary cost to the project and many interviews may be completed before or after school hours. With the decision made, Superintendent Moss called Dr. Wood to his office where he informed his assistant of the change.

At first the assistant superintendent gasped and questioned how the school board and city council might respond as co-sponsors of the project. Moss countered he was quite certain he had the necessary votes should it come to a vote. Wood surrendered his battle knowing that he, not the person hired to manage the project, would be in question. Plus requiring an inconvenient trip to and from the school district office daily served no real purpose and would add expense to the project. Although Dr. Wood was known for playing with the lives of people who worked for and with him, he knew the high school principal had beaten him. In a word, Wood was a well known lad.

As the superintendent walked Karen to the stairwell outside his offices, Karen said, "I hope this doesn't create any problems..."

"No, no Miss Gustafson. Your idea is more than reasonable. Don't worry about Dr. Wood's statements. He has a lot on his plate. He's married to my former wife and stepfather to my two sons," Moss chuckled as he said, "I'm certain I'll receive a call from her."

***

One could say the forces of good had won a skirmish. Others might reason that good sense had followed flexibility on the part of the school board's new hire. The next battle proved far more dangerous and offered opportunity to impact the community at large negatively. Rumor spread quickly that both Pilgrim Wayne and Adam Claymore were out of the picture, albeit temporarily. With Barnabas riding line and Rabbit at cow camp with Red's wranglers, Night Riders sought to take advantage of the new equation. In their madness, they believed two of three disrupters of the recent rave had been neutralized. Only Izzy and his father Ezra remained as the only naysayers with clout enough to thwart seizure of the Blair House, its water and mineral wealth. With the Sheriff and Councilman Brown in league with them, the McNaughton Corporation leaders ignored the potential effectiveness of the likes of Attorney John Law and Deputy Cotton Candy in not only swaying public opinion but also in rallying law enforcement agencies.

Izzy readied his troops at the Blair House. Ken Bond organized nightly prayer meetings in the second floor meeting room. With help, Ezra positioned fifty gallon drums on the ground throughout the stand of trees north of the house. They filled each drum with water tinted with bright red dye and set them to spill over on forceful contact. Earlier Ezra set webbing above the center of the grove where he was certain many would gather. Detective Caleb Jones coordinated with Deputy Cotton Candy to have sheriff's office vehicles ready to make arrests. Janine and Jill visited neighbors along Main Street, who committed to call the sheriff's office if something suspicious happened. Specifically, they were to ask for Deputy Candy and tell her that Operation Brazos was underway. While the intent was to function like a recent popular western movie, the way their plan played out was more like the chase scene from a movie titled the *North Avenue Irregulars*, a comedy where church ladies helped a local pastor overcome organized crime in their community. Once things started happening at Blair House, squad cars, trucks, and family vehicles were to barricade both ends of County Road 403 in and out of Jericho Springs. Pizza store manager and deliveryman, Jerry Sunday, set up surveillance throughout the town. On the north end of town, Donald Borden, the former pastor of the little Church in the Glen in Rock Creek, led a group from the Jericho Springs Baptist Church. Members of the pastors' group contributed help. Both groups committed to record license plate numbers and to write physical descriptions of all perpetrators.

At the convenience store in Jericho Springs, Mike Crowfoot supervised the south end barrier. Like road warriors, members of the McNaughton Corporation rolled into town from the south and parked vehicles along side streets off Main Street. Mike Crowfoot called Jerry at the pizzeria to alert those covering the north end of town and then called Izzy at the Blair House. Moments later Night Riders entered town from the north. Caleb Jones called Deputy Candy, who dispatched three other deputies plus herself. John Mark, Pastor Borden, and the Bond family had waited at Rachael McNaughton's home. They helped her cross the street to the Blair House, where she would play the piano and lead the hymn sing. After opening side and front windows, several neighbors and friends without ties to the McNaughtons gathered around Rachael to sing. Judge Randolph Parsons and his wife Aquila, Attorney John Law and his secretary Amanda with her mother Willa Sentry had waited in the bookstore. Kip had led them to join Rachael at the piano. More prominent guests were escorted from the library to sit with others in the piano room.

Meanwhile, no one noticed the yellow jeep passing from east to west up the road leading into the mountain valley. The jeep stopped at the hairpin turn and two very large men wearing gray cowls climbed from it and descended the road to little Huerfano Butte. Once there they opened a bottle that one had carried to the tree. Kneeling at the west and south base of the tree, they laid hands where each limb had been broken from the huge trunk. They prayed and then poured the contents of the bottle on the two scars. Like ointment they rubbed the liquid into each scar until their hands were sore. They then poured the residue on their sore hands. Pain subsided.

Before leaving the two lifted the dead branches from where they lay and carried them down the northwest side of the hill where they would be discovered later. Together they stood before Ezra Sr.'s carving, admired his work, and focused on the hooded figures around the podium where the naked man stood. Glancing at one another, they chuckled then looked at the house below, and turned to leave, but not before Izzy and Janine caught a glimpse of them.

Janine called out to them, "Have you been sent from the Lord or the Fisher King?"

Both waved and smiled in response.

"Praise God!" Izzy yelled to which both waved again before climbing into the yellow jeep and descending the mountain road before traveling quietly past those gathered at the south entrance of CR403. Only Mike Crowfoot took note of them and he realized he had experienced the end of a divine moment.

*** 

When darkness enveloped the valley, Night Riders, which were to gather, had arrived and merged with men recruited from Jericho Springs. From their midst a man dressed in black bear hide came forward from the crowd. Concealed in the darkness, Blair House residents stood ready on each of the three floors. They held baskets of fresh eggs and balloons filled with water. Morris teamed with Tim to launch balloons from a slingshot at the street end of the porch, while Hannah and Misty did the same at the other end. Jill distributed eggs to everyone on the first floor porch. Additional neighbors from across the street joined those gathered outside on the first floor and took up positions to participate in the fray. Some manned water hoses, while others stood ready to turn on faucets and launch eggs. Others brought their own supply of water-filled balloons.

As Izzy prepared to call out to the group that had gathered, Detective Caleb Jones watched Ezra run the length of the porch rail from the back of the house to the zip line. Making a mental note, he thought to himself that he had just seen how Ezra could have reached Sam Gelding on the footbridge without leaving finger prints. Izzy called out, "You there in the woods are trespassing. Leave now without impunity."

As torches flamed, a man dressed as a black bear moved forward out of the stand of trees. A roar from the crowd behind him encouraged him, as the roar became a growl. They moved forward within striking distance of those on the porches with balloons.

Rachael McNaughton pounded the piano keys and those inside loudly sang *"All Hail the Power of Jesus' Name."* Tim and Morris launched the red dye balloons as more balloons and eggs were thrown by those on the first and second floor balconies. Those at the faucets turned on full power. Ezra tripped the net over all but the torch bearers, the man dressed in the bear costume, and a few others. Ezra grabbed hold of the zip line and rode it to the largest tree in the stand. Dropping to the ground and rolling, Ezra pushed over the fifty gallon drums, which flooded the area with more water tinted with bright red dye.

Torch bearers ran forward from the web covered crowd and tossed their torches, as those on the porches, armed with cameras, took pictures. Two torches landed on each of the first and second floor porches, but were quickly doused by those operating hoses. Realizing their actions had been recorded, the torch bearers fled back into the crowd, which was covered with thick web netting. Under the netting, the crowd stood on ground soaked with red dye. Mayhem followed as many fell under the weight of the nets and slipped in the red mud to the ground. The torch bearers trampled those under foot as they rushed to escape. Growls turned to anguish, as Ezra Sr. took advantage of the situation. In the cover of darkness, he knocked down all who were still standing.

From the third floor porch, Izzy called out to those below, "Look there above Rock Creek. These men have set something on fire."

"Let it burn. We have bigger fish to fry right here. The fire is probably more devilment these men set a foot," said Deputy Cotton Candy, as the one wearing the bear suit had been cuffed. "Let's see what scum we have found."

"Check this out, Candy. Buddy Smith is caught under the net, but the bear is Van Allen from right here in Jericho Springs," said one deputy.

Another reported, "Look here, Sam Gelding's partner, the real estate man, Robert King!"

"Did the newspaper reporter and camera man show up?" asked Candy.

"Yes," answered Detective Caleb Jones, "the cameraman is taking pictures of all of them like we asked them to do. I've got plenty of my own pictures as well. Judge Parsons is here as is John Law."

"What about the CBI unit?"

"I recognize their unit. They just pulled in the driveway," Caleb said.

"Secure every one of them to the first floor porch rail and guard them. Use the twist ties if you need to. Let none get away," the deputy ordered.

"Ezra picked up some strays and has them in tow," reported Izzy.

"We must have more than a dozen here," another deputy reported.

Finally Sheriff Bailey arrived, introduced himself to the CBI investigators, took note of the catch and especially the one in the bear garb, and then asked, "Who is responsible for this?"

"Do you mean the attempted arson, trespass, menacing, and more, or do you mean the sting?" Judge Randolph Parsons asked Bailey, while John Law stood beside him flanked by the ranking CBI investigator, Detective Caleb Jones.

"The one dressed as a bear and all those who are repeat offenders against the Blair House will be transported to an alternate location of CBI's choosing, Sheriff," reported Detective Jones, "but we need to house the first time offenders, if any, here at your county jail. Is that okay with you?"

"Of course, it is," replied Bailey.

Caleb moved closer to Bailey and spoke quietly to him, "Right now CBI is at your office and your home with a search warrant. You too are a suspect in this case."

Typically, Bailey moved his right hand toward his service revolver, but stopped when Jones said to him, "Go ahead and make my day. If I find out you had anything to do with the death of my sister, I'll be coming for you."

"I didn't, and you'll find I had nothing to do with this," said Sheriff Bailey, "and you won't find anything at my office or in my house or garage."

While rounding up strays, Caleb began interviewing some of those throttled by Ezra. He chuckled as he asked, "How did that old man get the best of you?"

One said, "The old man nailed me straight away with a hit to my jaw. He may be old but he is powerful." Another, "I slipped in the mud, and he just kicked my arms out from under me when I tried to get up." A third one said, "He flipped me with his legs at my neck when he came off that line near the tree. I think it's a zip line."

One of those now cuffed asked to speak to those on the porch, "Most of us knew nothing about torching the Blair House. We're here because we were told the woman from the Asherah House is being held here against her will, we were told you Blair House people are... like a cult...but we saw her willfully rocketing water balloons at us and laughing with the others when we got hit. Van Allen's plan was for us to meet in the stand of trees, and then he told us we would go to the front door to ask about Misty. He said with all of us gathered on the porch, you would be certain to release her! We were duped by Van Allen and Buddy Smith."

Detective Jones asked, "Was Butch McNaughton with you?"

Willa Sentry added, "Was my son, Roy, here?"

The first speaker answered, "No, Mrs. Sentry, neither one of them were involved. I heard Butch is at the Stage Stop Hotel...and I heard he is the new manager there...maybe he has Roy working for him."

Attorney John Law asked, "The torch bearers wore ski masks. Are they among you? Do you know who they are?"

"No, they are not from Jericho Springs! We knew nothing about trying to set fire to the Blair House. They trampled over several of us to escape, after you started taking pictures. A few of us tried to stop them, but we got caught up in the net."

"Izzy, we know how the McNaughton Corporation has been treating you and your father..." their original spokesman said. "It is a shame, and if I may speak for those gathered, we support you, as long as you are not a cult. Most of us consider the Blair House as one of Jericho Springs' finest treasures."

"Our work here is to honor our savior," said Jill, "and Paul and Lydia Blair."

Noting his wife's relief, Judge Parsons whispered to Detective Jones, "How about writing down the names of those involved and uncuff them, except for Van Allen and the two torch bearers, if we find them. The rest will show, and if they don't, we'll issue warrants for their arrests."

Detective Jones' voice boomed, "Gentlemen, Van Allen is already under arrest. I will take your names and addresses, so have proof of your identity to verify your signature and picture match. You'll be expected to appear before Judge Parsons, but you'll receive a letter telling you when to appear, unless you have been arrested before for having done something with the Night Riders. If you have, I'll arrest you now!"

The spokesman raised his hand, and with a nod from Caleb, he spoke again, "After we gathered in the stand of trees, Van Allen had us circle up. He wore a bear costume, a black bear. What's with that?"

"The leaders of the rave wore black bearskins," answered John Mark.

"That being the case...one got away. I saw someone drop a costume in one of the barrels with the red water in it," said one oldtimer, whose pants were soaked.

"Did you recognize him?" asked the detective.

"I've seen him, but I don't know him, and I don't remember where it was I seen him," said another oldtimer.

John Mark stepped forward and asked to speak. With a nod from the detective, he said, "Have any of you seen or participated in a rave, either this week or sometime earlier?"

Those about to be processed looked at one another, as did those standing on the porch, and then, the spokesman said, "No none of us, except you and the detective. Who are you?"

Tim McNaughton stepped forward to introduce John Mark, and said, "You know me from the Cozy Corner Café. I live here now, and I get to help restore the Blair House. Perhaps you heard a story about a man who came to the restaurant where I work and how he told me scripture that met me right where I was. This is the man, my friend John Mark Cannikin."

"Does he live here too?"

"No," said Tim, "he lives in Rock Creek. He's the one restoring Mary Claymore's house."

A hush came over the crowd, and an old man said, as he nearly cried, "Like this house and the tree on Huerfano, Mary McNaughton

Claymore was full of grace and mercy...she blessed us all...and she was the real treasure in the valley."

Karen arrived with pizza from the Jericho Springs Pizzeria, and Izzy said to the crowd, "I know we soaked many of you with our balloons and eggs, but won't you join us inside for pizza. We had planned to have a hymn sing and pizza anyway. You can take a tour of the first two floors, where we've just opened a Christian bookstore. We'll tell you what we are all about."

Janine added, "Come into my home, the home of Paul and Lydia Blair and my husband Izzy. How many of you knew or had heard about the Blair family?"

"I came here for piano lessons with Miss Rachael," said one more oldtimer.

"I use to attend one of their Bible studies...Paul use to say something about truth and justice..." said another.

"Grace and mercy," said an older water soaked fellow, "that's the rest of the saying... Truth and Justice, Grace and Mercy," who then added with tears forming in his eyes, "Is that what you folks are seeking...Miss Lydia was always so kind to me and my family..."

"Where is the woman named, Misty?" shouted a younger man.

"Yeah, the one held here against her will?" shouted another.

Misty and Hannah appeared on the first floor porch and said, "I'm Misty. These folks rescued me from the Asherah House and I've been born again, I'm a new Christian, and it was fun throwing water balloons at you...I mean, no offense, but it was a lot of fun!"

"Hannah Rahab...is it you?" the first young man asked. "Do you live here too?"

"Yes, I'm Hannah... Misty and me go to the little Church in the Glen. I accepted Jesus as my savior, and I get to help with the restoration of Blair House. Come on in and take the tour. Be certain to go see the wood carving in the old tree. It is really cool! Come on now before the pizza cools off."

"We have dry towels you may use," Janine offered.

As the Brownings arrived, Rachael began playing hymns again, while Kip opened the bookstore door to welcome the visitors. Kat organized the pizza, set out plates and silverware, glasses with ice, and cans of soda pop. Twelve of the raiders joined the festivities with neighbors and others from the community on tours of the first and second floor before climbing the butte to look at Ezra Sr.'s carving on Freedom's tree. Jill stationed herself by the garden where she explained the plans to build a pole barn, plant the vineyard and garden, set up sheds for tools, the rabbit hutches, and the chicken coop. John Mark stood on the butte with a bright beam project lamp and helped each person express what they saw in the wood carving, while Izzy explained how the rock slide cracked the butte and diverted thermally heated water into the pond. Izzy explained how he was setting up a pellet mill to make fuel for his new pellet stove, which would be set up in the basement. Misty led Amanda and John Law on tour and showed them her room and where she had been helping with the cooking and cleaning. Karen talked with Ruth about her project and enlisted Ruth's help. Ruth reminded Karen that they knew they would be working together on something important after making their trip to the top of the butte. Janine stationed herself at the bottom of the first floor porch stairs where she could greet arrivals and say goodbye to those who were leaving. She concluded they had won the hearts of the people.

The spokesman for the raiders prepared to leave with the old man who had made the cherishing statement about Mary Claymore. The spokesman said to Janine, "Mrs. Freedom, thank you all for your hospitality. This was not at all what we expected, but I wish we had heard what John Mark was going to say."

"Another time," Janine said, "I'm certain he would have told you that those who wear the bearskins were trying to hide their identity..."

As the old man passed by Janine, he mumbled, "Yes, yes, truth and justice, grace and mercy, it is...that's what my friend Paul use to say..."

*** 

Meanwhile on the other side of the river valley in Rock Creek, residents presumed mischief was happening when they heard a thwacking of axe to wood up on the ridge. None in the hotel, Tobacco Store, or Asherah House paid attention to what transpired until after those in the yellow jeep drove into town and parked in the garage at

Adam's house. Undetected they entered the home where they had set up temporary quarters with John Mark.

The thwacking soon had been replaced by the updraft roar of a gasoline fire. It began to fully consume the Asher pole. The pole had fallen to the ground and landed on the ceremonial table used earlier at the rave. Two had cut down the Asher pole, soaked both pole and table with gasoline, and ignited a terrifying blaze. Residents saw the fire not only in Rock Creek, but also by those high on the foothills at the Blair House. Within minutes both pole and table, charred as pulp, became red cinders. As the two walked away into the night, what remained of the Asher pole was a wooden stump that looked more like a huge knuckle of a tree root.

# A Tale of Two Towns: Morning

## CHAPTER 12

"No one will be able to stand against you."
Deuteronomy 11:25a

wo towns in the Rock Creek River Valley had been impacted by actions of those seeking financial gain through human trafficking or by unscrupulously grabbing for gold and water rights. Jericho Springs had been under siege at the Blair House. Some townspeople had been duped by a local leader into believing a woman had been held there against her wishes. Hoping to make right that which was wrong, they laid siege at the Blair House believing the woman had been kidnapped by a cult. Instead, the townspeople learned the woman had been rescued from the Asherah House Bed and Breakfast where she had been the victim of human trafficking. Like a rock thrown into a small pool of water, this discovery led to a widening circle of discussion by all those who had been at the Blair House on the night of the raid. The ripple effect crosscut all social-economic stratus; however, not all were horrified at the thought of what may be happening in the valley. After all, the minority opinion stated, it served as a necessary social function and it's not like it was happening in our town. The Asherah House was only in Rock Creek.

Additionally, Rock Creek had been the site of recent Baal worship, conducted for profit under the guise of a dramatic musical event. Determining event sponsorship remained as murky as the storm clouds, which had thwarted the event. Red McNaughton owned the land and led the McNaughton Corporation. His involvement was certain. Determining who had helped to thwart the event remained partly cloudy. Baal worshippers blamed three sources of opposition for their failure and financial loss. Adam Claymore stood against them at the primary intersection in Rock Creek. Adam's wrangler, Rabbit Pinebow, tried to protect the church from a brown bear's attack on the entrance doors. Another wrangler, Pilgrim Wayne, desecrated the Asher Pole with one crack shot from his Sharps rifle, while on grand mesa known as Claymore Flats. Later he had been attacked by the same bear at cow camp.

Baal leadership incorrectly identified the third source of opposition. They presumed Izzy Freedom of the Blair House had disrupted their ritual when three horrifying men suddenly appeared out of the darkness in a jeep. Meanwhile, Baal leaders first had feared the roar of a bear below on the highway, but later they were encouraged by news that the bear had clawed both the doors to the Rock Creek church and the massive Live Oak tree which stands above the Blair House. Few leaders grieved when hearing that three non-residents had suffered injury, as the crowd fled during the storm and pushed the outsiders over the ridge. Only Betty Strong Bull's relatives had cried after hearing that she had died from the fall, and most of them lived in Wolf City. Finding out who had sponsored the rave, who had thwarted it, and why three people had been forced over the edge of the cliff proved more obscure than the terrible storm clouds.

Circumstances following the rave emboldened those wanting the gold and water rights. Red McNaughton's wranglers got word to him that Pilgrim Wayne had been mauled by the bear at cow camp. They said Adam Claymore had left the valley and had vowed not to return until either he or the bear were dead. Also, Red's wranglers reported Barnabas led a team repairing fences on Claymore Flats. They said Barney rode line at the end of the mesa near Wolf City. Last of their news was Rabbit would lead them driving the herd down to the mountain pasture. As a result, Red ordered Van Allen to organize the group that made the assault on Blair House, which not only failed but also had been used by Izzy and team to gain public support in Jericho Springs. The truth of the event prevailed as did justice when Van Allen and certain Night Riders were arrested, while those Van Allen had misled received grace and mercy from the Blair

House group. When they learned Misty remained at the Blair House by choice, the men who had come to rescue her were not only disarmed but also won over by Izzy and team. Night Riders suffered additional defeat the night of the attack on the Blair House. They were blamed for the fire above Rock Creek on the ridge. Townspeople presumed the Night Riders had been up to more devilment based on their previous harassment of the town and its people, especially newcomers. Red McNaughton and most of the rest of the McNaughton Corporation recoiled at how public sentiment shifted from uncaring to outright hostility toward them.

\*\*\*

The morning before the attack on Blair House and before Adam left on his quest to slay the beast, he had called Pastor Borden of the Jericho Springs Baptist Church and said, "Pastor, this is Adam."

"Adam, thanks for calling. I'm sorry to hear about Pilgrim and the church. I know you took a stand against the human trafficking and Baal worship. You knew persecution would come."

"Indeed I did, and I'm about to leave to kill the bear. It killed the parents of two young boys in Pryor, it killed Pilgrim's dog and broke Pilgrim's leg, it clawed the church door and the Live Oak tree, plus it broke two limbs off the old oak tree."

"Be careful! This is no ordinary bear, but you are no ordinary man. Too bad, you will miss our next hymn sing at Blair House," said Pastor Donald Borden.

"Maybe they will pray for me, and Lord willing, I'll be successful. What's the status of your plans for finishing the prayer walk we started in Jericho Springs?"

"Adam, my flock finished the walk earlier this week."

"Great, you have encouraged me!"

"There's more, Adam, I placed an order for outreach materials through the new bookstore at Blair House and my order recently arrived."

"You mentioned your plan at our pastor's meeting..."

"Yes...and some good news is some of the folks from the other churches want to help with the effort. It will be a combined effort of several churches."

"When do you start?"

"Thanks to what happened at the rave, people are ready to do something about what's happening around them."

"And?"

"Tonight, I have three teams from my flock delivering an outreach packet door to door to every house and business in town. It may take more than one day and night to complete, but we put a Bible, a children's book, a couple of Bible tracts, and a flyer about the Baptist church in plastic bags. My people will hang them on screen doors and door knobs and be on their way."

"Sounds great! What if someone comes to the door?"

"We are prepared to engage them, share Jesus, and give them a personal invitation to come to church."

"That's what will take more time..."

"Yes, and Adam, I took your suggestion."

"What suggestion?"

"We are going to ask the people if we can pray for them right then."

"I wish I was going to be with you."

"Me, too. It's a victory for both of us. You and I worked hard to get people to go into the community and risk rejection by sharing the good news of Jesus Christ."

"In His time..."

"There's more, Adam. I've talked with Aquila and Priscilla. I asked them to replicate their street corner ministry here in Jericho Springs. I called all the churches in the pastor's group you lead and I invited them to join, so it would be a community-wide effort."

"Wow! Donald, God is at work...and I'm leaving town..."

"I hope you will be back in time to help with the community prayer meeting."

"Prayer for Our Nation...*2nd Chronicles 7:14.*"

"Yes, if my people......"

"Pastor, let us pray," said Adam as he prayed for his former pastor, the Baptist church and the other churches in Jericho Springs. He prayed for the Jericho Springs residents, who had been inflicted with enough nonsense to finally leave their comfort zones. Adam prayed they would take back their community and claim it in the name of Jesus.

"Adam, one comment...You sat under my teaching when I pastored the Church in the Glen. I know you and you know me. I know you are bruised, not only by the loss of your wife, but also by how you have been persecuted in the valley when taking a stand for Christ. Adam, you are more earnest than anyone I know when it comes to following Christ. And...I have to ask you one question..."

"Pastor, I'm listening..."

"You've been called the Lone Ranger, a knight of the roundtable, one who seeks to make right that which is wrong, a defender of women and children...and I know you can be sidetracked. Sometimes your pride gets in the way and you take on responsibilities because no one else will do what is right and good."

"Your question?" asked Adam.

"Where is Red McNaughton in all of this? He is your partner, but he isn't going to cow camp with his wranglers. The two of you flooded your pasture in town, and he took his herd to the ridge, which, by the way, is where the rave was held. His boy has been caught doing a number of things, and now, Butch manages the Stage Stop Hotel. Your trailer that the Bond's lived in burnt to the ground. It was at the edge of Red's pasture and was conveniently eliminated prior to the rave."

"Surely, you don't think Red is behind the human trafficking?"

"Who owns the Asherah House?' asked Pastor Borden.

"I don't know...I've never checked."

"Who were the six men in the bear skins at the rave?" asked Donald.

"What really happened to Betty Strong Bull and the two outsiders who fell from the cliff?" added Adam.

"Why was Gloria Jones murdered?"

"We know Sam Gelding killed her and stuffed her body under the bridge on 403. I hear he is supposed to have murdered the teenager in Quail Point," said Adam.

"Have you noticed very little has been said about Betty's death?" said Borden.

"And public clamor about the death of Gloria Jones is negligible," Adam added.

"Adam, is it because Gloria was black and because Betty was an Indian? Or is it because Gloria was a newcomer and Betty lived in Wolf City? Or is it because neither fit into the plans of the McNaughton clan?" added Donald.

"Do you mean the effort to gain the water rights and the gold that goes with the Blair House or the human trafficking?" Adam paused... and said, "We seem to be on the same page...but Pastor, are you suggesting Red is behind all of this?"

"Adam, I'm just wondering...and my primary wonder is whether or not God has called you to go kill the bear when all of this is going on. Look at what has already happened and how the church is ignited for Christ. It baffles me that you want to go kill a bear when God is so much at work here. Has God told you to go do this?"

"It is heavy on my heart that the church was clawed, Mary's church, and that the Live Oak was scared, and that Pilgrim was wounded after rescuing the two boys. And it's heavy on my heart what Red might be doing."

"Adam, you may need to bend in the wind like the reed that doesn't break. Could it be that the bear is just a bear and not the embodiment of evil?"

"Or, Pastor, is there a spiritual connection between the grizzly and the black bears in the Baal worship at the rave?"

"You have probably been researching Baal worship and the Canaanite religion like I have...I didn't find any connection. Did you?" asked Borden.

"None...I don't know what to make of it..."

"Well, Adam, I know you can get help through John Law, and the other churches should join any effort to deal with Baal worship, but in the meantime, do you have others you can rely on to help?" said Donald.

"Folks at the Blair House...Karen Gustafson..."

"In Rock Creek?"

"Do you think that's where to expect trouble?

"Yes, Adam, like in the battle of Jericho where some Canaanite cities built a vestibule where the defenders met the enemy. Rock Creek seems to be like that..."

"And Rock Creek is the vestibule for the valley... hmm...what do you suggest?" asked Adam.

"I think there is value in you riding out as if to kill the bear. Make an appearance at cow camp so all of the wranglers see you, and then circle around north to where you enter the mountain pasture through Ezra's cabin site. Follow south across the creek and up the south slope of Huajatolla. Then, go down the west slope and cross the road to Wolf City where you can connect with your line crew. I think you will want to re-position them to where they build fence by the town of Rock Creek," said Pastor Borden.

"Pastor, did God tell you to tell me all of this?"

"No, he just said I should say what is on my mind when you called. He said you needed to hear from me."

"And so I have. Thank you."

"One more thing, Adam, have you been following the weather reports?"

"You are right...I've been distracted..."

"By evening we are supposed to have heavy snowfall."

"I'll call you when I get back...I did tell Rabbit to move the herd at the first sign of heavy snow. Once we have the herd in the narrows the cattle would head downhill, so long as the canyon is steep."

"Don't forget about the wedding! What if you do not return in time to do the wedding, or if the bear gets you?" asked Pastor Borden.

"Perish both thoughts, but I did ask Ken Bond to fill in for me while I'm gone...he would have to take care of the wedding, I suppose," Adam said with concern.

"Let's pray, Adam," and so they did.

\*\*\*

Although Adam left on his quest to kill the bear that had afflicted so many, he followed the wisdom of his friend. Pastor Borden led his flock to go door to door throughout the town beginning at noon. Adam rode into cow camp and spent time with all the wranglers. Later he rode north and stopped on the ridge above the camp in time to watch one of Red's wranglers ride toward Jericho Springs. Adam guessed correctly, the wrangler would report his whereabouts to

Red. Adam continued riding east on the back slope of the ridge and into a valley that would lead him to Ezra Freedom Sr.'s cabin by late afternoon, unless he met the bear.

*** 

Like Pastor Borden and Adam Claymore, early morning residents in Jericho Springs and Rock Creek had wakened eager to discover what had transpired in each of their towns. Many in Jericho Springs walked or drove to Blair House where they first met with Kat Bond. She invited them to tour the first floor of the house before walking through the forest glen and up the butte to see Freedom's tree. Kat showed them the small bookstore and gave each a flyer about Kip Powell's store, product specials, and part time employment opportunities. She explained how as a dealer they could do in home parties with their friends and neighbors. Many expressed genuine interest in the Christian books and music, while some wanted to attend an in-home party, and a few wanted to become a dealer of Christian books and products. Rachael walked over when the crowd arrived and began playing the Upright in the piano room. Three people signed up for piano lessons. To all, Rachael gave her flyer reinforcing the weekly newspaper article that announced her Saturday afternoon in-home book party featuring Christian resources for all ages.

Misty and Hannah served as guides for those wanting to see where the Night Rider group had staged their assault on the Blair House, then the visitors laughed as Hannah described how she and Misty with others held off the group with water balloons and eggs. The women had identified themselves, Misty formerly of the Asherah House and Hannah the former desk clerk at the Stage Stop Hotel. Enthusiastically, both shared how they were not only living at the Blair House, but also they were actively helping to restore the landmark. Both talked freely about being discipled by the women of Blair House. As the tour group explored the grounds, they discovered the trap door on the side of the hill that opened to the tunnel and ended at the coal bin in the Blair House basement. Unintentionally, they left the trap door opened allowing anyone or anything opportunity to explore the tunnel and possibly enter the house undetected. The visitors left marveling about what they had seen on the tree, about how different Hannah looked, and how innocent Misty appeared, except for those few who knew her from the Asherah House.

Those in Rock Creek first looked out the windows of their homes to see what destruction had taken place after the rave. Lawns had been damaged where a sparse grass covering once prospered, and the pathway to the game trail had been heavily trodden. Men, women, and children came out of their homes and from the hotel. Some walked the pathway leading to the ridge above town, while others strolled through the hotel parking lot a short distance south on the Valley Highway. They crossed the highway and followed the lane to observe the claw marks on the doors of the Church in the Glen. It was their church regardless of whether or not they attended there. From both vantage points, the groups witnessed the arrival of yet another peculiar passenger, as he exited the Trailways bus driven by Morris Goodenough, recently a new resident at the Blair House.

Unaccustomed to such girth, observers guessed the man's height to be above six foot five and weight around three hundred pounds. Comparatively, Morris was a big man, but the passenger stood well above Morris' height. Despite Morris' usual upbeat nature, the man's countenance rejected Morris' merriment and encouragement. The passenger projected seriousness both in appearance and manner-isms, but it was the brown bear skin wrapped around him that was both most disturbing yet attracting. Morris asked him for his luggage receipts and noted the man's name was Bear.

"Mr. Bear," Morris asked, "what brings you to the valley?"

Bear turned but did not yet smile at Morris, "Just Bear, I'm here to do what is necessary," Mr. Bear responded with a pained smile, which revealed his broken front teeth and accentuated scars spanning the length of the left side of his head and face, "My luggage, please. I expect to be leaving immediately. Please point me in the direction of the church where the giant of a bear clawed the front doors."

As Morris opened the luggage compartment doors, Mr. Bear continued, "Where were the imposters located?"

"Imposters?"

"Yes, those who wore my brothers' skins," Bear asked, "Were they black or brown?"

"The rave was up there," Morris pointed toward the ridge where the observers cringed and backed up so they could not be seen by Bear, "and the bear skins were black, but not like me. I'm black," Morris continued, "for real."

"I see that," Bear said showing more broken teeth, "and you are a nice man. I will see you again when this is over. We will have a pint of bitters together, you and I, and you will tell me why you are here and what God wants you to do."

Morris gasped as Bear shook his hand, and then picked up four pieces of luggage as if they were paper weights. One very heavy piece was long and narrow, while one was narrow except at one end where it formed a square. The other two pieces appeared well travelled with scuff marks. Morris, passengers on the bus, walkers returning from the church and townspeople on the ridge—all watched as the man named Bear disappeared in the glen between the church and the highway to smell the roses that climbed the grand mesa on the other side of the creek.

"Peace and granola," Bear said as he walked and sang, "It's beginning to look a lot like Christmas, snow is on the way..."

"He had six fingers," Morris said to himself, as he walked back to the bus door, "I think he had six fingers...on each hand...and a terrible scar from crown to chin."

***

Meanwhile Deputy Sheriff Cotton Candy placed a telephone call to John Mark requesting him to meet with her at the Church in the Glen at noon. Candy explained Priscilla and Aquila wanted to help him as did Ezra Sr. Candy said she had received five other telephone calls from his neighbors, who were ready to take back their town from the thugs. She said the rave broke the camel's back, but his neighbors expressed concern about the Tobacco Store, the hotel, and the bed and breakfast. As a result John Mark called Amanda Sentry and confirmed John Law's request to meet with John and friends at 10 a.m. in Law's office in Jericho Springs. Amanda asked John Mark to bring his rather large friends, two of which she had been pleased to meet.

Promptly at 9:40 a.m., John Mark and the red and blond giants exited the garage which they had finished restoring at Adam's house in Rock Creek. The red head drove the yellow jeep to the church where Mr. Bear quickly vaulted into the back bench seat next to the blonde.

"Hi, Brother," Bear said as he slapped the shoulder of his younger brother.

"Good to see you, Brother Bear, we wondered if you would arrive in time," John Mark replied for the younger brother.

"Are they still committed to a vow of silence?"

"Aye, they are, but they're terribly tempted to speak because of a beautiful young woman we will soon meet," John Mark said enthusiastically.

"Is she the one?"

"No, this one captured their hearts instantaneously, and regrettably her name is not Elaine!"

"Is she worthy?"

Both brothers looked at one another and shook their heads affirmatively, while John Mark said, "She is of good report...more so than the other..."

"Remember young brothers," Bear replied, "remember what Mother said—women have the power to bring out the best in a man..."

"Or the worst," John Mark added by finishing the quote.

"Did she make a choice?" Bear said, as both Drostan and Coinneach nodded enthusiastically. "And did she seal it with a kiss?" to which Drostan nodded.

"And yet, you say, she is not the one...well, have you located the one?"

"Yes, she is here and protected. Opposition has attempted to capture her. There are problems we will share later," answered John Mark.

Following County Road 403 to where it became Main Street in Jericho Springs, Brother Bear remarked about the massive tree and the three story house before it. To which John Mark replied, "That is one of the problems. The Live Oak tree is nearly dead and the bear destroyed the south and west limbs. Coinneach and Drostan applied the ointment to the scars, and the rest of the tree will have buds. Bear, good people live there and their hearts are bent toward serving our Lord like a light in darkness."

"How is it a problem? We will help them."

"Bear, gold and water rights go with the house, and some towns-people want to destroy the house and those in it, so they can have the wealth," said John Mark.

"Then the one we seek lives there," said Bear.

"Aye, brother, and she is with child."

"With child? Is there more to this story?"

"Yes, Baal worshippers are active. They want the baby."

"Our mission is complicated. The bear I must kill is linked to the Baal worship, I assume?" asked Bear.

"Yes, it has recently made an appearance at the church and at the Blair House. There at the tree," John Mark explained.

"The group, the light in darkness, is there, too, restoring Blair House?"

"Aye, Brother Bear! And they are discipling the woman!"

"Her name?"

"They call her Misty, but her name is Elaine McClaren," answered John Mark.

"You found the McClaren, yet she is not worthy?"

"She is who she is..."

"Has she accepted Christ as her savior?"

"Aye, Brother!"

"Then the Holy Spirit has work to do, and we get to have a part in what is required," concluded Bear.

"Yes!"

"Where is my other brother?"

"Niall is at Coyote Springs, a settlement south on the ridge. No residents, east of the highway from the canyon," John Mark reported as the men, both his brothers of the same clan and knights on a spiritual mission, arrived at the offices of Attorney John Law.

Coinneach and Drostan promptly climbed the stairs to the law offices above Bustos Family Mexican Restaurant without attracting much attention. Carrying flowers, the younger brothers struggled through the doorway to be the first to greet John Law's secretary, Amanda Sentry. The brothers waited like two hounds anticipating their beloved mistress. When John Mark and Brother Bear arrived, all proceeded to Amanda's desk and awaited her arrival.

Full of grace and charm, Amanda appeared from John Law's conference room having already escorted Ezra Freedom Sr. into the room. She paused, just briefly, swept her long hair from her face with a turn of her head, and then in full composure approached her desk, while the red head and the blonde bowed awkwardly and presented their bouquets of fresh picked flowers.

"You are sweet to remember me, thank you," Amanda said warmly, as she looked at both men and smiled.

Bear noticed his brothers' response to the beautifully feminine and modestly dressed woman, who had been genuinely pleased by the brothers' gift. John Mark had been equally impressed despite having seen Amanda previously. Elegant and wholesome, he thought and hoped Misty would become more like Amanda. It was Bear who spoke to Amanda, with a smile revealing both upper and lower teeth, "And you, Miss, to say you are a cute little human would not do you justice, but to say you compare well to the fairest of our homeland's maidens is the best of compliments from gentlemen such as we..."

"Brothers, let us not cause discomfort for the maiden, who is already aligned with our mission," urged John Mark.

Setting the flowers in a vase on her desk, Amanda beckoned the men to follow her, which would have happened without her invitation. She held the opened door for the brothers to enter the room, and each was stunned again by her fragrance. All four smitten, Bear said he felt sorry for their missing brother, who would soon be busy planting a Live Oak tree behind the stump of the Asher Pole on the ridge.

Ezra Sr. had watched the men enter the room and the effect Amanda had on them. His laugh sounded more like Hans Solo's friend Chewbacca than the beast himself. Last to enter John Law came in, sat at the end of the table, and began the meeting with, "Well, gentlemen, it is plain to see you have met Amanda. She is precious to me, like a daughter, had I one." Then looking at Ezra, "Thank you for coming, Ezra. I know you have met John Mark Cannikin, but let me introduce the brothers Tunnicliffe. Next to John Mark is the eldest named Bear, but his real name is Brian, which means strength. To his left, the red head is Drostan, which means sad and is translated as Tristan. Next the blonde is Coinneach, meaning fair haired one and translated as Kenneth. One other brother you will meet later is Niall, which means champion. He is the tallest of the brothers Tunnicliffe."

Next, looking at the brothers, John Law said, "Meet Ezra Freedom Sr., who happens to own the Blair House and the mountain valley behind it plus all the land north to the west peak of Mount Huajatolla. Like you, he is a formidable warrior."

The men exchanged greetings with John Law adding, "Ezra, the Tunnicliffes need to know some of your history." To which Ezra nodded. "Until recently, Ezra had been held captive long after the Vietnam War. When he returned here, he lived in his old hunting cabin not far in the mountains. Although very wealthy he did not let people know his true identity. He had left a couple, named Paul and Lydia Blair, in charge of all his properties, which includes the Blair House. They were to raise his son until he returned from war. If he did not survive the war, they were to manage everything until the son came of age. Upon learning the Blair's were not his parents, the son ran away from home not to return until last summer, just months ago. Fortunately, father and son have been united and both are dedicated to restoring the Blair House to its former stature as a light in darkness and a citadel on the high point of the valley."

John Law paused to let his words sink in and then began again, "Gentlemen, they have gathered together a team of volunteers who are committed to the restoration of Blair House both physically and spiritually. Recently, they brought two women there, who, having accepted Christ as their Savior, were in grave danger from people at the Stage Stop Hotel and the Asherah House Bed and Breakfast."

At the mention of Asherah, each Tunnicliffe gripped both arms of their chairs. Each looked toward the others in recognition of Baal worship, which not only included temple prostitution but also human sacrifice. Brian spoke saying, "Light versus darkness, good versus evil. Evil is part of why we are here. These two brothers are here on a quest and vowed not to speak until their quest is completed. My name is Bear Killer and I believe I am here to kill the bear that scarred your tree and the doors to the church in Rock Creek. I saw the scarring on the church door an hour ago, and I look forward to seeing the Live Oak tree up close."

John Law began to break in, but Bear continued, "We are here to plant another tree like our forefathers planted the Live Oak behind the Blair House. Tonight a Live Oak will be planted where the Asher Pole and Baal ceremonial table burned to ashes on the ridge."

Turning toward Ezra Sr., Brian the Bear Killer said, "Ezra, blood of our people, consecrated the ground where the tree was planted and we know what lies beneath."

Ezra moved forward in the chair with instant concern, but was put at ease with Brian's next words, "My people pledged no interest, no claim to what lies below. I have come to kill the bear that opposes the guardian of the Live Oak, another brother to follow a tradition, and these two brothers to look after a young woman at the Blair House. John Mark has a similar quest. All of us are pledged to support you, while we are here."

Brian looked directly at John Law and said, "When we leave, she may go with us."

John Mark added, "She may not want to leave."

As everyone leaned back in their respective chairs and realized John Law had not understood Brian's comment, John Mark continued. "That brings us to the reason for this meeting. Ezra, we need to establish a base for our operations. I came first and connected with Adam Claymore. God sent me to him. I've been working with the help of two of my brothers to prepare the house for a pastor who will lead the church in Adam's place. We are nearly finished. We have begun to draw attention primarily because of the size of the brothers."

Ezra nodded with understanding, and motioned for John Law to speak for him. "Gentlemen, apparently God has led the way. Ezra and I exchanged notes. He thought he needed to prepare to move to Blair House, because God planned to use the cabin. There will be no charge but he asks each of you help clear dead timber and stack it where he can get to it for use at his saw mill. Ezra sells cut wood in town and supplies it for the Blair House. Also, he mills the wood for the restoration project. He bags the saw dust and makes pellets for wood burning stoves and fireplaces. It looks like we are going to have a long, cold winter, so much wood is needed. He would like for each of you to work seven hours a week in exchange for the lodging. You will be able to hunt whatever game you need to eat."

"It is good," Brian said, "Lord willing, we will likely be here at least until summer."

"Then an agreement is made," said John Law, as the brothers reached across the table and shook hands with Ezra Sr., who thought any one of them may be able to kill the bear.

Noting the time, John Mark said, "I have another meeting back in Rock Creek. If we leave now, we could return to Adam's house and fix lunch for the brothers Tunnicliffe, before they go to the cabin. They drive a yellow jeep."

"Why not let me call Jerry at the local pizzeria and have what… three pizzas delivered to your door. I'll put it on my bill to Ezra to which Ezra nodded approval."

Disappointed, the brothers Tunnicliffe descended the stairwell from the lobby of Attorney John Law's offices. Amanda had left to join those gathered at the Baptist church to stuff plastic bags, which would soon be distributed to every household and business in Jericho Springs by evening. They climbed into the yellow jeep, made a u-turn on the side-street, and took the shortest route to leave Jericho Springs. They sought to return to Rock Creek and arrive at Adam Claymore's house before the pizza delivery. Speeding past the Blair House, they did not acknowledge the little old lady walking down the east side of the street. Recognizing John Mark from church, Rachael McNaughton had waved at him. Like them, she took her daily walk on a mission to the post office. Today she extended her walk by going to the Baptist church to help her friend Willa Sentry, Willa's daughter Amanda, and Rachael's former pastor, as they stuffed plastic bags.

Having baked pizzas for delivery in Rock Creek, Jerry Sunday, store manager and resident at Blair House, slowed his old Chevy when he came to the bridge over Rock Creek. He coasted across where the body of Gloria Jones had been found below. It gave him the creeps driving there, as he had parked on the road above her body to make a pizza delivery at the house across the street. Slowing at the stop sign, then looking both ways, north and south on the Valley Highway-US 85/87, he observed Karen Gustafson ascend stairs to the Stage Stop Hotel entrance. Inside Karen would make an appointment to counsel

261

with Sarah on Saturday morning at Sarah's house. Jerry honked his car horn and waved, as Karen turned to see him and shouted, "I'll see you tonight at the pizzeria."

Ready to turn south on the Valley Highway, somewhat of a traffic jam occurred. Cars and trucks arrived behind Jerry at the stop sign and autos entered Rock Creek from the north and south. They parked at the Stage Stop Hotel and also in the church parking lot and driveway. Wanting to deliver hot pizza to Adam's house, Jerry pulled forward at the stop sign but braked as other automobiles turned west from the highway toward Jericho Springs. Unbeknownst to Jerry, many from Quail Point as well as Ridge View had come to Rock Creek to investigate the remains of the fire on the ridge where sons and daughters, husbands and wives, friends and relatives had participated in the recent rave. Others had heard about the incident at the Blair House and had decided to go there not only to see the ground where the red dye stained the earth, but also to check out the new Christian book store. They had heard about and wanted to walk to the top of the butte to see both the bear claw marks, broken tree limbs, and the carving in the tree.

Taking advantage of multiple south bound cars making a right turn down County Road 403, Jerry successfully navigated his right turn and drove into the end of the driveway at Adam's house. Exiting his car and carrying three pizzas, Jerry walked around the back of his automobile to check to see if he had pulled far enough off the highway. It was then that he looked south and noticed a rather tall man somehow descend the ridge at the mouth of the canyon. The man hurried across the highway, entered the birch glen before the church driveway, and walked toward him. Stunned with the man's size, Jerry followed his progress to the driveway, then followed him to the side door of Adam's house where the man did not knock on the door but entered directly and closed the door. Jerry walked to the door and knocked, whereupon John Mark opened the door slightly and said, "Jerry! You are a welcomed sight. Come in with that pizza!"

Entering, Jerry set the pizza on the table and looked around the kitchen and front room of the house. Though he had just witnessed the arrival of a large young man, in all appearances no one was there other than John Mark. Somewhat stunned, he turned to John Mark who said, "John Law paid for the pizza, but here is a five dollar tip. Thank you for your prompt service."

"Thanks," Jerry said and smiled, "I've learned to expect the unexpected when I deliver to Rock Creek."

# A Tale of Two Towns: Noon and After

## CHAPTER 13

*"As the mountains surround Jerusalem, so the Lord surrounds his people both now and forevermore."*
*Psalm 125:2*

Back in the good old days, or so they were called, Texas neighbors came a runnin' when someone yelled Brazos. At first folks in a settlement gathered at a tavern to settle disputes or to hold church services, when a circuit riding judge or preacher scheduled a visit. Ultimately, God fearing folks banned together and built a church, which thrived until some of the folks argued over a trivial topic like the color of the carpet. As more folks became disillusioned with the settlement's church and built a school, the school displaced the church as the center of the settlement. At least that was what the museum director posted about the valley on a bulletin board with a map of the area with one exception. While the description generally applied to Wolf City, Quail Point, Ridge View, and even Coyote Springs, it had not characterized Rock Creek or Jericho Springs. Rock Creek began as a frontier fort with a pony express station and a stage line in what is now named the Stage Stop Hotel, while Jericho Springs grew near what is now called the Blair House.

When problems directly impacted one of the small towns or neighborhoods, some residents could be depended upon to turnout for a meeting. Others might show up, if it were convenient. Likewise, when problems were solved and needs fulfilled, leaders found it difficult to maintain a problem solving structure that helped to build a sense of community. Only Jericho Springs formalized by incorporating as a municipality. Its leadership persisted through waning interest and developed a formal legal structure, while Rock Creek remained unincorporated. The Rock Creek settlement continued with a knee jerk approach. When new issues stirred residents to come out of their homes, they banded together temporarily. One result was the volunteer fire department building, which was constructed on the northwest corner of the only four way intersection in the settlement. Unfortunately, it sits unused, unstaffed.

Finally, both Jericho Springs and Rock Creek residents could no longer ignore three tragic deaths. They were jarred out of denial and into involvement to resolve immediate problems. In Rock Creek three deaths had occurred—one, the murder of a newcomer, a young prostitute from the Asherah House; another, the apparent accidental death of a rave participant from Wolf City, a relative of Janine Freedom and Mike Crowfoot; and the third death that of a well known businessman, local insurance agent of many and husband of the high school secretary. In Jericho Springs, attempted arson reflected the extent to which one prominent clan would go to gain wealth for itself at the expense of oldtimers and newcomers. All longtime residents feared rumors of human trafficking might prove to be true. They also came to believe the McNaughton clan would go to any lengths to gain the water and mineral rights of the Blair House. Long time residents realized that meant no one was really safe from the McNaughtons, including other members of the corporation. All except the perpetrators themselves had been negatively impacted by intimidation from Night Riders, who were young men from the community. Although the Night Riders primarily targeted newcomers, their activities produced significant collateral damage. Beatrice Jaramillo, a McNaughton grandmother had been struck in the head with a beer bottle and left unconscious alongside the highway. Violence and mayhem reflected common threads of greed, covetousness, envy, and avarice. Fortunately in Rock Creek and Jericho Springs, individuals came forward to lead an effort to resolve problems, which included their solving the three murder mysteries.

Newcomer Karen Gustafson had been busy implementing a school district/city council sponsored project. She began by interviewing those in leadership positions in order to uncover less obvious informal leaders. Through the project, both formal and informal leaders shared their perspectives on community problems and resources to resolve those problems. Meanwhile, others had resolved to take matters into their own hands. In Rock Creek sheriff's deputy Cotton Candy used her position and new assignment with neighborhood watch to bring town residents together in the name of public safety. Cotton believed she would have to seek leadership from a newcomer, a person not afraid of the existing power structure and not bound by family connections for income or approval. She sought help from John Mark Cannikin, a recent arrival. Cannikin had been hired by well known and well respected rancher, Adam Claymore, to restore the house of his deceased wife. Since he stayed at the house, while working on it, Cannikin both lived and worked in Rock Creek, at least temporarily. In Jericho Springs, Attorney John Law had earlier met with a group from the Blair House, who felt passionate about making right that which was wrong. The group began with the restoration of Blair House, the object of much discussion and unrest not only in Jericho Springs but also throughout the valley. Neither Deputy Candy nor Attorney Law had realized the magnitude of the motivation behind John Mark Cannikin and the Blair House group.

Candy had contacted John Mark early in the morning and requested to meet privately with him at the Rock Creek Church in the Glen. When she arrived there at noon, Candy parked her cruiser along the lane leading to the churchyard and out of sight of residents at the Stage Stop Hotel or occupants of vehicles parked in the hotel parking area. First feeling deep claw marks on the front door of the church with the tips of her fingers, Candy then scanned her surroundings. At first, she was distracted by the roar of truck and auto engines from busy highway traffic. Next, she watched canyon wind flitter birch leaves on the trees in the glen. Inhaling the intoxicating fragrance of the roses, which climbed the canyon and mesa walls, she listened to the rush of water and imagined how it hurried around and over rocks in the creek. Then she picked up and touched sharp edges of glass fragments from the broken yard light, which had been shattered by a bullet shot from the ridge during the rave. Not seeing any sign of John Mark, but stepping onto the massive brown bear's tracks, she followed the footprints toward the back of the church building. She could see a trail led to both the church graveyard and the footbridge, which crossed over Rock Creek and led to a north/south trail. She remembered to the north on County Road 403, a bridge spanned the creek. In a crawl space under the bridge, the body of Gloria Jones had been found earlier. To the south the trail led through a raspberry patch where it became a footpath surrounded by tangles of strawberries. The path led to the top of the mesa where a metal bench perched like a sentry watching over the valley. Candy paused, sat on the steps leading to the pastor's office, and briefly felt at ease, while she visualized the land around the church and smelled the flowers.

Resuming her walk toward the back of the building, Candy felt the chill as a crisp breeze blew through the canyon. Again, she smelled the fragrance from rose bushes lining fence, which marked the creek from the cemetery to the mouth of the canyon. She turned and saw how roses bloomed on tendrils, which had climbed from the ground at the base of the cliff. Her eyes followed the path of the tendrils, as they spread along the wall leading to its top thirty or so feet above her. Candy wondered whether the blooms would survive the projected snow storm.

Next, Candy watched John Mark as he prayed while systematically walking amongst the graves in the church cemetery. Her gaze shifted left to the bridge where both Karen Gustafson and Buddy Smith had fallen to the ground. Karen had been one of Sam Gelding's victims, while Buddy had been a perpetrator. It had been Buddy who struck Beatrice Jaramillo with a beer bottle and knocked her out. Candy remembered her conversation with John Law and Detective Caleb Jones. They speculated about what had happened to Karen and about how Sam Gelding's body had come to be held by the whirlpool in the creek. The investigation gained no finger prints and found no signs of violence. Only one section of the bridge rail had been scuffed and only the end post had been stained with blood.

Tall, handsome, and muscular John Mark sensed Candy's presence and spoke without turning toward her. "Each of those buried here has a story. I wonder how they would feel about what happens in their town now that they are gone...I wonder what they would do in response..."

"To the gambling, the prostitution, harassment of townspeople, the disrespect toward women, and who knows what else," Candy echoed, as she walked to the entrance gate to the cemetery.

John Mark turned and smiled as he walked toward the deputy. Almost pretty he thought of her, a nice smile and eyes twinkling in the sunbeams, "the rave, Baal worship, and more. What about the school district offices?"

"The insurance agency, real estate office, post office, and convenience store..."

"And a volunteer fire department without volunteers..."

"A boarded up building that used to be a grocery store."

"There is more, I suspect, though I've never researched," responded Cotton Candy. "You would enjoy visiting the library and historical society's museum."

As John Mark reached the gate, he thrust his hand toward Cotton and said, "Deputy, I'm glad you called me. I'm here to listen to you."

The deputy grasped the carpenter's hand with surprise at its gentle strength. "Why are you here, man willing to listen?" she said.

"You called to meet me..."

"No, I mean why have you walked to this town from out of nowhere...and now you are restoring Mary Claymore's house? How long will you be here?" Cotton asked with piercing eyes.

"Good questions...now you are listening, albeit with suspicion. No, with curiosity." He explained, "Since Adam hired me to do a job, I'm here at least until the job is done, until my assignment is completed. Other than you being law enforcement, why do you ask?"

"I want you to help me."

"I know..." he pondered. "You said so after the rave when we met at the church."

"As promised, I've got all we need to get started," said Candy.

"Deputy, you are on the right track. God is with you," John Mark said, while his eyes searched hers.

"Do you work at being mysterious or what? I wonder if you're here for another reason?"

"I'm about my father's work..."

"Didn't Jesus say that?"

"Yes. Sorry Deputy, you may have heard about what happened at a recent church meeting where I helped a young woman from the Asherah House."

"And…"

"I merely committed to help her keep away from their clutches."

"Then you are the one I need to help me."

"How?"

"John Mark, the people here in Rock Creek have been terrorized by the same group that's after those at the Blair House," began the Deputy. "Between the gambling, the rave, the Night Riders, hotel patrons, and drunks at the bar, the people here need more help than what the sheriff's office can provide alone."

"Especially with the death of Gloria Jones, the assault on Karen Gustafson, and the death and injury after the recent rave," added John Mark, "as well as the bear's visitation."

"Add in the porn and drug dealing through the convenience store."

"Plus all the traffic we've had with people so curious about the fire on the ridge. Deputy, what do you have in mind?"

"I've been wanting to get a neighborhood watch organization started here, where people watch out for one another, and if they see something suspicious going on, they call one another and contact me at the sheriff's office."

"How do I figure in?"

"I need you to help get it started and to provide the initial leadership," Candy said, "I mean I know it's not likely you will stay around here forever, and frankly, it would probably be longer lasting if someone who has lived here a long time would shoulder the responsibility."

"So a newcomer helps the oldtimers get started but then assumes a secondary role."

"You understand?"

"Yes, I do. I suppose you want to have an organizational meeting," John Mark said, and then asked, "When do you want to do this?"

"Tonight!"

"Tonight? Kind of short notice."

"Admittedly, but with what happened at the rave and the fire on the ridge the other night, I've gotten phone calls from most of the people here in town. I think they are ready to get involved. Will you help me?" Candy said as she opened a box, which she held under her arm. "I made flyers announcing a meeting tonight at the senior center located on the back side of the school administration building. It won't take long."

"You want me to pass out flyers?"

"Only on this side of town...you only need twelve or so," she replied, "and talk with the people if they are at home. You don't go to the businesses. I'll take flyers to folks on Indiana Avenue."

"And you won't deliver a flyer to the businesses including the Asherah House, the Tobacco Store, and the hotel," confirmed, John Mark.

"Correct, I know you wanted to meet at the church, but based on my phone calls, I need for us to meet at a neutral setting, so we will meet at the senior center, where I will present the idea and lead the meeting. I'll introduce you and tell people you have agreed to help me get things started."

"Ok, what do you want me to do at the meeting?"

"Here's a sign in sheet. Get everyone to sign in and provide their name, address, and telephone number, so we can have a telephone tree from the start. Pass out flyers and other handouts I'll have. I'll have a window sticker for each house that identifies their home as members of the Rock Creek Neighborhood Watch!"

"I'll do it, Deputy; I'll knock on each door and talk with all I find. I'm working at Adam's house the rest of the afternoon, so I can check on folks when they come home."

"We won't get everyone to attend our first meeting on such short notice..."

"But we'll get started, and I'll follow up with those who don't attend," said John Mark.

"And John...be willing to speak from your heart...please...what I need you to do is to be as real as you seem to be."

"I know that is what you need from me," replied John Mark.

Parting ways by giving one another the thumbs up, Cotton drove to Indiana Avenue, while John Mark headed for the house next to the church. She parked in front of the Asherah House and crossed the street where she began at the house opposite the bed and breakfast. He left a flyer explaining the Sheriff's Neighborhood Watch program with a notice announcing tonight's meeting at the senior center. Lunch time proved effective as he found four people at their homes including Lila Longdon. Both she and her daughter worked at the Stage Stop Hotel. Lila welcomed the contact, especially after learning he was her next door neighbor. On Indiana Avenue, Deputy Candy matched his results by contacting all nine houses, and her contacts garnered productive results. The lady directly across from the Asherah House reported she had been terrified by those attending the rave. Two doors to the west of her house, an older gentleman promised to supply a lengthy list of license plate numbers of the johns frequenting the bed and breakfast. He owned and operated the antique store sandwiched between the tobacco shop and the real estate office recently shared by the deceased insurance agent, Sam Gelding. Additionally, the old gentleman owned the other shops along the east side of the highway. One of the deputy's contacts proved especially promising, as the mother of five on the corner had leadership experience. She had helped organize a neighborhood watch program in metropolitan Denver, and she promised to help!

Inside the hotel restaurant, Karen had sat watching Deputy Candy's arrival and departure and John Mark's door to door canvassing of the houses along the highway. Karen presumed he had continued to do the same with the houses bordering the county road to Jericho Springs. Suddenly a yellow jeep with three large occupants emerged from the driveway next to Adam's house. Their departure had been so quick not even the convenience store clerk noticed as the jeep sped left around the corner and proceeded west on the county road. She watched John Mark wave as the occupants sped by him toward Jericho Springs and on to Ezra's mountain cabin. Karen concluded John Mark knew those who rode in the mysterious yellow jeep,

\*\*\*

Keeping her promise to not forget Sarah, Karen waited for the waitress to have a few minutes to sit with her and make an appointment for later that night. Just before Sarah sat down at her table,

Karen watched Sarah's mother Lila as she walked from her house to the hotel and joined them at Karen's table.

"I know you girls wanted to talk, but I've got some important news about our dreamy neighbor," Lila said, "and Sarah, honey, you've got to meet him."

"In my condition," Sarah said as she patted her tummy, "I have no interest in meeting any more men!"

Nearly laughing, Karen hid her humorous response with a quick hand covering her mouth, "You must be referring to John Mark Cannikin. He is restoring Adam's house next door to your place."

"I know he's staying and working there, and there are others there too," said Lila.

"Oh... I hadn't heard that," Karen replied.

"John Mark is big, but you ought to see the others. One drives a yellow jeep. I've seen them working in the garage," informed Sarah.

"Anyway, let me tell you the news. John Mark gave me this flyer about neighborhood watch and this one about a meeting tonight at the senior center. We need to go to it," urged Lila.

Karen took the flyers and scanned them before passing them to Sarah, then said, "I'd like to go with you."

"Great, then we can talk after the meeting," Sarah replied with a smile, and when Karen nodded affirmatively, "I knew you would follow through with me."

\*\*\*

Meanwhile in Jericho Springs, twelve gathered at the Baptist church. Eight Baptists and two each from the Methodist and Lutheran churches began stuffing plastic bags with what Pastor Borden had purchased at the Blair House bookstore. Each bag included a Bible, a children's book, Bible tracts, and welcome messages from each of the three churches.

Rachael McNaughton arrived to help as did Amanda Sentry, secretary to Attorney John Law, who spent her lunch hour preparing the bags for the others to distribute. As Amanda stuffed bags she thought about the Tunnicliffe twins, who were meeting with Ezra Freedom and her boss. She wondered what they would do with the

Live Oak sapling, which she had watched over for years. They had exchanged two large planters for the one sapling that they took from her file room. She remembered how they had poured some liquid on the soil in each planter directly above the acorn that they had planted. She had kissed Drostan the Red...only, while Coinneach the Fair smiled. It had been impulsive, she thought, to kiss the man, the magnificent man. Today, both arrived again, the one with flowers, the other without. Quite taken with both of them, she had surprised herself when she kissed Drostan earlier. She bore a reputation for being reserved and even distant, but not now, not with either of them. It was good, she thought, I had an appointment elsewhere, so I would not be there when they left the meeting. Who knows how I would have responded to either or both of them...and then she remembered something her boss had told her when she first started working at the law offices.

Mr. Law had come out of his office one afternoon after opening a box that he had received from the British Isles. He held an acorn in his hand and told her to order a large pot from the lumber and hardware store in Ridge View. He said it should be delivered here with a bag of potting soil and a bottle of Alaskan fish fertilizer. Amanda remembered once the order had been delivered, she had helped Mr. Law plant the acorn, and she had watched as he poured the fertilizer on the dirt above it. "Then I watched him pray over it," Amanda said softly, "and then he told me that someone was coming here to plant the tree, and we will give it to them. Next, he looked at me and a tear came to his eye as he said revival is coming and all will be restored. I was just out of high school...eight years ago."

"What did you say, Mandy? Did you say revival is coming? I agree and I knew I had to get to work at the Blair House..." said Rachael, as she struggled to remember something. "Oh, goodness, my dear, I'm not sure how to get home...will you help me?"

Pastor Borden gathered the group together to pray over the five hundred bags that they had prepared to deliver door to door to all the households in town. He proclaimed to the group, "Much has happened in our town, our valley. People are unnerved by witnessing what our friends and neighbors will do to gain wealth that does not belong to them. We've had three deaths in our midst, one of a man who had apparently been responsible for one death here in the valley and probably another in Quail Point. The truth needs be told, justice must be served, and yet grace and mercy need be extended to the innocent. I don't know what part the recent rave had to do with any of the deaths other than that of the spectator from Wolf City. I do know the pagan god Baal was being worshipped, and for that very reason, we need to be active in our community. A malevolent force has entered our community, a giant of a bear left its mark on the entry door to the little Church in the Glen in the town of Rock Creek, a church I used to pastor. People are unnerved, frightened. All need Jesus! Let us pray, let us share a prayer. One of you begin the prayer and I will end it."

One by one the church members prayed asking God to bless the people who were to receive each bag that they had stuffed. They prayed that the beauty of Jesus be seen in them. They asked the Holy Spirit to lead in what they said to people that they might meet along the way. And then it was Amanda's turn to pray.

"Father God, thank you that we can crawl up into your lap like little children and you keep us safe and secure in your promises, your character. Protect us from the Night Riders, the advocates of Baal worship, and the human trafficking. Watch over those, who are yours, who oppose evil in our town be it from those that attack Blair House or our churches. Watch over the newcomers to our valley who come here and have often been harassed only because they are new or may have a claim to the water or mineral rights here. Thank you for sending reinforcements to deal with the bear, seemingly a manifestation of evil. Most of all Father, thank you for Jesus!"

"Thank you all for being here," the pastor said. "You have your maps and you are going two by two, one on each side of the street. We will walk for an hour, so keep track of where you make your deliveries. Another team will walk this evening, so don't worry if you have leftovers. Remember all you have to do is place the bags on screen or door knobs. If someone is in the yard or comes to the door, be bold and courageous. Tell them who you are and that you are from this church or your own, and then hand them the bag of gifts. Pray over each house, the people there. Ask God to bless them and for him to bring the residents close to him. Pray for their salvation," Pastor continued, "Remember the promise of *Second Chronicles, chapter seven, verse fourteen, 'If my people, who are called by my name, will humble themselves and pray and seek my face and turn from their wicked ways, then I will hear from heaven and I will forgive their sin and will heal their land' (2Chronicles 7:14).* My wife will drive our station wagon and keep tabs on all of us. We should be finished in an hour. Let us go out singing together..."

All those gathered began singing, "Yes, we can, yes we can...we can grow as better people, halleluiah, yes we can..." as the six teams left Jericho Springs Baptist Church located adjacent to the high school. They delivered door hanger bags to the one hundred fifty-two households south of the post office to County Road 403 on the south end of town. Later in the evening another hundred would be delivered to houses north of the post office. The pastor planned to use the rest to deliver along CR403 to Ridge View and further north.

\*\*\*

Adam had meandered back and forth in the valley looking for bear tracks around the front side of the west peak of Mount Huajatolla. It had been three hours since he left cow camp and stiffness settled into his back. He rode looking for fresh bear scat or large bear tracks along a tributary, which led to the north branch of Rock Creek. Adam departed from the creek bed to traverse back over a ridge, which would lead back to Ezra Freedom's cabin.

In another hour Adam approached the cabin where he could see Ezra working with his draft horses in the corral by the barn. From a high point Adam watched as a yellow jeep turned off the mountain road by Ezra's saw mill. He watched as the jeep climbed the access road to the cabin, and he noted three rather large occupants. Taking his spyglass from his saddlebag, Adam focused on the riders in hopes that he would recognize if they were friend or foe. Each wore a gray hooded cloak. Deciding to time his arrival with that of the jeep, he cautiously made his way down the rugged slope, while still searching for bear tracks and scat. Although once entertained by songbirds and squirrels, he realized he no longer heard them. Since he left the creek in the valley the other side of the ridge, all he could hear was his horse's grunts as it struggled down slope. Big Foot had been running through the meadow and into stands of Ponderosa on both sides of him, but suddenly appeared next to him. Footers pointed west to Adam's right and growled.

Reaching again for his spyglass, Adam steadied his horse on a level where he could focus on the stand of trees. He watched birds fly overhead toward him from the trees. Uncharacteristically, Big Foot stayed by him instead of running to the stand of trees. At first an unearthly silence prevailed, until deer bolted from the woods directly toward him before veering away. Peculiar he thought, as he returned his spyglass to his saddlebag and pulled his Winchester from its scabbard. Peculiar for deer to run toward him, he thought, when they had been safely out of sight. Something more frightening than a man on horseback spooked them. Adam dismounted and loosened a short rope from the laddigo strap which tied it to the saddle. Carrying his rifle, Adam threaded the rope through an o-ring which dangled from the hackamore bridle and led his horse down the rest of a steep slope, while he kept an eye on the stand of trees. Big Foot remained vigilant by his side.

At the cabin the Tunnicliffe brothers greeted Ezra at the corral and unloaded their gear from the jeep. Ezra led them to the cabin and gave them a quick tour of the limited facilities. There were two beds in the loft, a couch downstairs next to the loft ladder, an overstuffed chair on the south side near the entry door, a table with four chairs by the front window, and a pot belly stove near the east wall. The kitchen filled the northwest corner and a cook stove lined the west wall with wood stacked against most of the north wall, except for an icebox located in the middle by the back door. One could look out a window above the cook stove and west of the back door. The other three walls featured one window each, but the west wall had another window. One could sit at the table and look out and see both the barn and corral to the west and the saw mill to the south. Earlier in the week, Kat Bond, Misty MacNaughten, and Hannah Rahab of the Blair House had cleaned the cabin for Ezra, which provided the Tunnicliffes with a false impression of Ezra's tidiness.

Of course, Big Foot arrived first at the back door of the cabin looking for Ezra. Since the door had been opened, Footers pushed quickly on the back screen door, which caused it to bounce open enough for the excitable dog to get his nose between the door and the frame. In he came with his fluffy black tail wagging. The Tunnicliffe twins dropped down to the main floor from the loft with such force that once the dog saw the size and bulk of them, Big Foot bolted out of the back door to where Adam had just dismounted.

"What ho in the cabin! I'm looking for Ezra. Tell him Adam is here!"

Each twin came out the back door to meet him, first the blond and then the red head. Next came Ezra and then Bear, who spoke, while holding a javelin that he had pulled from a travel case less he had need of it, "What ho, yourself, Neighbor!"

Ezra put his hand on Bear's arm to restrain him, and Bear continued, "Aye, you must be a friend of Ezra. We are three of the brothers Tunnicliffe—I'm Bear Killer, Drostan the red, Coinneach the fair, and my name is Brian."

"Speaking of bear," Adam said, "I've been tracking the great brown since morning and just discovered he has probably been tracking me. I believe he is in the stand of Ponderosa up the slope."

The red and the blonde bolted back through the rear door and fetched two javelins each from Bear's travel case in time to follow after Brian, who already ran a third of the way up the slope from the cabin. Both sprinted uphill after Brian and caught up with him before he crossed the clearing to the stand of Ponderosa. Having leaped into his saddle from the back porch, Adam soon caught up with them leaving Ezra behind. Protecting his draft horses, Ezra took a Winchester off the wall and ran to the barn where he closed the doors and locked them from the inside. Climbing the ladder to the hay loft, he opened the north loft door in hopes of seeing and shooting the bear.

Each of the Tunnicliffes entered the forest twenty yards apart. Drostan the red found fresh bear scat, mounds of it, and he found and followed the great brown's tracks long enough to prove the direction it had taken. Clanging his javelins together, Drostan caught the attention of Brian and Coinneach, and then pointed the direction. The twins broke into a sprint through the woods, while Brian followed along the edge of the stand.

"Adam, the great brown was here and he's taken to a southward path. Moving quickly he is and apparently not wanting to meet his death yet. Would you ride to the road, while we flush him out like a scared rabbit soon to be stew in the pot?" asked Brian.

"Aye!" said Adam with a smile, "He is likely to cross the creek and head over the mountain or circle west around where my herd has been easy pickins for him. But...the sly beast may head east for town or southeast toward my ranch...I'll head for the road. Come on, Big Foot! We may soon have the grizz!"

Each hunter sprang into action. Adam rode for the dirt road that parallels Ezra's saw mill. The Tunnicliffes ran through the woods with hope of catching up with the bear. Ezra moved from the north door of the hay loaf to the south door above the corral and opened it, so he could keep up with the action. Big Foot stopped and listened. Adam ignored the dog in hopes of catching the bear where the road runs between the forest and West Rock Creek.

Having circled around the Tunnicliffes and climbing over rock, the bear eluded his trackers, except for Big Foot. The great brown lumbered stealthily down slope to the meadow directly toward Ezra's cabin undetected. Adam waited by the road and spoke as if Big Foot were at his side. The brothers emerged from the forest and climbed onto the road.

"Have you seen him, Adam?" asked Brian.

"No, were you able to follow his tracks to here?"

"Lost them and thought he would be here."

Big Foot's barking interrupted the hunters, who looked toward the barking dog in the field by the saw mill. Having caught their attention, the dog pointed toward the cabin with nose out front, tail level with his back, and left leg folded to his chest. The men abruptly followed his lead, and looked to the cabin where the bear had been clawing the cabin's front door. As if laughing, the great brown stood on its back legs and walked across the porch to the stairs, and on all fours, it bounded down the stairs, turned left, and climbed up the slope, passed over the ridge, and out of sight.

Once angry at being outfoxed by the grizz, the men laughed at the bear's antics and respected its craftiness. This would not be an easy hunt, Bear Killer thought, which stirred painful memories of the bear that had scared his face. Ezra pointed at his mouth and rubbed his stomach to invite the men to eat with him. They returned to the cabin, examined the bear's signature on the sturdy cabin door, and teased Ezra for not responding to the bear knocking at his cabin door. Big Foot earned their praise for finding the bear.

Since the red and the blonde did not speak, but did laugh, Brian had to tell their story to both Ezra, who could not speak, and to Adam, who had not experienced such laughter for years. But first, the Tunnicliffes needed to bring the rest of their gear into the cabin and set up for a long stay, while Adam stabled his horse with the much bigger draft horses. Ezra stoked a fire in the cook stove to heat a dish, which Jill had left for him in the icebox. With his Winchester in hand, Adam walked the grounds where he speculated the bear had travelled to the crest of the ridge. He did not break the horizon, as the crafty bear could be waiting on the other side. He wondered how far his wranglers had moved the herd toward the pasture directly across the road from the saw mill. Returning to the front porch of the cabin, Adam approached the door and placed his hand on the center of the claw marks.

"Where have you gone? Will you circle around and return here, or will you head for my herd? You crafty old boar!" Adam said, then vowed, "Either me or one of my friends will get you. You have marked those who stood against the Baal worship—the Rock Creek church, the Live Oak at the Blair House, my wrangler Pilgrim Wayne, and now this cabin. If you are somehow inspired by the evil one, what is your next target? Or has all of this just been happenstance and you have just been acting like a crazy old bear following my herd?"

# A Tale of Two Towns:
# Evening into Night

## CHAPTER 14

*"Ask and it will be given to you; seek and you will find;
knock and the door will be opened to you."*

*Matthew 7:7*

oth radio and television weather forecasters predicted a massive storm would blanket all of Colorado with heavy
snow. The weathermen said to expect the heaviest accumula-
tion on the Rockies' eastern slope, especially Monument Hill on the
Palmer Divide near Colorado Springs to Raton Pass by Trinidad. They
stated residents of Rock Creek Valley and its connecting mesa should
prepare to receive up to three feet or more snow. Moisture laden
clouds entered the valley by mid-afternoon, and the temperature
dipped from the mid-sixties to thirty degrees. Essentially, forecasters
advised people in the valley to get ready to just "chill out" and stay
at home, as soon as the storm moved in.

While Adam fellowshipped with Ezra and the three Tunnicliffe
brothers, Adam and Red's wranglers broke camp. The drovers started
moving the herd down the mountain road alongside the West Rock
Creek waterway. Following Adam's orders, Rabbit, the trail boss,
intended to halt their combined herds in the lush mountain pasture just south of Ezra's saw mill. Adam planned to have the herd
held there, until the Jericho Springs pasture dried and a new crop of
grass had grown. If the snowfall proved to be as forecasted, Rabbit
Pinebow knew to follow Adam's alternate plan where the herd would

bypass the mountain pasture and go directly to the Jericho Springs pasture. Unless roads became impassable, wranglers would feed the cattle by dumping bales of new mown hay from a pickup truck. If roads had not or could not be cleared of snow, fun loving wranglers previously had volunteered to toboggan and cross-country ski to the Jericho pasture. They would load bales of hay on the toboggan from the other side of CR403 where bales had been stacked. Strays would be rounded up later, held temporarily in the mountain pasture, and united later with the main herd. If necessary, Ezra could be depended on to set bales in the pasture or on the field near the saw mill.

Another group of Adam's wranglers had nearly finished repairing fence on the southern border of Claymore Flats. They had been mending fences from Wolf City east over the mesa toward Quail Point. Rather than fight the incoming snow, Barnabas, the line foreman, ordered the wranglers to gather their tools and head for the line shack where they would spend the night. Barnabas sent the two boys from Pryor home to the ranch house with one lineman under orders to assist Pilgrim and to enjoy sleeping in their own bed.

\*\*\*

Meanwhile at the Blair House, most team members looked forward to the night's activities. Jerry Sunday invited others to help prepare the dining room for group building activities that evening. He stoked the fire in the dining room fireplace and photocopied materials in the second floor office. Morris Goodenough, the bus driver, and Mike Crowfoot, the convenience store manager, gathered blocks of wood from the back porch and filled a storage area built into the hearth. Mike had walked less than a block up Main Street from the store to get home. After finishing a round trip to San Francisco, Morris hitched a ride from the bus terminal to get home from Ridge View. Pizza store manager and deliveryman, Jerry had volunteered to lead the team in group building activities. He assembled and set out Lyman Coleman's materials, a popular 1970's collection of work to build Christian community within small groups. Each of these men fit in easily.

Others fit in easily. Karen quickly gained prestige in the valley for two reasons. She had just been hired to teach in the school district. She had impressed the community by ending an altercation by shooting the bully, Roy Sentry, in the foot. Her marksmanship became renowned. The third reason for her prestige was she was dating Adam Claymore. Also, brother and sister, Mike and Janine fit in easily. Of course, Janine married into great fortune, but also they were oldtimers of good report. There was one exception in Rachael McNaughton, who had just finished a piano lesson in the adjoining room. Rachael was a McNaughton grandmother, matriarch of the valley's prominent family. Rachael lived across the street from Blair House, but served as a full fledged team member.

Both Hannah and Misty struggled with their own judgment of themselves. Both felt inadequate. Though a life-long resident, none knew Misty from her work at the Asherah House Bed and Breakfast. All noted how Misty had fawned over John Mark and were embarrassed by her bold behavior. Some met her when she attended church in Rock Creek and sat with the Brownings. Others first met her when the Brownings brought her to Blair House, and the team learned she would be joining them. Most knew Hannah from the story of how Karen had helped rescue her from the clutches of Butch McNaughton after a school board meeting. As desk clerk, Hannah recognized some of the group from when they had dined at the Stage Stop Hotel, so she was known by many and had pleasant conversation with them previously. Hannah and Misty thrived in the acceptance they had already experienced at Blair House. Misty began to think beyond herself, while Hannah began to open up to others. What bothered Misty and Hannah was neither had really participated on a team before, nor had they had genuine help with sharing or goal development. Hannah and Misty talked about the meeting before going downstairs to the dining room. They discussed how Karen and Jill had been counseling Misty and how Katarina and Janine had worked with both of them around the house.

Misty said, "You know, I think we can trust them to help us out."

"We can sit next to each other and you can kick me under the table if I'm making a fool of myself," said Hannah.

"And you with me," Misty laughed, and added, "then let's high five when we're on target!"

"Cool beans..." answered Hannah.

Misty became silent for a moment and concluded, "We can be ourselves...There's no need for drama..."

"Okay, but promise me we will talk later..." Hannah said to which Misty nodded agreeably.

Soon others arrived, while Rachael waved goodnight to those in the dining room. She greeted Tim McNaughton as he descended the front stairwell. When Janine and Izzy came from their apartment down the hall to greet Rachael, Ken Bond waved to her from the kitchen as did his daughters Kristin and Krystal, who had washed and dried the dinner dishes. Katarina Bond and Kip Powell emerged from the bookstore where they had reviewed the day's sales and prepared to mail several new orders.

"There you are newlyweds. When is the ceremony at school? Am I still playing the music, I hope?" Rachael asked for affirmation.

"None but you will provide the music, dear. Jill has the two solos with you playing for her. Misty and Hannah are in charge of the guest books and gifts," said Janine.

"Remember everyone has a job..." said Jerry, who used the conversation as a segue to the group building activities.

The group shouted out, "All for one, and one for all!

"Goodnight to all of you," Rachael said with some envy, "this old lady is soon off to bed. I hope tonight is peaceful."

"Thank you Rachael! I trust your lesson went well," Janine inquired.

"We were blessed by it upstairs," said Tim.

"When is the next hymn sing?" asked Kip.

"And another book party?" added Katarina.

"I'll pray about those tonight," Rachael responded with a smile, as Tim opened the front door for her. "Look there," she added, "It is snowing already. All of you keep warm tonight."

"We will, Rachael," Izzy said. "Tim, please walk her home and see to it her thermostat is working."

Rachael paused to give the group a blessing, "I know you are working tonight and my buddy Beatrice is watching over Pilgrim and the boys from Pryor. I just got a chill, where is Karen? Where's your father, Izzy?"

"They are all right, dear," Izzy replied. "My father is at the cabin, but he should be home later this evening."

"Trouble is coming," Rachael whispered with only Tim hearing her, "a quick prayer covering over all of you...remember in *First Chronicles* that Jabez was more honorable than his brothers. Over you I pray, "*Jabez cried out to the God of Israel, Oh, that you would bless me and enlarge my territory! Let your hand be with me, and keep me from harm so that I will be free from pain. And God granted his request*" (1 Chronicles 4:10).

Izzy opened the screen door and embraced Rachael there on his porch, "Be assured we seek God's plan for us individually and as a team. Tonight, we do group building activities and we hope to be pain free. We don't want any of us to be the cause of pain especially at the hands of one another. We ask for the Holy Spirit to teach us and guide us."

"But Karen isn't here?"

"She's about the Father's work. Karen is with Sarah and Lila Longdon."

"The Longdons...in Rock Creek...the ones at the Stage Stop? Wonders never cease!"

"John Mark is helping Deputy Candy start a neighborhood watch for all of Rock Creek, and Karen and the Longdons are attending the meeting," Izzy said, "and the others are accounted for...except for Caleb Jones."

"No doubt he is investigating something!"

"That's what detectives do..."

"Bee is at Claymore Flats...You will call her tonight, won't you?" asked Rachael, who then whispered to Tim, "I so like watching Columbo. My husband liked Perry Mason."

"She said she would call later."

"I didn't see Ezra...is he with my husband?"

"Not yet...God still has work for him here," Izzy gently said.

"Oh, that's right, Izzy...I'm just...forgetful," Rachael said, "and memories seem real."

"Afraid when you don't see loved ones?" Izzy offered, "Ezra has guests at the cabin. He will be here more often now."

"Never figured hospitality'd be one of his gifts..."

"Look at all of us," Tim offered.

"God's wonders never cease," Rachael concluded with a smile unfolding across her face, and turning, she grabbed Tim by the arm, "Come on young man. Take me home."

As they descended the front sidewalk, Tim told Rachael about the rules for small group sharing. He said, "Rachael, what is great about our meetings is everyone contributes, and we are all expected to listen to one another. Only one person speaks at a time, and every idea is considered."

"So nobody is made to feel stupid or unwanted?"

"Nobody..."

"Red and yellow, black and white," Rachael sang, "we are precious in His sight...

\*\*\*

In Rock Creek, John Mark joined Deputy Candy at the senior center in the old high school building. It had been repurposed to house the school district administrative offices, the senior center, the valley's museum, and secrets. The building bordered the Valley Highway, US 85/87, and it stood across the road from the only vehicular entrance to Indiana Avenue. It was the only way in, other than footpaths—one north from the water tower, the marsh below it, and an open space between the hogback and the highway; another east, the game trail leading to and from the ridge; and a third, south from the Stage Stop Hotel and the Tobacco Store. While the museum recorded and displayed some secrets, they were maintained in the memories of residents like the ones attending the senior center...and all paths led to the Asherah House. John Mark and the deputy reviewed their plans for the meeting as well as the purpose, role, and functions of a neighborhood watch in Rock Creek. It was a matter of public safety, as it had always been.

"One other thing, John Mark, I was at the bridge before coming here. I dusted for finger prints from the center of the bridge top rail to the end. Did you notice anything out of the ordinary when you looked to the creek from the bridge and saw Gelding's body?"

"You asked...what I noticed, which was the enthralling fragrance from the roses, the crisp air blown my way by canyon winds, and the dew resting on my cheeks. I noticed how perfect the timing was for me to be standing on the bridge leaning on the top rail. The water lowered and the current released the body from the clutches of the whirlpool. I noticed how dust became mud and cloaked the top rail, but I saw no smudges where hands may have gripped the rail. What I did see along the path on the bank was bear scat amongst strawberries and raspberry bushes. But it's what I didn't see...nothing, no one had disturbed the ground, nor had anything crushed the tall grasses leading to the creek bank from the footpath," said John Mark, and then, "Oh yes, the tree at the east end had one branch that had been bent or broken. I saw a couple of prints, not shoe but footprints, no toes...maybe moccasins...and at the other end on the ground...It is amazing how the cool wind brings so much moisture. It is almost muddy. The soil there has a deep red tint to it."

\*\*\*

Karen parked her Nova near the highway in front of Adam's house where John Mark and the Tunnicliffes had been staying. She walked next door where she met Sarah and Lila Longdon to walk to the senior center for the neighborhood watch meeting. The neighbor immediately south of Adam's house, caught up with the women and engaged them in conversation. He introduced himself and explained he was the highwayman, the truck driver who kept the canyon opened during the winter. Additional small groups of people joined their walk from four of the seven houses along CR403. Walking north along the Valley Highway, they noticed many people crossing the highway from Indiana Avenue, which represented half the houses from the street.

Cloud cover darkened the streets and no lights illuminated the dusk other than those from the hotel and the convenience store on the corner. A fourth Tunnicliffe from Coyote Springs made his way to the birch glen between the highway and church driveway near the mouth of the canyon. In the glen he had stored a mixture of sheep and peat, wood chips, a spade and long handle shovel, five gallons of water in a can, plus the Live Oak sapling that his brothers had claimed from Amanda at the law offices. One by one he carried five packages across the highway and repeatedly scaled the rock wall by climbing a rope ladder securely fixed at the top of the rim. Once on top with all the packages, he moved them to where the Asher pole had been chopped down and burned with the ceremonial tables. With his long handled shovel, he gathered the ashes from the burn, set them aside in a pile, and then focused on digging a hole to plant the sapling.

With everything gathered at the site, he hammered one long spike into the ground, took a four foot length of rope from one backpack, and tied it loosely around the spike. Holding the other end of the rope at his waist, he walked counterclockwise. He prayed as he walked in Gaelic, until his path had been clearly marked, and then he reversed his direction. As he prayed he asked God to protect the tree and bind all evil from disrupting the success of his mission. Next, he proceeded to dig a hole within the circumference of the path he had walked, until the hole reached a half length of his four foot rope. After mixing the sheep and peat with the soil he had removed from the hole, he placed wood chips in the bottom of the hole, set the sapling on the chips, and filled the hole half way with soil mixed with sheep and peat. He stepped on the soil to compress it, wrapped biodegradable tape around the trunk, and spilled some water from his five gallon tank. Finally, he finished by spreading more soil mixture to cover the circumference of the hole, compressed it again, and then he spread more wood chips on top. Once planted, he removed a vile from his pocket, poured its contents into his water drum, and sloshed the water around to mix it. Pouring the mixture over the ground, he gave thanks and loosely tied three ribbons around the sapling trunk.

He said aloud, "Father, may this white ribbon represent the advent of your holiness to the people of this valley," as he tied the white ribbon, and as he tied the red ribbon, "Father, may this red ribbon represent the blood Jesus sacrificed that all may live including those in this valley," and then he said, "May this purple ribbon represent the royalty of Christ in the hearts of all here who accept Jesus as Savior and Lord!" and then he continued, "As this tree grows to symbolize both the battle won here to defeat Baal worship again in this valley, may it bring comfort to the people below with its shade, and like the citadel on the hill across the valley, may you raise up those you would have to be lights in darkness."

Finally, the young giant of a man took to his knees and prayed, "Thank you for allowing me this quest, and may you always enable me to live up to my name Niall, champion, and may you continue to use me to champion your causes, be it here or elsewhere, amen...," and then he bagged the ash and put it in one of his backpacks. Niall gathered his tools and returned to the edge of the ridge by the mouth of the canyon.

***

Meanwhile, on the valley floor below, Karen, Lila and Sarah Longdon, and the rest of the group followed the residents from Indiana Avenue around the back of the school district building to the senior center. Deputy Candy greeted them at the entry door, and inside John Mark had each sign in noting their name, address, and telephone number. He handed them a copy of a sheriff's report covering crime and calls for assistance from the town of Rock Creek. Neighbors greeted one another and renewed past acquaintances. Most had not spoken with one another since the volunteer fire department's last picnic at least three years earlier when the volunteers disbanded.

Deputy Candy convened the meeting and stated their purpose, "You are all aware of what's been happening here in your town. Someone forced you into darkness by shooting out your street lights. The rave the other night ended with the death of Betty Strong Bull and injury to a couple of visitors to the valley from Denver."

"I'm a newcomer, and all of you have lived here longer than me. Your home is your castle. What goes on inside it is your business, and you should be able to live there in peace. We share the land around us, and it makes sense for us to watch out for one another. I think we would agree recent happenings have shattered that peace. I suspect there is much more going on I don't know about. Folks, this is your community. It's time to take it back! Take back your community," John Mark urged fist pumping his right arm.

"Yeah, and all the drunkenness from the bar spills over into our neighborhood regularly," said a resident from Indiana Avenue.

"And the prostitution at the hotel and the bed and breakfast is disgusting," said another from Indiana Avenue.

"It is a disgrace…" said a resident of County Road 403.

"A public nuisance…" said someone else from CR403.

"And all the stuff the Night Riders are doing…poor old Beatrice got hit with a beer bottle…" said Lila Longdon, a resident on the highway.

"She moved out of the hotel…" added Lila's daughter, Sarah.

"What about the hotrodding up and down highway 96 to the interstate?" asked the highwayman, another highway resident.

"We need a cop right here all the time…" said an old man who lived on Indiana Avenue.

"They don't have enough personnel to cover everything, and that's where we come in," said the lady with previous neighborhood watch experience, "and we need to organize and take back our town."

Candy seized the moment and said, "That is our purpose tonight, to set up an organization, a neighborhood watch organization, which not only builds community for all of you but also functions as the eyes and ears for the sheriff's office."

"A lot of good it will do…" someone said sarcastically, "that's where Butch McNaughton works, and we all know he is behind a lot that happens."

"Butch is no longer a deputy sheriff," Candy said.

"That's right," Lila said, "he's no longer a deputy, but he's still here. His dad made him manager of the hotel."

"That can't be too good," said Karen.

John Mark pitched in, "So our purpose is to organize a neighborhood watch, so we can take back our community. How do we do it, Deputy?"

"Everyone has a role. Specifically, you look out for your neighbor to the right and left and the three directly across the street. If you see anything suspicious, you call one another and you call your block captain. You do not engage someone doing something wrong. Place a call to your block captain or John Mark Cannikin. He will be my primary contact for now. Who will be the block captains for Indiana Avenue, one for the county road, and one for south of the convenience store?"

After captains were identified for each roadway, the Deputy continued, "Now block captains get the names and telephone numbers for those who live on your street. Block captains will need to contact those who are not here and tell them what we are doing. If they want to join our organization, give them a window sticker. All of you get one as well."

"Will signs be posted telling people we have a neighborhood watch?" asked the experienced lady, who volunteered to be captain for Indiana Avenue.

"Yes," said the deputy, "I'll order a sign to be posted on all three entrances to the town."

"Everyone will know we have organized..." the resident from a house near the church said, as the crowd clapped spontaneously.

"Say, aren't you the one who plows the highway when it snows?" said the widow, who lived next to the church.

"I'm the one. I work for the highway department, and I'll probably be busy tonight."

The deputy continued, "Remember you are our eyes and ears. We now have a telephone tree. Make note of what's going on."

"Like license plates of people who go in and out of the Asherah House?" asked the owner of the antique shop on the highway.

"Yea! The Tobacco Store runs numbers and keeps book. It's a gambling hall. Should we write down license plates of people coming and going from there, too?" said the antique store owner.

"Absolutely!" Candy said, "and be discreet."

"Something bothers me," said a retired lady, who lives next to the bridge on CR 403, which spans the creek.

"What bothers you most?" the deputy asked.

"Prostitution and gambling mean scary people are doing things in our midst!"

"Hopefully, no one here is a spy," another man said, as people looked at one another.

"Gloria Jones was murdered and her body was stuffed under the bridge next to this lady's house," one man said, as he pointed at the lady, "I'm frightened about that and the fact Sam Gelding's body was found in the creek by the church cemetery, of all places."

"Two people murdered within a block!" said Sarah.

"And Betty Strong Bull died from a fall during the rave," said a CR403 resident.

"Make that three deaths..." said an Indiana Avenue resident.

"Or three murders," said John Mark.

"Does anyone here know who organizes the raves? This isn't the first one," asked the highwayman.

"Who owns the property?" asked Karen.

"Red McNaughton," reported Sarah.

"Who owns the convenience store?" asked John Mark.

"Van Allen?" said the lady, who lives by the bridge. She volunteered to be block captain for CR403.

"Yes, and he's the one who duped a lot of people in Jericho Springs and got them in trouble!" said Sarah.

"I'm embarrassed to go to the corner store with all the indecent magazines..." admitted Karen.

"She's right! You walk in and you're hit in your face. You can't miss 'em. Is that part of neighborhood watch?" asked Lila.

"Absolutely, as a group you can notify the owner and staff about your objections," said Deputy Cotton Candy, who added, "and you may find out the manager has removed offensive magazines from the racks!"

"They're probably hidden but available from behind the clerk's counter," said the old lady who lived by the bridge.

"What I hear is a lot of pot is sold by someone who works there," said a father of high school students.

"What if we have drug dealers in our midst?" asked Sarah, "We should make notes for Deputy Candy!"

"Perfect! Good notes should include date, time, and location. Make and color of any vehicles as well as license plate numbers... and physical description," explained the deputy.

"Who owns the Tobacco Store?" asked Karen.

"I don't know," said Candy, "that would be good to find out."

"I'll bet it's either Van Allen or this Red McNaughton person," guessed the experienced woman.

"I don't think so," Lila said, "but you better be careful, if you go lookin' to find out."

"I use to own it, but I had to sell it to the bank, so I could pay my taxes. I still have the antique shop and I own the insurance building," said the man who lives across from the Asherah House.

"For now, let's just get ourselves set up," Deputy Sheriff Candy said as she recaptured the floor. "Tonight we are organized. You have a telephone tree, sticker signs to place in your windows, and road signs, announcing your organization is on the watch."

"We have a job to do too! We need to collect data and recruit those who are not here," summarized the experienced lady. "It would help if we waved whenever we see one another."

"Good point," said Candy, "check on each other, especially those who are older or alone."

"Winter is coming. We are supposed to have heavy snow tonight," said a CR403 resident.

"Put your stickers on your front windows!" said the lady with previous experience.

"Let's leave our porch lights on to show solidarity!" John Mark urged, "Let's shine some light in the darkness! Let your light shine!"

"Good idea, especially tonight when I'm out plowing snow. I may need to contact the block captains," said the highwayman.

"Please re-enforce the structure. John Mark is my contact with you. Contact him, then he will contact Lila and Sarah for the highway, Mrs. White-the lady next to the bridge for CR403, and Mrs. Calahan, she's the one who has neighborhood watch experience," said Deputy Candy.

"Deputy, when is our next meeting?" asked John Mark.

"You may want to meet together before our next scheduled meeting, which would be fine," said Candy. "Our next meeting is here the same time, the same location in one month. Let John Mark know if you want to have a block meeting, which would probably be at the block captain's home. I would try to attend at first, otherwise, I'll depend on John Mark to be there for me. Thank you for coming!"

Residents applauded the deputy, shook hands with one another, and left as a group to walk home through heavy snowfall. The Indiana Avenue group broke off first and the antique store owner switched on a flashlight, so his group could walk home together with light. All parted amicably and promised to keep in touch with one another.

Only the woman with experience knew otherwise. Since she lived in the first house on the north corner of Indiana Avenue, she had less contact with the others down the street. In accepting the role of block captain, she knew she would have to work at maintaining the effort and enthusiasm. Those from the other neighborhoods continued walking to the intersection of CR403 and the highway. The CR403 neighbors walked up the street together. One man with a flashlight made certain Mrs. White was secure in her home by the bridge, and then he walked back to his home. The highwayman walked Karen, Sarah, and Lila to the Longdon's door on the highway, before he continued home in the dark.

* * *

Earlier at the cabin, Adam sat with Ezra on the front porch after dinner and watched as the snow began falling. Of course Ezra said nothing nor could he without his tongue. Occasionally, he would grunt and nod his head, as he thoroughly enjoyed Adam's conversation. Adam, as it were, profited most from the talk. He never worried about his transparency before Ezra, and Ezra never gossiped. He would sometimes vociferously respond when Adam needed to take action or be taken down a notch or two. Such was their conversation tonight.

Adam explained his telephone call with Pastor Borden. He shared how he had taken the pastor's advice by leaving town, riding to cow camp, and ending up at the cabin. Next Adam said, "Sitting here I'm wondering about the bear and whether or not it is just being a bear or if it is the embodiment of evil. The bear wrecked havoc on those who opposed the Baal worship. I mean how coincidental is it ...the bear shows up when the bear ceremony was taking place above on the ridge. Rabbit and Pilgrim were already in Rock Creek. I sent them to the end of the Flats. Rabbit ran down to the church, while Pilgrim fired at the Asher pole. Meanwhile, I had driven to Rock Creek and made as much noise as I could. The bear was already in town. With my noise, the gunfire, and all, plus the lightening, why would a bear, a grizzly at that...why would it stop its flight to leave its mark on the church doors in the glen?"

Ezra just shrugged his shoulders and kept looking ahead.

Adam continued, "Did the bear actually know Pilgrim fired the shot that nearly split the Asher pole itself? Did the bear follow after Pilgrim and go on to Pryor when Pilgrim stopped for lunch in Wolf City? Why would a bear seek the family in Pryor and kill the parents, then purposefully follow after the children when Pilgrim showed up and rescued them? Why would a bear kill so much of my herd, the newborn, and not eat them? I mean, it should be eating a lot before hibernating. Even after the two boys were taken from cow camp to the ranch house, why would the bear seek out Pilgrim and attack him only to be deterred by my cinnamon growler? Does it make sense to you?"

Ezra shrugged his shoulders and looked at Adam and then cocked his head to the side.

"I get your point," Adam said. "How could those be coincidences? And what's a grizzly doing in Colorado? And why would a grizz climb Huerfano and leave its mark on the Live Oak after breaking off what appeared to be dead branches? I know you shot at the bear and chased it away when you ran up the hill after it. Another coincidence?"

Aroused now, Ezra cocked both arms before him and clenched his fists, then shook his head side to side.

"If the bear is truly the embodiment of evil, it must have presumed those at Blair House had helped break up the ceremony."

Ezra nodded affirmatively.

"I found no track this afternoon. Nothing...and I circled from cow camp around the mountain, up and down the slopes, in and out of the creek, and saw nothing...no deer, no birds, nothing until I came up the ridge behind your cabin. And then I realized the bear had been tracking me like I was prey like a rabbit, it followed after me and undetected at that. I'm the only one the bear has not marked."

Ezra stood up and looked toward town through heavy snowfall.

"That's what I've been wondering. If the bear is after those who disrupted the rave and it missed on me, thanks to the Tunnicliffes and you, where would it go next?"

Ezra pointed at Adam, and then southeast toward Adam's ranch.

"You mean the bear would go for Pilgrim and the boys at my ranch house, if it were evil?"

Ezra nodded.

Adam vaulted over the porch rail and ran through deep snow to the stable where he saddled his horse and whistled for his dog. Big Foot came a running and caught up with Adam as he reached the saw mill. At that point dusk had nearly snuffed out full light, and the cattle had begun to fill the mountain pasture. As Adam entered the road, he motioned to trail boss, Rabbit, to continue to move the herd toward town. Adam spurred his horse to a canter, as it seemingly flew down the canyon road toward the Blair House despite the snow, then turned right on the road, which led across Claymore Flats toward Wolf City.

With more urgency than good sense, Adam arrived at the side of his ranch house, dismounted, climbed the steps, then followed around to the east side of the porch where he met a frantic Beatrice at the front door.

"Lord God!" Bee said, "He is fast answering my prayers. How did you get here so fast?"

"Was it the bear?"

"I hope to tell you, but here, let me show you what the terrible beast did to the house," Beatrice said, as she took Adam by the hand and dragged him toward the front of the porch. "Look here, where he practically shredded these posts!"

Gasping, Adam had been startled by the depth and width of the marks. He said, "This is worse than all the others. Did he try to get into the ranch house?"

"No...

"Adam, is it you? The bear is after the boys," Pilgrim said, as he hopped across the porch with his leg in a cast to Adam. Both examined claw marks on main beams, which brace both the porch and cross beams to the house.

"What do you mean? You said the bear was after the boys," asked Adam.

"Just that! The boys rode in from the line shack with a wrangler when it started snowing," Pilgrim said, "and they heard the bear clawing and growling. They'd seen what the bear can do!"

"And the bear had chased them before."

"I told them to leave, to ride east for the end of the mesa, then to leave their horses and go to the hotel where there are people who can help them," said Pilgrim.

"They wasted no time leaving. I just got off the phone talking with Janine. They had just finished group training and thanked me for the warning. Someone will go to the hotel to help the boys. Others there will walk the perimeter of the property in case the bear changes direction," reported Beatrice.

"What head start does it have?" asked Adam.

"About ten minutes, Adam, the beast covers ground," urged Pilgrim. "You be careful, that bear wants you, too!"

Like the Lone Ranger would, Adam whistled for his horse. Silver came around to the front of the porch. Adam leaped from the porch into the saddle and rode off in the direction of Rock Creek through the snow.

"There he goes, again, to rescue someone in distress," Beatrice cheered, "Adam Claymore, the Lone Ranger."

Pilgrim added with a smile, "Hi yo, Silver! Oh my, he's gonna' feel that in the mornin'."

*** 

Earlier the Rock Creek residents left the neighborhood watch meeting, while John Mark and Candy straightened the meeting room at the senior center. The respective groups walked home together. After Karen, Lila, and Sarah parted company with the group heading for their homes on CR403, Lila crossed the highway to report for work as night clerk at the hotel. The cook and waitress knew she had arranged to be late, so she could attend a meeting at the senior center. Lila knew Butch would be watching her.

Sarah and Karen watched the highwayman walk down the road toward his house. Although he seemed nice enough, both women wondered where he had been. Karen hadn't seen him in church, and Sarah didn't recognize him as one who ate at the restaurant or drank in the hotel bar. Apparently, he just kept to himself. They concluded unless he was a regular at the bed and breakfast or frequented the Tobacco Store, he was probably a good guy.

After Karen and Sarah watched the man walk down his driveway, the women began walking toward the church. The snowfall increased, but Sarah wanted to see the valley from a different point of view. They walked through the churchyard, past the cemetery, across the footbridge, and up the path to the top of the mesa. As Karen led the way, she began asking Sarah about herself. Sarah revealed she and her mother had never attended church until now, and her mother had grown up in the valley and had never married. She explained both had only worked at the hotel and both had participated in a rave, which accounted for Sarah's own birth and her pregnancy. Snowfall increased rapidly and made the climb more difficult.

At the top of the trail, Karen said, as they both laughed, "This will be a short visit here. Good thing we have our jackets. Over here, come sit in the snow on the bench. We'll be able to look out over the entire town."

"I managed to have gloves in my pockets. I've always wondered what it would be like to see the valley from up here!" Sarah said, as she paused and turned where she could see the valley below, "It is so beautiful!"

"Down below on the left are Adam's orchards. Of course, across the road are both hogbacks, which circle the town...we can see everything from this bench that Adam built for his wife Mary."

"Karen, she was a wonderful woman and apparently a great wife to Mr. Claymore. I've heard and seen the two of you together. You make a good looking couple. Any hope there?"

"I think so," said Karen, "but Mary will be tough to follow."

"Indeed! You're kinda spunky though."

Sitting down close together, they huddled as the chill proved the temperature had dropped. They sat silently observing the town below, while watching where newly lit fires billowed smoke out of chimney stacks at the houses. While Karen looked west to where Blair House would be, she wondered about the team building activities she had given up to be here on the bench with Sarah. Somewhat awestruck, Sarah looked below and smiled at the scene.

"Look there," Karen said, "on Indiana Avenue. We can see several porch lights!"

"Which is the only light over there. Normally, street lights would be on by now. Look how the light from the hotel makes a difference, but look over on the ridge. There's a man doing something near where the Asher pole used to be," reported Sarah.

Turning to where Karen could see, she squinted her eyes, looked through the snowfall toward the scene that Sarah had described, and said, "Looks like the Night Rider boys did us a good turn."

"What I hear at the café is it wasn't them, who set the fire, and they are spooked!" Sarah said with a laugh, "It's good to watch the intimidators be intimidated!"

"They're bullies!"

"More than you would guess. I've lived here all my life, Karen."

"What do you suppose happens over there?" asked Karen.

"That's where I got pregnant. They said it was a dramatic production, part of the rave, a cultural experience," Sarah said, "but really I'm with child because I was part of the ceremony."

"And you were going to end the pregnancy."

"Yes, but you helped me see things differently when you said God knows and it's not the baby's fault."

"Should I apologize?" asked Karen.

"Heavens, no, if God wants my baby to be born then it will be. I wouldn't be here if my mother had done what I planned to do. She attended a rave or something and had me too!"

"So this has been going on for a long time...have they always been on the ridge?"

"The ceremony has been happening for a long time, in one form or another, or so my mother says, but not publicly through a rave, but always with impunity," said Sarah.

"No one was ever caught, or turned in to the police?"

"Karen, not that I know of...I don't exactly know why, but my mother somehow wanted to have a relationship with whoever my father is or was," said Sarah, "and I don't look like anyone I've ever seen."

"And you were raised without a father by a single mom..."

"She did a good job..."

"No doubt...I'm not judging her...it's just that when there is no father, it is hard for a child to imagine God as a loving father or that

God will never leave or forsake us...I realize how fortunate I am," said Karen.

Pointing toward the ridge, Sarah said, "Look there, Karen, whoever he is...and he is a big one...he has finished what he was doing and now somehow he's climbing down from the ridge to the trees."

Both women rose to their feet and watched, as the man slipped tools between himself and a backpack, then rapidly descended the rope ladder to the snow covered ground below. They moved closer to the edge of the mesa to watch what he did next. They lost sight of him as he remained hidden in the trees east of the Valley Highway. They watched as he quickly crossed the highway and disappeared again in the birch grove near the church. He reappeared on the church lane but without the tools or backpack. Once he passed before the front of the church, they lost sight of him walking northward.

"Watch to see if new smoke comes from one of the houses."

"The second house belongs to the highwayman, the third is Adam's, and the forth is mine. Can't be the forth since Mom went to work."

Moments later, "See the smoke...the third one...Adam's house..."

"But we left John Mark at the senior center with Deputy Candy... Adam's big but not that big...besides he left earlier today hunting for the grizzly bear..."

Snowfall intensified, and from behind, the women heard horses whinnying, as the boys slowed the cantering steeds to halt at the bench where Karen and Sarah stood watching in snow up to their mid-calves. The older said, "Are you Miss Karen, Adam's friend...the one who lives at the Blair House?"

He turned and looked behind himself and quickly dismounted as did his younger brother, who said, "There he is, the bear, he's after us."

Both women moved to where they could see around the horses, as the boys slapped the haunch of each horse, which galloped away to escape the bear. Without waiting, the boys fled down the snow covered trail from the mesa. In their descent both tumbled down the path, gained scratches and scrapes, before reaching the bottom.

Stunned, Karen and Sarah watched how quickly the roaring bear had been covering the snow covered ground from the stand of trees to themselves. They screamed and fled, as Sarah slipped and struck the end of the bench. She fell, over the side of the mesa, onto the trail and rolled downhill, not stopping until she slammed against a boulder next to the footpath. Karen had been last to descend the path more familiar to her than Sarah or the boys. She caught up with Sarah quickly as did the boys, who had stopped at the bottom of the trail.

Knocked out with a gash above her forehead, Sarah attempted to rise to her feet and did with the boys help. She grabbed her stomach, and said, "Karen, the baby…"

"Come on, boys, let's get her down from here…but you," Karen said to the younger boy, "you go to the hotel, ask, no tell the clerk to call for an ambulance, now!"

Hearing the women's screams and the bear's roar, the man, who had entered Adam's house, emerged from it, as the highwayman came out from his house just south of Adam's. Both bent on helping the women, the highwayman intercepted the boy and took him into his home to call for an ambulance. The other, cloaked in a dark cowl, raced through the snow to the end of the footbridge by the cemetery where he placed a long sheathed instrument on the bridge rail and opened a large can of fluid. Quickly, he brushed away snow with both hands and feet, as he generously poured fluid from the can on each top rail, on the ends of eight floor boards, and then on the end posts and along the final plank of the bridge.

Within seconds, the man in the cowl met Karen, Sarah, and the older brother near the end of the footpath. He scooped Sarah in his arms and carried her like a limp doll to the middle of the footbridge. Karen and the boy caught up with him, while Deputy Candy and John Mark arrived in her cruiser and parked before the pastor's door of the church. The younger boy called for an ambulance in the highwayman's house, and the man helped the boy tell their location, while the bear lumbered mid-way down the footpath.

Hurrying around the church corner, John Mark paused near the cemetery fence and motioned for Candy to stop, "Watch," he said, "this will be one for the ages."

"But the bear…" the deputy said.

"Just watch a moment…trust me," urged John Mark, "the man and his brothers have done this before."

At the top of the mesa stood Adam, who enthralled in the moment, also watched as Karen, Sarah, and the boy moved to the far end of the footbridge. Karen caught a glimpse of Adam, where he stood, and waved to him. Catching her eye, he whistled for his horse, and leading it by the reins, Adam began his descent with his rifle in hand, while heavy snowfall increased and the footpath became more treacherous.

The bear rushed toward the end of the footbridge, and the man in the cowl struck a match and lit the fluid he had poured out of the can. With a startling flash, the fluid ignited and lit up the end of the bridge. The man grabbed his scabbard, and as the grizzly stood on hind legs and roared, the man roared mightily, threw off his cowl, and stepped forward, while unsheathing his long sword. The bear roared again and charged, but stopped short of the flames, while the man began swirling his sword back and forth, round and round overhead, until it made a sound as if it were singing. Confused, the bear rose again on its hind legs, and as its head followed the motion of the sword, the pitch of the sword's sound became higher and sharper like that of a Scottish fife. Niall whistled as sharply as the sword's song. As he rotated the sword in one hand from side to side, he held the can of fluid in the other and squeezed it. He squeezed the can so hard it sprayed a steady stream of fluid to soak the bear's foot and hind leg, and then Niall tapered the stream to the burn line where it ignited and set the bear's foot and leg on fire.

Watching the fire, Candy said, "Well, there goes the area I wanted to check for more prints."

Candy would not be held back any longer. Drawing her service revolver, she climbed the tree at the church end of the bridge. John Mark helped Karen and Sarah as well as the older brother inside the church. Around the corner came John Mark's neighbor and the younger brother who watched spell bound. As John Mark returned to the footbridge where Candy perched in the tree with gun drawn, Adam reached a midway point down the trail from the top of the mesa where Sarah had fallen. He drew his rifle from its scabbard and fired at the bear, as Candy also pulled the trigger of her thirty-eight caliber pistol.

Hit by bullets from above and before him and his foot and leg on fire, the bear came out of the trance the man with the sword had put him in. The bear turned and ran on all fours while bleeding from its shoulder and reeling from the fire on its leg. As Adam reached the end of the trail from the top of the mesa, Karen sprinted toward him through the snow from the church. She passed Deputy Candy as she descended the tree and stood on the bridge rail. Niall looked first at Adam and Karen with a scowl and then the same at Candy. He sheathed his sword, put on his cowl, and left in disgust before anyone could thank him.

John's neighbor attempted to stop him and said, "Thank you!"

"Aye, I would have killed," the man said in his Gaelic accent, "but it's just as well. My brother has that assignment."

Their reunion made with a brief kiss, Adam climbed back-in-the-saddle again and said to Karen, "I hope to finish this..."

"Adam, I don't think you should follow the bear in this snow," said Karen, as she noted Adam's look of disbelief, "but if you must go, please be safe."

Adam turned Silver and followed the bear's tracks through the snow. Within minutes those at the church heard one shot from Adam's rifle and then no more. The snow now blanketed the tracks of both bear and horse. Karen asked John Mark to go with her to find Adam, while Deputy Candy stayed with the boys and waited for the ambulance to transport Sarah to the hospital. Sarah told Karen to go find Adam. John Mark insisted on driving Adam's car to where the road to Wolf City intersected with CR 403. He told Karen if Adam killed the bear, he would probably ride home to his ranch, but if the bear got Adam, he would be laying in the snow, and the bear would likely cross the road and head west. If that were the case, the bear's tracks likely would not yet be covered. Karen agreed judging the time between Adam's leaving and the rifle shot had been long enough for Adam to cover significant distance away from the footbridge. Either way it was a toss of the coin, so they prayed for direction.

John Mark retrieved the Winchester from Adam's house, while Karen started Adam's old Chevy. Together, they planned to ride to the intersection of CR 403 and the road to Wolf City. The ambulance arrived to rush Sarah to the hospital with Lila as a passenger. Also,

Big Foot arrived and stood against the driver's window of Karen's car. He barked, hopped down from the window and moved toward the church, then returned to the car and jumped again at the window.

Karen told John Mark to drive Adam's car to the road to Wolf City, while she would follow Big Foot to Adam. John Mark began to protest, but Karen said she would get help to go with her. She said she had to do this. Out from Adam's house came the man who held the singing sword.

"You need my help?"

"Please, the bear may have gotten Adam Claymore, whose house you just came from. He is a good man. I fear he is in trouble, if not dead. Who are you?" Karen asked.

The man bowed and knelt before Karen with his sword drawn and held upright against his forehead, and then he said, "My lady, I am your servant, Niall Tunnicliffe. The bear will be gone, but we must go now! Follow me and try to keep up."

Snowfall increased, and while no one watched them, the boys from Pryor slipped away.

Watching Niall, Karen thought, rather dramatic but mystifying. She ran after Niall alongside a row of trees in the orchard toward the road leading to Wolf City. John Mark drove Adam's car to the intersection. Once there, he turned left on the Wolf City road to avoid the herd coming from the mountain pasture. Rabbit led the herd through the intersection at Main Street and down CR403 toward the pasture where he would open a make shift gate for cattle to pass through. John parked Adam's car on the side of the road and looked for bear tracks. He found the bear's trail, but snowfall increased, and the herd blocked a return to the county road.

Meanwhile, Big Foot led Niall and Karen to Adam, who lay face down in the snow beside his horse, Silver. Turning Adam over, Niall listened for a heartbeat and finding one, he said Adam lives. Hearing the herd, Niall wrapped Adam's belt around his left arm near the shoulder as a tourniquet. Quickly, Niall picked up Adam and carried him, as he walked briskly back to Rock Creek.

"Run for the church, Miss Karen, we are closer to the church than back to the car. We won't get the car through the herd in time. Call for another ambulance, if we are to save his life or his arm. He will never be a pretty man. Run! Run quickly!"

Snowfall increased!

Sobbing, Karen ran for the church, and when arriving, she stopped at the door to the pastor's office, broke the window, reached through to open the door, switched on the office light, and called for another ambulance to the same location. She told the woman who answered the call, "Hurry again to the church in Rock Creek! The bear got Adam Claymore. He is badly hurt! Hurry!"

"Adam Claymore's hurt," the woman repeated to her fellow workers. "Send another truck to the church in Rock Creek! Everybody pray for Adam!"

And they did, while snowfall increased!!

The ambulance arrived shortly after Niall had carried Adam to the church and into the pastor's office. Adam awakened to Karen's tears streaming down her face. The medic completed an initial examination and ordered a stretcher to carry him to the ambulance. It wouldn't be necessary, as Niall picked up Adam and carried him inside the ambulance and placed him on the stretcher. Karen jumped into the ambulance, and when the medic said she could not go with them, she raised her fist and told him that she would not leave and they had better get going. Niall smiled with admiration and stepped off the ambulance.

Before the ambulance door closed, Niall bowed again to Karen and said, "My lady, his life is saved for you and our Lord's work!"

Smiling back at him, Karen thought he certainly had a flare for the dramatic. The roads became slick, but the highwayman led the ambulance as his highway truck plowed a path all the way to the hospital.

And the snowfall increased again!!!

Unfortunately for the humans, the grizzly had fled from the horse it killed and the man it partially shredded but had not killed. When the snowfall kept increasing, the bear had crossed the road to Wolf City. It made its way west on the road leading into the mountain valley. As it climbed, it diverted its assent above little Huerfano when it heard the approaching herd. The grizzly turned back toward Blair House once again, but lumbered down the northwest side of the butte and ambled northward. Coming upon the opened trap door to the tunnel, the bear literally looked around to see if anything had seen its arrival. Neither seeing nor smelling man through its dog bitten nose, the bear caught snow with its tongue before passing through the opened door and settling down for a long winter's sleep and much needed healing.

***

Inside the Blair House, as Izzy's team had finished the group building activities, he asked them, "Today, when the visitors toured our house and the grounds, someone opened the trap door to the house...did any of you see it open and closed it?"

Misty raised her hand and said, "I know where it is. I saw it opened. I'll go close it."

"Do you have boots? The snow is really coming down!" asked Jill.

"No, but I'll be all right. I've never been out in the snow before!" Misty said with glee.

Entering the front door, Deputy Cotton Candy arrived with the boys from Pryor in tow. Detective Caleb Jones followed her inside. All four brushed the snow off their coats and stomped their boots on the throw rug at the front door.

"We've had quite a night!" said Caleb, "For the better part of an hour, I was stuck behind Deputy Candy, as we had to wait for a herd of cattle to get off the road."

"You've only heard half of it," said Candy, "and I can't stay long enough to tell you the whole story! Let me just tell you quickly."

"Tell them what you can..." Caleb advised.

"Sarah rolled down the mountain and fell against a boulder. Karen's at the hospital with Adam. He and I shot the bear, but it got away... it was on fire...there's a fourth Tunnicliffe, and he is magnificent! He had control of the bear with his sword. Adam chased the bear, but it killed his horse and hurt him badly. John Mark is somewhere with Adam's car. And I couldn't find the boys from Pryor!"

"How do the boys fit into this?" Jill asked.

Candy reported, "The bear followed them across Claymore Flats where they met Sarah and Karen at Mary's bench. The bear chased all of them down to the church. Niall literally stopped the bear at the bridge. During the fracas, the boys fled for town. I searched for the boys in town and found them hiding in a room at the hotel. Somehow they managed to enter a locked room. Together we watched the comings and goings between the hotel and the Asherah House. It proved to be very informative. I bought them dinner, so you may just want to send them to bed somewhere. Look folks, there's more snow out there than I can remember. I've got to be on my way before I get snowed in. The boys can help fill in the details. They have had quite a day!"

As Candy closed the front door, the Blair House team looked dumbfounded at one another, but Caleb offered, "Did I hear you need to close the tunnel door? I'll go with one of you ladies, if you like…"

"Great!" said Misty, as she scampered to Caleb, and taking him by the arm, she led him out the front door, around the first floor porch, and up the slope toward the trap door.

Once there, Caleb amply closed the snow laden door with the grizzly asleep inside. He looked up at the falling snow and said to Misty, "I love the snow. It is like Jesus."

"How so?" Misty asked.

"When we accept Jesus as our savior, his righteousness covers all our sin. God sees us clean, white as snow, through Jesus!"

Misty declared, "Covered like snow, my sin is forgiven!"

Together and holding hands, they looked around and saw even their foot prints had been filled in with snow, as had been the tracks of the great bear.

"Snow melts and no longer covers the ground. Here's where the metaphor ends, except the snow eventually melts, and like our sins, the snow has been washed away," said Caleb.

"Does it mean the covering over me doesn't go away?"

"Yes," Caleb replied to her, realizing the importance of her question, "once saved, always saved…since you accepted Christ as your Savior…"

"And Lord…Savior and Lord?"

"Yes again Misty, both your savior and lord, and your sins will not be revisited. They're removed, taken away, as far as the east is from the west," Caleb said, as he looked down at Misty and smiled at her.

Misty trembled and wept…as her friend Caleb walked with her back to her home.

# Snow, New Venues, and the Cross

## Chapter 15

*"The Lord your God, as he promised you, will put the terror and fear of you on the whole land, wherever you go."*                    *Deuteronomy 11:25b*

S now fell heavily the following week. Meteorologists reported record breaking totals, as snow fall records were broken not only for Rock Creek Valley but also to the south on Claymore Flats, south through Rock Creek Canyon to Quail Point, west in the mountains around Wolf City and Pryor to Mt. Huajatolla. Residents in Jericho Springs and Rock Creek measured snow by the foot with long handled shovels, as they stepped outside their homes and lodged shovels in snowdrifts. Not only had heavy snow fallen but also the temperature steadily declined to single digits and lower. Fortunately, winds remained calm.

Basically, since snowfall rendered roadways impassable, community life took a prolonged pause. Motels and hotels filled to full capacity, and only a skeletal crew staffed health facilities. Snowplow drivers struggled to keep the Valley Highway opened from Ridge View to Quail Point. County roads had just begun to be plowed, but side streets remained unaddressed. Schools closed both Tuesday and Wednesday, as neither staff nor students could get to schools by sidewalks or roadways. Parents could not drive children to school, nor could school buses reach rural feeder areas. Delivery services to local businesses ended.

Traffic on the roads and highways depleted to only the lonely high-wayman, who lived next to Adam's Rock Creek house. Plowing snow into the creek and barrow ditches alongside roads, the highwayman kept clearing a single path both ways through Rock Creek Canyon to Quail Point. He would turn around and head back through the canyon all the way north on the Valley Highway to Colorado 96. At ninety-six, he turned east to Interstate 25 and drove back again. Once back to the Valley Highway, he turned north again and continued to Ridge View. He plowed through downtown to the Interstate and back to the north end of CR 403. At the county road, he had been ordered to turn right and proceed to the utility lineman's house. At the Browning's home, the plowman made a turn around and returned to the Valley Highway, so Rob, one of the valley's utility linemen, could report to and from work in Ridge View easily. The highwayman returned to his route and began to push and pile snow where he could. In Rock Creek he pushed snow into the marsh east of the highway by the hog-back and west of the highway onto the old football field. At the other end of town, he piled snow at the south end of the hotel parking lot. Since only state highways had been plowed, regular community life stopped, until the highwayman could address county roads.

Local workers mostly enjoyed staying home. Teachers called the school district offices to notify the automated system of their absences. Karen received a 4:00 a.m. call to schedule her for a sub-bing assignment to teach eighth grade social studies at the high school. The assignment had been cancelled an hour later by an auto-mated call that announced school closures. Teachers living at the Blair House, Janine, Karen, and Jill celebrated in the kitchen with Hannah and Misty over hot chocolate before going back to bed. Caleb the detective, Jerry the pizzeria manager, Mike the convenience store clerk, Tim the waiter, and Morris the Trailways bus driver stoked fires throughout the house and restocked wood at each fireplace, while reviewing the Denver Bronco 23-14 loss to the New England Patriots compared to last year's 45-10 victory. Finding more to brag about, Caleb switched the conversation to talk baseball and how the Denver Bears had won the West Division of the American Association 1980 season with a 92-44 won-loss record. Izzy crossed the street and checked on Rachael. Kat Bond trudged through the snow to help

Kip Powell prepare new book orders and packages for his mail order customers.

Some local workers managed to get to their workplaces. Since Ezra had run a power cord to his truck and placed a light bulb under the hood, he had no trouble starting his four wheel drive truck. He attached a plow blade to the front end and drove toward his cabin only to find his road impassable; however, much to his delight he watched the Tunnicliffe brothers at work. They had already set bales of hay for his horses inside the barns and had filled pans of cracked corn for his chickens and ducks in their coops. Footsteps across the road led to where they had tossed two bales of hay for strays from Adam's herd. As a result, Ezra backed down the road to the hairpin turn and turned around. He began a full day's work helping the high-wayman by plowing the mountain road to the intersection with Main Street.

Systematically, he plowed snow off Main Street down to Bustos Family Mexican Restaurant and began clearing side streets to the high school. Once the highwayman plowed County Road 403, Ken Bond stocked copies of the Tuesday, Wednesday, and Thursday editions of the *Denver Post* and *Rocky Mountain News* in newspaper boxes along the highways and county roads. Later in the day, Ken drove to Ridge View and picked up the weekly Wednesday edition of *The Out Cry* from its publisher. He filled business boxes with the current edition and delivered copies to the households he could reach. Mike Crowfoot walked to the convenience store at the south end of Main Street and opened the store for business. He was in time to give a free cup of fresh coffee to both Ezra and the highwayman, as they passed by with their plows.

Blair House friends went about their duties. Deputy Candy spent most of her time with other deputies at the sheriff's office catching up on paperwork as did most of the other staff. Across the street from Blair House, Rachael made quart jars of her recipe to share with friends and relatives. Beatrice tended to Pilgrim at Adam's ranch, while Karen caught a ride to the hospital to visit Adam. She rode behind Rabbit on the back of a snow mobile. Wranglers at the Claymore Ranch either rode to the line shack to bring back those who had been fixing fences, scattered bales of hay for the herd on the Flats, or headed for the Jericho Springs pasture to feed the cattle. Some rode toboggans, others skied, and one drove a ski-doo, while one attached a blade to the ranch pickup truck and pushed snow to the edges of the yard and entrance to the ranch, before plowing a trail on the road to the pasture. Once wranglers hauled hay bales to the pasture, they opened fence and used the skidoo to carry bales throughout the pasture. Along the way they searched for cattle trapped in the deep snow. Theirs would be a long sad day as some cattle had been trapped in deep snow and froze to death. Most managed to gather around the hogbacks where they found shelter on the north side. Once the highwayman cleared the highway and county roads, he shoved snow to the end of Indiana Avenue. John Mark and Niall Tunnicliffe cleared the sidewalks of houses along the highway, CR403, and Indiana Avenue.

By Thursday afternoon most residents had begun to dig out of their driveways only to discover side streets had yet to be cleared. A team of men and women from Blair House shoveled their neighbors' sidewalks and left a flyer, which said compliments of your friends at the Blair House. By early Friday morning when intermittent snowfall ended, the highwayman had successfully cleared highways and county roads including the road across Claymore Flats. Finally, he was able to focus on side streets and roads. Rock Creek with only Indiana Avenue had been easy to maintain. Jericho Springs proved more difficult for him, while another truck, which had been assigned to maintain Interstate 25, cleared side streets in Ridge View and country roads to the north and west. Thanks to Ezra's help, the highwayman finished Jericho Springs by the end of Friday.

\*\*\*

Both the bear in the Blair House tunnel and the sapling on the ridge survived the storm and cold. When planting, Niall had protected the sapling by wrapping the trunk with bio-degradable covering and had layered absorbent under the wood chip mixture. With a projected twenty-five year life span, the old boar had suffered multiple wounds while roaming the hostile environment amongst man in the Rock Creek Valley. The man in Pryor had hoed him. The woman had stabbed him in his chest savagely with a butcher knife. Later he killed the cinnamon colored dog that had bitten him on his snout, and he had gotten even with a man who had sent a rifle shot through his nose below what would be like sinus cavities. He had marked his territory at the old white building by the mouth of the canyon. After hearing a gunshot, he ran across the creek to the butte where he had marked the tree and tried to sleep on the big branches. An older, smaller man had hit him in his rump with multiple painful pellets.

Later the bear enjoyed getting away from the big men who chased after him at the cabin. When he had marked his territory on the ranch house, he ran after the two boys who had eluded him earlier in Pryor. Scary had been the strange man who brought fire to the bridge by the strawberries and raspberries that he loved. A woman had shot at him from the tree at the end of the bridge as had the man pulling a horse down from the mesa. The grizz had run pigeon-toed for awhile in a short burst of up to thirty miles per hour, while slipping occasionally in the snow before slowing to an amble through the orchard grounds. He had looked for the side of the hill where he had begun to dig out a den for the winter, but could not find it in the deep snow. He had enough, when in the midst of the blizzard in the orchard, he heard the man on horseback chasing after him with rifle ready to fire. The old boar rose up full height and straightened his humped back to more than eight feet. As he elevated his full length, he confronted the horse and then the man. With razor sharp claws and bone crunching jaws, he lit into the horse, which he had brought down and killed with one blow. He missed the man and saddle by inches. Biting into the horse's neck and crushing vertebrae, he landed a glancing swat across the man's head and shoulder, as the man discharged his Winchester. Horse dead and the man named Adam laying still, the bear had turned and resumed his flight toward the mountains.

Fleeing from the man in front of the herd, he climbed down from the butte and entered the tunnel opening minutes before the arrival of a woman and a man, who closed the tunnel door. Feeling warmth from further down the tunnel, the boar inched closer to its source until tunnel walls narrowed. Impervious to what happened around them, both tree and bear should survive the winter until the sapling

311

awakened with spring, while the old boar laid down to hibernate and to heal for over two hundred days.

\*\*\*

At sunrise Friday, life normalized in the valley and beyond. Ken Bond drove from Jericho Springs toward the Interstate outside Ridge View to meet the morning newspaper delivery truck. He knew his route would be difficult to complete. Since he had to deliver back issues to most of his customers, it would take longer to finish his route in a timely manner. Two passengers rode with him. Tim McNaughton rode shotgun in the front, while Morris Goodenough sat in the middle of the bench seat behind them. Ken left Tim at the Cozy Corner Café in time to open for business, while Morris Goodenough rode on with him to the bus terminal arriving in time for an assignment. All three benefited from their fellowship together.

Tim greeted everyone as they entered the café. Customers who intended to interact with others usually sat at an open area with tables. Others, wanting to speak more privately or not at all, sat at the counter or gathered in the booths that lined the front wall. Today, almost everyone suffered from cabin fever, so they sat in the open area with tables. Members of the McNaughton Corporation sat there, as well as unaffiliated Night Riders. People, who had prayed at intersections with Priscilla and Aquila, sat there, as they hoped to share their experience with others. Some had been at the café when Tim shared about Jesus and Adam Claymore led them in prayer. They hungered for more! The corporate members were outnumbered.

One man started the conversation asking, "Hey, some of you were here when Tim shared what he said was the Ambassador's Toolkit. Do you remember seeing the two men who blocked the door?"

Several said, "Yes!"

"What about it?" said another, "I wasn't here..."

"Has anyone seen them?

"I heard Lila, you know, the night clerk at the hotel in Rock Creek... she said she might have seen them working on the garage behind Adam's house."

"Could be, but I know we delivered some lumber and paint there to John Mark. He stays there and is restoring what was once Mary Claymore's house," said Irv Moss, employee at Red's hardware and lumber company. "I didn't see evidence of anyone else."

"You know what, another real big guy, wearing a brown bear skin coat...he got off the bus in Rock Creek at the hotel."

"Yes, and he had several scars across his head and face. He must have been over six feet five, bald, and ugly. Weighed three hundred pounds or more and big as a door frame," a postal worker from Rock Creek said.

"Anyone else?" the first man asked.

"Yup, I seen 'em in a yellow jeep and more than once when I stopped at the convenience store."

"What have you been smokin'?" asked another, which caused much laughter.

"Tim, have you seen them? Say, where you living these days?" asked a man stirring the pot of potential trouble.

"No... not at all today," Tim replied.

"I didn't know you had moved, Tim, where are you living?" asked one of those in the McNaughton Corporation.

"I joined those restoring Blair House and moved in with them. They're good people," Tim replied.

Many in the room turned to face Tim, and one asked with a scowl, "What's going on there?"

"Well, I'll tell you. I get to live there rent free..."

"You'll need it if you lose your job here..."

Like minded people came to Tim's aid, "How many of you lived here when Paul and Lydia Blair were alive? How many of you remember what Mary Claymore said she wished would happen in the valley?"

Many raised their hands and one responded about Mary with a tear in his eye, "I remember what that precious young woman would say. She worked for it too! She hoped we would all get along with one another and that we would watch out for one another."

"When the Blair's were alive, it was like the Live Oak tree shaded us all...not literally, but things were good and people were kind, at least those who knew the Blair's...at least for awhile."

313

"Blair House, the building was magnificent and the pool on top of little orphan, Huerfano, was warm and refreshing to bathe in."

"Blair House was like a spiritual oasis…"

Tim interrupted, "Hold right there! Both of you just restated what's going on there. We are trying to restore Blair House as a place of beauty, both physically and spiritually, an oasis in the midst of dry ground, a desert."

"How's that happen?" asked a customer.

"Well, for one, I get free rent in exchange for working a minimum number of hours cleaning the insides, replacing boards, painting rooms…those kinds of things. I'm also studying the Bible and trying to apply it."

\*\*\*

Ken Bond arrived with newspapers to fill a box near the front door, which was soon accessed by many. Removing coins from the box, he knew his profit would be minimal.

"Say, Ken," said Red McNaughton, "do you live at the Blair House?"

Ken suspected Red may have ordered the torching of the trailer his family had lived in, so he studied Red before answering him, "No, I live with my family in the house where Janine and Jill use to live. You know it, just like you know the trailer I used to live in. It was next to your land on the ridge. Why do you ask where I live?"

"Oh nothing much…we were just asking about whether or not anyone had seen some rather large men in a yellow jeep. Do you know anything about them?" asked Red.

"What I've seen are the ruins of the Asher Pole and the ceremonial table used for Baal worship during the rave. They have been torched by someone. Now they're covered with snow…Red…Did you hear the Colorado Bureau of Investigation searched Sheriff Bailey's office and home after the assault on the Blair House?" Ken replied. "Red, what do you know about it?"

Red stammered…

Ken continued, "Here's another one, Red, do you know where your partner is, the one who went into the mountains for you to take care of both your herds, while you remained here?"

Red rose from his seat sensing the challenge, as Ken turned to the crowd and continued, "Like Red, all of you can read about both of these in this issue of the weekly newspaper," Ken said, and continued, "Adam is in the hospital. He's alive, but he encountered the bear that has been plaguing Red's mountain herd. You will want to read how a man, a newcomer, rescued Adam and carried him to safety. You'll want to read the editors comments about what's been going on in the valley… about the rave and human trafficking. You'll want to read Penelope Quick's letter to the editor. And…sadly, you'll read the notice of Sam Gelding's obituary as well as an announcement that Janine and Izzy's wedding is postponed until further notice. Read about these things and more in your weekly newspaper. It's available right there in the newspaper box. Oh, by the way, there is an ad where CBI invites information about the rave and Betty Strong Bull's death."

"Who's CBI?" asked one oldtimer.

"Like the FBI?" replied a cop show enthusiast.

The oldtimer said, "Then it must be serious business…anybody know anything?"

While many hurried to purchase a copy, Ken stood by so no one would hold open the door to the newspaper machine for others to steal a copy. Ken said, as Red put a quarter in the coin box, "Sorry, Red, I meant no real offense, I'm just trying to sell newspapers."

"Right!" Red replied suspiciously, as his mind churned with thoughts of how all newcomers had been trouble and still needed to be eliminated.

Turning back to the crowd again, Ken informed them, "I'll be filling in for Adam at the Rock Creek Church starting Sunday. I'm preaching a series of messages on eternal rewards and wages," and then looking directly at Red, Ken said, "All of you are welcomed. The light is still on at the little Church in the Glen."

"If you can find a place to park," Tim said, as his girl friend, Heather Ross, sashayed into the diner, strutted over to the juke box, put a quarter in the record machine, selected her first song, and began dancing seductively for Tim and the rest of the men.

Interesting timing both Ken and Tim thought, as Ken made his exit.

315

\*\*\*

As in Ridge View, customers arrived early in Rock Creek at the Stage Stop Hotel. Although many paused for breakfast before heading into the Rock Creek Canyon, locals had planned an early morning neighborhood watch meeting at the restaurant. Surprised, new hotel manager, Butch McNaughton, watched as the group occupied two tables. Having been self-relegated to manage this morning from the kitchen, he learned his new trade on-the-job with the same manly bravado, which he had used as a deputy sheriff. Patrons soon loved the portions he served, but his cooking was a work in progress. Even Butch accepted the humor of his situation, as did his co-workers, including old Lila Longdon at the front desk and her daughter Sarah, who waited tables.

Ken Bond soon arrived to service the newspaper boxes in the hotel lobby where he greeted Lila. Supplying both the *Denver Post* box with old afternoon newspapers and the *Rocky Mountain News* with new editions, he also placed Wednesday's copy of *The Out Cry* in the weekly's box. Knowing the prevalence of newspaper theft, he emptied a meager number of coins from all three boxes. Before leaving, Ken gave Lila copies of outdated *Rocky Mountain News* editions for her to distribute at the tables in the restaurant.

Lila set at least one copy on each table and announced, "These are free, but if you want today's paper, put your quarter in the coin box for each paper you take. The man's got to make a living. If you're too cheap to buy one, ask to borrow a copy from someone else."

After several laughed and Butch glared at Lila, she continued as new arrivals filled seats, "I just scanned the weekly headlines. Sam Gelding's obituary toward the middle, but you'll want to read the letters to the editor, one letter thanks someone named Penelope Quick for the kind letters she's been mailing to people. Hmmm... check out today's editorial about the misbehavior of many of the valley's so called upstanding citizens," she paused and looked toward Butch, as he peered over the counter from the kitchen.

"What else, Lila?"

"There's an article about the bear that clawed the church door during the rave. Did you it nearly killed Adam Claymore? You know he's still in the hospital in Ridge View," she reported.

Wiping his hands with his apron, Butch came out from behind the counter and into the dining room, and asked, "Did you say Adam's in the hospital nearly dead?"

"Yes, I did Butch. Your uncle, one of the finest men in the valley, nearly died after trying to protect this town from the grizzly bear."

Genuinely concerned, Butch said, "I didn't know..."

"Hey, there's a letter here from someone who participated in the attack on Blair House. He thanked folks at the Blair House for their grace and mercy. Seems the attackers were fed pizza and soda pop!" Lila laughed and continued, "What do you make of that? Anyway go buy your own copy, but put a quarter in the slot." Then she paused again, "There's an article about the folks at these two tables here. We now have a neighborhood watch in Rock Creek!"

Laughing one patron asked, "What kinda watch?"

The lady with previous experience rose from the table to speak, as John Mark entered the dining room and joined her table, "We're taking back our community! We are fed up and angry about all the nonsense that has gone on here in Rock Creek!"

"Whoa, lady, did someone just let the genie out of the bottle?" an oldtimer asked.

"It's a program sponsored by the sheriff's office," Butch said before retreating back to the kitchen, "Deputy Candy heads up the effort."

"Your old friend, Butch..." said a Night Rider.

"Hey Guys, Candy's a good cop...better than I was..." said Butch.

Murmuring took over the conversations, as all the residents processed Butch's confession. One oldtimer asked, "What does a neighborhood watch do?"

The lady continued, "We watch out for one another, you know like how people did in the old days. If we see something suspicious, we report it. If one of us has trouble of some sort, we come to their aid, like with the snow storm. Those who could, shoveled snow, and then we gathered for hot chocolate and fresh baked cookies."

"Sounds pretty good," said another oldtimer, "I coulda' used help...I only have footprints from the house to my car..."

"We bring out our concerns and we address them," the lady continued.

"Like what," asked a curious customer.

"Like who shot out the street lights before the rave! It's not safe in the dark. Our kids wait for the school buses before full light, and soon it will be dusk by the time they get home from school in Jericho Springs."

"I always said we never should have closed the school here," echoed a third oldtimer.

"Did you know two people laid in the dark injured when they fell over the cliff?" said a man from Jericho Springs.

"Betty Strong Bull died where she landed. She fell over the edge during the rave. She may have laid there for awhile before dying, but no one saw her. Someone shot out the street lights. Even the businesses turned off their lights,"

Lila added, "Someone could have seen her, could have helped her, but now she's dead."

"There were no lights," said John Mark.

"Betty Strong Bull is a relative of mine..." said a customer from Wolf City.

"What about the bear! It came back to town and nearly got me over in the church parking lot," argued Sarah the waitress, "but thanks to Karen Gustafson, Deputy Candy, Adam Claymore, and two other men I'm okay."

"Didn't you have to go to the hospital?" asked a member of the neighborhood watch.

"Yes, and I almost lost my baby when I fell..." Sarah reported before realizing she should not have said what she said where she said it, because Baal worshippers were present and they had future designs on her.

On cue one of the oldtimers shifted the conversation, "You know the rave is just a bunch of kids having fun up on the ridge. It's a musical presentation with a drama that's included. Betty Strong Bull fell over the edge when the people tried to flee when the darn jeep arrived and the rifle shot split the Asher pole."

"And the bear roared!" said a rave participant.

"And the heavens opened and the storm gods flooded the ground with rainwater that later turned into the heaviest snowfall we have seen for this time of year...thirty-six inches!" said another rave participant.

"We've all seen the ruins of the rave. Snow covers the ashes from someone burning the Asher pole and ceremonial table. Old and young attended the rave!" said the antique shop owner.

"Who organized the rave?" asked a neighborhood watch leader.

"Someone must have gained permission or rented the land? Who owns it?" asked the CR403 block captain.

Since most oldtimers knew the answer to the questions, they looked toward the kitchen where Butch worked oblivious of how the conversation had shifted, which was answer enough for the neighborhood watch members. Butch rang the bell for Sarah to pick up and deliver more meals for patrons, and re-entered the conservation. "Has anyone seen the huge man who got off the bus and ate here? The one who wore a brown bear skin? He certainly looked suspicious. Where'd he go?" asked Butch.

"I think he was just here for awhile and moved on," lied Sarah.

"Oh, no, honey, ask John Mark. He was at Adam's house with the two men in the yellow jeep!" Lila said, and then flushed red at her daughter's glance.

John Mark clarified, "Oh, an acquaintance of mine, who has moved on elsewhere, as have his friends in the yellow jeep."

"One other question for you oldtimers," said the neighborhood watch leader.

"Go ahead, lady, we are getting an education from you this morning," a forth oldtimer said.

"Why is it all the deaths in the valley, other than those traffic related or of natural causes...Why have they all happened right here in our little town?" she said. "And I mean Gloria Jones, Sam Gelding, and Betty Strong Bull?"

Friendly conversation ended, when Butch burped loudly from the kitchen, while like his father Red, Butch murmured about how newcomers caused all the problems.

\*\*\*

319

The publisher of *The Out Cry* had completed a survey of its readers to identify the best places to eat in Rock Creek Valley. The Bustos Family Restaurant gained the most votes for breakfast, lunch, and dinner categories. The distinction came not only as a result of its food and service, but also people voted for its atmosphere, décor, and Friday specials. Since the management featured beef enchiladas smothered with green chili as the Friday lunch special, Attorney John Law and his secretary, Amanda Sentry, ordered by telephone before leaving their offices. It was a short walk down the stairs from the John Law offices.

The lunch crowd already had filled half the seating before Kip Powell entered the front door. He carried a counter pack of books to replace an empty carton. He greeted Marisa the hostess and hugged her affectionately. She frequently visited the bookstore at the Blair House, and her mother had sponsored an in-home book party for Kip.

"Aw, my favorite hostess, it is good to see you!" Kip had said.

"And you also, Mr. Kip," Marisa replied.

"Here is a new counter pack of books to replace the ones you sold."

"I loved Janette Oke's *Love Comes Softly*, what's the new title?"

"New book from the same author titled *Love's Enduring Promise*. I'm certain you will like it. Maybe someday a movie will be made about both of these!" said Kip.

"I would see it at least twice, I'm sure," Marisa asserted as Kip completed the invoice for the first book carton and prepared a statement of books left on consignment.

"Please give this to Mrs. Bustos for payment," asked Kip, then noticing the pending arrival of Ken Bond, "Here comes Ken Bond with a load of newspapers for your bookshelves."

"Oh, good, customers have been asking for back issues due to the snow storm," said Marisa, as she held the entrance door open for the newspaperman.

Ken Bond entered the restaurant with a hefty bundled of papers that he set on the floor before the newspaper shelf. "Thank you, Miss Marisa! May God continue to bless you for your kindness to old men like Kip and me! Hey you!" Ken said to Kip, and then back to the hostess, "And how is the lovely Miss Marisa?"

Marisa gave him a thumbs up, as she counted the left over papers with Ken and signed an invoice for the new delivery. She picked up a copy of The Out Cry and began thumbing through it. "Oh look," she said, "I love the word and picture games in the back. I always read the letters to the editor and the editorial from the owner of the paper."

"Say fella," one of the restaurant's regular customers addressed Ken, "Why should I want to buy a Wednesday paper you're delivering to newsstands today?"

"What are the headlines?" asked another patron at a different table, which caused people from more tables to look their way including John Law and Amanda Sentry.

"Let's see," said Marisa, "there's news here about the churches doing prayer walks in both Rock Creek and Jericho Springs followed by gift bags put on all residential door knobs in the Springs...get this... the Baptist, Methodist, and Lutheran churches worked together. Rachael McNaughton held an in-home book party, and a group of women have been praying with people at intersections in both Jericho Springs and Ridge View. There's news about a committee being formed to bring Christian music to the valley...cool beans...I look forward to Christian tunes on my radio."

"Surely there are more important headlines than those!" the first patron asked.

"Depends on your perspective, I guess," said Kip.

"Mister newspaperman, why would I want to buy the fish wrapper in your hand?" he said without respect.

"You mean, of course, about more grizzly things like the recent rave, crime, and scandalous behavior by both men and bears. It's all in here and you can read about it for a quarter," answered Ken.

"Now you are talkin'," said the first patron and others raised their hands for a copy of *The Out Cry*.

"Let me help, Ken," said Kip. "Neither of us is surprised at man's preference for mayhem and malice."

"Newcomer!" the first patron replied.

As the conversation took on a life of its own, another patron said, "You know, don't you, the bear probably followed Red's herd to town."

"I saw Rabbit Pinebow hauling hay toward Rock Creek. They must have moved the herd during the blizzard."

"The bear just about killed Adam Claymore," said the patron who purchased a newspaper.

"Is Adam in the hospital?" a fifth oldtimer answered his own question, "Yes, there's an article in the paper about it and the bear, a grizzly, it got away."

"I heard the bear was in Jericho Springs," said an earlier oldtimer.

"At the Blair House," said Kip. "Earlier the bear sat on Freedom's tree and broke two giant limbs off it. Izzy and his father, Ezra, chased the bear away. Adam Claymore and Pilgrim Wayne chased after it after the rave. The bear got both of them. Which is why Adam's in the hospital."

"Did you hear about a Ute Indian who fell over a cliff during the rave in Rock Creek?" asked someone from Ridge View.

"She was from Wolf City..." answered someone from there.

"Just a bunch of kids is my guess..." the oldtimer said.

"Don't bet on it. There is more to the story..." added a neighborhood watch member.

Finally, one man rose from his chair and asked for all to listen to him, "You'll read in the paper about the assault on the Blair House and that Van Allen and Robert King, the Rock Creek realtor, were arrested when it happened. I could have been right there with them, if it hadn't been for these two men, the book man and the paper carrier, and Mr. Law over there," the man said as he pointed in the attorney's direction, "and that goes for Miss Sentry too."

"What are you talking about?" asked the rude patron.

"A group of men, mostly from Jericho Springs but also from Ridge, which included some of the McNaughton Corporation's Night Riders... Well, we were recruited by Van Allen and Robert King to make a raid on those at the Blair House," said the man who had accepted Christ as his Savior. "We believe we were doing what was right by trying to get Misty away from them at the Blair House. Van Allen told us she was being held against her will, like some sort of a cult."

Ken asked, "What did you find out?"

"You know, Kip, you live there!" and when Kip nodded, the man continued, "We found out those folks are really nice people. Old Rachael McNaughton was playing a piano and leading a hymn sing.

Judge Parsons and his wife Aquila, her sister Priscilla, and Amanda Sentry were all there."

"Tell them the rest," Ken said.

"I'll be glad to tell," the man said. "Misty and Hannah Rahab hit us with water balloons and eggs, while Robert and Van Allen lit and tossed torches onto the balconies. That's when we figured we had been lied to. Both Misty and Hannah sure had a good time."

"Robert King and Van Allen went to jail as did Night Riders who had attempted other foolishness against the Blair House," said the man who had been the spokesman for those who had been duped by Van Allen and Robert King.

"Grace and mercy," said Ken.

"Yes, you are right. The rest of us were invited inside despite some of us having been soaked in water or caught under a big net."

"I was soaked and some guy rode a zip line into the trees and threw me to the ground with his legs. I never seen it before," said another patron.

"So you went inside and had tea and cookies?" the rude patron said.

"Pretty much! We were served snacks and pizza like we had been invited guests instead of the scoundrels we were."

"That's not all," Ken interjected.

"They gave us a tour of the lower floor of the house. You should see Kip's bookstore! I bought a Bible and two CD's, one by Sandi Patty and *My Father's Eyes* by Amy Grant," said one of those who had participated in the assault on Blair House.

"Unbelievable. You guys went there to kidnap Misty; they forgave your foolishness and fed you, then showed you around their place. And you bought a Bible," added another patron.

"I never had one before..." the man said.

"All of that and one more," added the second participant.

"We walked up the hill, now this might spook some of you, we walked up the hill led by this guy with a big flashlight, a real powerful one."

"And we looked at what old man Ezra had carved in the tree," said someone else.

"What did you see?" asked the rude patron, who now was interested.

"Jesus! I saw Jesus crucified on the cross."

"I did too, and then we prayed. I think it was Izzy who led us in a prayer."

"No, it was the manager of the pizzeria, Jerry Sunday," still another said.

"I accepted Jesus as my Savior," said the first confessor, "which is why I needed to buy the Bible! I went home and confessed to my wife what I had done and how the people at Blair House treated us. Then you know what, my wife wept. She wept and told me she had prayed for my salvation for nearly five years."

Touched by the confession, Amanda briefly reached over and placed her hand on that of her boss, John Law, and said, "These people don't know, but I do. None of this would have happened if you hadn't found Izzy Freedom for his father Ezra."

"Thank you, Dear one, all praise to the Father. This old man just listened and did what I was told to do."

"God truly does have a plan for each of us!" Amanda surmised.

"Indeed! You heard the murmuring...oldtimers say the newcomers are the source of their troubles and that may be, because a lot of the oldtimers don't bend with the wind. Wait till they see the CBI ad on page three."

\*\*\*

Detective Caleb Jones sought help from Mike Crowfoot and his cousin, Rabbit Pinebow. Jones needed them to arrange a meeting with Ute tribal leadership about the death of Betty Strong Bull. At first both men had been hesitant to make the contact, but conceded when they learned the chief had referred to Caleb as "Ta-ton-ka," which means buffalo for both his coloring, upper body strength, and hair. Flattered, when told how he had found favor with the chief, Caleb had looked forward to the meeting. Mike volunteered to go with him.

Ezra Sr. loaned his four wheel drive truck to Caleb, so he could travel the road from Jericho Springs to Wolf City over Claymore Flats and back. Ezra drew Caleb a map to and through Wolf City. He marked a rutted road Caleb could follow and connect with the road, which passes by Ezra's sawmill before coming up behind Blair House. Ezra warned Caleb the road might not be passable.

Rabbit had asked Caleb to stop by the Claymore ranch barn to load Ezra's truck bed with bales of hay to drop over the east fence ten miles south of the ranch entrance. While there Caleb stopped at the ranch house to visit both Beatrice Jaramillo and Pilgrim Wayne, whom he found to be in good health and spirits. Big Foot had met Caleb and Mike at the door, and after initially meeting the man, the dog ran onto the porch looking for Adam his master. Beatrice removed a quart mason jar from a kitchen cupboard and filled it with green chili before giving it to Caleb. On crutches Pilgrim greeted Caleb from a bedroom then came to the kitchen.

"Mike, did you warn him about the Chief?" asked Pilgrim.

"No, I was just going to let it evolve," Mike answered, "Which is why I took the day off work to ride with him."

Looking at both smiling men, Caleb asked, "What have I gotten myself into?"

"I think you will enjoy this," Mike said still smiling, "but just in case you don't, remember you asked me to get you a meeting with the Chief. So forgive me in advance."

"You are big enough, strong enough," Pilgrim said, "but the Chief will want to arm wrestle with you right at the beginning. If you agree to wrestle, you are in and he will help you whenever you need him."

"Is Chief still up to his antics? I thought an old man like him would have given up his wrestling around," commented Bea.

"The meeting is at the Wolf City Café," said Mike sheepishly.

"The Chief still is the line coach for the high school football team..." added Pilgrim, "and he coaches the wrestling team."

"Does the café still have a ring set-up?" Bea asked with enthusiasm.

"Of course," added Pilgrim, "if you arm wrestle and lose, the competition is over and he will look at you and think you are okay, but if you win, the Chief will want you to get in the ring with him."

"Has Adam wrestled him?" asked Caleb.

"Lost every time!" said Bea.

"Butch? Red?" Caleb asked mentioning more men of girth, while the three of them nodded affirmatively.

"Ezra Sr.?"

"The Chief beat Ezra every time before the war, but he won't wrestle him since Ezra came home," said Beatrice and the two men nodded affirmatively.

"Hmm..." Caleb murmured, and then asked, "Let us pray about my meeting with Chief...what is his name?"

"Strong as a Bull," the three replied in unison.

\*\*\*

Stopping ten miles south of the Claymore Flats ranch house, Caleb and Mike unload ten bales of hay, which would later be distributed to a hungry herd on the grand mesa. Caleb backed the truck to the barbwire fence. From the truck bed Mike struggled to lift and toss three bales of hay over the barbwire fence, while Caleb worked from the ground and tossed the remaining hay bales over the fence. Once back inside the cab they continued their conversation until entering Wolf City.

"Who was Betty to the Chief? I mean other than a tribal member."

"Betty was a granddaughter...and a cousin to me and Janine."

"I'm sorry to hear that, Mike. I wonder what she was doing at the rave..." said Caleb.

"We've all asked that..." Mike said, "and I think all the relatives of each of those women, young and old... the relatives ask the same question. Everyone of them is somebody's daughter or sister. I think all of us who are believers know it is a spiritual issue."

"I know Gloria broke my mother's heart. She and my dad took us to church, raised us to be good people...people with good sense..." said Caleb.

"Yet something went wrong..."

"Well, God has sons and daughters and Jesus brothers and sisters..."

"But no grandchildren..." added Mike.

"I keep wondering if it has something to do with discipleship..."

"Perhaps you are right...look how often the *Old Testament* tells of a good or great king whose children don't continue to live in goodness after the king passes," said Mike, while remembering the accounts of kings in the Bible histories.

"We all do have free will...make choices... and are tempted," said Caleb.

"Have you noticed how Misty acts toward men...primarily John Mark?"

"He certainly has opportunity there, and he works at being chaste... it has something to do with his mission here, or so I've heard him say."

"Have you heard about my sister, Janine, she kept herself pure in hopes Izzy would do what he said he would do."

"And he did. Why are some able to do that and others don't?"

"I know my sister is a prayer warrior and reads and studies the Bible daily. I know she makes certain to budget her time, so she is available to do the Lord's work. She talks to me regularly to work for what makes an eternal difference."

"Izzy is a fortunate man..."

"Indeed! Like in *First Chronicles*, chapter four, verses nine and ten," added Mike.

"Have any of the women who participated in a rave," Caleb asked, "Have any of them been married?"

"No...I can't think of any..." answered Mike, who added, "Most have been young with rare exception...like Sarah..."

Passing through downtown Wolf City, Mike imagined how Pilgrim had ridden into town and hitched his horse to the rail outside the café. "That's the Chief's horse. Don't get too close to it, so Ezra's pick-up doesn't get kicked."

"You've made it sound like we've entered the Wild West," said Caleb.

"Not really, it's just the horse is rodeo stock."

"Not sure what that means..."

"Let's get inside, I don't want to keep the Chief waiting," Mike said as they bounded up the stairs and opened the front doors.

Wolf City Café sported a western motif with pictures of Indians and cultural artifacts on every wall. A bar spanned one wall and the wrestling ring occupied the center back section, while tables neatly covered the front and booths lined the other wall. Only two booths sat alone toward the front corner where Pilgrim had sat looking out the window earlier.

The Chief grimly rose from the front booth to greet his grandson Mike Crowfoot and Detective Caleb Jones. The Chief looked into Caleb's eyes to size him up, and then rolled up his shirt sleeves.

"I trust Mike shared stories about me on your drive over here. Right hand or left?"

"You were serious," Caleb said as he looked at Mike who nodded.

"It's tradition," Mike responded.

Having noticed the Chief had stirred his coffee with his right hand, Caleb rolled up his sleeves and said, "Left hand..."

"Ta-ton-ka, crafty you are...I like that. Are you here to find out who murdered my granddaughter...or are you here to clear some white man's crime?" the Chief said as they grasped left hands.

"I'm here to find out why my sister was murdered...perhaps instigated by those responsible for your granddaughter's death," responded Caleb, who had not yet cracked a smile.

As the two grappled, Mike invited a crowd to come watch the match. Some folks came in off the street to see if the one the Chief called a buffalo could last long against their chief.

"Chief, I ask for your help to find the instigators..."

"Mike, see to it none can hear us. The answer lies in who runs the rave."

"Sorry," Mike said, "I shouldn't have brought the crowd...come on folks, go about your business."

"Do you know why my sister was killed? Your granddaughter too?" asked Caleb.

"Baal worship, they were both temple prostitutes. Gloria ended her pregnancy, and since the ceremony was disrupted, Betty served as a sacrifice," the chief explained.

"Before or after they participated in a rave."

"After...that is why your sister died," answered the chief.

"Do you have proof?"

"Yes!"

"Did you go to the sheriff?" asked Caleb.

"Yes, but you are part of CBI Human Trafficking Taskforce. You know the answer. You searched Bailey's home and office and found nothing. You searched Gelding's home and office, but found nothing, and you know that someone had cleaned out Gelding's files despite how tidy things appeared," answered the chief angrily.

"Had you given Bailey your proof?"

"He asked for it, but I didn't give it to him. I just said I had proof."

"I don't trust him either," Caleb said, and then asked, "Other than the participants, do the people in the valley understand what is going on?"

"No, but Adam knows, he won't want to admit it, but he knows here," Chief Strong Bull said as he touched his chest before his heart.

"Are you saying he is involved?" asked the detective.

"No, not at all, but he knows the temple priest, and I believe he knows who wears my brother bear suits. They won't want to come on my land, our reservation."

"Why do you suppose?"

"I don't know, perhaps they would think they would disappear or not make it out of my ring," the Chief said sternly, "and they won't want to come to any ballgames here against Wolf City High School."

"What about the fire on the ridge...do you know who set fire?" Caleb asked.

"Warriors on our side..." the Chief said as he began to gain an advantage against Caleb.

"I wondered...what do you make of the bear, how it killed the couple in Pryor and attacked the church, Pilgrim, Adam, and Freedom's tree?"

"The man was foolish, the woman brave, the children terrified. The bear hibernates now for six moons or more. It is wounded many times. Maybe it won't heal. If not, someone will have to kill it, maybe the warriors I mentioned. Maybe someone else. It is a grizzly, but it hunts man. Most animals flee from where whites congregate. I think it's their odor," the Chief said and laughed, "Haven't you noticed?"

"Not really," Caleb said, "they do all look alike," which brought laughter from both.

"Have you seen Ezra's carving in the tree?"

Caleb nodded and asked, "What do you see?"

Looking above Caleb's head, the Chief replied, "Hmm...I wondered if you would ask. I see the cross, of course, but I see the underworld, which is all going on below the surface. What we have talked about. I see Adam conflicted with what to do. I see the four who recently arrived, the big men who are cloaked with disguise—they are warriors on a mission. Perhaps they are angels in disguise. I see the hand of God reaching down to man, ever present and in charge. I see him waiting to see what choices are made. I know you are one of the reinforcements and there are more that have arrived. I look forward to the restoration of Blair House."

"Me, too..."

"Do you realize Janine is my granddaughter?" asked Strong Bull.

"No, I didn't, but I see where her strength of character comes from."

"Yes," the Chief said, "I helped to disciple her. Her strength comes from the Lord..." and then he let go of Caleb's hand, and continued, "I don't really take people to the mat if they beat me arm wrestling. I coach wrestling and have the team do some practice sessions here, but we have tournaments here sometimes."

"Speaking of temple prostitution, do you know of any human trafficking involving the high school and the students here?" asked Caleb.

"Yes."

"Any idea how the children were contacted?"

"I'll look into that...this is reservation land and we may handle things differently from what you are used to," the chief promised.

"Understood...do kids leave high school whenever they want to?"

"Not any more they don't."

"You mentioned you had proof and you didn't give it to Bailey. May I have it?" asked Caleb.

"I've been waiting for you to ask," the Chief said as he reached the seat beside him, picked up flyers and his granddaughter's diary, and then handed them to Caleb, "This is my café, and we have professional boxing here as well. You should come over sometime."

"I will and if I call for help, can I count on you and your people?"

"You have my word," the Chief said, as he crossed his heart with his fist. "We welcome newcomers who might make a difference, truth and justice."

"Grace and mercy," Caleb replied, as he rose to leave.

The Chief seemed regal as he rose and shook Caleb's hand and said, "Don't expect help from Osteen. Have Karen Gustafson do your research there if you can. And Caleb, say hello to Ezra for me, we speak together often."

"You mean Ezra not Izzy?" said Caleb.

The Chief nodded, and added one final comment, "The widow Gelding...there is something about her that just isn't right...When you were searching Gelding's office and Mrs. Gelding's home, did you search the trunk of her car?"

"It wasn't at her home and I didn't see any cars in the office garage..."

"Of course not," the chief responded.

***

Caleb drove on to Quail Point without Mike, who stayed with the Chief to have dinner at the café. Although Caleb was to meet with April and May Osteen, daughters of Mayor August Osteen, Caleb was given a message from the mayor at his receptionist's desk. It advised Detective Jones the mayor's daughters would be interviewed only through his police department. It said Caleb and CBI would have to work through and with the Quail Point Police Department.

# RESTORATION

## CHAPTER 16

*"Then build a proper kind of alter to the Lord your God*
*on the top of this bluff."*                    *Judges 6:25c*

"I wish you could have been with us this morning,
Adam," Karen told him. "We are having a good time together,
and each has found acceptance from the others. Jerry leads the
small group lessons. They are a blessing! Misty wrote us a song she
had been writing for us, so we adopted it as our own. You will have
to hear us sing it!"

"Sounds like you have become an effective small group. I'm
jealous," Adam responded, "but it is good to be here at home in my
own bed. I wasn't so certain I would ever be back here."

"You're not the only one," added Karen, who sat beside him on
his bed. She leaned over and kissed him, "and I have missed you!"

"Was I in that bad of shape?"

"You know how scalp wounds can be, plus your arm was terribly
cut! Isn't it amazing what doctors can do these days?"

"Indeed, I remembered as soon as I became coherent..." Adam
said, as he reflected, "I pictured myself in the hands of Jesus. I confessed on my own I am not able to deal with this, and then I opened
my eyes and there you were, and I wasn't alone."

"I was by your side all night and the next day praying for you.
Others prayed too. I think most of the community did."

"You are a blessing to me, Karen, I love you..." Adam said, which
caused her to cry. "Do I look as bad as I feel?"

332

"It is wonderful to see you on the mend. You will have reminders..." Karen replied, "just by looking in the mirror. Deputy Candy stopped by yesterday to interview Jill and me again."

"Together or separately?"

"Separately..." Karen answered, and then paused, "What do you make of it?"

"My guess? She didn't want you influencing what the other one said or remembered. What was she looking for?"

"She wanted me to recount the sequence of events about Gelding's attack on me...but I think she really wanted to know what I remembered about who rescued me and how the attack happened..." Karen paused again, "I think she's trying to figure out how Gelding ended up caught by the whirlpool."

"From the bridge to the whirlpool...there's one just south of the footbridge and one north of the county road."

"Yes, and I have no idea, no recollection of seeing Ezra before waking at the cabin. Candy did say whoever rescued me would not be charged, because they came to my defense. It would be ruled self-defense."

"My guess is she is looking for Sam's motive, as if it may not have been a sexual assault."

"I don't get it, I mean I am a newcomer..."

"And you've been poking around...listening and taking notice of things...perhaps someone fears you will uncover what others want to remain hidden..."

"And they know I'm good with a gun..."

"You, my dear, are a force to be reckoned with, and you made a difference in Quail Point..."

"Where I just came from..." Karen reflected, "Jill and I talked afterwards. She said the conversation got back around to Ezra and what he had seen, if he shared anything with her about what had happened. I'm certain Candy tried to interview him, but how could he testify at least out loud."

"Look what he did at the raid on Blair House..." Adam concluded.

"You mean the zip line that put him behind the group in the trees..."

"And he dropped the net and caught them in a snare..."

"And soaked them in red dye water..."

"They were marked to be hung out and tried..." Adam said, as he chuckled.

"Some went to jail, while the others received grace and mercy, pizza and soda pop!" Karen said and laughed.

"Hmm..." Adam reflected, "Something is afoot. I knew it when Red didn't join our roundup or the bear hunt. The roundup had always been something we did together. Whoever kills the bear will have lifelong bragging rights...Add Caleb to the mix. He is here as part of the Human Trafficking Taskforce, which involves Hannah and Misty as participants during the raves and Jill as a witness of his sister's death. Now he is staying at the Blair House, where Hannah, Misty, Jill, and you live. Is he trying to resolve his case, or is he there to protect the four of you?"

"Let's extend your thought," Karen said. "Who owns the ridge where the rave took place? Who pastures his cattle there? Who arranged to have your presence removed from next to his pasture? You know...the torching of your trailer...which removed your eyes and ears."

"How do you mean?"

"Adam, had the Bonds been there during the rave they would have paid attention to what was going on. Ken would have investigated it. Most believe Butch torched the trailer, but who would have given the order?"

"Red, in all those cases...I'm sure he wanted me gone when I made a fuss about the raves, and I wouldn't help finance them. The stated motive was to bring in more business to our valley," Adam said, "I thought the fire was about scaring off another newcomer who might have a claim to the water and mineral rights, but you are suggesting something more than that."

"Then Red is at least one of those behind the raves, which somehow makes them connected to human trafficking," concluded Karen, "and Red leads the McNaughton Corporation."

"Based on what has happened, I'm sure the two are connected. Red introduced the idea during a corporate meeting, but he clearly said it was a community project and not a corporate project. But who else would it be?"

"I might find out with the project I'm doing..."

"And that may well be why you were targeted..." added Adam.

"I'll bet Red owns the Stage Stop Hotel, the Tobacco Store, and the Asherah House too!" Karen guessed.

"My guess is he is part owner of the hotel, or Butch wouldn't be managing it. I don't know about other partners. All three of those buildings along the highway used to be owned by the man who sells antiques, and I think he lost ownership of the tobacco shop when the interstate construction allowed most of the traffic to pass us by. He sold it to save the other two buildings. My question is who owns the bed and breakfast? To my knowledge, it has never been for sale. I know it hasn't always been the Asherah House...but I don't remember the name...it might have been named after a prominent family," Adam said and then pondered, "Have Caleb check with the county clerk and recorder to find your answer, instead of you, please. My guess is he already knows."

"What would be wrong with me asking? I would just be doing research..."

"Trust me...I want you to have a future here. I don't know the answer and, frankly, I don't want to know...at least not now...because if I know, I'll probably feel compelled..."

"To do something about it and right now you can't," Karen empathized, "I'll respect your wishes and let Caleb make the discovery."

"I heard you delivered pizza to the Blair House during the raid," Adam said, then asked, "Are you working every night?"

"No, Sir, I don't work Wednesday night or on Sunday. If I have interviews scheduled when I'm supposed to be working, Hannah will cover for me," Karen explained. "Jerry approved our arrangement. He won't have her make deliveries with all that is going on," she paused, "and in case you are wondering, I get off at eight and with your permission, I should be here to check on you by eight-fifteen."

"Sounds complicated, Karen," Adam noted. "He's jumping through some hoops to accommodate your schedule, which is nice of him, but he's not the owner of the store."

"And I should not take advantage of his willingness to accommodate what I want to do," Karen replied, "which he may be doing because we both live at Blair House."

"Maybe you should switch roles with Hannah..."

"You mean for her to have, perhaps a full time job with me occasionally filling in for her or somebody else."

"Who else works there?"

"Gloria King opens at ten and works until school is out at three thirty. She works a full eight hours on Saturday," Karen added, "She makes the pies and manages the store, while Jerry makes deliveries."

"No wonder Jerry is so accommodating," Adam said. "It's too bad Misty couldn't help out or Kat, but she will soon be moving to my Rock Creek house. It's almost ready."

"And our primary mission is to help restore Blair House," Karen concluded. "We all need to pray God will send more help to Blair House and the pizzeria. Thank you, you would make a good partner..."

"Thanks for noticing," Adam said, as he thought Eve was made from Adam's side. She wasn't made to be a doormat or to rule over him. Eve was made to be a partner. "Ken Bond stopped by this morning when delivering the morning and weekly newspapers. I asked him if anyone had killed the bear, and of course, he said no one had seen it since the big snow. I was probably the last one to see the old boar. I had asked Pilgrim to loan you his Sharps, so Pilgrim asked Ken to take it to you," Adam continued earnestly, and then leaned upward and gently grasped Karen's arm, looked into her eyes, and continued, "Karen, kill the bear! Don't give it a chance, don't feel kindly toward it as one of God's creatures, it's not just a bear..." then he reclined again and shut his eyes.

"After what it did to you, I welcome the opportunity to put it away," Karen responded, "and speaking of dealing with unpleasant bears, Ken had a confrontation with Red when he was delivering newspapers at the Cozy Corner Cafe. Of course, Ken believes Red is responsible for torching your trailer, and we all think Red is behind a lot of what goes on with the Night Riders and the raves."

"I'm afraid you are right about both and more..."

"Did Ken say anything else?" asked Karen.

"Just that Morris had done a real fine job filling in for me on Sunday morning."

"He has! He is a good man...but he needs to be able to go when he has a bus trip to drive."

"I asked Ken to take my spot at church as interim pastor beginning next Sunday and to plan to move into my Rock Creek house as soon as John Mark is finished there. I guess John and the brothers Tunnicliffe have really done well restoring my house."

"John was saying it probably would have taken most of the year to really do a quality job, but with the brothers' help, it has become a job of just a few months...John said he would miss being in Rock Creek with the work the neighborhood watch had accomplished there."

"Neighborhood Watch, Candy's program?" Adam asked to Karen's nod, "What's happening in Rock Creek?"

"Well, you know Red has Butch managing the hotel...and despite Sarah and Lila working for Butch...they and others have been adamant against the nonsense that goes on there! Drunk and disorderly behavior, the traipsing through people's backyards to get to the Asherah House."

Laughing, Adam asked, "What else have they done?"

"They went to the convenience store as a group and told the clerks to tell the owner they would not do business there if they didn't get rid of the trash on the magazine racks. They also told Mike Monroe they knew he was selling drugs at the store and they were doing surveillance in and around the store and taking names and pictures. Then they had people shop there armed with cameras! Mike quit and left town. The manager thanked the members of the watch and cleaned up the message board too..." said Karen, who then asked, "So, Ken's in the pulpit when?"

"Tomorrow morning...Ken will baptize Andy Browning instead of waiting for me to do it. I asked Ken to stop at the Brownings and ask them to get Andy ready. I need to talk with Izzy and Janine too."

"That's short notice for someone to prepare a sermon..."

"Admittedly, which is why I told Ken to just share his testimony, and I also asked him to teach about rewards and wages and the Bema."

"The Bema?"

"The judgment when Christ returns," proclaimed Adam.

"I've never heard much about the topic. Never heard much from the book of Revelations."

"Nor I and it is time we all hear!"

337

While Karen and Adam continued their conversation, occasionally snuggling and fondly kissing, Beatrice Jaramillo answered the knocking on the ranch house front door to the tune of "Good morning, good morning, we're happy to see you this morning!"

"Good morning yourselves, Miss Janine and Mr. Izzy! I hope you have not forgotten about me or tossed my belongings out on the Blair House front porch."

"Not on your life, Gramma Bea, but we all miss your good cooking. Rachael sure misses you too, and you should hear how well the Bond girls are playing the piano. In fact more times than not, Rachael is in the piano room teaching someone to play. Bea, your good friend said to tell you she was going to take you to a fancy restaurant when you get home. She said to tell you she has made a pile of money and she was willing to spend part of her earnings not only from piano lessons but also from her book party sales!" Janine laughed as she reported and then asked, "Are Adam and Pilgrim available?"

"Well, Pilgrim's out at the barn on crutches pokin' around. He misses not being with the crew building fence now that they can navigate the snow. I guess they still want to fence in the mesa before hard winter."

"How far have they gone?" asked Izzy.

"Barnabas was here over night reporting to Adam then left early this morning. He said they had finished everything heading south along both sides of the county road to Wolf City, east to Quail Point and then midway across the end of the mesa toward the stream that empties into the canyon. I 'spect he meant to where the stream flows over the mesa and into the air. You know it rarely makes it to Rock Creek by the canyon highway."

"It's like the creek on Grand Mesa near Grand Junction. Water from the mesa just empties into the air and you can see the mist as it dissipates, if you drive by on the way to or from Delta."

"Yes, but ours ends up moistening the town of Rock Creek and my orchards..." said Adam from the bedroom.

"Plus the beautiful rose bushes..."added Karen, as she entered the vestibule to greet them, "follow me, I've just been trying to torment my Mr. Wonderful with a gentle kiss now and then to try to motivate him to get well soon."

"It's working," confirmed Adam with a shout from his bedroom.

"Try not to be stunned," Karen warned them with a whisper...It didn't work.

Both entered Adam's room, and Janine broke into tears and rushed to her hero and hugged him. Shaken as well, Izzy choked a little as he spoke and handed a get well card to Adam, "It is good to see you here at home. Here's a card everyone from Blair House signed. Everyone asks how you are doing. And it looks like you scared off the bear. No one has seen it."

"I must be quite a sight...thank you for the card," Adam said, as tears swelled to his eyes. "That's what my men say, but the bear is still here. It will come hunting for us again. My guess is it's hold up somewhere and will be back come spring, if not sooner. It's hibernating now. Shoot it on sight. Give it no quarter, no mercy. It is not a person who can be redeemed."

"Will do," said Izzy.

"I had Ken Bond take Pilgrim's rifle to Karen. Be ready to shoot it. My bet is she will bring it down and probably with one shot!"

"Adam, we want to talk to you about our wedding," interrupted Janine. "Most everyone knows we went to the justice of the peace instead of having a church wedding."

"Gossip can really sting, especially in the church. Don't let it bruise you and rob your joy. What is so significant about your story is that Izzy returned as promised, and you, Janine, acted on your faith in him. You preserved yourself for him, while you waited. You have my blessing if you want someone else to perform the ceremony, I understand."

"We decided to wait until you are well. We want you to be the one to marry us," added Izzy.

"Aren't you tired of people asking you about it?"

"Oh, yes, we are Adam," Janine continued, "but we already made the mistake of not following Friar Laurence's admonition that they stumble who run too fast. It will be a once in a lifetime occasion, and we want you to do the ceremony, so we will wait."

"Understood...I have a favor to ask of you two."

"Anything...what is it?"

"I've asked Ken Bond to take over at church for me. Hopefully, it will be a permanent arrangement. As soon as John Mark is finished remodeling my house in Rock Creek, I'll want him to move there not only to be close at hand to the church and town, but also to occupy my house and to work with the pastoral group in the valley. Did you know he has a Bible college degree and some seminary?"

"No, he hasn't said anything about it..." said Izzy.

"He will Sunday..."

"Are you asking us to support him?"

"Yes, Janine, I know not all of your people at the Blair House will be attending church there due to your overall mission, but you know what happened to Pastor Borden."

"Yes, he got very discouraged..." answered Janine.

"I'd say brokenhearted..." Adam added, "Ken will be able to continue his paper routes and maintain the boxes around businesses, but eventually Kat and the girls won't be able to do what they do at Blair House."

"Which means Kip will need some help with the bookstore. Adam, it is something we'll deal with. We know Kip will be excited for Ken to be able to do this!" Izzy concluded, as he and Janine left the room.

"Adam, thank you...we have a lunch meeting at the Blair House, and I know Janine and Izzy will need to get ready for it. We've invited John Mark and Amanda to join us. I hate to go, but I will call you later after I complete two other interviews. Thanks for doing yours," Karen said, as she leaned over to kiss him, but his kiss stunned her into saying, "Hmmm... Mr.Wonderful, I'm thinking I'll be calling you Mr. Hotlips...at least in private."

\*\*\*

Promptly at noon, team Blair House gathered for lunch and a weekly meeting. Both Tim and guest Amanda came through the front door together, while Morris, Mike, Ezra, and Kip descended the front stairwell. Caleb and Karen parked their cars in the lot between the house and stand of trees then entered through the back porch. Jill washed garden soil from her hands in the kitchen sink, while both Izzy and Janine emerged from their first floor apartment. Hannah and

Misty finished setting the dining room table, while Kat stood stirring a pot on the wood stove. Ken and John Mark shook hands, as they met on the front porch and entered together. Jerry arrived with some dessert pizza. Only Beatrice was missing, as the boys from Pryor also slowly descended the stairs to sit at the table.

While eight sat on each side, Izzy assumed the helm of the table. Before Jerry had led them in part of the Lyman Coleman series, the men would sit on one side of the table, while the women on the other. Since the members of the group had become more comfortable with one another, seating arrangements changed. Those currently working on projects together gravitated to one another. Several of the men who sat together continued their banter about the Denver Bears' recent season. Some felt second baseman/left fielder, Tim Raines played best with a .354 batting average, while scoring 105 runs. Others lobbied for first baseman Randy Bass, who batted .333, hit thirty-seven homers, and scored 106 runs. Meanwhile as the guest, Amanda had been invited to sit between Misty and Karen. When Amanda sat down, those sitting across from her stopped talking and looked at the three women briefly, then began chatting again.

Quick to notice what had just happened, Karen looked at both Misty and Amanda and whispered to Amanda, "Amanda, ask Misty on the other side of you if she noticed what just happened," which Amanda did.

Misty replied to Amanda, "Oh, they were just checking me out. It happens all the time..." and then to those across from her, "Doesn't it, guys?"

Kip answered, "I don't know about Tom and Jerry, I mean Jerry and Tim, but I haven't been around either of you much. I am just surprised at how you look like each other."

"They could be sisters," said Jerry.

"Or twins," said Tim.

Kat brought a mixing bowl of creamed tuna to one end of the table, followed by Kristin carrying a large bowl of rice. Krystal followed Janine and carried a bowl of tuna with a bowl of rice. Kat said, "Except for the hair style and make-up, definitely twins."

Janine joined in with, "Maybe not twins, but they sure look like sisters."

Seeing no end to the comparison, Amanda picked up a bottle of hot sauce, looked at Misty, and said, "Well, my dear, they have us pegged."

To which Misty, not knowing how to respond, said, "I just don't see it," while looking toward John Mark.

Quick to gain closure, John Mark commented, "I think all three of you look lovely!"

Others chimed in, while Izzy said, "Grace and mercy, let's pray," which diverted the situation.

When the lunch fare had been quickly consumed, Jerry brought the dessert pies from the top of the wood stove, and served tasty slices of apple and cheese pizza.

Izzy opened the team meeting with prayer followed by his asking, "Has anyone seen signs of the bear anywhere? Tracks? Scat?"

Since no, none, nowhere had been the replies, Izzy followed with, "Does anyone have an announcement for us to put on our calendars?"

Ken spoke first, "I'm honored to share with you that Adam Claymore asked me to sub in at the pulpit in Rock Creek, so Morris can follow his regular bus schedule. Morris and I have talked, and he will make certain I know the ropes at church. And when John Mark finishes remodeling Adam's Rock Creek house, Kat, the girls, and I will be moving there to carryout related church duties. Adam said the intent, if everything works out, is that I would likely become the pastor, but I will need to continue to have my paper routes."

"The paper routes will probably help develop the church once people make the connection between you and the Church in the Glen," said Jerry.

"I can finish inside as soon as I lay carpet and swap out the appliances. We've cleaned and painted the inside and upgraded the plumbing and bathroom and kitchen fixtures. I'll need to paint the exterior, but it can be done later. The garage is finished, I did it first. I had the driveway poured today."

"A cement driveway?" asked Jill.

"That's got to be the first in Rock Creek!" added Janine.

"Or just about anywhere else in the valley," said Tim.

"Of course, it has to dry, but so long as a hard freeze doesn't hit, it will be useable in a few days," John Mark clarified.

"God is good," said Misty, "all the time!"

"All the time, God is good," countered Amanda, and the two who looked alike gave the other a high-five.

"Well," said Izzy, "looks like we will have to make some adjustments here. Kat has played a major role in cleaning and cooking here with Beatrice helping on both ends. Kristin and Krystal have done fine jobs too."

"I guess, Kat, you won't be working for me after you move to Rock Creek," concluded Kip.

"I could and would like to work on a scheduled basis, but the truth is it's best if someone from here were able to do it."

"I'm new at being a Christian," said Hannah, "but I'd like to be considered for the position."

"I'll help more in the kitchen and with the cleaning. I hope to need more cooking and housekeeping skills soon," Misty said, and then glanced at John Mark, who became very uncomfortable.

"Well, no decisions need be made now, but I think it is fair to say we are all happy for the Bond family and for Adam who has wanted to return to being a deacon instead of pastor," said Janine, as she concluded with, "and thank you both for stepping up to help!"

"Amen to that," everyone said including the Bond girls, but the boys from Pryor sat unengaged.

"I attended the meeting at the senior center when the neighborhood watch was formed in Rock Creek," Karen said to help change the topic. "John Mark helped Deputy Candy begin the meeting. I think we should consider helping the deputy start one here in Jericho Springs."

"Ken and Kat, you will want to connect with the effort in Rock Creek," said John Mark.

"What do they do?" asked Kat.

"They are taking back their community," Ken replied. "They watch out for one another."

"In Rock Creek? There will be opposition from in the Asherah House..." reflected Misty, "the Tobacco Store, hotel, even the convenience store...who does that leave?"

"The people? Some kids too!" Krystal blurted out.

"Exactly!"

"Why not ask Deputy Candy to come here and make a presentation? I know she wants to talk with Jill and Karen," offered Detective Caleb. "Neighborhood watch is about empowering people to take responsibility for their neighborhood. They help the sheriff by becoming the eyes and ears for the police. They are not to stop a crime or to confront a bad guy, who is doing something bad...that's not what it's about. It is about caring enough to watch out for one another."

"Sounds like our ministry like a light on a hill..." said Hannah, who drew nods of approval from the rest.

"I'll invite Deputy Cotton today," said Izzy, "as well as some of our neighbors."

Misty leaned toward Amanda and whispered, "I thought the deputy we would invite would be Candy..."

"Her name is ...Cotton Candy..." Amanda whispered back.

"Sweeeeet!" countered Misty, who offered another high-five, which Amanda returned with a smile.

"I have something I need to announce. I can't tell you much yet, but I need for all of you to watch out for signs of human trafficking and where it may be happening," urged Caleb.

"Like at the rave," said John Mark.

"At the hotel and the Asherah House," declared both Hannah and Misty.

"Yes...and we know something about those...I mean..." explained the detective.

"The schools...you need for Jill and Janine and me to be on the watch at the schools," concluded Karen.

"And in the community too...often during school hours," Caleb added, "like with neighborhood watch...become aware of what's going on around you. Bad things are happening to some people. If you suspect it, report it directly to me or John Alden at the high school."

"I take it you mean go to the principal in person and not to leave a note with the secretary or counselor," Jill asked to which Caleb nodded. Karen and Janine looked toward Jill and one another and nodded together.

"I have an agenda item," Jill spoke up. "Morris and Mike have been helping to move field stone to the base of Little Huerfano. You know we want to build a wall around the butte and fill in a mixture of manure, soil, and wood chips, which will help the longevity of the Live Oak tree."

"Like part of a healing..." added Ken Bond.

"Repair what was damaged...restoring..." said Izzy.

"I assume you need help moving field stone as you rototill the gardens..." John Mark asked and received Jill's nod. "I've shoveled several yards of soil into piles when we dugout the space for the concrete driveway. We used some of it to grade the backyard at Adam's house. It will help drain rain water and snow melt away from the foundation. Can I bring it over here and dump it for you to mix with cow and horse poop and wood chips?"

"Yea!" said Jill, "but will you need a truck?"

Immediately, Ezra Sr. flashed a smile across his face and raised his hand.

"Here's another announcement," said Kip. "The pastor's group now includes a couple more pastors from Ridge View. Next Saturday, they would like help with a prayer walk through the downtown area and around the residential area."

"They should start in the parking lot at the Cozy Corner Café. One road swings north around town and the other leads through the center of town," urged Tim the waiter.

"What time?" asked Jerry.

"Nine in the morning to noon..." informed Kip, "Will some go with me?"

John Mark, Amanda, Misty, Karen, Ezra, the Bond family, and others volunteered, as Izzy said, "That's part of spiritually restoring Blair House. Misty, stay with a group."

"I'll be by her side, and I think I know some others may look forward to participating..." smiled John Mark at Misty, who became radiant.

"If there are no other announcements, let me get into a couple of agenda items," Izzy stated. "I wanted to help clarify what we mean when talking about both physical and spiritual restoration of Blair House... a lot has already happened with today's agenda...beginning with how we started..." Izzy paused as most soaked in the thought. "Physical restoration is about our making new what once was...about repairing Blair House and making upgrades, which will take some time. It is about making good use of the land that goes with the estate. As you know my father owns the house and the land around it plus the mountain valley and north along a ridge beyond the creek north of the cabin. It extends up the west peak of Huajatolla and south toward Pryor where the boys lived. Local ranchers have used mountain pastures to graze their cattle, and we will be hunting the woods for game. To the south we border Adam Claymore's land, while to the north it becomes either national forest or BLM land. I'm certain you have noticed how my dad has been harvesting the dead and downed timber, which keeps with the idea of physical restoration. The property includes the water and mineral rights."

"Are we going to work on all that?" Jerry asked.

"No, our primary focus is right here, but we can dream a little. There is plenty to do right here, but the potential for creating jobs that would affect the lives of people in the valley may one day become a realization, and it is what the opposition is really about, the McNaughton Corporation, I'm certain."

"That clarifies some things..." said John Mark.

"On the spiritual side of things, we are seeking to restore the spiritual influence of Blair House as a light shining in darkness, that we would regain what God had the Blair's establish. Lydia and Paul were good people. Folks have said the beauty of Jesus could be seen in and through them. Right, Dad?" Izzy asked his father, who eagerly nodded with a smile, "While my dad was off fighting the Viet Nam War, the Blair's raised me. I owed them a lot, but when I found out they were not my parents, I didn't respond well. Janine can tell you...I kind of flipped out. I got drunk, stole a chest of gold, and then lost it. Janine, can tell you. I guess Karen can too, since I came back to the valley on the same bus she arrived here on. Anyway, I'm still looking for the gold I lost."

"Just a minute," said Janine with a Cheshire Cat grin, "I found it and hid it," as she got up from the table, walked to the fireplace, stood before the upper air vent on the right hand side of the mantle, pulled the face plate out, reached in, and extracted a wooden chest. Struggling to carry it, she brought it to Izzy and gave it to him saying, "I hid this in hopes of using it for a honeymoon, Izzy, I know now we need to use the wealth that's enclosed to pay for the restoration. What's left over is left over, if any."

Both Izzy and his father were flabbergasted by Janine's revelation to the extent that Izzy did not open the chest. He resisted his desire to glance at the gold, so as to not provoke jealousy or covetousness amongst their friends. Izzy continued holding the chest and prophesied, "This could become a spiritual problem we do not want. What we do want is your help in re-establishing Blair House as a spiritual force for God in the Rock Creek Valley. Let our light shine. The rave and Baal worship are opposition, and so is the bear, I think. Our goal is to submit to the Lordship of Christ and to follow his plan for us as in *First Chronicles*, chapter four, verses nine thru ten, to be salt and light as in *Matthew*, chapter five, verses thirteen thru sixteen, to work for revival as in *Second Chronicles*, chapter seven, verse fourteen, while following the great commission of *Matthew*, chapter twenty-eight, verses eighteen thru twenty. All the while, each of us will be laying up eternal rewards and wages in heaven."

"Please, no one mention you saw the chest," John Mark said, as his countenance became serious, "and understand the real wealth of this moment on the part of Janine."

Unfortunately, again they did not listen or comprehend what John Mark had meant, as Jerry spoke, "I mostly followed you, Izzy, and I don't need to fully understand. I do think God is with us, especially based on the results of the attack on us to kidnap Misty. We turned public opinion when we showed grace and mercy to the attackers who had been deceived by Van Allen and probably others."

"We are winning the hearts of a lot of people. You should hear what people are saying in town. I think it is important to know what the townspeople think," said Ken.

"Including the Indians," urged Mike Crowfoot, who looked at his sister Janine when he spoke.

"It includes both Quail Point and Wolf City," offered Caleb.

"Especially, the oldtimers in Ridge View," argued Tim the waiter.

"And working people like those in the Rock Creek Neighborhood Watch," mused Karen.

Izzy asked, "What about Jericho Springs?"

"The battle for Jericho is well underway. Ken, Kip, and I got an earful at Bustos Mexican Restaurant," Amanda interjected, "and we got support from an unexpected source, a high school student named Marisa."

"Excuse me for a minute, Miss Amanda and Izzy, let me either lead off or bat second or maybe start off with Mike and follow with me," offered Caleb, "I think the sequence will be important for our understanding." Seeing no opposition, he proceed, "In nice little Quail Point where a nice little girl was allegedly killed by her much older lover and her body stored under a bridge, we have the mayor who was incensed when we held his two teenaged, smart mouthed, rave participating daughters, after an event where a man and wife were injured and another girl died from a fall off the cliff. Whether the daughters were there to participate in the Baal ceremony, we don't know. How they got information about the event we don't know, because the father won't let me directly talk to them. Karen may be the way to reach these girls, because she taught there and because I'm a cop. Dad doesn't seem to believe his daughters could be involved in the likes of what he knows or feared was happening. Either way, the parent was not receptive to me, and I'm an outsider, black, and a newcomer."

"You are talking about April and May Osteen. I know them well. The father is Mayor August Osteen. I could talk with the mayor's wife, January," answered Karen, former teacher in Quail Point, "and the answer, I think, is dad is overwhelmed by the idea of his daughters being involved in human trafficking like other girls at the high school. I think his first concern would be about what that would mean for his political career. The mother would not hesitate to deal with the girls."

"Okay let's not get into solutions yet," advised Izzy, "I think we should put ourselves in the girls and parents' point of view. What about Wolf City? What have you heard coming out of there?"

"Let me give my point of view and switch the microphone to Mike, pun intended," continued Caleb, "the death of Betty Strong Bull appears to be a tragic accident. There has been no public clamor to find answers to how and why the death happened. It has just been accepted that, sadly, someone's daughter died when attending the rave. I think there is more to it, so do some others. Like Betty's grand-father, I feel the same way about my sister's death, there was little response from the public compared to what it would be if the two deaths had been April and May Osteen."

"Because your sister was black and Betty a Ute Indian?" asked Mike Crowfoot.

"Maybe, I know that's what I thought initially, and I guess it's easier to claim that, but when I met Betty's grandfather, a grandfather to Mike and Janine as well, I realized the theory doesn't work. Chief Strong Bull is the power structure. Their roots here go deeper than everyone else. But he is not part of the McNaughton Corporation and does not live directly in the valley. I wonder if the issue comes down to money."

"Caleb symbolically handed the mic to Mike Crowfoot, who said, "Ta-ton-ka speaks well, Caleb." He paused and looked directly at Janine, "He hit it off with our grandfather. They arm wrestled to a draw."

"And that doesn't happen..." added Janine.

"I stayed with Grandpa, while Caleb went to Quail Point. I think the issue is spiritual. If some kind of battle comes our way, Grandpa will be on our side. He is a friend of Ezra's, and we will be okay, so long as we are true to our faith."

"You mean we must be real?"asked Kip.

"I think it means our yes is yes and our no is no," answered Janine.

Misty leaned over to Amanda and whispered, "I think it means no lying..." to which Amanda nodded affirmatively.

"Basically, my people don't trust the system, which is why we tend to take care of things ourselves, but then again, we are on a reservation. Our experiences haven't been good with treaties when some form of money is involved."

"We are in a spiritual battle. It didn't begin with the rave or when the McNaughton Corporation formed or when the Asherah House began to prostitute women. Look again at Ezra's carving..."said John Mark.

"Well said...who can tell what we're hearing out of Jericho Springs?" Izzy asked.

"Let's see if I can capture what Kip, Ken, and I recently heard at Bustos'," asserted Amanda, "and they can jump in to clarify anything. Not all, but a lot of my friends and neighbors, friends of my mother too...they express a real disdain for newcomers. They blame a lot of what happens on newcomers, and when youth are actually caught doing something like the Night Riders, oldtimers say it's just boys being boys. As if it were acceptable for boys to do mischief, even if people get hurt, and God forbid anyone hold them responsible. After all, if they were prosecuted, it would ruin their lives!"

Kip added, "A lot of people are easily influenced by someone they trust. Sometimes that is good and sometimes not. Most of those involved in the assault on Blair House came here because they believed Misty and maybe Hannah were being held here against their will, which is what a man named Van Allen and maybe others told them. Too bad they didn't check out the facts before acting. But look what happened when Tim bore witness for Christ at the Cozy Corner Café."

"And when the guy stood up and confessed he had been wrong to do what he did...then he was unashamed to tell everyone he had accepted Jesus as his Savior!" added Ken.

"Couldn't you have cheered when Marisa spoke up?" asserted Amanda. "John and I were so proud of her!"

While those, who had been listening, chatted in response to Ken, Kip, and Amanda, Izzy said, "What about Rock Creek? Karen, John Mark, help us out..."

"Even bullies can be redeemed...and I think that includes Butch McNaughton. Adam thinks so too! Adam not only led Butch to Christ, he followed through by being his mentor at least for awhile. Too bad there was no follow through at home. Butch became upset when he heard Adam was in the hospital, and I mean genuine concern. Although they have been on opposite sides a lot, Butch has real respect for this genuine man who invested his time in Butch. I think Butch knows Adam is the real deal. He has seen the light of Christ in and through Adam."

"No hypocrisy, flawed and bruised, but real," said Janine.

"Butch has reached a real low...from Deputy Sheriff to cooking and washing dishes. He is doing what his cousin Harper used to do at the hotel. Butch shamelessly ridiculed Harper to the point it was probably Harper who shot Butch twice in the back..." Karen said,"...and with my pistol!"

"Look what happens when there is a breakthrough," said John Mark. "We prayed at the Church in the Glen for God to reveal to each of us what he wanted us to do. Street corner prayer, neighborhood watch, prayer walks, churches working together, public testimony."

"The opposition is confused, and they don't know what to do," Jill said. "People they considered as weaklings rise up and challenge the bully's comfort zone!"

The room became quiet, as all around the table pondered the input, until John Mark spoke up, "One lady asked an insightful question."

"What was it?" several asked.

"Why is it all the deaths that happen in the valley, other than those caused by traffic or natural causes...why have they all happened in Rock Creek?"

"Hmmm..."said Morris, "The battle is the Lord's."

"Anything different in Ridge View," asked Izzy.

"No," said Tim, as he looked Ken's way and referred to Ken's encounter with Red McNaughton, "Power of the press again, as people are willing to confront evil where they find it."

"Are they really Baal worshipers? You should compare the placement of the Asher poles on the ridge to Little Huerfano," John Mark said, then whispered, "Izzy, read chapter fourteen of *First Kings* about the poles being placed before spreading trees."

The boys from Pryor heard, but they had been left out of the discussion and were basically ignored. They smiled at John Mark and said, "We listened and we heard. We will watch, John Mark..."

Deep in thought, Izzy did not listen, did not hear, but looked up and down the sides of the table alternately smiling and frowning, as the team went their own ways. He churned the thoughts in his head. He rested his eyes on his bride, and said to Janine, "I think I've got at least part of it figured out, "Newcomers have an advantage over the oldtimers."

"Really, how do you figure?" asked Janine. "The oldtimers are well rooted here. They have friends, family, and a history."

"True, and most people are related somehow to all the other oldtimers. Inbred," he said, "and relationships are more important than the issues."

"True," she added, "and to survive, a newcomer has to walk a thin line and learn who is in control and who is related to whom."

"Good and evil become obvious..." said Tim.

"To those who pay attention..." added Jerry.

"Bliss is superficial..." Jill surmised.

"Maybe that's why oldtimers resist having anyone dig too deep..."concluded Karen.

"Kinfolk are more important than issues..." Janine added.

"Except when the local economy was decimated by the construction of the interstate highway and the schools were reorganized," Jill countered, "both really rocked valley culture."

"No matter how positive, people resisted change..." Mike explained.

"Especially, when the proposed change arrived by-way of a newcomer as the change agent...So, what is the newcomer's advantage?" said Karen.

"Newcomer's come here from other places. If things don't go well, they can move on to somewhere else, but the oldtimers very existence is at risk. Like in the *Grapes of Wrath*, the family's blood, sweat, and tears were invested in the land. It brought death to the man who lost the homestead when his family had been forced to move on. A newcomer can lose here and easily leave without much heartburn, but if an oldtimer loses, like Red, he loses family, friends, history."

"Well said, Izzy..." said Mike.

"I wish my father could speak," said Izzy, "I'd like to know his perceptions about the valley and its people. He has attended so many meetings—city council, school and church board meetings...all kinds of get-togethers."

"And what did he do?" said Janine.

"He hunted me down and brought me home..."

"To make right that which was wrong..."

"To restore Blair House," Izzy concluded, "and for mercy's sake, let us neither cause or receive pain."

"Except in child birth..." said Janine.

Shocked, Izzy whispered, "You're not..."

"Not yet..." she whispered back and coyly smiled, "We will have time to play, but I just wanted to help put things into perspective?"

# New Pastor, Old Enemies

## CHAPTER 17

*"But when he, the Spirit of Truth, comes, he will guide*
*you into all the truth..."*                    John 16:13a

I f one were to create an historical timeline for a Christian family, wouldn't you expect to find major markers posted on a Sunday morning? Such would be the case this morning for the Bonds and the Brownings. Happenings on this Sunday would forever link the two families.

For the Bond family members, their day began with the delivery of the Sunday *Rocky Mountain News* and the *Denver Post* newspaper editions. They delivered news to the valley not only on a door to door basis, but also through newspaper stands placed at businesses. Delivering newspapers had only been a prelude to the good news that would be delivered later Sunday morning. Getting up at 3:00 a.m. to meet the newspaper delivery truck at the interstate highway outside of Ridge View, husband/ father Ken Bond felt blessed to have the support of wife/mother Katarina and daughters Kristin and Krystal. The task today had been completed as a family venture, but a milestone came later with the literal realization of a dream that was about to come true. The family had left New Jersey at God's direction for them to return to Colorado and to go into the mountains. To do what, they didn't know. They had lived the winter of 1979 in a mountain cabin near Central City, and the girls attended school in Nederland, Colorado. And then they came down from the mountain. Dad entered seminary and worked as a church custodian. Two days

before starting as an assistant pastor for youth and Christian education, he survived congestive heart failure and the widow maker, a
moderately severe myocardial infarction to the pumping chamber of
his heart at age thirty-five.

For the Browning family wife/mother Ruth had risen earlier than
her husband Robert and son Andrew. Putting on her long white bathrobe and fuzzy red slippers, she sat on the front porch with their white
boxer, The Princess Frieda Louise. Tucking her feet under her, she
watched for the Bond's station wagon to cross the bridge, which covered Rock Creek. She thought about how her husband had called for
her and her son Andy to come to the valley to repair their fractured
marriage and family. Arriving with two other newcomers on the same
bus, she entered the valley with her new friend Karen Gustafson and
Izzy Freedom, the rightful heir of the Blair House estate. Spotting the
Bond's station wagon, Ruth walked briskly to the end of her driveway
with The Princess beside her. Ruth hoped to greet the Bonds, as they
delivered her copy of the *Denver Post*.

Seeing Ruth at the end of her driveway, Ken slowed to a stop
to hand Ruth her newspaper and said, "This is the day the Lord
hath made!"

Ruth responded with, "Let us rejoice and be glad in it!"

From the front passenger seat, Katarina called out, "What a great
day for Andy!"

"He is excited! We all are thrilled for Andrew to be baptized this
morning!" said Ruth.

"And Daddy gets to baptize him!" said Kristin.

"I can hardly wait to congratulate him," followed Krystal.

"All of you are precious to him, to us all!" Ruth smiled with tears
in her eyes. "Be safe! The bear hasn't been found."

"There hasn't been any sign of the bear since the snow storm is
what I've heard," Ken said, as he removed his foot from the brake
pedal and let the car ease forward as it idled. "See you in a couple
of hours."

Taking the rubber band off the tri-folded paper, Ruth read the
flyer Katarina and the girls had inserted in all the papers for home
delivery. "Good for Ken to announce he will begin preaching this
Sunday at the little Church in the Glen. Soon move to Claymore house

in Rock Creek. Same phone number..." Ruth said, "...Good for Pastor! If people didn't know before, they'll know now he's a Christian, which puts a target on his back...and Kat and the girls too."

Entering the front doorway, closing the door and leaving The Princess outside, Ruth shouted out, "Wake up, get out of bed. Come on you sleepy head..."and then she sang in her best voice, *Morning has Broken*... to which both father and son sat up and listened to her melodious song. Captivated, both hurried down the stairs to draw near her and sing as well.

Coming up behind her, Rob took her in his arms, turned her around, and planted a long kiss on her lips, and said, "I love to hear you sing. You've been singing a lot lately..."

"It's easy to sing when you tell me you love me..."

"It's easy to say I love you when you have asked me to please do something..."

Interrupting, Andy slid feet first onto the kitchen throw rug singing, "I've got Mohawk in the morning..."

To which both parents replied, "Oh no, not the Mohawk in the morning song," and the dog howled to be let in and join the merrymaking.

"Come on, Rob, let's fix breakfast for our little man. Andrew's getting baptized this morning!"

"Dad, am I a little man?"

"You sure are, Son," Rob said. "We are very proud of you!"

"Are you very proud of me too, Mom..." Andrew paused, as Mom nodded affirmatively, "so you aren't mad at me for anything when you called me Andrew?"

"No, my little man, I'm very pleased with you, and I called you Andrew because you've done a big boy thing...and the Bond girls said they couldn't wait to congratulate you."

"Kristin and Krystal? You talked to Krystal and Kristin...do they have their bubblegum plexion?" Andrew said as he clasped his hands, raised them to his right ear, and rested his head on them, "I can't wait to see them. Dad, do you suppose, I'll get to hug them?"

"Maybe," said Ruth, "and you remember to be a gentleman."

"Can we invite them to go to the movies with us this afternoon in Peeblo?"

"Let's see what's on," said Mom.

"We may have a hard time finding a suitable movie," said Dad, which gained him an appreciative smile from Mom, "but I've got a backup plan."

With Andrew at her knee, Ruth found the entertainment section of the paper, and read, "Hmmm...the ones that look good are not G rated..."

"What are they?" asked Dad.

"R rated, *'Private Benjamin'*; PG rated, *'The Elephant Man'*; and PG rated, *'Somewhere in Time'.*"

"I've read the reviews and they all look good but not for someone not yet six...how about going to the Cheyenne Mountain Zoo in Colorado Springs!"

"Could still be cold, they got more snow than we did," said Mom.

"Mom, Dad, we don't have to do anything special. Nothing could top me gettin' baptized, and there's nuthin' much to do here..." offered Andrew.

"What would you like to do?" asked Dad.

"Let's just stay home, eat popcorn, watch football, and play Sorry!" answered Andy, while he clapped his hands.

"Ruth, there really isn't much for kids to do when you can't go outside and play. Maybe we should take a drive and explore our surroundings?"

"Wahoo," shouted Mom, "then let's eat breakfast and go to church!"

\*\*\*

Normally, Adam would have arrived first at the little Church in the Glen, but since he lay recuperating in bed at his Claymore Flats ranch house, John Mark arrived first. He set and stoked a fire in the potbelly stove near the front of the chapel seating, and then checked the windows and doors for any break-ins or mischief. Walking the grounds, he looked for signs of the bear, and finding none, he breathed a sigh of relief. Next, he checked the water temperature in the baptistery tub, which was located behind a curtain at the front of the sanctuary. Since he had filled the tub the night before, he found the water lukewarm as predicted by Adam. As John Mark tested the water from the steps leading to the tub, he wondered first about the tub's construction, and then about whether or not the water would be used to irrigate the landscape.

Earlier in the week John Mark had made some repairs and arranged for others. He replaced a broken window in the outside door to the pastor's office. Despite multiple calls to the rural electric company, no one had come to replace and repair the lenses and bulbs, which had been destroyed by rifle fire during the rave. Finding replacement bulbs and one spare lens on a shelf next to a rod with dusty choir robes, he had prayed God would send someone to climb the church's light pole. John Mark had sat on the chair Andy would use the following Sunday to change his clothes and put on a white linen robe for the baptism. John Mark had prayed there for little Andy Browning and for God to use him mightily. Sitting on the chair he had realized Andy's father was the solution to the yard light problem. John Mark called Rob who promised to replace the bulb the next evening.

Wearing spiked shoes and a belt with pole strap, Rob Browning had arrived on his way home from work Monday afternoon. Before climbing, he made certain the light switch had been turned off in the pastor's office, and then he shinned up the pole effortlessly with the lens and bulb secured in his backpack. In what seemed only minutes, he had reached the top of the pole. Rob secured himself to the pole with his spikes well set into the wood. He leaned out from the pole with his body strap preventing a fall, unscrewed the remains of the lens and bulb, and successfully replaced both. Next, Rob waved for John Mark to switch on the light, which once again brightly illuminated the side and back of the church building. Beyond in the graveyard and on the footbridge, dusk began to fade and would soon give way to night. During the night, the yard light would produce shadows, as trees and bushes would partially block its shine. Further back the light would diminish and only part of the lane leading to the county road would be seen, as would the landscape in front of the church along the driveway. Seemingly, the effect of the light would end with the leaves in the birch grove or across the creek where climbing roses clung to the mesa wall. Effectively, the light set parameters, as someone in the light would be forewarned against something evil lurking beyond the limits of the light.

While at the top of the pole, Rob had looked beyond the church property to watch as the sun reclined behind the mountains. Watching the mountain shadow darken the valley west to the eastern ridge, he caught a glimpse of where the rave had been staged. His glimpse captured the remains of the Asher pole and ceremonial table as well as the wispy form of a sapling supported with four dowels. He questioned the reality of what he had seen and thought he could see but not determine its shape. Curious, he had thought before descending the pole, if it is a tree, it had to have been planted after the rave. Rob asked John Mark if he had noticed anyone working on the ridge. John Mark shrugged his shoulders and claimed he had not, which was true. John Mark thought wryly, I did not see Brother Niall plant the Live Oak, but I did see Andy's father restore the yard light at the church, and I hoped the light of Christ would shine brightly through Rob's son.

Aquila Parson and Priscilla King arrived first, made an urn of coffee, and set it on the white linen tablecloth on top of a folding table at the back of the sanctuary. They added fresh baked cookies they had made the night before. Aquila always brought three dozen raisin nut oatmeal cookies, while Priscilla made chocolate chip ones. The ladies, as hostesses, checked and filled a supply of Styrofoam cups, paper napkins and plates as well as plastic spoons, sugar, and powdered dairy creamer. Looking at one another, they nodded their approval, and then grabbed dust mops they pushed over the hard wood floors. While Priscilla shook the dust mops out the door to the pastor's office, Aquila used a feather duster on the lectern, piano, and organ. Replacing their cleaning tools, they told Pastor Ken that all was ready.

"You won last week," Aquila said, "so mine goes closest to the entry way!"

"Which means if yours disappear before mine this Sunday," Priscilla replied, "I buy you lunch on workday, Monday."

"I'm switching to peanut butter cookies, if you win three in a row," promised Aquila.

Judge Randolph Parson arrived simultaneously with Arthur King, the elementary school principal, who were promptly greeted by their wives. Both had become regular attendees after the attempted arson at the Blair House. A procession of Rock Creek residents made its way down Indiana Avenue, County Road 403, and the Valley Highway. Almost all of the neighborhood watch families and single adults merged together at the highwayman's house just south of Adam's Rock Creek house. The group assumed a swagger, a presence, a countenance reflecting their unity of purpose, pride, and sense of belonging. They had come not only in support of their leader John Mark, but also for Ken Bond, who delivered their newspapers and had been appointed to preach today. One neighbor had notice Ken Bond's announcement tucked inside the newspaper and activated the telephone chain. Others called the neighbors, who had not attended the neighborhood watch meeting, to spur them forward. Sarah and her mother Lila Longdon had asked to have Sunday morning off from work, so they could attend church. When Butch consented, they invited him to meet them at church. If he would, Lila promised to serve him a fried chicken and mashed potato dinner after church. Lila promised to serve him Olathe sweet corn, fresh baked bread, and pie made from cherries, which she had purchased in Paonia during the annual Cherry Days Festival.

Heads turned as bad-boy Butch McNaughton entered the sanctuary and sat down next to Sarah and Lila Longdon. A buzz hovered over the congregation as more attendees arrived from Jericho Springs, Ridge View, and the plains and mountains north of Ridge View. When Priscilla and Aquila stepped forward and greeted Butch at the end of the isle where he sat, Priscilla said welcome home to him and the buzz stopped. The congregation's attention shifted to the little boy who happily entered the church lobby and proclaimed he was getting baptized today. Andy went up and down the aisles telling the adults that he had accepted Jesus as his Savior. He told them he knew his sins were forgiven even if his mom still spanked him!

Butch engaged in conversation with Sarah and Lila and others in the row in front of him. He told them he once had attended the little Church in the Glen and that his Uncle Adam Claymore had discipled him for years. He said he had drifted away from church before becoming a deputy sheriff. Assuming they knew of his shameful exploits, he credited Sarah and Lila for his being at church today.

Meanwhile, the group from Blair House arrived and took seats near the front of the sanctuary. When Misty and Hannah sat directly in Butch's view, he groaned in dismay and hung his head in shame. Sarah put her hand on his shoulder, comforted him with words of encouragement, and trusted his feelings were of genuine remorse. She too had felt the brunt of his abusive actions. Wranglers from Claymore Flats arrived escorting one of the McNaughton grandmothers, Beatrice Jaramillo, and they sat directly behind Misty and Hannah. Butch remembered his friend Buddy Smith had thrown a beer bottle at Gramma Bea and knocked her down into the barrow ditch on the west side of the highway in front of the church. Butch realized Adam was not present and would not be preaching, and his own father should have been with Adam hunting the bear, which had ravaged their herd. What happened next brought forth memories that shook Butch to his core.

While Pastor Ken and Rob Browning helped prepare Andrew for baptism, Jill Lowenstein led the congregation in singing hymns and praises. Rabbit Pinebow read the announcements, asked visitors to fill out a visitor's card and place the card in the offering plate, and then he led the congregational offertory prayer. Mike Crowfoot and Jerry Sunday passed collection plates, and then gave them to Priscilla and Aquila for counting. Dressed in his wading boots and white gown, Pastor Ken and Andy's father, Rob Browning, came out from the dressing room, and stepped into the baptistery. Pastor read scripture in preparation for Andrew's baptism.

"Most of us know Andrew as Andy, but as his mother and father have said, Andrew has made a big boy decision to follow Jesus not only as his Savior but also as his Lord. My wife and I and my daughters, Kristin and Krystal, have known Andy from the beginning of the Brownings' arrival in the Rock Creek Valley. We have prayed for Andy's salvation regularly. So how is it one can be saved?" Pastor Ken paused, "You know all have sinned and fall short of the glory of God. The wages of sin is death, but God provided a way out of those consequences. Jesus is the way, the only way. He paid the price for you by dying on the cross. If you believe in your heart and profess with your mouth Jesus is your lord and savior, then you will live forever, for Jesus died so all may live. *"For God so loved the world that he gave his one and only Son, that whoever believes in him shall not perish, but have eternal life" (John 3:16).* Eternal life, eternal salvation begins the moment you invite Jesus into your heart. Today, you have an opportunity to accept the finished work of Jesus. Let us pray.

Pastor invited Andrew to step into the baptistery, and said, "Andrew, how's the water?"

"Kinda chilly, but I'm okay. My dad's here. We could be in the creek or the pond by my house."

"Shall I call you Andrew or Andy?"

"Today, I'm being called Andrew, my mom and dad say so because I've made a big boy decision, but I'm really just Andy and that's what Jesus calls me."

"Jesus calls you by your name?"

"Yes, Sir."

"Did he say anything else?"

"He said love one another like how he has loved us."

"What does that mean, Andrew?"

"I'm to love my parents and do what they say."

"Anything else?"

"No...not yet, but I know there is more to come..."

"Well..."

"But there is more, I know I'm to talk with him every day. I've been praying for a lot of months already. And I'm to learn to read as soon as possible."

"Why are you to learn to read?"

"Oh, I think it's obvious!"

"Did Jesus tell you that?"

"No, I've watched Mom and Dad read the Bible and they pray together. Sometimes I get to pray with them. Things have been real good since they do that. Our family's not broke anymore."

"So you know you need to pray and talk with God, and you need to learn to read the Bible. Do you have a children's Bible or do you think you can handle a Bible like your mom and dad's?"

"I'm going to listen to Dad. He said I'll start with a children's Bible. Dad said Jesus will help me understand. I think Dad can tell me what I don't understand. Dad already ordered a Bible for me at the Blair

House. There's a bookstore there. I saw Krystal and Kristin there, Mr. Pastor," Andrew smiled dreamily at the thought of them.

"So Andrew," Pastor said, as he moved into position to baptize Andrew, "Have you accepted Jesus as your savior?"

"Yes Sir, so my sins are forgiven and I'll have 'ternal life."

"Eternal?" Pastor asked and Andy nodded.

"And you want Jesus to be your Lord?"

"Oh, yes, I really like him...I want to be like him..."

"Hold your nose with your hand and hold your arm close to your chest and bend your knees like I showed you. Rob, you stand beside me like I showed you."

"Yes, Sir..."

"Andrew Browning, based on your confession of faith in Jesus, I baptize you in the name of the Father, and of the Son, and of the Holy Spirit..." Pastor said, as he and Rob submerged Andy under water, and then Pastor said, as he raised Andy from the water, "Dead to sin, alive in Christ."

The crowd clapped, cried tears of joy, and took pictures, as Pastor raised Andrew from the waters, then he said with an infectious smile, "Meet Andrew Browning, who has been born again."

While Pastor, Rob, and Andrew changed clothes, Jill led the congregation in singing, *Power in the Blood.* Pastor quickly exited the room where he changed his clothes and joined Jill at the lectern. She left the stage and sat down, as Pastor began speaking.

"I have mixed feelings about speaking before you today. It means a very kind person, Adam Claymore, is not speaking. Adam came to my rescue when my family was burned out of the trailer we rented from him on state highway 96. We lost everything but what we had with us, which meant the clothes on our backs and our Bibles. Adam took us in at the Claymore ranch house and not only gave us food and lodging, but also provided us with another place to live when Jill and Janine moved into the Blair House and became a part of the team helping to rebuild it. Now, he invited me to fill in for him with the prospect of my becoming the full time pastor here. I welcome the opportunity. It has been a heartfelt goal of mine to pastor a flock in a local church, a goal I had worked for and nearly died, while trying to fulfill it. There's more to my story, our story," Pastor Ken said, while pointing toward his wife and two daughters.

"I accepted Christ as my Savior, while attending a church my grandfather had been forced to leave. My grandfather lost his wife in the birth of my father. As a widower, he had a difficult time dealing with his loss. As a result he had to leave his church at the discipline of his pastor. To my knowledge, my father never darkened the door of a church again, except when my sister and I married. Although my father had nearly completed college to become a veterinarian, he had to drop out of college in his last year when his father and he lost their real estate holdings on Denver's north-side."

"Eventually, my father became an alcoholic, and he moved us to the country near the junction of what are now Orchard Road and the Valley Highway, which is better known as Interstate 25. We lived on Yosemite Street, which was bordered by thirty-five acres of farm land. My father had the opportunity to buy the acreage for five thousand dollars, but to do so, he would have to borrow the money from his mother-in-law, my grandmother, who out of hatred toward him, refused to lend him the money to buy the farm."

"When my father stopped drinking, we moved to town and lived in an apartment above South Pearl Street Grocery Store across the street from Grant Junior High School. My brother's friend invited my brother, sister, and me to attend a Baptist church on South Logan Street and all three of us thrived there. I participated in the youth group at church and got to attend Camp Id-ra-ha-je, I'd rather have Jesus. Our youth group attended a Youth for Christ program at the Denver Auditorium and I went forward at the invitation to receive Christ as my Savior. A short time later, the pastor of the Baptist church baptized me. Much later, I found out the man who baptized me was the same pastor who had removed my grandfather from the church. I found that coincidence particularly of interest, because I don't believe in coincidences. God had a plan that happened despite what men had done."

"One of the first things I did as a new believer was to pray God would raise-up a godly woman for me to marry. He did! I met her as a senior at South High School in Denver. We started dating on February 1, and on February 22, I told her I had gone home and told my folks I was getting married," Pastor Ken said, as he pointed again at Katarina, "...and she said, oh yeah, who to? So I said we are getting married... and then I said okay? She was kind of floored by that, but she said yes. We married in Kat's church, and soon became the adult advisors for the junior high school youth group. We had started right, and we read the Bible and prayed together. It was then I figured I should become a school teacher. "

"I mostly worked washing dishes in a bowling alley off of Colorado Boulevard and pumped gasoline on West Alameda Avenue. Kat was a legal secretary straight out of high school. I made $200 a month and she made $270. I figured out I would have to go to college, if I was ever going to support Kat and have a family. So...I went to school and worked nights as a copyboy at the *Denver Post*. I finally graduated and became a teacher in Commerce City. We saved our money and bought a house, because we qualified for President Johnson's War on Poverty Program. My daughter Kristin came along, and I started working after school as an elementary school coach until 5 p.m. and for two hours more at the corner grocery store. Each summer I went to a Bible college in hopes I would one day become a pastor...and that work pattern pretty much followed me up to my heart attack. My solution to problems was for me to work harder. I didn't want to end up like my dad, who seemed to have been defeated by life's circumstances. I failed to see his victory in overcoming the bottle. Unfortunately, he lived a generation too early. Had he been in my generation, well, he would have survived the heart disease. To his credit, he worked every day he could after his heart attack until he had another that took him."

"So what's my point you might be asking. I hope you are asking... here's a few. As a young couple my wife and I started right. We prayed together and read the Bible together. We had a date night every week, but we got side tracked. Let's work more to strengthen marriages rather than to have divorce recovery as a main goal. Two, from the start our marriage had been Christ centered, but we really needed to be discipled by and in the church. That will be a focal point of my ministry here. Three, Instead of working harder, we are going to grow in what you have been doing. This church is known to be a praying church, and you have reached out to the community. By God's grace...

and his mercy, we are going to seek his plan, his direction instead of striving. Four, by God's grace, we will carry the good news of Jesus into the community. Ours is to share the Gospel, it's up to the Holy Spirit to convict others to accept Jesus into their heart. Five, I should have had more compassion for my father's circumstances. I should have extended more grace...and mercy toward him...like Adam Claymore has done toward my family. We were without food and shelter and he took us in..." Ken paused, then continued, "Perhaps I've gone too far... you know I deliver your newspapers... I will have to continue. I will be a bi-vocational pastor. I will need your help, and, of course, we will talk more and pray more about what I have shared and about what is on your hearts, too. My family continues to be blessed by Adam who is going to provide us with housing. We will be moving into the finest home in Rock Creek," Ken said with a swagger, "and you know we have a master carpenter in John Mark who is finishing the remodeling of it. Later we will have an open house there."

"One more thing before we have a coffee and cookie fellowship... next week I'll be preaching about the Bema and the rewards and wages we will receive...or not...when Christ comes again. Meanwhile, let us hold one another in prayer, and please pray especially for Pilgrim Wayne and Adam Claymore, as they heal from injuries, while defending others from the great bear that has plagued our valley. Also, be certain to greet Andrew Browning and his family."

As Pastor gathered his family, Butch moved toward the front of the sanctuary. The rest of the attendees milled around the coffee and cookies, and then exited through the lobby and onto the church lane. Kat noticed Butch's approach first and grabbed her husband's arm to get his attention and said, "Ken, Butch McNaughton is coming to talk with you...I think..."

Butch said softly, "Pastor, I'm sorry the trailer was set on fire. I'm sorry you lost most of what you had. I'm glad all of you are safe and that my uncle took you in. He's like that you know..."

"Thank you, it's Butch isn't it...your name..." responded Pastor Ken.

"Yes, Sir, Butch McNaughton, I used to attend church here when I was young. Pastor Borden served here then, but it was my uncle who led me to the Lord. He discipled me...please tell him I was here, if you will, he'll be pleased. Tell him I haven't forgotten," said Butch.

"And has your father and mother attended here…"

"My father use to come here before Adam married Mary McNaughton."

"And your mother?"

"I never met her, and apparently, neither has anyone else…"

"What a mystery…Butch…I'm glad you came. We will be here every Sunday…you are always welcomed to worship here."

"We'll see…just be careful…if you don't mind, would you let me slip out of here through the pastor's office? I'm a little bit embarrassed," Butch confessed.

Pastor Ken led Butch to the pastor's office and watched as Butch crossed the floor to the exit door. Butch turned to wave toward the pastor, but noting Pastor had already turned to join the crowd inside, he quickly stuffed a wad of paper into the lock jam to prevent the door from fully closing.

Sheepishly, Butch walked past the cemetery, crossed the footbridge, and followed the path to the bridge over the creek, and continued on CR403 to the Tobacco Store where he entered through the back door.

"Is it true, Butch, you actually attended church this morning?"

With a smirk on his face, Butch admitted, "Just as planned, I even sat with Sarah and her mother, Lila Longdon. The wedding's been postponed."

"What was it like?" several asked.

"Actually, it was quite a moving experience!" Butch shared, contemplatively, "The little boy, whose ducks we set fire to…he got baptized. It reminded me how important Adam Claymore had been to me growing up…and how he was one of very few who visited me in jail."

"Oh, brother…" Red growled, "here it comes…"

"Where the father gets slammed and the uncle gets whatever…" said Ralph of Wolf City. "I've got something I've got to tell you!"

"There's some truth to that…" Red confessed, as he ignored Ralph.

"What else, Butch?" asked Van Allen.

"I gave them those ducks…" said Ellis Moss.

"Remember the family who lived on 96? The ones who lived in the trailer we torched?" Butch continued.

"The guy delivers the newspapers?" clarified Irv Moss.

"He took on Red at the Cozy Corner Café the other day!" clarified Ellis.

"Yes," Butch continued, "he is the new pastor. He and his family were taken in by Adam after the fire. Now Adam is going to set them up in his house on Main Street, as soon as John Mark is finished restoring it. You know that house belonged to Adam's wife Mary." Butch paused, and then said, "The Pastor talked at length about what it was like for him growing up...Did you know his woman helps at Blair House?"

"My wife says she runs the Christian bookstore," said Seamus.

"We need to do something about that place..." urged Van Allen.

"They always toss the paper on my porch..." added Seamus.

"And the church...they've got people doing things all over the valley!" noted Roy Sentry.

"And Cousin Tim too! He hears too much, and he's joined the group at the Blair House," Robert King said angrily.

"And Izzy, too bad the bear didn't get him like it got Pilgrim and Adam, speaking of which, we need to find out what Adam knows," urged Buddy.

"In the works," Red growled, and then asked his son directly, "Butch, did you do what you were supposed to do?"

"Yeah, I did...I stuffed a wad of paper in the jam of the door, so it will stay depressed when the door is locked. We will be able to go inside without breaking in," Butch answered, "but I don't feel good about it...I remember when Tim was baptized...so was I..."

"What about Aquila and Priscilla on the street corners?" asked Buddy Smith.

"What are you, stupid? That would cause us more trouble than you hitting Beatrice with a beer bottle!" growled Red.

"We wouldn't have to hit them...just toss a few eggs in their direction..." Buddy clarified.

"*Lord of the Flies,*" mumbled Butch contemplatively.

"Flies are all dead, Butch, what did you have in mind?" Ellis asked.

"Nothing, I just remembered a book I read in school about a group of boys who threw rocks at one boy that wore glasses," Butch replied. He then turned in his chair to face his father directly and said, "Dad, don't you realize what will happen when we do what's already planned?"

Red neglected answering his son, but growled as he said, "We need to get the water and mineral rights...and we need to be able to conduct the raves without interference. Look how the opposition gains strength. The pastor at the Jericho Springs Baptist Church got other churches to join with him and go door to door with gift bags. We need to divide and conquer."

"Cool, who's the pastor?" asked Ralph.

"Donald Borden...he use to be the pastor in Rock Creek," explained Robert King, the realtor.

"I've got something I've got to tell ya..." Ralph said anxiously.

"Shut up!" growled Red.

"My mom and sister go to the Baptist church in Jericho Springs," said Roy Sentry.

"Don't you have problems with that?" growled Red.

Cowering, Roy countered, "You sound like that grizzly, Red...I'm just sayin'...I mean I'm already in a whole lot of trouble with my family and the law."

"I'd like to know who took the rifles out of the back of my truck and let the air out of my tires," Robert stated.

"So would I...Cotton's been snooping around the evidence room and discovered where the rifles came from. They were all gathered from previous crimes," answered Bailey, who was visibly shaken, "Caleb Jones has interviewed people all over the valley. He's part of CBI. They searched my office and my home. What about the missing girl who fled into Red's pasture?"

"Don't know, Sheriff, that's kinda your department, don't you think?" asked Robert.

"That includes Wolf City and Quail Point," added Ralph, "Jones has been there too!"

"Jones left the hotel. What I heard is that he has one of the rooms at the Blair House," said Seamus.

"I'd like to see what the old man carved on the tree..." said Butch.

"Did you hear what they said about the tour?" asked Irv Moss.

"He means those who weren't arrested in our failed attempt at Blair House," Butch explained.

"I sure didn't expect that," Ellis Moss added, "I mean we were obviously enemies, and they fed us soda pop and pizza. Old Miss Rachael played songs and we all sang along."

"Hymns, she played hymns," said Butch.

"Hims?" Ellis wondered, "All I know is everyone says they had a good time."

"You know, what I never hear anymore?" Butch asked.

"Your mommy, calling you, 'Butchie, come home now'?" Roy teased.

"No, we never hear the old man's truck go cough, cough, sputter, cough, sputter, boom," Butch answered, "and it warned us when he was around like he was watching over the valley, and now we have the four big men who help the old man deliver wood."

"I just got the creeps..." Butch added, "he could be watching us right now."

"And now there's the neighborhood watch who probably has an eye on us," Red surmised.

"Who's that?" asked Ralph.

"Everybody who lives in Rock Creek," Butch answered, "except for those who live at the Asherah House."

"They're not the only ones watching..." Ralph tried to explain again.

With that said, Red's meeting ended and the group disbanded hastily like cockroaches in a room when the lights were turned on. Out of the darkness of the room, both Maurice Wood and Chauncey Brown emerged together, and Chauncey said, "Red, you have lost them. This was terrible. Detective Jones is on track and will soon have things figured out. We don't have any pregnant women left, do we?"

"Only Misty...and maybe Sarah. I wish Sam was here..."

"Well, he isn't! You know what has to be done!" ordered Dr. Wood, "And we all need to scatter."

"Do the mischief at the church and Blair House. I'll get rid of Tim from the café, so you can meet there without having him listening to what you are planning. Have Heather visit him at Blair House. She will know to case the place. Then lay low and wait until spring and take care of Misty then. Our goals are still the same. You stated them. We need to rebuild our organization," instructed Chauncey.

"The church will run out of steam; it always does," echoed Maurice.

"I'm not so sure..." mumbled Red, as he and Maurice left the building out the back door.

Once outside, all were captured on film by the lady with previous experience, except for Chauncey, who waited for the cover of darkness to leave.

While Red met with Dr. Wood and Chauncey Brown, Ralph finally got someone to listen to him outside in the parking lot. "Listen, Butch, I tried to tell your dad, but he just wouldn't let me speak."

"I know...he's very disturbed..."

"Caleb Jones was in Wolf City, and he met with Chief Strong Bull at the chief's café. Rabbit Pinebow was with Jones, until Caleb started talking with Chief."

"What about?"

"I didn't get to hear and the chief never told anyone then, but he ordered me to meet with him later that afternoon."

"He ordered you! Ha! And you met with him," Butch said, as he mocked Ralph.

"In Wolf City, you don't cross the Chief. If you do, you'll be in the ring with him. Look, Butch, I'm tired of you and your dad. I think you both have some come-up-ins coming soon, and I don't want to be a part of it," Ralph accentuated, "I won't be."

"What are you going to do about it?" Butch said menacingly.

"Butch, I'm not going to be around to be a part of it. The Chief said they would let me leave, if I left now. I just came by to let the group know."

"Leaving? The Chief doesn't run things in the valley."

"I've got what I could get in my truck," Ralph said as he pointed to his truck, "Look around. What do you see?"

Butch scanned the hotel parking lot, "Someone's sitting by himself on the porch, there's a truck parked in front of the fire department, a guy is pumping gas at the convenience store or appears to have been pumping gas."

"They're all from Wolf City. Don't turn around, but someone is on the roof above the tavern taking pictures, and someone is at the mouth of the canyon."

"I see what you mean..." Butch whispered.

"You didn't sound too thrilled with what your dad had to say tonight. I think you have had enough as well. The law might catch up with us all, but in the meantime, I'm leaving. For your own sake, tell your dad to shut everything down in Wolf City and you might live," Ralph advised, as he grasped his truck door handle, slid into the cab, and started the engine, "I'm outta' here!"

# Burnt Ends

## CHAPTER 18

*"The weapons we fight with are not weapons of the world."*                  *2 Corinthians 10:4a*

Loose ends! They can be like burnt ends, tasty and satisfying or sometimes dried out and covered with too much sauce to mask the reality of their condition. Either way, they had to be handled for good or ill, pleasing or disappointing.

Sorting out the real story behind the family that occupied the farmstead at Pryor proved intriguing. Karen thought she knew the story, until Caleb revealed what he had discovered through the Chief and Deputy Candy. By chance or divine appointment, they both had wandered outside their second floor rooms to the east end of the Blair House above the front door on the first floor. They sat in chairs on the porch, as they watched the sunrise. The sun appeared to climb on the horizon, while its light lowered behind them on the Spanish Peaks, which the Ute's call Huajatolla, Breast of the Earth. Caleb started to share his story first about what he and the Chief had learned about the boys from Pryor. Chief Strong Bull had conspired with Detective Jones in conducting an investigation which produced surprising results. It involved the story behind how Deputy Cotton Candy located the boys after the bear attack. It took a few hours, but she found them at the Stage Stop Hotel.

Karen broke into Caleb's narrative to explain that after the bear chased the boys into the town of Rock Creek, the bear met strong opposition near the footbridge. It had followed the boys to the end of the mesa, but the boys fled before it could get to them. Instead, while descending the mesa trail, it attempted to attack Sarah Longdon and her near the footbridge. It balked before a giant of a man who challenged it at the end of the bridge. The old boar retreated before a wall of fire set by Niall Tunnicliffe, the champion by name. Niall ignited the end of the bridge with a sudden burst of flames, and then he waved a long sword over his head so violently the sword sang. In the midst of the blizzard, he stopped the bear's charge long enough for others to join the fight. Bullets rang out from before and above the bear, as Adam Claymore fired his Winchester rifle from above on the footpath and Deputy Candy fired her service revolver, from where she had climbed the tree at the end of the bridge.

What neither knew was that completely thwarted, the grizzly had fled into the night and away from the champion only later to maul Adam Claymore and his horse, Silver, in the orchard. Having gained some satisfaction, the old boar fled through the snow and up the mountain road only to be thwarted again. Meeting the lead drovers driving the mountain herd of cattle, the bear fled again from the road, but successfully found refuge as it fled through the trap door to an underground passageway to the Blair House.

Meanwhile Caleb tried to steer the conversation back to include what the Chief had discovered. Caleb said, "The Chief and his hunting party, a small band of Ute braves, had set out on horseback to find the bear that had mauled his friend, Adam Claymore.

Karen said, "Remember you and Candy arrived at the Blair House at the same time and that she had little time to tell us what happened to her with the boys...The boys revealed to Candy that they had fled to the Stage Stop Hotel to escape the bear. I guess they climbed the fire escape at the east end of the hotel from the front deck. When they got to the second floor, they said they had followed the same path Hannah and I used to escape Butch McNaughton and his friend Roy Sentry, earlier in the summer when I was here interviewing for a job!"

"I remember ..." said Caleb, scratching his head and wondering how Adam managed to communicate with Karen, "that's before Harley used your pistol to shoot Butch in the back."

"Poetic justice?"

"Indeed," Caleb said, "but how did the boys elude discovery?"

"When Butch was after Hannah and me, we shimmied along the second floor ledge to the façade over the front deck. The boys went the other direction around the west side and down the north side of the building. They recounted how they tried to enter rooms they passed by through opened or unlocked windows, but found none until midway up the north-side of the building."

"That put them outside the room you stayed in, 219."

"Yes, remember, Hannah had been the desk clerk. I asked her to get the window repaired, so I could lock it," Karen laughed. "Apparently, it still isn't fixed, but anyway, the boys say they climbed through the window. Once inside they wedged the chest of drawers between the door and bedstead in hopes they could keep the bear out of the room."

"Just like you did to keep unwanted company from bothering you!"

"Yes, meanwhile after Adam had been taken to the hospital and everyone returned to their homes, it must have occurred to Candy that the boys were nowhere in sight. I know she told me she checked back with John Mark and the highwayman who lives next door to John. She went to the convenience store as well as the hotel. Candy told me she actually walked the trail leading to the Asherah House and also the opposite direction through the grove of trees along the ridge to the mouth of the canyon."

"The boys were nowhere to be found?"

"No, and she walked down Indiana Avenue and over to the water tower and down the highway back to her cruiser in the hotel parking lot. And all of this while it was snowing."

"Heavily," added Caleb, "Is it true they broke into the kitchen and helped themselves to some leftovers, while the night clerk slept on the couch in the hotel lobby?"

"Lila, you know, Sarah's mother," Karen laughed again, "but turns out it wasn't leftovers. It was food prep for the morning that Butch had prepared earlier. What a stitch!"

"Even little boys have been able to thwart Butch."

"I know," replied Karen, "and I almost feel sorry for him..."

"But not really..."

"No, a whole lot people have given him a chance to turn around, especially Adam."

"He has nearly hit bottom," frowned Caleb.

"At least his dad has him managing the hotel," Karen said sympathetically. "Caleb, have you ever heard any mention of a Mrs. Whitney 'Red' McNaughton? Or of Butch's mother?"

"No...if they are married, she keeps a low profile. My guess is she divorced Red long ago..." offered Caleb, who then asked, "Were the boys ever caught?"

"The boys, no, they said they walked out the door from the east end of the second floor and went over to visit the Asherah House."

"No one discovered them there?"

"No, they said they walked down the exterior stairwell and into the back parking lot, while Butch was shouting at Lila for getting into the refrigerator. They scampered through the deep snow and entered the back porch, and then they refused to talk about what happened next."

"But Deputy Candy picked them up a couple of hours later, when they walked in the back door to the kitchen. She bought them something more to eat and took them to the Blair House for safe keeping," said Caleb.

"And they've been here ever since, while she is trying to locate relatives to come get them," said Karen, "but...Caleb, didn't you say Chief Strong Bull shared something about where the family came from?"

"Yes, yes I did...I would have liked to have seen them ride out...it was like a hunting party, and in the snow," began Caleb. "The Chief and three of his braves rode through Wolf City in full regalia and out to Pryor...horseback it was. He said he was sending a message to the town, his people, that this would be handled the old way. They went to the farmstead where the boys lived with their parents."

"Did they see the bear?"

"No...and the Chief was specific about it," the detective said, "but they did find a flat bed truck hidden in a stand of Aspen. There was a huge crate on the bed...no he said it was a cage with long bars."

"A cage with long bars?" Karen asked. "And I would imagine powerfully built..."

"I see where you are headed," he responded, "and that was what the Chief concluded as well."

"The cage was big enough..."

"To hold a bear, a grizzly bear...but why? If that were true, why did they have it?"

"Why did they turn it loose?" Karen wondered.

"I wonder if they were trying to reintroduce a grizzly to Colorado..." said Caleb, "or if they rescued the bear from somewhere."

"Whatever the reason, they received no thanks from the bear. It killed both the boys' mother and father."

"If they were the boys' parents..." Caleb questioned.

"Which may be why Deputy Candy has had difficulty locating the next of kin," Karen said, and added, "Now that's a wrinkle I had not expected at all!"

"Remember the bear followed the boys when they fled the cabin in Pryor with Pilgrim. It attacked Pilgrim at cow camp..."

"Then it showed up at Ezra's cabin and escaped the brothers Tunnicliffe..."

"Only to show up at Adam's ranch house..."

"Then it followed the boys to where Sarah and I were sitting on the bench above town. The boys had ridden their horses there and barely paused before descending the trail to the Church in the Glen."

"The boys are the common denominator..." Caleb concluded; "and apparently there is some kind of relationship between the boys and the bear."

"I wonder if they raised the bear. Clearly, they are afraid of it, and they knew what it could do," Karen said. "As you said, the bear killed their parents, if they were the boys' parents."

"Maybe they are not the parents," Caleb added, "but they do share a history! Somehow the four of them appeared to be a family, and who would suspect anything different. They lived in Pryor, which is more of a ghost town than anything else."

"Could that be why Candy has not found their next of kin...or the boys' relatives? Perhaps they have given the bear enough reason to chase after them..." Karen offered, "and now the boys are at Blair House!"

"If the bear isn't hibernating, my guess it will show up soon enough, otherwise not until spring…" Caleb speculated.

"If it doesn't die from the gunshot wounds …Adam had Pilgrim loan me his Sharps rifle, and he said not to give the bear a chance. He was insistent that I was to kill the bear on first sight…"Karen paused, and then prophesied, "Caleb, I think Adam fears what might happen if the bear isn't killed soon."

"He has a right to want the bear killed. Adam is the foremost protector of the valley and without him, we are all at more risk," Caleb asserted. "I don't think his response is out of fear. He's a man of God who walks closely with God. I'd listen to what he has said."

Karen smiled and suggested, "What if it is not a wild bear? What if it came from a circus?"

Caleb laughed, as they started to feel a little foolish, "Go on, and play out the idea…"

"This is like Jerry's group building rules…"

"Where every idea is accepted and explored…"

"And no one is made to feel stupid…"

"I wonder if the bear wears a collar, or maybe one of its ears has been clipped…"Karen said.

"Hopefully, it does have some sort of identification," Caleb replied, "because that would explain a couple of unanswered questions."

Karen and Caleb parted their ways, she to her interviews and he to his investigation, both committing to reconnect and to share what each thought would be helpful to the other. Both recognized the other's need for confidentiality.

A tasty morsel, these tidbits! Not completely satisfying…in need of resolution, hopefully, before Thanksgiving, but spring may be more likely.

***

A solution to another loose end had been instigated by Ezra Sr. He travelled one evening to Rock Creek where he parked his truck in the Stage Stop Hotel parking lot. Instead of entering the hotel, he crossed the highway to visit with John Mark at Adam's house in Rock Creek. In minutes Ezra communicated his purpose by opening his

Bible. He pointed two fingers at John Mark's eyes and then at *Second Kings*, chapter twenty-two. Ezra followed the text through chapter twenty-three. Next, he handed his Bible to John Mark and pointed his two fingers back to chapter twenty-two. Before reading, John Mark prayed for discernment, not just to understand the scripture, but also to understand Ezra Sr.'s purpose. Within an hour, a plan had been struck. John Mark had been chosen to be Ezra's mouth piece at a meeting two nights hence only to include the four Tunnicliffe brothers, Tim McNaughton, and Mike Crowfoot.

When John Mark parked Adam's old Chevy on the hairpin curve above Huerfano Butte, he noticed the others sat circling a small fire in the dry pool not far from the Live Oak tree. The brothers Tunnicliffe wore their cowls and had their hoods pulled over their heads. Ezra, Tim, and Mike flanked them. John Mark prayed as he descended the slope before greeting those gathered, and the others rose and shook his hand when he entered the circle.

John Mark began his assigned role to share Ezra's dream that the others would soon have opportunity to fulfill. He said, "As you know Ezra physically cannot speak. That ability was taken from him by enemies who imprisoned him. He escaped his tormentors to return home. Coming home he was saddened to learn tormentors wrecked havoc in this valley, a valley he sought to protect by fighting in Vietnam. Those tormentors abused innocent people, especially women, children, and the aged. Many sought what does not belong to them, specifically property that belongs to Ezra and his son, and now his daughter-in-law. But it doesn't stop there. All newcomers have been threatened, harassed, and intimidated in hopes they would leave. Ezra has watched, and he has waited. His friend, Chief Strong Bull in Wolf City, shares his point of view, especially because of the recent death of a granddaughter, Betty Strong Bull."

"Is there a plan?" Tim asked.

"Yes, the other night Ezra shared his ideas with me first by having me read what Josiah did in *Second Kings*. I know the Tunnicliffes, as well as myself, came here to fulfill quests. Coinneach and Drostan have made an oath and pledged not to speak until they have fulfilled their quests," John Mark paused and smiled before continuing, "since we arrived here together, most of the time I've enjoyed the silence."

"But you walked here and they drove their yellow jeep," then looking toward brothers Brian and Niall, Mike asked, as the others laughed at John Mark's comment, "Are the two of you here on a quest?"

"I'm here to kill a bear," responded Brother Brian.

Brother Niall, the champion, smiled at Mike, and then replied, "Which is why I didn't kill the bear on the footbridge...I believe I will hear tonight more of why I am here. I've chopped down the Asher pole and burned it and the ceremonial table...but I know there is more to do."

"And you planted a Live Oak sapling..." added John Mark.

"Not only because the ceremony at the so called rave was a fraud and a sham, but also I would have chopped down the Asher pole and burned it with the Baal ceremonial table anyway. They know not what they do..."

"Their ignorance does not excuse them?" asked Tim.

"Taking on the appearance of Baal worship, they are such, even though they did not attempt to perform the ceremony before a spreading tree like Ezra's Live Oak. When those dressed as black bears pushed Betty Strong Bull and the Andersons over the cliff, it was a woman and her unborn child who died..." concluded Niall, "but why do they wear the black bear..."

"Costumes?" added Tim. "To hide their identity is my guess!"

"But notice how their folly became real with the arrival of the grizzly..." said John Mark, "and they believed their storm gods opened the sky and soaked the land...as if they were true Canaanites and the town of Rock Creek a vestibule behind the city gates."

"My grandfather said you were not from this land. He said you have come to the valley...let me see how shall I translate this...he said you were sent," said Mike Crowfoot. "He said the same about you too, John Mark."

"Did Chief Strong Bull send you here to represent him?" asked John Mark.

"Why, yes he did."

"Since Tim is a McNaughton, is there personal risk for Tim and is there not risk for you in being part of what we are going to do?"

"As there is for you and the Tunnicliffes," answered Mike, "but not as much."

"I don't know about that," said Brian. "We will leave when we are finished, successful or not, but you will stay and these are your neighbors and perhaps some are your friends."

Brothers Coinneach and Drostan nodded affirmatively as did Brothers John Mark and Niall. Brother Brian, the bear killer, said, "Aye, we are all sent warriors!"

The Brothers laughed and punched one another, before John Mark became serious again, "Really, we don't mean to be melodramatic, but if you have a study Bible, you may want to check it out, especially if you have a Bible with archaeological study helps on biblical history and culture," John Mark explained and then asked, "Are all of you ready to hear Ezra's plan? It is patterned after what Josiah did."

"Yes," said Tim, "but I'm not at all a warrior like the rest of you."

"My grandfather always tells me to be strong and courageous. He tells me to leave my comfort zone when the opportunity comes to do a mighty work for the Lord..." Mike reflected, "and then he tells me any work directed by God is mighty."

"We are all like Bilbo Baggins when we are called out of our comfort zone...here's the plan as I understand what Ezra has meant and Niall has already begun...number one..." said John Mark as he moved the agenda, "We are to gather all the articles used at the rave. What is wooden must be burned, smashed, and ground to powder."

Interrupting, Niall offered, "I have the remains in the back of the jeep!"

"Then you are to take the remains and pour out the dust over the grave of Cristabel MacNaughten in the cemetery behind the Church in the Glen in Rock Creek. Scatter the dust lightly so as to cover all the earth on her gravesite. Spread the rest along the paths in the grave yard where it can be stomped into the ground. What she started has become perverted," said John Mark.

"I'll do it tonight," Niall promised.

"Although most of the Night Riders are in jail or pending sentencing, we need to get rid of them. Just as they have harassed newcomers, children, women, and the aged, we will seek justice. We will be agents for truth and justice. We will confront evil where we find it...I'm not saying we will break the law. I am asking you to thwart what they attempt. It will be best to go into the community at least two by two. In Rock Creek, Niall and I will work with the neighborhood watch. We will ask Deputy Candy to help get one started here in Jericho Springs," said John Mark.

"Confront evil where you find it," whispered Mike.

"Three, expose those who wore the bear suits. The sheriff will be up for election, and Deputy Cotton Candy would be a good replacement. Some may be on the school board or city council. They may be facing an election."

"My grandfather took care of Ralph. He won't be back in the valley, and if he returns he will be dealt with swiftly," said Mike, "and Van Allen and Robert King have already been exposed during the raid on Blair House. King took off his suit during the attack and escaped, but Van Allen identified him, when Allen copped a plea. Who are the others?"

"I can find out just by listening where I work. I'll find out," offered Tim, "but we already know Red and Butch are also deeply involved ... which totals five!"

"That will lead to more strategy, and the goal is to expose them. If one is a business man, it would be easy to organize a boycott," said John Mark, as Ezra pumped his fist in the air, "and we need for Brian, Coinneach, and Drostan to spend the next several weeks here at Blair House with Ezra, while Niall stays in Rock Creek with me, until we finish the remodel."

"Is there more?" Tim asked as he heard activity from the kitchen in the house below them, then added, "Why haven't you sought the help of Deputy Candy and Detective Jones?...I mean he is right here, living right here..."

"Good question! As we get into things, we may have to involve them and others as well. Mike knows the Chief ordered Ralph to leave the valley and he left. People know not to mess around on reservation land, but we neither have the Chief's clout, nor do we have the legal support he enjoys. The Sheriff's office and home were searched in an attempt to locate a bear skin costume. If CBI didn't find a bear skin and if Caleb didn't, I think it is because no one looked in the right place. We need to think about where else the bear suit might be," said John Mark. "When the Sheriff runs for re-election, we are thinking Cotton Candy needs to oppose him. Because I think she could win, she should not be tied to what we are doing in case we are viewed as vigilantes."

"And because Caleb is busy trying to identify the source of human trafficking in the valley," Mike said, "and we don't want to muddy his effort either."

"As sure as I know I can throw my javelin into that tree, I'll wager that when we find out who is behind the rave and who wear the black bear costumes, we will have found who is behind the human trafficking," concluded Brian the Bear Killer, and no one disagreed.

"That's a perfect segue into our last goals," said John Mark. "Number four is to tear down the dwelling of the temple prostitutes... what Josiah did...which means to dismantle the Asherah House Bed and Breakfast. I'm not certain how to do it...I mean we are not going to commit arson, but dismantle could mean destroying a business. At this point, Ezra is working with his attorney John Law to find out who owns the property as well as who manages the business there, and I'll work with the neighborhood watch to gather data on who comes and goes there."

"Number five?" asked Tim.

"Josiah burned the chariots of his enemies," said Brian with a smile.

"Now that would be fun," said Mike.

"And you said the three trucks on the ridge were minus their plates," Niall said.

"But our detective friend said he was close to finding out who owns the trucks based on the description I gave him," said John Mark, "so we let him sort it out, and we will match the names of who has the bear skins and who owns the trucks."

"And then? Letters, similar to those written by Penelope Quick, should be sent with evidence and letters will be written to the newspapers and to the pastors of churches..." Tim said.

"Complete your thought, Tim," Niall encouraged.

"I like it," said Brian, "We will pray about who to send the letters to...we will know when the time comes!"

All rose from the center of the pool. Ezra let out a pleasurable moan, as he walked quickly to his Live Oak tree, which had been barren on the south and west sides. Coinneach and Drostan smiled at one another, as the others gathered around the tree. They noticed two new sprouts had grown out of the scars the bear had caused when it broke off the dead limbs.

"New growth," Mile Crowfoot proclaimed, "not only does the tree live...there is new growth, new growth from where it was...dead!"

How satisfying, Ezra Sr. thought, How sweet to see how my Lord is restoring Blair House...

\*\*\*

Hurriedly, Niall retrieved the remains of the Asher pole and ceremonial table from the yellow jeep parked on the hairpin turn above Huerfano Butte. John Mark opened the trunk of Adam's old Chevy, and Niall placed two large boxes there. Both signaled each other a thumbs up sign of approval, and John drove Adam's heap back to Rock Creek on CR403. Turning right at the intersection of CR403 and the Valley Highway, he quickly entered the drive way to the little Church in the Glen, parked where the headlights lit up the cemetery behind the church, and sought the tombstone marking the grave of Cristabel MacNaughten.

Bringing the shovel, John Mark asked whether or not Niall had found the tombstone to which Niall had said he had not. They separated and made a deliberate search of the cemetery. Noting the names of the deceased as they proceeded, they called out each name for the other's benefit. Niall found the old weathered stone and read her name.

"Cristabel MacNaughten. John Mark, the spelling of her last name is not the same as the other McNaughtons. And she is buried alone, no husband or children. No other graves with the same spelling."

"That's the old way of spelling the name. More like it's spelled on the Isles. I wonder if there is a McClaren amongst the stones," Niall said, and then getting on with his mission, he returned to Adam's old Chevy, removed a good sized box of ashes, and returned to the gravesite. John Mark found a long handled shovel in the lean-to where cut wood had been stored and protected from stormy weather.

Niall set the box next to Cristabel's grave effortlessly. John Mark joined him with the shovel and handed it to Niall, and then prayed over the effort. Next John Mark said, "King Josiah burned the implements of the Baal worship and scattered the ashes as dust over the graves of common people. We know not who Cristabel really was to this town, except that she found favor with the people of this church to be buried in this cemetery. Though she apparently had no kin amongst those gathered here, you and I know and ken that she made a difference in the settlement of this valley and in what happened in Rock Creek, good or evil."

"Aye, we may ken her value here, but others are not likely to understand her contribution," said Niall.

Scooping a shovel full of ashes from the box, Niall shook the handle and sprinkled the ash over the head of the grave, then took other loads of ashes from the box until it was emptied and the grave covered. John Mark retrieved the final box of equal size and set it at the entrance to the graveyard, while Niall finished the quest by sprinkling the pathway from the grave to the entrance.

Niall proclaimed, "This part of my quest is ended and I am freed of my oath to destroy the fraud and replace it with a tree of life, a Live Oak tree, and to burn the evidence of the Baal worship and spread the powdered remains over this grave. May some good come from the dust returning to the earth from which it came, no longer man made symbols of a false god. May the sapling I planted above on the ridge grow to great heights and spread out like Freedom's tree on Huerfano Butte to the west of the valley."

"Two other seeds are planted and safely hidden," said John Mark.

"Aye and I think I know where they are to be planted, north and south."

"Where the path leads to this grand mesa?"

"And where fowl were sacrificed on the banks of Eden's pond to the north is my guess."

"Time will tell, Brother Niall, time will tell, perhaps in your life time and mine."

"Aye...and you are nearly finished restoring this Blair House in Rock Creek," said Niall.

"But only when spiritual leadership of this church, of the town, returns to reside in it."

"When the Bond family moves in and Kenneth is officially the pastor, and then we have to help root out the temple prostitution."

"Then the prayers of Mary McNaughton Claymore will have been fulfilled, and her mother's home will have been restored, both physically and spiritually," John Mark said with a smile.

"Aye, God is good all the time!"

"Aye, All the time, God is good!"

"Which means one Live Oak sapling will need to be planted behind Mary's bench on the mesa..." concluded Niall.

"Aye, a tree of life to the south...if there were true Baal worship, the Asher pole would have been placed before a spreading tree. What happened on the ridge was a fraud, but what happens at the Asherah House is not," said John Mark, "and I think I'll do some research about it at the library and local museum."

"That is why one of Ezra's strategies is to tear down the bed and breakfast," added Niall.

***

Remember the axioms that no good deed goes unpunished and that where God is at work, one can expect Satan to be around to rob someone's joy. Knowing Tim McNaughton shared the gospel one morning at the Cozy Corner Café, many McNaughton relatives knew there would be trouble. To make matters worse, Tim moved into the Blair House and joined with the group to restore the building and grounds. That infuriated Whitney "Red" McNaughton, childhood friend and partner of Adam Claymore as well as the head of the McNaughton family corporation, which coveted the water and mineral rights connected to the Blair House. Frustrated in all their efforts, including the failed attempt to convince the city council to condemn the Blair House, the botched raid on the Blair House, and the unsuccessful rave on the ridge above the Stage Stop Hotel in Rock Creek, Red's countenance visibly changed. Once well groomed with neatly trimmed red hair and a dashing mustache, he let both his beard and red hair grow to shoulder length. When he spoke, his voice growled.

Red also presided over the Night Riders, the informal group of younger men bent on harassing all newcomers to the Rock Creek Valley. At the instigation of the McNaughton corporate leadership, the Night Riders set out to get Tim fired from his job as waiter at the Cozy Corner Café. Meanwhile, Tim volunteered to eavesdrop when Red met at the café with those Tim suspected as being Night Riders. Also, Tim listened to the conversations of members of the McNaughton Corporation leadership with hope that he could discover who had worn the bear costumes during the recent rave.

To set a snare, Red asked both the corporation leadership and members of the Night Riders, now formally recognized, to meet him for an early breakfast. Tim arrived at his usual time to open the café at five. Assistant Superintendant, Maurice Wood, and Banker, Chauncey Brown, stood at the door with Red, while Night Riders waited in their cars and trucks. Seamus, Van Allen, and Robert King arrived just before Sheriff Bailey. When Butch arrived, Tim knew something was afoot, so he began memorizing who was present.

"Sorry I'm late," Butch said, "I had to get Sarah and Lila to cover breakfast for me."

"Come in, blabbermouth," Red replied to his son, who visibly withered before his father, "I guess Ralph will be late driving in from Wolf City?"

"Guess you didn't get his message…"said Butch.

"What message?" Red replied as the others filed in and the corporate leaders assembled at the round table.

"I saw him after we met at the Tobacco Store," Butch lowered his voice, "and he said he tried to tell you but you wouldn't listen to him. He said he was leaving town for his own good."

"What do you mean?" Red asked.

"Dad, we are in trouble. The Chief told Ralph he could leave the valley but not to come back or he would deal with him."

"Strong Bull would take him to the ring?"

"Ralph seemed to think it meant something more permanent."

"He can't do that…"

"Look what we've been doing. And what do you have planned for here?"

"Come on in and you'll see…" said Red and a grim smile crossed his face.

Tim, the waiter, promptly took a few orders immediately when the first of the pack sat down, and the cook had already begun cooking meats and potatoes when he saw the group begin to arrive in the parking lot. Tim filled the early orders with immediacy, then took additional orders, passed out menus where needed, and prepared and delivered a tray of water.

"You're a good waiter, Tim, probably the best in the valley," said Maurice.

"He could probably get a job anywhere if he were available," added Chauncey.

"Ya anywhere but where we hang our dirty laundry," said Van Allen.

"Then what good will it do to do what you're planning, Tim's a cousin and so was Harley?" Butch asked.

"You do remember Harley shot you in the back, and Tim has done the same, in effect, by moving into the Blair House," Red said.

"But I was messin' with Harley's girl friend, and I gave him a bad time about only bein' the dishwasher and part time cook at the Stage Stop!"

"You sayin' Harley had a right to shoot you twice in the back?" growled Red.

"I'm saying, Father, I'm beginning to realize how far off I've been," Butch said loudly, "and I'm tired of regretting what I've done and what we are planning to do. I'm not going to be a part of this!"

Maurice said, "Don't leave!"

"Don't do this to your father," Chauncey added.

"You two are really something else," Butch paused when he stood up and threw his napkin on the table, "I'm done."

"Well, I'll be…" said Robert King, as the rest of the crowd murmured between each other, while Tim listened as he took orders and filled them quickly.

As Tim delivered meals to Red's round table of corporate leadership, Red shouted angrily, "You've been listening to all of this haven't you? Tim, you're a traitor."

"How could anyone miss what you shouted? I'm just doing my job, Red, as fast and as well as I can," replied Tim.

"You listen all the time, don't you? Then you report back. This is where me and the boys have met for years. We should be able to have private conversation without worrying about who is listening in."

"Then maybe you should be at the Tobacco Store or Robert's office right now, Red, so you can have a private conversation with your board members and your Night Riders," Tim fired back.

"Young man, you should consider whom you are talking to!" bellowed Chauncey.

"You forget who you work for!" added Dr. Wood.

"As do you, Mr. Assistant Superintendent!" the cook shouted from the kitchen.

"This has gotten out of hand. Tim, I'm going to arrest you for disturbing the peace, if you don't settle down!" Sheriff Bailey asserted.

"Me...I'm Just doing my job. Red is the one who's out of order," shouted the cook, "and we know all of you are part of this. Each of you is either a Night Rider or a member of the McNaughton Corporation, and you are targeting Tim not just for where he lives now, but because he is a McNaughton who stands on his own feet."

"You either fire Tim, or we won't be back!" said Dr. Wood.

"In the last several weeks what Tim has done truly has blessed this café. Why, we even have Bible studies meeting here now, and some of the churches have groups meet here for lunch on Sunday afternoon. We are blessed by the change that has taken place," said the cook, "Mr. Brown, this is your café. If you want Tim fired, you are gonna' have to do it."

"Tim, you are fired!" Chauncey said.

"Wow! That's the first time I've ever seen Chauncey flustered," admitted Roy Sentry. "By gosh, this is kinda funny!"

The cook threw down his apron on the table before banker and city councilman, Chauncey Brown, "Since you fired Tim, I quit, and I will tell everyone, all I know. You can expect to have competition when you run for re-election."

"Tim's fired and the cook quit, then I'm leaving too!" said a member of the McNaughton Corporation.

Another walked by Red's table, and said, "Red, Chauncey... Maurice, sometimes you guys are real idiots. I'm done with the corporation. This has all been a foolish gambit. First the Blair House and now how you have treated Tim," pausing he spoke directly to the others at the table, "Robert, Van, and Seamus—we know you, Butch, and Ralph are the ones parading around in the bear costumes. Bailey, regardless of CBI and the detective not finding the bear suit at your office or home, we know you guys are the ones who have worn them at the raves."

A local pastor stood up and said, "I have been a member of the McNaughton Corporation, and I didn't know about any of this. My own fault, I guess...but now I wonder about the rumors I've heard about what's going on in our schools as well as at the hotel..."

"And the Asherah House..." said the cook.

"I should have guessed," said the pastor, "Folks, I think it is time to leave the corporation leadership here to simmer in the pot of stew they have conspired to make. I will be mailing my formal notice to them. I'm withdrawing my participation in the corporation."

"Let's go," said another.

And as the pastor walked by Red's table, he said, "May God forgive you..."

Only Buddy Smith, Roy Sentry, Irv and Ellis Moss remained and pulled up chairs to sit at the round table, and Roy said, "Red, I've never heard Butch talk like that...I mean he hasn't said anything about it to me, and I'm his best friend."

Looking at the young man who tried to comfort him, Red growled, "Well, that says a lot about his good sense, not to tell you anything!"

"I think you just tried to insult me, Red, to make me feel bad. You do that a lot. Usually, I just kinda shrivel inside, but you know what," Roy said, "you really look bad and you should go to a doctor...one of those mental ones. I quit too! My mother will be glad to hear it!"

"She's not your mother!" Red said. "You weren't even adopted, neither you nor Amanda!"

"Neither me or Amanda not even adopted," Roy said as tears burst forth and he ran from the café toward home. "I'm going to ask my mother..."

"Will you shut up! You are sabotaging everything! I'm leaving, call me when you come to your senses. Wait I can't leave, I own this place and now, I've got to figure out how to get my café covered. Get out of here! All of you, before other customers arrive," Chauncey demanded.

"Chance, I'm sorry…" Red growled. Maurice and Ellis took each side of Red and escorted him to the café door, while Irv opened the door for the three of them. Robert, Van, Bailey and Seamus followed after them.

Van Allen was first to say anything, "I'll stay here and help Chauncey, but you guys know we need to follow through with what's already planned at the church and with Heather Ross. She's our wild card."

"I'll stay here for the morning shift," said Ellis, "I'm not scheduled to work at the feed store today."

"But…my bet is I'll need you this afternoon," said Ellis' brother Irv, "Red doesn't look too good, so I will open the store and let's see where we go from there."

"Heather is set to visit the Blair House tonight. She'll charm Tim and case the place," said Seamus, "I'll see to it."

Robert added, "All I'll need is Irv and Ellis tonight at the church. But you guys be certain to bring the buckets of red paint."

What had been planned, as a savory means of disposing with Tim the waiter, turned into a bitter end for the conspirators and their allies at the café. God had a better plan for Tim and the cook, who stood with him against the bullies.

\*\*\*

In Jericho Springs, Tim the waiter and the cook from the Cozy Corner Café, arrived within minutes of each other at Bustos Family Mexican Restaurant to ask for a job. There had not been an opening posted for a short order cook, but Tim was hired on the spot to start work the next day. Tim felt sorry for his friend the cook, who countered with, "Tim, I know there is an opening at the truck stop at the Ridge View exit. I'll snag a job there. Don't worry about me. Like you, I have a good reputation. I don't feel bad at all. We had to do what we did. Chauncey Brown and the others are into things I'd prefer not to be around. Everything's falling apart for them, and I think their end's coming soon. It was good to work with you who knows, maybe we'll work together again. Hey, I'll see you later."

After getting the job, Tim went home to the Blair House. He found Misty finishing the dishes and prepping for lunch, while Kat and Hannah worked with Kip in the bookstore. Hannah dusted the shelves, as Kat and Kip filled mail orders. Tim greeted them and went upstairs to his room to shower and take a nap. Kip asked Kat and Hannah to join him in praying for Tim, and then they returned to their work.

"Hannah, when you finish dusting, please vacuum the floor. You'll find the vacuum sweeper behind the stairwell door that leads to my room," said Kip.

"Sure thing!" Hannah replied with enthusiasm. "And then I'll sweep the porch and fluff the pillows in the rocking chairs like I did last time."

"Kip, when she's finished, can she help me check the packing slips in the shipment we received yesterday?" asked Kat.

"I'm finished in the kitchen," Misty said from the hallway. "Can I help you, Kat? Is that okay, Mr. Kip?"

Both Kip and Kat looked at each other and smiled with approval, and then Kat said, "I'd be glad to have your help!"

Encouraged, Misty informed them, "Tim arrived home. He said he got fired at the Cozy Corner Café for listening. Said he'd tell folks about it later, and then he went upstairs to his room. Oh, he also said he got a new job waiting tables at Bustos. I've never eaten at a Mexican restaurant. Do they speak English? What kind of food do they serve?"

At first Kip thought the answer to both questions had been obvious, and then he realized Misty had asked sincere questions, so Kip offered, "Misty, would you join me for dinner once Tim begins working there?"

"He starts tomorrow tonight! Could we go sometime this week?"

"I'm gone the rest of the week, but when I get back, it's a date, Misty. I'll look forward to that," said Kip as Kat and Hannah watched each other for a response.

Pleased with the invitation, Misty turned to leave, until Kat reminded her that she was going to help her. Misty turned to enter the book room, when she noticed a woman climbing the stairs to the porch and said, "Now she's no lady and those shorts belong to a huntress!"

"What did you say, Misty?" asked Hannah.

"The vixen who's about to knock on the door! She's on the prowl, and she's trouble. I should know. Mind if I answer the door?" Misty said with a catty meow.

Watching Misty, Hannah and Kat moved to the book room door and Kip looked out the window. Heather Ross, Tim's girl friend, knocked at the door, and Misty opened it briskly. "Hello, Welcome to the Blair House. How may I direct you?" Misty said curtly.

"Oh, sure and thanks," Heather said, while popping her chewing gum and pushing on the heavy door to open it more completely; however, Misty withheld her advance with a firm grip on the door.

"Miss, are you here to shop at our bookstore, or are you making a house call?" Misty inquired with a smirk.

"I'm Heather, Timmy's fiancée! You must be the maid. Would ya tell him I'm here?"

"Wait here, please. I'll inquire if he is receiving any callers," Misty pronounced, as she closed the door and climbed the stairs to the second floor.

"Moxie, that girl has," said Kip, "and clever too."

"This is going to be fun to watch," said Hannah, "I know of Heather and she is a tough cookie."

"Shouldn't we let her in? After all we could engage her, while Misty finds Tim. This part of the house is a business," suggested Kat.

"As you two would say, she may look like a tramp, but Jesus died for her too!" Hannah urged.

"Invite her into the store..." concluded Kip, "Well done, Hannah."

Hannah went to the door and invited Heather into the Blair House and said, "Good morning, Heather, come on in. We've been working in the store and overheard Misty telling you she would find Tim for you."

Kat added, "Come in, and take a look around in the bookstore, won't you?"

Somewhat startled and perplexed, Heather said, "Oh, I'll just go upstairs and find Tim."

"Sorry, house rules are a woman is not allowed in the room of a man and reverse. Please join us in here," Kip insisted pleasantly, as he motioned for Heather to enter before them.

"A gentleman, how nice...don't mind if I do. So the other one is Misty, and you three are?" asked Heather.

"Yes, how rude of us not to introduce ourselves. I'm Kip Powell, and I operate this bookstore. This is Katarina Bond, the new pastor's wife at the Church in the Glen..."

"And I know Heather, but she may not remember me from the Stage Stop Hotel..."

"Yes, I do, you must be Hannah. Mrs. Bond, I'm pleased to meet you. Tim has spoken well of all of you," said Heather, as she rested her gaze on Hannah, "but who answered the door? I've never seen her before. She's rather attractively sassy!"

"I'm Misty, perhaps you have heard of me," said Misty as she sashayed down the stairs from the second floor with a smirk across her face, "I had to interrupt Tim in the shower to let him know he has a... guest..."

Kip, Kat, and Hannah gasped, before Heather responded, "Hmmm...I have heard of you. You were at the Asherah House until these fine folks rescued you. I must say you hardly show," Heather paused, then continued, "and others will be pleased to know you are safe here ...and still...pregnant."

While Misty and Hannah knew well Heather's intended meaning, Kip and Kat looked confused. Fortunately, Tim arrived in time to avoid a real cat fight between the three women who one time or another had been involved in a rave ceremony. Misty changed her countenance when she noted Kip and Kat's response, and she felt camaraderie with Hannah.

"Well," Tim said having descended the stairs quickly, but slowed his pace after hearing the conversation, "I see all of you have met. Heather, it is good to see you. I have much to share with you."

Heather met him on the bottom stair, once he had passed Misty in his descent, and thrust herself against him, "And I have much to finally share with you...can we go to your room?"

With pained expression Tim looked at Kat, Kip, and Hannah, who shook their heads back and forth. Tim replied, "No, my dear, it is a house rule that no women are allowed in a man's room, and no men in a woman's room. But I can take you on a tour here of the first floor and the grounds. There is something I'd like to show you...on top of Huerfano Butte. The view is spectacular."

Lower lip protruding, Heather pulled Tim by the hand into the bookstore and directly to the shelving by the open door leading to Kip's second floor room. She pretended to look at the titles on the west wall shelving, and then turned to her left, so she rotated before the doorway. Strategically, she noted the unlocked exterior window bordering the stairs, the door to the right, which she would soon learn led to the library and study. Heather noted a pull string led to a light bulb from the ceiling above the stair well landing.

No one noticed her focus on the window in the stairwell, but intuitively both Hannah and Misty had been suspicious of Heather's timing. As she proceeded counter clockwise about the room, Heather noticed the locked front window, as she pretended to be interested in the gifts collection on the front table under the window. She paid attention to the closed lock.

Before leaving the bookstore, Heather said, "Tim, I stopped by the Cozy Corner to see you. I heard you had an important question to ask me. My answer would be yes, but I heard Chauncey Brown fired you this morning. Is that true?"

Quickly thinking, Tim wondered why Heather had chosen to ask the question now and in front of his friends, who already knew he not only was fired but also hired to wait tables at Bustos restaurant. Tim replied, "I'm sorry you heard the bad news from someone at the Cozy. I'll have to look for another job. Meanwhile, there is plenty of work for me to help with right here, and I'll probably be reading a lot of books from the bookstore. I guess I will have to delay asking you that question."

"Maybe you ought to go back to Chauncey and plead with him to let you come back, and that goes for the cook too," Heather said. "I'm sure you will be able to save face, and you really must have a job."

From behind her, Misty stuck out her tongue at Heather and looked cross-eyed at Tim. Kat held her back, as Tim responded,

"Heather, I'm not going to worry. My situation is in God's hands. I'll seek no revenge, and I'll keep out of the way of what God might do there."

"My guess is God has already been at work," said Hannah.

"Yes, I'll bet a job is already waiting for you," added Kat.

"Don't you think with how he has ministered at the Cozy Corner Café, people will follow him to another location? Why, I'll bet Chauncey or someone else put you up to urging Tim to tuck his tail and beg to come back. Don't you think that's the case?" Kip said, as he looked around at the others.

"That's my guess," said Tim, "Come on, Heather, I want you to see the valley from the top of the butte out back."

"Okay, but I really think you should go back to the Cozy," Heather said, as she walked out of the room and into the lobby, "Come along, Timmy!"

As Tim followed obediently, he smiled and whispered to the others, "Delilah."

Tim wrestled the lead from Heather and firmly led her by the hand across the hall and into the piano room, where he said, "This is where we had the hymn sing and served soda and pizza to those who had attacked the Blair House. It was humorous when Hannah and Misty hammered the attackers with water balloons. We all laughed afterwards including the attackers, as we sang together. Really, it was a grand time."

"But Van Allen was hauled off for throwing the torches," whined Heather.

"Yes, the others had no idea he was going to do that," Tim reported. "They said they came here with the idea of rescuing Hannah and Misty from being kept here against their will."

"They seem to be enjoying themselves," said Heather with surprise.

"Come on into the dining room," Tim invited and said, "This is where we have our meals. We do group studies here to build our relationships with one another. Above here on the second and third floors, we have a TV room and a study area. Come on, I'll show you where we do laundry and cook meals."

"Who does the cooking?" asked Heather.

"Kat and her girls, Kristin and Krystal, plus Hannah and Misty primarily... so long as Gramma Bee is taking care of Adam at his ranch on Claymore Flats."

"Beatrice Jaramillo lives here too!" Heather responded, "I'll bet Red isn't too happy about that!"

"Well, you remember it was one of Red's Night Riders, Buddy Smith, who hit Gramma Bee with a beer bottle one night after Butch got into a fight with Hannah, Deputy Cotton Candy, and Karen Gustafson."

"When Hannah just about knocked Butch's lights out!" Heather said enthusiastically.

"And Karen shot Roy Sentry in the heel..."

"Then Hannah and Harper ran off together...I'd forgotten a lot of that," said Heather.

Escorting Heather into the kitchen, Tim said, "To the right is our laundry area and the left is food prep."

"Wow, two brand new washers and a dryer!" Heather said, and then concluded, "You may be cooking on a wood stove, but you've got the latest when it comes to washing clothes, and I see the back porch spans the width of the house and is filled with cut wood!"

"We're ready for a cold winter."

"I'd be willing to come stay cold nights and snuggle with you..."

"Thanks, but you may not like the life here. The rooms are mostly small, and we share one bathroom per floor," said Tim.

"Are there separate bedrooms for everyone?"

"Yes, and we swapped out the old hardware on the doors and installed deadbolt locks," Tim said as he led Heather along the hallway, "and to your right is where our lovebirds have their own individual apartment."

"Really, I thought their wedding was postponed until Adam Claymore is well enough to officiate their wedding," said Heather snidely.

"True, but unfortunately they had a civil ceremony at the courthouse, but still they want to have a ceremony in the Church in the Glen in Rock Creek."

"They admit they made a mistake?" said Heather and continued at Tim's nod, "Good for them...they're married, but they admit they made a mistake by not waiting to be married in the church. I like that."

"Next, here we have the library and study," said Tim, as he opened the door and switched on a light, "and over there is where the bookstore stairwell door opens into this room. Now let's go outside."

"Wow! The book collection matches the library in Ridge View. It would be fun to see all that is here."

"You mean to catalogue them?" asked Tim, "That's a winter project several want to do. Come on, I want you to see the outside. Let's go to the left."

"No, no," she tugged on his hand, and Tim relented, "I want to go right, so I can see the fabled hot spring ponds."

Heather led the way, and Tim watched as she turned her head to verify the unfastened lock. Just as I thought, Tim realized, she is not here to romance me, she is here to case the place. Saddened, it was something he knew he needed to know, but he persisted to have her see Ezra's carving in the tree. Perhaps...he thought, perhaps she will meet God there, he hoped. He followed her to the pond where she dipped her hand to feel the warmth, and before she could take her shoes off, he took back the lead from Heather and noticed the women were watching them from the window in the stairwell from the bookstore.

Tim prayed, while they silently climbed Huerfano. He prayed for Heather's salvation and vowed if that didn't happen he would end his pursuit of her. She no longer had him wrapped around her little finger, and even now in her tight jean shorts and pale blue halter top with loosely tied knots behind her neck and back, he knew he must resist her advances. Reaching the crest they paused at the dry pool.

"What a neat place for a campfire!" Heather said, and then turned around to face the east where she had a panoramic view of the valley. "I can see all the way to where we had the rave."

"It is quite revealing, isn't it, but come see what's on the other side of the tree."

"Oh, look Tim, those are huge scars where a bear left its mark, and there's new growth on the tree. It's coming out of the..."she came close to touch the scars, "brokenness...and there's a new sprout in the center of this scar. Was this where the bear broke the branches off the tree?"

"Yes, Heather, the tree appeared to be dead and now look, we have life renewed on the south and over here on the west side, but come around here and maybe you'll have your life renewed."

"You sound like this is mystical...the tree was dead and now it is alive...my life renewed...as if I were going to be born again," said Heather mocking him.

"Not really...I don't mean to say it like that. I'm sorry I did. It's not the tree, but some people have been blessed when they see what's on the north side. Heather, please choose to come over here and decide what you see."

Heather rounded the west side of the tree and immediately noticed what some have called the knuckle of a root erecting from the ground, "Tim, this is special, an Asher pole once stood here before the spreading tree! How sad..." Heather said, "Baal was once wor-shipped here, but the Asher pole was cut down and probably burned, and only the weathered stump remains. This was the real thing, and not like the pole that stood on the ridge for the rave. Everybody knows it was fake!"

"Everybody?"

"Sure! The raves are only here to bring money to the valley... they're for show. Ask Hannah and Misty...they both participated at one time or another...I'll bet on it...but now they look different. I wonder why?" Heather genuinely asked.

"Check this out," Tim said as he stood framing the carving with his hands and then moving away to see if she could determine what was carved into the old Live Oak. "Do you see anything?"

"How sad! Someone or something marked this side of the tree too! It doesn't look like a bear though," said Heather, as Tim prayed God would choose to meet her here. When it didn't happen, he knew he was not to ask her to marry him, at least not today and maybe never. If his suspicions were accurate about her being here to case the house, he knew he would see her less, but he would earnestly pray for her salvation.

Heather and Tim climbed down the hill, and at the bottom, Heather made a lame excuse about needing to leave. Without pas-sion, without a kiss, she said her goodbye...a not so pleasant burnt ending to their relationship. Inside the house the ladies clapped their hands and watched Heather walk away and out of Tim's life, while he felt the loss of an insincere friend.

# Setting the Stage

## CHAPTER 19

*"Also our enemies said, 'Before they know it or see us, we will be right there among them and will kill them and put an end to the work.'"*　　　*Nehemiah 4:11*

Since Chauncey Brown could not immediately hire suitable replacements for the popular cook and waiter he had run off, he made a nearly fatal mistake by closing the Cozy Corner Café for the rest of the week. As if it were a church split, most patrons bitterly swore they would never return to the Cozy Corner for two reasons. They had become quite fond of the cook and the waiter, Tim McNaughton, especially after he had shared the gospel one morning at Adam Claymore's urging. When the waiter and cook gained new jobs, angry patrons shifted their allegiance to both the Truck Stop Diner by the interstate highway in Ridge View and Bustos Family Mexican Restaurant in Jericho Springs. The other reason for patrons to not return to the Cozy Corner Café was they learned banker, Chauncey Brown, not only owned the café but also served on the McNaughton Corporation Board of Directors. As the public became aware of the notorious activities of the corporation and its splinter group the Night Riders, favorable sentiment shifted away from men like Chauncey in favor of newcomers like Izzy Freedom. The corporation's violence and greed was about to come down on its members, and they were about to fall into the hole they had dug for themselves. With truth revealed, justice prevailed.

Tim was guilty as Red had charged. He had listened to what had been said at his tables. One of the conversations Tim noted was about the planned vandalism to the Church in the Glen. He shared what he had heard with Ken Bond, the new pastor. Ken met with John Mark and Niall and shared the information with them. John Mark contacted Deputy Candy. Together they forged a plan to thwart the effort. Since Butch had wedged the paper stuffing in the door jam, they figured he would be one of the vandals. In setting a snare, Ken Bond made certain to keep the stuffing in the jam, so the vandals would think they had not been discovered. He also did not switch on the evening yard light. Ken called the neighborhood watch block captains and alerted them to what might transpire. After dark, Niall pitched a tent each night in the grove between the church parking lot and the highway. He carried with him his javelin and an M-80 fire cracker. John Mark had bought a timer, plugged it into a wall socket near a table lamp, and plugged the lamp cord into the timer. He set the timer to switch off the lamp nightly, so it appeared all were asleep at Adam's house in Rock Creek by nine each night. John Mark then walked to church, waited out of sight in the pastor's office, while perched on a folding chair.

Irv and Ellis Moss had been assigned by the corporate leaders to help Robert King implement the next phase of terror on their opponents. When they arrived at the insurance agency, Irv parked behind the building, and they waited for Robert King to come out from the back door of his office. Across the street, the Indiana Avenue Neighborhood Watch block captain noticed their suspicious behavior. Each carried a gallon sized paint can in each hand as they walked south on the highway. Immediately, she called the church office to implement their counter plan. She told John Mark the vandals were on their way and he would recognize them as the local realtor Robert King with Irv and Ellis Moss, employees of Red McNaughton at the lumberyard. Next, the block captain called her telephone tree members after first calling the block captain on County Road 403. Last she called Deputy Candy and said "Brazos! Come quick!"

The plan called for all to arrive together. They wanted to shock the vandals with their unity. Candy left the sheriff's office, waited briefly in the parking lot to see if she were being followed, and then drove toward Rock Creek. John Mark lit a candle and held it briefly in the pastor's office window for Niall to see. Hidden in the trees, Niall put on his gray cowl and grasped his javelin. Armed with cameras all neighborhood watch members waited for the deputy's arrival.

Robert, Irv, and Ellis joked with one another as they walked down the highway. A car passed them, so they took on a more serious tone. More carefully, they walked past the Stage Stop Bar and through the hotel parking lot. They noticed no lights shined at Adam's house, so they crossed the highway just opposite the lane leading to the church parking lot. They rounded the front of the building and walked to the pastor's side door. Inside the pastor's office, John Mark repositioned himself from the folding chair to sit in the sanctuary on the middle pew next to the south wall.

Only then did Robert say, "Okay, we go in, use the bottle openers to pop the lids to the paint cans once we enter the sanctuary. Don't turn on any lights. Pour the paint on the organ, the piano, and the lectern first. If you have any left over, spill it on the wooden floor. We are in and out within minutes."

"Then we just walk back to your office?" stated Irv.

"I'm going to cross the highway and return by way of the grove of trees by the ridge. We can make it all the way back to the path leading to the Asherah House without being seen," said Robert.

"Too bad you didn't think of that earlier," said Ellis.

"Nobody saw us come here. We will be okay," answered Robert. "Let's go!"

As the vandals entered through the door to the pastor's office, Niall sprinted and stood to the right of it. Once inside the sanctuary, the vandals set the gallon paint cans on the floor, took out their bottle openers, and began to open the lids. Suddenly, John Mark struck his stick match, lit the M-80, dropped it into a metal bucket, and shoved it with his foot toward Irv, Ellis, and Robert. The light from the match had startled the vandals, but the fizz of the wick frightened them. Ellis wet himself, and all three stood just before the explosion.

Forgetting their mission and the paint cans, they ran for the exit, but John Mark met the two slowest in the air, as he yelled, "You came to desecrate the House of the Lord, now feel my wrath." Both Irv and Ellis Moss fell against the church organ. As the Ellis brothers attempted to regain their footing, John Mark first blackened one's eye and then the other with a right and left hook. He broke both of their noses with another fist to their faces. Irv managed to crawl to safety, while John worked over Ellis.

Robert King fared no better. He proved quicker than the Moss brothers, but as he made his way out of the pastor's office, Niall jammed his javelin into the door frame high enough for Robert to trip over it. Falling face first to the driveway gravel, Robert rolled over and looked up to see the nearly seven foot Niall standing by the doorway with his javelin ready for his next victim.

"Stay down, if you know what's good for you!" Niall said with a controlled yet menacing voice.

"Oh, no!" King uttered in despair, when he heard Deputy Candy's siren.

By then townspeople had begun to arrive from the highway and down the driveway in time to witness Irv Moss fall face first onto Robert King. Each hit the other's head like cymbals clanging. John Mark switched on the yard light before appearing with Ellis Moss in tow. John led Ellis down the stairs by the nap of his neck and deposited him with the other two in a heap.

As the townspeople circled around the vandals on the ground, Niall bent down so only the vandals could hear him, "That was for Beatrice Jaramillo, Gramma Bee, and all the others the Night Riders terrorized. If we hear you have harassed any more people, we are coming after you first! Got it?" Niall asked with his javelin pointed directly in front of Robert King's face.

"Got it!" King said followed by the two others repeating his words.

"Who are you?" Irv asked.

People milled around as Deputy Candy cuffed the three men, and the crowd recognized them despite their bloodied faces. "Robert King, you should be ashamed of yourself. I'll be transferring my home and auto insurance to another company," said someone from Indiana Avenue.

"It's the superintendent's boys, Irv and Ellis Moss. They work at the lumber yard. I mean the assistant superintendent's stepsons. You were nice boys before your mother married that Wood fellow," said the CR403 block captain.

"But I don't sell insurance..." Robert King said, meekly, "I'm the realtor."

"Do you mean the former wife of the superintendent of schools married the superintendent's assistant?" asked the CR403 block captain's neighbor.

"I wonder if that was a condition of employment," laughed his neighbor from across the road.

"That only happens in a small town!" added another CR403 neighbor.

"Did they trash the inside of the church?" asked John Mark's neighbor, the highwayman.

"No," John Mark said, "we stopped them just before they spilled paint over everything."

"I'm glad for their sake that they were stopped before they desecrated the Lord's house," said another neighbor from CR403.

"I heard King is one of those who wore the bear costume during the rave..." said another from Indiana Avenue.

"He's part of the McNaughton Corporation..." clarified the block captain from Indiana Avenue.

"Irv and Ellis are Night Riders..." added one more resident from the county road.

With Deputy Candy's permission, the block captain for Indiana Avenue stood on the stairs to the pastor's office and shouted out, "Listen folks, what happened here is a real community tragedy, but it could have been worse. As a neighborhood watch, we are to watch out for one another and report suspicious behavior. We are not to confront the bad guys. Our heroes, John Mark and the man in the black shirt or coat...whatever it is he wears...he has disappeared. Anyway they took on these men, because they crossed the line and entered this church to desecrate it. I don't want you to get the idea that we are vigilantes. Understand we worked with the police. Deputy Candy was part of this effort from the beginning. Look what we can do when we work together with the police."

"You mean we need to be careful to not be part of the problem," said the highwayman.

"Yes, we work with the police, their eyes and ears," she paused, "and what should we do now?"

Priscilla King had arrived and said, "We should go inside the church and pray. Please, enter through the front door."

"Good idea! Let's go inside..." said the owner of the antique store.

As she walked by Robert King, the CR403 block captain told the people from her street, "I know what I'm going to do. I'm cancelling all the insurance I bought through Robert King, and I urge all of you to the same!"

Robert hung his head in shame...

"Rock bottom, Son," Priscilla said to her son, "You've hit rock bottom..."

As the people entered the church, they began to sing, "There is power, power..."

"Deputy, before everybody gets inside and someone handles the paint cans, please retrieve the evidence. I made certain the cans were not touched in the scuffle, but they are opened," John Mark advised.

"Scuffle, it was you who fought the three of them in the sanctuary, and they didn't land a punch did they?" Candy asked, and turned to notice other deputies had arrived. She turned back to finish talking with John Mark, but he was gone, "Who is he?"

"I think the question is what is he?" said the Indiana Avenue block captain.

From inside, Candy heard Priscilla King leading the people in prayer. Candy regretted having to go inside and telling the people to disperse because the sanctuary was temporarily a crime scene.

Heather Ross, who had introduced herself to the women at Blair House as Tim's fiancée, went directly to Red McNaughton's ranch house on the north end of the valley to make her report. Red's housekeeper escorted Heather to his private bar at the back of the house. The housekeeper told Heather that she was required to wait there for Red. Heather had anticipated a warmer reception, one that would validate her importance to Red. Instead, the wait gave her time to analyze what had happened to her at the Blair House.

Like other women caught in a tangled web of manipulation after participating in one of the raves, Heather had learned to cope with the duplicity and treachery of those who organized and conducted the events. Taking on those traits, she played upon the lust of men by wearing alluring clothing and by dancing seductively before them. She knew Hannah had been treated like a rag doll after a rave. Hannah had been played with, tossed around, mistreated, and forgotten, until someone wanted attention that she had been eager to give away. Gloria Jones, the detective's younger sister, had attended a rave, never went home, and had become a prostitute at the Asherah House Bed and Breakfast. She became pregnant during the rave ceremony, but was murdered by Sam Gelding, local insurance agent, after she ended the pregnancy. Sarah, a waitress at the Stage Stop Hotel, had intended to end her pregnancy. She relented but nearly lost her child when she fell against a boulder, while escaping the grizzly. Recently, a high school girl from Quail Point had been murdered by Sam Gelding. Apparently, she too had ended her pregnancy. Rumor had it that Betty Strong Bull had been pushed over the cliff when the mob fled from the last rave. Apparently, she died not because she ended her pregnancy, but because the rave needed a sacrifice to end the ceremony. If Sam Gelding were still alive, Heather thought, he would probably have been given the assignment to eliminate her. Heather knew little about Misty, except that Red and the others were bent on getting her to come back to the Asherah House Bed and Breakfast where she had apparently spent all of her life. What Heather did know was Misty was pregnant after participating in a rave ceremony. Other than those women, Heather did not know how many others may have had their lives totally altered by those who organized the raves.

Heather went to Red's bar, filled a glass with ice, and poured herself a soft drink. How have I gotten so involved, she thought? Half the time Red calls me his dog. Tim is no longer enthralled with me. He was supposed to ask me to marry him, and when I saw him at the Blair House, it was like he didn't want me at all. And what was with Hannah and Misty? They were working in the Christian bookstore, laughing and having a good time, right alongside the older woman named Kat and her father Mr. Goodie-two-shoes! "And they really like one another. They were such losers..." Heather paused, "but why is it I'm the one who is miserable? At least Red wants me, but it's at his convenience...and here I am waiting, and Tim is surrounded by women who like him."

"I should have paid attention to what Tim was trying to show me. I didn't even look at the tree or what was carved on it. I knew it had been important to him, but I just wanted to make him squirm and do what I wanted..." she said slowly, "which no longer works."

Heather found a notepad next to Red's telephone and quickly wrote him a note telling him about the one unlocked first floor, front window on the south side of the house. She lied and wrote Red to tell him that her mother was sick, so she had to go home for a visit. Finishing her note, she picked up her purse, quickly left out a back door, and ran around the side of the house to her car. Heather sped away, went to her room where she boarded, packed most of her things in her car, left the valley, and went home to Wild Horse, a very small town in eastern Colorado where the air was clean, the water fresh, and her mom's home cooking waited for her. As Heather distanced herself from the valley, she realized she had escaped Red's hold on her. She likened her experience to an unsavory burnt end that needed to be removed from the grill before it became a crispy critter. Heather escaped and was no longer Red's dog, the Canaanite term for a temple prostitute.

*** 

While Niall and John Mark protected the church in Rock Creek, it had been Ezra's plan to have Brian, Drostan, and Coinneach join him in protecting the Blair House. He knew that he could also count on Detective Caleb Jones to help, but he knew his warriors might need to go beyond what Jones would consider lawful. Victims may be perceived as perpetrators. He knew Jerry Sunday worked late managing the pizzeria as did Mike Crowfoot at the Jericho Springs Convenience Store at the south end of Main Street. Tim McNaughton used to work early hours at the Cozy Corner Café, but now his schedule had not yet been set at Bustos Family Mexican Restaurant. Older than the others, Kip Powell found it necessary to spend a lot of time on the road servicing his Christian bookstore accounts, while Morris Goodenough's bus driving schedule usually included overnight trips. Ken Bond lived a few houses down the street and would help, but he may have to protect his family should evil come their way. All would be reinforcements. Besides, Ezra thought, the brothers Tunnicliffe were bear hunters and keen with both sword and javelin.

Since Izzy had received an anonymous phone call from a woman warning him of pending trouble, he shared the message with his father, who seemed to relish the prospect of seeing some action. At first, Izzy had scoffed at the prospect of another assault on the house. The previous attempt produced hilarious results, but he consented to have the Tunnicliffe brothers move in temporarily and occupy the remaining unused third floor rooms. Ezra thought differently, took the threat perhaps too seriously, and sought the counsel of Adam Claymore and Chief Strong Bull. Both advised Ezra that anything was possible because of Red's compulsion to gain the water and mineral rights, because of Sheriff Bailey's apparent involvement, and because of the long list of McNaughton Corporation members.

Each night Ezra's tribe of defenders watched the grounds from the third floor, wrap-around porch in teams of two. Members of each team served alternated nights with one sitting at the northeast corner and the other at the southwest. On Ezra's duty nights, he always took the northeast corner where he could watch the full length of Main Street in front of the house. Also, he watched the trees north of the house where his zip line could reach. He placed his shotgun, with a load of salt in each barrel, in his corner. Wearing their dark cowls, Brian the Bear Killer and Coinneach the Fair shared coverage of the southwest corner. They monitored the backside of the house, the butte with Freedom's tree, the dry pond, and the hairpin turn on the mountain valley road. The pair watched over the hot springs pool all the way to the Bond's residence as well as to the county road to the south. Stacks of small wooden logs radiated in both directions from each corner. Defensively, the wood not only blocked the view from the ground below, but also the logs would be propelled as assault weapons against all invaders from any approach. If under attack, Ezra assigned the tossing of the small logs to the boys from Pryor.

The woman, who had called to warn the defenders of the Blair House, also confessed she had cased the house for Red McNaughton. She informed Izzy she had told Red about the unlocked window behind the staircase door in the bookstore and that Red intended to have his men enter the house through that window. As a distraction the assault would begin in the Christian bookstore. The informant said Red's invaders would not only include men and older boys from the McNaughton Corporation and the Night Riders, but also Red had ordered some of his wranglers to join with him. Finding it hard to believe, Ezra knew if it were true, it would mean up to thirty men might join the fray against him.

Based on what Tim had learned by listening to the table talk at the temporarily defunct Cozy Corner Café, Izzy figured the invaders could include all those who had worn the bear costumes. Tim recorded what he heard and made a list, which included Sheriff Bailey, Councilman Chauncey Brown, Red McNaughton and his son Butch, Ralph from Wolf City, Van Allen, Seamus, and Assistant Superintendent Dr. Maurice Wood. Also, Tim reported a rumor that Butch McNaughton and his friend Roy Sentry had a falling out with Red, the corporation, and the Night Riders. Tim confirmed it had become well known Ralph had been told to leave the valley forever. A newspaper article reported Irv and Ellis Moss had been wounded enough to be hospitalized during their unlawful entry and vandalism at the Church in the Glen. Another article announced Robert King had transferred to an out-of-state real-estate office. Tim noted King left the day following his involvement in the unlawful entry at the church. This meant two of the eight who wore the bear skins had left the valley.

Since Izzy shared the news of the woman's telephone call with his wife Janine, the Blair House women discussed their options at length when the men were not around. Kat, Hannah, and Misty confirmed Heather Ross had come to the Blair House after Tim had been fired from the cafe. Jill and Karen gave Misty high fives when the trio shared how Misty had handled Heather in her short shorts and halter top. Their estimation of Tim increased as well. They knew if another assault were coming, it wouldn't be dissuaded by volleys of water balloons. Janine organized both the women of the house and the neighbors along Main Street to meet with Deputy Candy to organize a neighborhood watch for their block. Mission had been accomplished, except for one additional detail.

Karen had a dream and in the dream, the grizzly bear made a final attack and it had been up to her to kill the bear. Not wanting to alarm the others with her serious reaction, she loaded Pilgrim's long barrel Sharps rifle, carried it one late night first down the stairs to the basement from her second floor room, and then tipped toed up the stairs of the secret staircase to the third floor. Once there she stood the rifle upright in the corner outside the closet of the northwest room and then retraced her steps down the stairs then back to her room.

Later in the week, Red mobilized his troops for the final attack on Blair House. No one wore the bear suits, and due to their positions in the community, the Sheriff, Chauncey, and Dr. Wood did not participate, nor did Roy Sentry and Red's son Butch. In Butch's absence, Buddy Smith took over the leadership of the Night Riders, and he led those that still remained active. Seamus and Van Allen eagerly volunteered to be the ones to violate the Christian bookstore. Despite Red's threats to fire them, only six of his wranglers joined him in a ride to the Blair House through Ridge View, down the Valley Highway, and then across the pasture, which Red shared with Adam. Red's wranglers tied their mounts to fence posts inside the pasture and walked through a subdivision and west on a side street that brought them north of the convenience store. Seamus and Van Allen parked Van's truck a block north of Blair House and walked toward the grove of trees beside the building. Van Allen warned those with him to watch for the old man, who might descend on them from the overhead zip line. Buddy led the Night Riders on foot behind the row of houses west of Main Street toward the garden. Although Kip's bookstore had been the primary target, Red also gave orders for the men to pour paint over Rachael McNaughton's piano, to rip out the garden Jill and others had planted, and to pollute the hot springs pond by pouring paint in it. Red said he wanted to be the one to destroy the carving Ezra Freedom had crafted on the Live Oak.

All waited. Storm clouds swept over the mountains and into the valley. Cloud cover favored the attackers, which also meant the defenders were not detected. Seamus and Van Allen began the attack from the north, while Red alone advanced from the south quietly. Although they made slight noise, the defenders had been instructed to let their enemies enter the house through the south window, so they could be charged with unlawful entry. Seamus and Van crept out of the trees, across the parking area, and up the wooden steps leading to the first floor porch. They tiptoed around the front of the house to the first window on the south side to open it.

Meanwhile, a neighborhood watch member on south Main Street and one to the north called Rachael to alert her, and then she called Janine inside the house to alert the women. Next, Rachael called Deputy Sheriff Cotton Candy to tell her the attack had begun, while the neighborhood watch members activated the telephone tree. Like the episode at the church in Rock Creek, Cotton headed for Jericho Springs from Ridge View.

Seamus opened the window to the stairwell, and Van Allen climbed through it. He took the paint cans Seamus handed him. Seamus crawled through the window, while Van Allen waited for him and searched for the light string to turn on the stairwell light. Pulling down the window shade, Seamus whispered for Van Allen to move forward, to open the bookstore door, and once inside, to feel for the light switch on the wall. Van Allen stumbled as he felt along the wall, and Seamus stood upright on the staircase landing. Kip pulled on the light string he had been holding, while Caleb Jones flipped on the light switch. Izzy raised the front window shade, so all would know the invaders were inside.

Kip shouted, "Hey cockroach, now what are you going to do?" as he threw blocks of wood at Seamus in rapid fire. The first barrage knocked Seamus against the library door. Seamus dropped his paint cans and tried to raise the window shade to climb back out the window. Kip nailed him in the back of the head with the next barrage. Seamus fell to the floor before the window in slow motion.

Looking perplexed, Van Allen reached for books to throw at Caleb, who smiled and clenched his fist before knocking out Van Allen with one fist to his face. Van Allen fell backward and landed in a heap on top of Seamus. Caleb quickly cuffed them, Van Allen's hand to Seamus' ankle. Caleb picked up one of the logs Kip had thrown, gave it back to Kip, told him to clobber one or both of them if they wakened. Caleb followed Izzy out the front door to battle the wranglers. Hannah came to help, grabbed one of the logs, and said to Kip, "You clobber one, while I clobber the other!"

"What fun, Miss Hannah, what fun!" Kip responded.

From the third floor the boys from Pryor began throwing the small logs at Red's wranglers and hit them effectively, but the wranglers moved away from the house toward the pond. Coinneach climbed down from the southwest corner to engage the wranglers, while Brian did the same to catch up with Red. Climbing the hill, Red pulled his Bowie from its scabbard to deface the tree. The six wranglers set down their unopened paint cans and turned to face Coinneach the Fair, while Brian followed after Red. Brian shouted they were destroying the garden and rabbit hutches.

Responding, Ezra rode his zip line to the grove of trees and landed behind the Night Riders, while Drostan climbed down the footholds Ezra had carved into the huge post at the northwest corner. Telling Janine to lock and guard the front door and Karen to do the same to the back door, John Mark raced toward the garden to engage the Night Riders. Hearing that someone was ravaging her garden, Jill bolted past Karen and ran out the back door with a broom in hand. She ran toward her out buildings followed by Misty, who said, "I have to help her, she is my friend!"

Locking the rear porch door, Karen smiled after Misty, and had been one of the first to see the flaming arrow cross the sky toward the county road south. Moments later another arrow landed on top of Huerfano Butte, another landed in the garden, another by the pond, and then a flurry of arrows fell safely to the ground outlining the rear of both the Night Riders and wranglers. Karen heard hooves pound pavement, so she abandoned her post to see what was coming. Dark clouds parted slightly, and the moon illuminated the scene. On the hairpin turn above the butte, Karen saw what looked like a scene from an old time movie. Lined single file across the horizon above the road, there appeared to be thirty warriors shouting war chants and waving spears and bows above their heads.

When Adam arrived with his wranglers, Rabbit, Barnabas, and Pilgrim, Red's six cowhands stopped fighting Coinneach and surrendered. From on top Huerfano Butte, Chief Strong Bull sat stoically without emotion on a magnificent black stallion. His stone face changed as a smile flashed across his face, his horse reared, and he first called Adam's name followed by Caleb's, "Ta-ton-ka!" Then he pointed toward the tree and shouted, "They fight!"

412

On top of the butte, a burning arrow struck the Asher pole stump. Red McNaughton had attempted to scrape Ezra's art in the bark from the tree with the Bowie knife that he carried in a sheath attached to his belt. Brian had arrived in time to keep Red from destroying Ezra Sr.'s carving of Christ on the cross. Brian knocked Red over backward. Red gathered himself with his knife still in hand. Looking at the size of Brian, Red asked, "Who are you?"

Brian shook off his customary bear skin robe and smiled as he said, "I am your worst nightmare for I am Brian the Bear Killer. Some call me Bear, but it is you who have had much to growl about."

Red lunged at Bear with his knife, and Bear easily avoided him and said, "You have become an ugly, evil man."

From below Coinneach launched his javelin and stuck it in the Asher stump. "Aw," said Bear, "my weapon of choice has arrived. Have you killed with your knife, as I have with my spear?"

"You will soon find out," Red replied, as he lunged again. "Why are you here?"

"I thought I was to kill the great grizzly, but now I think it is only you I am here to destroy," Bear said as he jerked his spear out of the stump and began to circle Red.

"I hate you newcomers!" Red said as he lunged and missed again.

In an instant it had been over and from below Adam shouted, "Is it over?"

Chief Strong Bull laughed, "It was too easy...Red lunged with his knife and the man called Bear shoved his spear through his shoulder. It probably separated when Bear twisted the spear. I heard the bones snapping!"

"I claim your weapon," growled Bear, as he twisted the spear again in Red's shoulder. Red reluctantly dropped his knife and collapsed to the ground, as Bear stripped him of his belt and sheath.

"Are you going to finish me off?" asked Red, who believed he was going to be killed.

"No," Brian the Bear laughed, "I no longer kill men. I only kill bears. You are not worthy." He put his foot on Red's chest and continued with a jerk on the javelin, "Here, it is better for you for me to pull it out quickly."

"Ow! Help me! I'm bleeding everywhere," Red pleaded.

Bear yelled for two of the Night Riders to come take Red inside, "Come here, now! Take Red inside to the ladies you came here to terrorize. Help save his sorry life, and call for an ambulance."

As the two Night Riders attempted to carry Red to one of their vehicles, Bear menacingly shouted, "No junior, you are not taking him anywhere. You are waiting here for the cops to come arrest you for unlawful trespass and destruction of property. Seriously, you had better hurry!"

The boys on the third floor shouted, "Hey you guys! Somebody just kidnapped Misty. The big guy, Buddy, put her over his shoulder and ran down behind the houses."

John Mark rushed past the two that hauled Red down the butte to where Adam stood holding the reins of his horse, "Adam, lend me your horse. Buddy Smith just kidnapped Misty," which drew the attention of Red's wranglers who cheered, as John Mark leaped into the saddle and quickly broke into a cantor.

"Some good came out of this!" bellowed one of Red's wranglers.

Coinneach decked him with a punch to his face with his massive fist. Izzy asked, "There now! Anyone else looking for the same."

In full regalia four of Strong Bull's braves gave pursuit and caught up with John Mark, as he passed Bustos restaurant. Not believing their eyes, late night patrons inside rose from where they were seated at the sound of the hoof beats and blurred vision of the horses flying passed the windows. Toward the end of town by the pizzeria, John Mark rode next to the driver's side of Buddy's clunker of a car. War ponies came along the passenger side, and with drawn bows, two braves let loose arrows with steel tipped heads that pierced the front and rear tires. The Indians peeled off the pursuit and slowed to a trot, as the tires on Buddy's automobile flattened. Buddy continued on the flat tires, until he saw Deputy Candy had blocked the county road with her cruiser. The deputy waited for Buddy with pistol drawn and pointed at him.

Buddy stopped his car, got out, and tried to run when John Mark caught up with and passed him, then stopped and dismounted Adam's horse. Buddy nearly ran to him, but stopped and prepared to battle John Mark, who rushed him and tackled Buddy to the ground.

Candy arrived and cuffed Buddy before he could get up. She said, "Misty is still in the back seat."

John Mark ran toward Buddy's car followed by Adam's horse. Misty climbed out of the back seat, as the braves surrounded the car to protect her. She paused and waited for John Mark, and then leaped into his open arms and hugged him. She said, "You kept your promise, you rescued me from evil."

And with his Gaelic accent, he said, "Aye Lassie, I feared I had lost you, and now I know I am the one who must stay here with you and not just to protect you."

Letting his words sink in, Misty melted in his arms, sought his mouth, and kissed him like the first day they met when she buckled his knees. She returned his brogue and said, "Aye, Laddie, I have my sights on you. I want you to be the father for all my children."

Tear drops fell from his eyes to her shoulder and they kissed again, as Candy watched, while holding Buddy with one hand and her night stick with the other.

The braves sang out, "Whoop, whoop!"

Helping her onto Adam's horse, before climbing up behind her, John Mark asked, "Why didn't you get out of that guy's car?"

"Are you kidding, Farm Boy, I've never seen Indians before now, and I was surrounded by men who shot the tires with arrows! That was pretty exciting, but you were the one who was impressive. Catching up with the clod! Who is he and why were they tearing out the grape vines and fruit trees from the garden?" Misty asked, as their mount began retracing its steps south down the center of Main Street, escorted by four braves dressed in loin cloths, leggings, and moccasins.

"Brrr..." said one brave, "I hope the Chief doesn't take long. I want to get to the motel and take a hot shower."

"Yeah, it may be Indian summer to the pale faces, but it got chilly under the cloud cover. Maybe the Chief will let us change back to our street clothes at the Blair House," said another.

"This is what it will be like, if we pass the audition."

"The circus or movie?"

"Sounds like both, or the one will lead to the other."

"Come on guys, let's let these lovebirds enjoy their moment!" a third said with a smile.

"I hope it's the silver screen...come on, let's stay in script and whoop it up!" said the last brave, as they raced past Misty and John Mark in front of Bustos restaurant.

"Here they come again!" one customer said.

"And there they go..." said another.

"Who's the couple?" asked the woman, as Adam's horse walked leisurely by the audience.

Tim the waiter said, "That's Misty McClaren and John Mark Cannikin. She lives where I do at the Blair House, and you probably heard about John when I was waiting tables when the Cozy was open!"

"He's a big man...big, bad, John," the woman said. "I'd like to be sitting on a saddle with him."

"You should see the others..." said the first customer.

"They're probably newcomers..." replied another oldtimer sorrowfully.

"Only John Mark...Misty is a McClaren, one of the MacNaughtens... and the Indians are from Wolf City," Tim explained.

"A McNaughton? I've never seen her before," said the second customer.

An older woman, the cook, joined the conversation as she came out of the kitchen, "Tim, you said she was a McClaren, then she must be M a c N a u g h t e n..." she spelled out, "I remember... Beatrice and Rachael may also, Timmy. Cristabel MacNaughten owned the bed and breakfast in Rock Creek...back when it was respectable. It was before, when it wasn't called the Asherah House...just a minute, I'll remember. It was well kept then...a vacation spot for some...for me a sanctuary."

"Are you the cook?" asked the woman customer to which the old lady nodded, "I love your green chili, the enchiladas, your queso dip, and salsa!"

"Why thank you, dear, I am the cook and the owner," the old lady said, "and I remember now...It was the Blair House...the Blair House Bed and Breakfast. Cristabel was a MacNaughten, who was related to the Blairs. I don't remember what happened that it changed to the Asherah House, but you could find out at the museum. It was in the newspaper... Cristabel was a grandmother. She had twin grand-daughters. Blair must have been her maiden name. I don't remember exactly, but somehow Mary Claymore's family fits in somewhere there. Perhaps Mary's family were Blairs too, but folks it's ten o'clock and this old lady needs to go to bed. Timmy, please close the shop."

"What a great story!" said the woman customer. "I learn something new every day!"

"Me, too!" said Tim, as he pulled the latest edition of *The Out Cry* newspaper from the newsstand, "Look here at the front page head-lines," as the customers came around him to see. "Here's the answer to the Indians, the article says our local Indians, under the direction of Chief Strong Bull, will be auditioning for a movie part with a circus which arrives in Ridge View tomorrow."

A customer bought a copy, and read, "Says members of the circus will perform in each of our towns as an introduction. Says they'll do a one act play...one performance will be on the Stage Stop Hotel, front deck!"

Another patron began to pull a newspaper from the opened machine, while the first paid for his copy, Tim interceded by saying, "The pastor makes a living delivering those newspapers..."

After sounding a humph, the customer put his coins in the slot, and then said, "The article says the circus will set up next to the feed lots outside of Ridge View."

*** 

Reluctantly, Sheriff Bailey arrived at the Blair House, as had an ambulance to take Red to the hospital. Red's wranglers had been las-soed by Pilgrim and strung together. Van Allen and Seamus sat back to back tied together to a floor to ceiling post on the first floor porch. Several Night Riders were caught, including the two who carried Red into the Blair House to get his bleeding stopped. The Night Riders sat next to Seamus and Van Allen looking forlorn, but the two who car-ried Red inside were shown the bookstore where they purchased a New Testament and were reading it aloud on the porch.

"Hannah said she had been told to read the Ambassador's Toolkit and gave us a copy of this paper she got from Tim," one Night Rider said to Seamus, and then he started with *John 3:16, "For God so loved the world..."*

The other Night Rider said, "Then even now in our stupidity, there is hope for us..."

Seamus broke in and said, "They never give up."

"It's a whole lot more promising than what you guys in the bear skins have to say. Look where following you has got us," he said as he hit Seamus hard in his shoulder, "So shut up and listen! This sounds like truth none of us deserve."

The Chief had his braves retrieve their arrows, except for the one stuck in the Asher pole stump, which he purposely left there as a souvenir for someone to treasure. The thirty braves assembled and made ready to leave. Before saddling, Chief Strong Bull said to Adam, "It is good to see you in the saddle, my friend, but you still are not healed of the wounds from the grizzly."

"Thank you for showing and for signaling me when to arrive," said Adam.

"Just as planned," said Izzy, "I'm amazed at the accuracy of your archers!"

"Fortunately, there was no wind," the Chief said, which brought laughter to most, and especially Ezra Sr., "otherwise we may be handcuffed."

Detective Jones came forward, and the Chief addressed him directly, "It was good to fight with Ta-ton-ka by our side."

Jones said, "We'll look forward to the movie you make, Chief, and in the mean time, we'll see you at the circus!"

"There is something you all should know about the bear, and the boys from Pryor can help fill you in, if they will," the Chief said, as he looked around for the two of them. "Earlier, several of my men rode with me to Pryor to look for sign of the bear. We found a flatbed truck with a large metal cage on its bed. I checked who made the cage, had my secretary contact them to find out who they sold it to, and that's how I came in contact with the circus. One thing led to another, and I found out the circus planned to stop here. They said movie company officials will meet them here in Ridge View tomorrow, and again, one thing led to another."

"Cool beans!" said Rabbit.

"But, what about the boys?" Detective Jones asked.

"They were runaways, joined the circus, and took on the appearance of being a family with the couple the bear killed in Pryor. The boys tormented the bear when it was a cub, and the couple who took them in actually stole the bear and the truck. They tried to hide in Pryor. Apparently, their purpose had been to turn the bear loose and reintroduce a grizzly to Colorado."

"So that's why the bear was so intent on catching the boys!" said Pilgrim.

"I guess so," the Chief replied, "it must have been a love-hate relationship."

With her yellow hair loosened to waist length, Jill came forward from the crowd that had gathered from the Blair House and the houses on Main Street. She stood before the Chief, who looked down from where he sat and dismounted to talk with her. He removed his headdress as she spoke. Jill touched his forearm and said, "You have always been a hero to me, as you know, thank you for saving my garden," as she rose to her tip toes to kiss him.

His lips met hers, and though both wanted to linger, the Chief said, "Yellow hair, you make my heart sing. I have burned with savage intent toward these men who have sought to harm my friends and to destroy the things about my God in the bookstore. With one kiss, you have made me at peace. May God allow me to always be around when you, Dear Child, face trouble."

Jill kissed him again and fled to safety on the front porch.

Karen said to Janine, "There's more to the story, and I want to hear it."

"Probably, but what I want to see is how you greet Adam…" responded Janine.

"If I ever get a chance!" interrupted Karen.

Sheriff Bailey started to quarrel with Deputy Cotton Candy over whether or not the invaders should be booked. Noting the crowd became unruly at his resistance, Bailey said, "It's your collar, you book 'em, you interrogate them."

Caleb stepped forward and suggested, "Sheriff, you are going to need several cruisers to get all of these to jail, why not deputize some men, myself included, haul them to jail, and I'll help Deputy Candy interrogate them with Deputy Harley's assist."

"Caleb is part of the CBI task force, and Harley just arrived," offered Deputy Candy, with the support of the murmuring crowd, to which Bailey relented and deputized the detective.

The Chief had remounted his horse and signaled for his men to move out, when Adam said to him, "My friend, the Sheriff has gotten himself into trouble I was not aware of. He may do something stupid. While you are in Ridge View, be watching, Chief."

"And you here, my brother..." the Chief replied, as he crossed his chest with his clenched right fist over his heart, and looked toward Karen, who smiled, "and you, my friend, have someone, who eagerly waits for you."

As the Chief made his grand exit down the Blair House driveway, thirty of his braves rode behind him. Unofficially, they rode out to parade through downtown Jericho Springs after ten o'clock. The sheriff, detective, and deputy organized transportation to deliver Red McNaughton's invaders to jail. Porch lights along the path switched on, as residents along Main Street either had been awakened from their sleep or left their television to witness the strange event. Many braved the cool night air, stepped out on their porches to witness the sight, and waved at the horsemen, while others closed their curtains and peered through the slits between their drapes. The switch board at the sheriff's office lit up with callers either complaining about the noise or proclaiming they feared they were about to be attacked by Indians. Others, who had read the newspaper article about the circus coming to town, grabbed their cameras and took pictures. They assumed the parade to be a late night promotion, and so it became!

Izzy and Janine Freedom, with her arm around her father-in-law Ezra, invited the defenders of the Blair House to come inside their home to have freshly made ice cream. Pilgrim Wayne, Barnabus, and Rabbit dismounted their horses and climbed the stairs to the porch. Ken, Kat, Kristin, and Krystal Bond joined the party and greeted all who stayed. Members of the South Main Street Neighborhood Watch crossed the street to celebrate the first of many victories they would share. Residents Kip Powell, Mike Crowfoot, Hannah Rahab, Misty McClaren, and Jill Lowenstein joined in, while late workers, Tim

McNaughton, Jerry Sunday, and Morris Goodenough would arrive home later. Brian the Bear, Niall, Drostan, and Coinneach—the Tunnicliffes relished having homemade ice cream. John Mark helped Rachael McNaughton up the stairs before joining Misty. All but Karen and Adam went inside.

***

Sheriff Bailey knew none of Red's wranglers would speak ill about him or the assault on Blair House, nor would any of the corporate members dare to reveal the inner workings of the McNaughton Corporation. He also knew Red controlled the Night Riders without mercy. They would be closed mouthed to a fault. Knowing none of those arrested would disclose anything to risk what the corporate leadership would do to them, Sheriff Bailey felt no fear in allowing Detective Jones and Deputy Candy interrogate the Night Riders or Red's wranglers no matter what shape Red was in. He did fear losing face at the hands of his ever popular deputy. She shattered Bailey's ego. Also, he feared what might be done by those who weren't at the raid. Chauncey Brown and Dr. Maurice Wood didn't participate due to their strategic positions, but it was what Red's son Butch might say and do Bailey feared most. Wallowing in his own defeat, Bailey decided to self medicate by going to the Tobacco Store to try to salvage his re-election bid and then to spend the night at the Asherah House Bed and Breakfast.

From the recliners on the first floor front porch, Karen and Adam watched the Sheriff leave and follow the county road toward Rock Creek. Sitting on Adam's right and holding his hand, Karen said, "Maybe we should follow the Sheriff to see where he goes."

"I take it you don't trust him?"

"Not any more, nor does it seem anyone else trusts him. I know Cotton and Caleb don't!"

"I know and I wish they didn't have good reason not to trust him. Red's men won't say anything Bailey has to worry about, nor would Seamus and Van Allen. Red's wranglers won't say anything, nor will any of the Night Riders."

"Did you notice Butch was not here?"

"Yes, and his friend Roy Sentry wasn't here. Butch's conscience is working on him. He wants to meet with me. I'm pretty certain he wants to tell me things Bailey would fear."

"Hmmm...now that is interesting!"

"As Ken Bond says, indubitably! And as for our checking up on Bailey, it's already taken care of. The Chief has surveillance in Rock Creek, here, and in Ridge View. Besides, I'd rather just sit here with you," Adam said as he leaned over and kissed Karen and kissed her again.

Of course, Karen responded well, and then said, "I can't wait for you to be able to hold me with both arms. I want more," she continued as she stood up and sat on his lap.

\*\*\*

A late night telephone call from his neighbor awakened John Law from a deep sleep. Somewhat shocked, he asked, "What has the school board done now?"

"It's about Amanda..."

"Is she all right?"

"Yes, dear, Amanda is fine....now that I've shared some things and calmed her down..." Willa Sentry said.

"Sounds ominous..." John replied.

"Could be, but I don't think so," Willa continued somewhat enthusiastically, "I think the timing is right to make things right...to expose some dirty laundry..."

"Go on...explain..."

"Amanda told me about what Mrs. Bustos said a few nights ago," Willa explained, "when the cowboys and Indians rescued Misty from the Night Rider, Buddy Smith"

"What did she say?"

"Mrs. Bustos told her customers that the Asherah House use to be better...when it was the Blair House Bed and Breakfast, and Cristabel MacNaughten owned it," said Willa, "and do you remember her maiden name was Blair and I think her mother was a McClaren from Scotland...or something like that."

"What do you have in mind?" John asked.

"John, we have the opportunity to help finish the restoration of Blair House," Willa said, as she began to weep, "You and I are the only ones who can make this happen, and those at the Blair House are making such a good effort in advancing the cause of Christ. Please arrange a meeting...around Thanksgiving."

"Bless you, Willa, I'll do it..."

# Giving Thanks

## Chapter 20

*"Rejoice always, pray continually, give thanks in all circumstances; for this is God's will for you in Christ Jesus."*                    *1Thessalonians 5:16-18*

"Have you noticed how pieces of a puzzle begin to fall into place once you recognize the pattern?" Adam said, as he and Karen assembled a puzzle picture of a lion lying down with a lamb.

"I like to find the edges and corners, so I can set the parameters, and then I work on locating connecting colors," Karen replied, as she snuggled closer to him on his brown leather couch.

"Here is some fruit for the two of you lovebirds," Beatrice said as she added a fruit bowl to the circular puzzle table, "and you have fifteen minutes to wash your hands and come to the table. Rabbit and I've made breakfast enchiladas smothered with my famous green chili with shredded potatoes, two eggs on top over easy, beans and rice."

"Gramma Bee, you have been a delight to have in my home! Good company and great cooking!" said Adam enthusiastically.

"And now you are well enough for me to go home…I confess I'm kind of sad to leave, but I'm needed at the Blair House…and have you noticed how the inside is so nicely restored. It is how I remembered it was when Paul and Lydia lived in Blair House," a McNaughton matriarch said.

"They were wonderful people, weren't they, Gramma Bee?" asked Karen.

"Yes, and like now with Izzy and Janine, people gather there to eat, fellowship, and speak of things of the Lord."

"And Rachael played hymns then and we gathered around her in the piano room," added Adam.

"I have been blessed just by having a room on the second floor where I have been able to look out the window and watch the birds pick through the seed in my cabin bird feeder," added Karen, "but it would be good to live there without the strife."

"I've thought everyone has gotten along well," Adam wondered.

"We do! I meant to say, strife from outside...the bitterness," Karen attempted to explain, "and community attitudes I've discovered through my interviews. I'm sorry to have said that...I'm really in a very good mood, and I'm glad to be included in things."

"Karen, you are such a dear," Beatrice said. "How can we expect non-believers to act as if Christ resided in their hearts? I don't think we can expect them to act differently than they do. Grace and mercy are what they need, and you are one of those called upon to give it to them."

"You'll be glad, Karen, when the pieces to the puzzle all fit together," Adam replied, as he put his right arm around her. "You are so thoughtful and considerate. Just like how you sat down here on my right side instead of my left."

"So you could put your arm around me."

"And you drove your car over here to pick up Beatrice to take her home."

"So I could see you early in the morning."

"And you volunteered to help move the Bonds into their new home in Rock Creek."

"So I could work alongside you."

"And you played alongside me to put this puzzle together."

"So I could speed up the completion of my own puzzle..."

"Thank you for being so motivated...you know, Karen," said Adam, "it has been important to me to have John Mark restore and update my Rock Creek house, so the Bonds can move in there as the pastor family for the church."

"One of your puzzle pieces?" asked Karen.

"Yes...it is part of me moving on...it will be okay for me to..." Adam reflected, "I can go back to being the church deacon, and I don't have to serve as pastor."

"Sounds like you are getting ready for a new life," Karen interrupted, "and I see a puzzle piece fitting together with another."

"Interesting...how so?"

"Well, your Mary was a McNaughton, but her mother was a Blair," Karen surmised, "and her mother's family home is now restored and an intact family with children will be living there in Rock Creek."

"True..."

"And although the Blair House was owned by Ezra Freedom, Paul and Lydia Blair lived there raising Ezra's son," Karen added.

"The house was magnificent, and the Blair's radiated with the beauty of Jesus! The tree seemed to dominate the town's landscape, and people came there for fellowship and conversation that brought them healing. We soaked in the thermal pond on the butte, and its waters heated the Blair House. Really, it was a spiritual oasis."

"And the building is mostly restored, and the grounds now include rabbit hutches and a chicken coop, and a pole barn is planned."

"And those gathered there have helped cause a spiritual awakening in the valley. Let me count the number of tools God has used by counting them on my fingers on both hands," Adam summarized, "One was the prayer walks; two, the door to door gift bag hanging; three, street corner prayer ministry; four, the pastor's group; five on my little finger are hymn sings; six, the bookstore and seven, in-home book parties; eight, the neighborhood watch; nine, just bringing people together, and ten, most important...how the folks at Blair House responded to the opposition."

"I see what you mean, both physical and spiritual restoration..." Karen said with a smile, "but you left off one Mr. Humble. Number eleven is the protector of the valley, who with his men confronted evil, thwarted the Baal worship, and chased the bear away."

"The bear is wounded and gone for now. He may not survive the winter, but at least I should have time to heal before he resurfaces," Adam sadly said.

"I hope the bear dies, and you don't have to face him again," Karen said earnestly.

"He has cost me my cinnamon growler, my horse Silver, and my good looks," Adam said as he quickly rebounded.

"Time to eat," shouted Rabbit from the kitchen, "my guess is help has already begun to arrive at the Bond's new home."

\*\*\*

After breakfast Karen helped Beatrice pack her belongings in Karen's Chevy Nova, and they sang *Oh, Happy Day* all the way home to Blair House. Help, which could, had gathered outside Adam's rental on Main Street in Jericho Springs, while more waited at his house in Rock Creek. Adam and Barnabas rode in Adam's Ford F-250 pick-up, while Rabbit had to stay home to clean up the kitchen and complete food prep for Thanksgiving dinner at the Claymore ranch. Since school had closed for Thanksgiving, Jill and Janine had already spent a couple of hours helping Kat pack her house. Krystal and Kristin packed their clothes in their bedroom and placed them in the front room. Izzy, Ezra, Kip, and Caleb had already loaded Ezra's truck and waited for the caravan to form along Main Street. Mike had to work at the convenience store, Jerry at the pizzeria, and Tim at Bustos restaurant. The Tunnicliffe brothers joined John Mark at the Rock Creek house to help remove stored boxes from the attic. Discovering the labels on the outside of the boxes, John Mark moved them and more to the garage. He knew Adam would value opening each box, so John Mark locked the garage side door. After wedging a rod in the overhead door rail, no one could enter the garage without the door key. The boys from Pryor had been busy feeding the chickens and rabbits, while Misty and Hannah focused on preparing for the Thanksgiving dinner. No one awakened Morris, as he had arrived home late after driving the Trailways Bus to and from Chicago.

All involved in the move understood its significance. The Bonds had lost all their possessions earlier in the arson fire, which totally consumed Adam's trailer on the ridge off highway 96. All their furniture, dishes, tableware, bedding and more had been donated by members of the little Church in the Glen and some of Ken's newspaper customers. Kat cherished all they had been given, and she longed for her husband to return home from delivering newspapers throughout the valley.

When Ken arrived, he rushed from their station wagon to the door, while waving at those there to help him. He bounded into the front room shouting for Kat. He said, "Kat, Kat, where are you? Where are you?"

"What's the matter, Honey? What happened now?"

"It's a God thing! It's a God thing!"

The girls rushed from their rooms saying, "Daddy, Daddy, what happened?"

Ken stopped jumping up and down long enough to repeat himself, calmed down, and released Kat from his grasp, and said, "Look here, what I've got in my hand!"

"What is it?" Kristin asked.

"It's a gold ping-pong ball!" Krystal proclaimed. "Do we have enough room for a ping pong table at our new house?"

"No, Darling Daughter, it is a gold nugget!" said Ken.

"Ken, where did it come from?" asked Kat.

"I did my routes and filled the boxes. I stopped at Bustos and saw Tim McNaughton, who said someone handed him the nugget with a note. The note said it was for the Bond family to use in furnishing their new house from head to toe and to replace all the moths had eaten and the defilers had burned. The note said the giver had been told to bless us with the nugget, and the giver was just being obedient. Tim said we wouldn't believe who gave it to him. Tim said it was someone who has been an enemy to you and everything going on at the Blair House. Tim said he was pleased to be sworn to secrecy."

"Just being obedient, as if it were easy..." said Kat.

"I asked Tim, if Ezra had given it to him, and he handed me the note. I've seen Ezra's crippled handwriting, and this is beautifully scribed," Ken explained, as he handed his wife the note.

"A woman wrote this..."

"Let's see, Mama," said Krystal, who read the note and exchanged it for the nugget and gave the note to Kristin. Krystal marveled at the nugget, while Kristin broke into tears reading the note.

"Lovely Daughter, are you dreaming about what this means?" asked Ken.

"I sure am...this is answered prayer...I asked God to forgive those who did evil to us, and I asked if they had one time been saved, that he would bring them back to him," Kristin said, "I gave up my right to revenge. I gave them to God, and I got out of the way!"

"You thought about your life verse didn't you?" asked Kat.

"I did Mommy, said Kristin. "It's *'So do not fear, for I am with you; do not be dismayed, for I am your God. I will strengthen you and help you; I will uphold you with my righteous right hand''* (Isaiah 41:10).

"Me too, I prayed for them, and I asked for truth and justice to win. In a way I think something is going to happen... the grizzly bear is going to get someone that wears the bear skin costumes we have heard about," Krystal said, "and while you are all listening to me, my life verse is like Mommy's, *'Consider the blameless, observe the upright; a future awaits those who seek peace'* (Psalm 37:37). How about that?"

"Wonderful, mine is *'In the same way, let your light shine before others, that they may see your good deeds and glorify your Father in heaven''* (Matthew 5:16), Dad said, as Kat listened and Ken pulled another paper out of his pocket, "and Mother there was one stipulation...we are not to move our old furniture to the Rock Creek house. Instead, we are to use this voucher to stay at the Stage Stop Hotel. Free meals and lodging for up to three rooms for three days. What do you think about that?"

"If it is not a snare, I think we follow the terms. We share this with those outside, we ask Adam if he would want the furniture and house wares, so he could rent the house furnished. If not, we can have a yard sale here," Mom replied, "Either way, we ask our help to move our things back in here. If we have a yard sale in late November, we donate the proceeds to the church. And we spend the day after Thanksgiving, Friday, shopping...after you do the paper routes."

The girls eagerly added, "It will be like a mini-vacation! We could shop in Colorado Springs or Pueblo or both!"

"As you wish, Mother," said Dad, and then he led his girls in a prayer of thanksgiving. Eagerly, the Bond family went outside to share their blessing and good fortune with the others.

Ken shared the blessing with great joy, showed his friends the gold nugget, and asked what the others thought. Adam confessed he was somewhat reluctant to tell them, but he recognized the hand-writing on the note. He refused to tell who had written it, and asked Ezra if he had been the one who provided the nugget. Delighted, Ezra shook his head to the contrary.

"Well, what do we do now?" asked Izzy.

"Suggestion," offered Adam, "Let's unload and put everything back in the house. Ken and family bring your clothes and personal items. Call the Stage Stop Hotel and reserve the rooms you need. Stay at the hotel tonight, get measurements tomorrow, and begin your shopping on Friday. I'll take your nugget to John Law, who will represent you at the bank. He will get the correct amount of money for it without anyone else learning of your good fortune. You should be able to pick up the cash from John on Thanksgiving at the Blair House. No one says anything until after the Bonds have made their purchases. Okay?"

When everyone agreed, Adam continued, "I think we should all go to the Rock Creek house. We need to do a prayer walk around the perimeter of the grounds. We need for God to place a hedge of protection around the house, and then we go into the house and re-dedicate it for the Lord's purposes..." Adam paused, "Didn't John Mark say he and the brothers had found things in the attic that I should look at?"

"Yes, I think he set some boxes in the garage for you, Adam, and he locked them in there securely," Karen said and added, "If you like, may I offer to help..."

"Thank you, Karen, I think that would be good," Adam replied. "It must be old things, perhaps from Mary's childhood or older."

"Ken, Kat, if you have any trouble, the only telephone is in the lobby."

"Thanks, Karen, we will be certain to locate the telephone booth, and we'll have change in case we need to call one of you," Ken said, as tears continued down the cheeks of Kat and the girls. "One other thing, Adam, if you would want to, we would like for you to have the household furnishings, so you could at least rent the house partially furnished. Consider it a thank you from us for all your kindness and for taking us in."

"I will consider it a blessing," Adam said, and then the Bond girls collectively hugged him.

Promptly, the caravan prepared to depart for the Rock Creek house. The Bonds gathered their clothing plus personal items, while the others laughed as they unloaded the vehicles that they had already packed. All the men who loaded goods in the trucks piled into two vehicles. Barnabas, Caleb and Adam rode with Karen, and Jill and Kip with Izzy and Ezra, while Janine decided to stay at home to help prepare dinner. The Bonds happily rode together and led the way to their new home.

Upon their arrival people from the church gathered from the immediate neighborhood including Lila and the highwayman. John Mark and the Tunnicliffes had just finished hauling treasures from the attic to the garage, securely locked the garage and joined the group. All were surprised passenger cars arrived but no trucks.

With Ken's permission, Adam took the lead and said, "Thank you all for being here! There has been a change of plans, a good thing. The Bonds won't be moving their furniture here, because they will have all new things."

The people cheered!

Adam continued, "This is a new beginning for us as a church. This house is fully remodeled and restored. Restored because as many of you know, this was my wife Mary's childhood home. She had a heart for this town, and she prayed regularly Christ would become Lord of every household and everyone in each house. When she died, I kept her house, which had been built for Mary's grandmother. I worked so her dream would be fulfilled."

The people cheered!

"Tradition has been the pastor of the Church in the Glen and his family, if he had one... would live here. John Mark as well as the Tunnicliffe brothers have totally updated the inside, restored the out-side, and repaired the garage, laid a concrete driveway, and upgraded the yard."

"This is really nice, Adam," said Lila.

"This morning we want to dedicate the house for the Lord's work. First, we will walk the perimeter of the property. John Mark will lead us, and we will each pray as we walk," Adam instructed the flock,

"This is important as we will establish a spiritual hedge of protection around the property. Then we will go inside the house, where we'll go room by room and pray, and then we will have shared prayer over the Bonds and the house to rededicate them and the house for the Lord."

"There's more to this, isn't there, Adam?" asked Karen.

"Yes, thank all of you for being here. This is very important for me. As you know, about fifteen years ago, I lost my wife to death. She's with the Lord, but I'm still here. I never healed from the loss of Mary. There has been a hole in my heart and now restoring this house, named after the maiden name of Mary's mother. This like the one below the great tree was known as Blair House. With the new pastor and family, with the restoration of the dwelling, all has been made new. I ask you to take wholeheartedly the prayer walk and dedication of our new pastor and his family's new home."

And so it happened wholeheartedly.

***

Preparation for Thanksgiving dinner had begun the day before. The Tunnicliffe brothers had built a four by eight foot table, made of one inch thick plywood and saw horses. They added it to the two formal dining room tables, which had been fully extended with additional leaves. When put together the usual spaces for eighteen became a comfortable setting of twenty-six seats. Across the street, Rachael McNaughton baked a spiral ham to go with the twenty-four pound turkey Janine roasted in the wood stove oven. Before moving to the house in Rock Creek, Kat made three pumpkin and three fruit pies-apple, blueberry, and cherry- and left them in the refrigerator at her old house. Ruth insisted on bringing three pumpkin pies and whipped cream. Misty and Hannah wrote name tags, prepared party favors, set the table, and assigned the seats so that the four brothers would not sit together. John Mark's name card had been placed next to Misty's, and the tags for Coinneach and Drostan flanked both sides of Hannah. Across the table they placed Jill's card with Tim's to her right and Jerry's to her left. Beatrice's had been flanked by Bear's and Ezra Sr.'s cards. Cards and place settings were prepared for all in attendance, including the three Brownings and the four Bonds.

Kristin and Krystal asked, "So Andrew Browning is coming?"

And then Krystal added, "I'll bet he brings us bubblegum."

"For our 'plexions!" added Kristin, who lit the room with her smile, while Krystal nodded agreement.

Additional folding chairs had been gathered to accommodate the many visitors who would arrive after dinner for dessert. Once all had gathered and were seated according to their name tags, but before the hot food had been served, all listened to hear Izzy pray. Leading the prayer, Izzy said, "This reminds me of the old days when I lived here with Paul and Lydia. As was their custom, twenty-six seats are filled and one is open. That was intentional, as Paul Blair would say the prayer and invite Jesus to come occupy the vacant chair at the end of the table. This day is significant for Janine, my father, and me. The inside of the house is clean, and most things have been repaired, washed, and painted. Some new features have been added like the bookstore and the staircase which leads to Kip's room on the second floor. Outside a garden plot has been prepared, grape vines and fruit trees planted and replanted..."

Laughter interrupted Izzy in response to his reference to the recent assault by Red's clan, and Janine said, "Go on dear, we are nearly ready to serve hot food."

"We have outbuildings and a pole barn is under construction, and like the *Old Testament* book of *Ezra*, we have had to have watchmen at the wall holding spears and swords to protect the builders," Izzy continued.

"Aye," said the Tunnicliffe brothers and "That's right, like in the book of *Ezra*," others added with Jerry saying, "Praise the Lord, we prevailed."

Izzy concluded, "We have had hymn sings and Kip's bookstore has ministered throughout the city."

"Prayer walks," said one, while another added, "Hanging gift bags with the gospel," and a third, "Prayer, fellowship, and Jerry's group building activities."

"Thank you one and all...it is by God's grace and mercy that the Blair House is now restored, both physically and spiritually," Izzy said, voice trembling, as his father cried, and those assembled clapped.

Izzy motioned for Jerry to give thanks, which he did, then said, "Izzy's plan was for us to eat and, while we are eating, for each of you to think of just one thing to share you are thankful for. We will share later around the piano. A real treat, we have the Deputy Cotton Candy from Ridge View, Adam and some of his wranglers from Claymore Flats, and John Law with the lovely Amanda and Willa Sentry from Jericho Springs coming to have dessert with us followed by a hymn sing!"

Janine added, "And with the Bonds, newly from Rock Creek, here for dinner...our table will be shared by friends from all three communities in Rock Creek Valley."

Next came a parade of food as Karen, Jill, Hannah, and Misty helped serve, while Beatrice and Janine loaded serving dishes with sumptuous food. First, the ladies served condiments of pickles, green and black olives, celery stuffed with cream cheese, and trays of sardines, smoked oysters and mussels and more. They followed with bowls of salads, an assortment of dressings, cottage cheese, and sour cream. Next, came the main course, the meats and vegetables, which included cuts from a standing rib roast from Adam's meat locker, the twenty-four pound turkey, and the spiral ham from Rachael for the three tables. As the meats were passed around the table, the ladies followed with fresh string beans, mashed potatoes and gravy, thin sliced French bread and butter, and stuffing. After Karen returned to her seat, Misty rushed back to the refrigerator and came back with a cranberry and pomegranate salad, which she placed in front of Karen.

"I've never done this before, but I wanted to prepare one of Karen's favorite dishes for her," Misty announced, and said, "thank you for letting me be your friend."

Mealtime conversation proved uplifting. Surrounded by the four Tunnicliffe brothers, two who did not speak due to their vow, Hannah enjoyed doing the talking and interpreting their responses, which they would confirm or deny. Jill became fascinated with Bear's stories of his time with a circus and his appearances in a repertoire group as well as his description of his homeland. Deputy Candy announced her candidacy for sheriff. Of particular notice had been the change in how Misty carried herself though pregnant. She interacted appropriately with John Mark. Her mentors—Jill, Karen, and Janine—nodded approval at her, as she mouthed a thank you instead of sticking out her tongue at them. Since her arrival they had worked with Misty to help her become "ladyfied," which is how she referred to her discipleship.

Mike said, "I'll eat like pig, be stuffed like turkey."

Bear added, "Them's good groceries!"

As they dined and finished their dinners, Hannah and Misty took charge of removing the serving plates, bowls, and leftovers of which little remained. All the meat, potatoes, bread, and vegetables had been devoured, but some salad and condiments remained. Salad and dishes were taken to the kitchen to be stored or washed later. Karen and Jill brought out dessert plates, forks, and additional coffee cups. At Janine's request some of the men brought folding chairs and interspersed them around the table amongst the other chairs, while the boys from Pryor cleared the dirty dishes from the table. Janine, Beatrice, and Rachael brought pies for Gramma Bee and Rachael to cut and have served.

Visitors began to arrive. First, Adam and his men cheerfully joined the others as Adam sat by Karen, while Barnabas, Rabbit, and Pilgrim sat in chairs near the Tunnicliffe brothers. Next, John Law entered and took a chair by his client and friend Ezra, Willa Sentry sat with Rachael and Beatrice. And then, Amanda entered the room. Both Coinneach and Drostan rose from their seats and bowed as Amanda shyly entered the piano room and stopped as she realized all eyes focused on her. She looked around and nodded. Without trying, she naturally captivated both men and women, boys and girls. It hadn't just been her appearance, but also how she moved. She made no pretense, and her regal presence and Christ-like countenance had been natural.

"May I sit by you, Elaine?" Amanda asked Misty, as she crossed the room behind some of the others and reached an empty folding chair.

"You remembered my name from the church meeting. How nice of you," said Misty, "Please do sit next to me."

Eyes shifted from Amanda to Misty and back again. John Law looked at Willa, who nodded. Detective Jones noted their reactions as well as those of the two silent Tunnicliffe brothers and John Mark, who had grasped Misty's hand. He glanced at Karen and caught her eyes and moved his hand to his ear and mouth to indicate he wanted to call her. Surprised, she nodded. Brian the Bear Killer pounded on the table and distracted all, when he said, "What a fine dinner!" and then he led those gathered in clapping for the lady's of the household.

Izzy gained attention by rising and clanging his glass with his spoon, "Earlier tonight I asked eyeryone here to think of one thing to share briefly that you are thankful for. This includes those who just arrived. I already shared mine about the restoration of Blair House, but please share yours one by one as you feel moved to do so."

Janine rose immediately and said, "I am thankful Izzy kept his word, came home, and married me like he promised."

Karen was next and said, "I am blessed by you all. Wounded by previous experiences, I'm here surrounded by wonderful friends... with a real purpose to serve Christ in this valley."

"I too have been wounded and sometimes grouchy and depressed, but that is changed and I am grateful my house in Rock Creek is restored. Pieces of my puzzle are coming together," Adam said, as he looked at Karen, who smiled.

Next, Jerry said, "I came to the valley for whatever purpose I didn't know. God has a plan for us and it has only begun to be fulfilled."

Tim rose and said, "I'm thankful for John Mark who I met one day at the Cozy Corner Café. I've been redirected and Mr. Claymore had a major role in that. Thank you both!"

"I am grateful I finally get to serve God in the church and by delivering newspapers to almost all of you," said Ken Bond, which brought forth laughter.

"I'm grateful for our new house in Rock Creek and for my Daddy to be able to preach at church," said Krystal.

Rachael rose from her seat awkwardly and said, "Age neither disqualifies nor excuses a believer from seeking to live out God's plan for us to help build his kingdom here on earth. I am grateful for the unique ministries he has given me to do!"

Caleb rose and said, "I'm grateful to have learned who murdered my baby sister and that we are well on our way to making right that which is wrong!"

The Tunnicliffes and John Mark pounded on the table to affirm Caleb, and Niall rose and said, "Much of what you have said is keening where we come from. Many of you have been mourning something as have we, and I am grateful to be among you to share your joy."

Others chimed in until only John Mark was left to share, he rose and said, "All of us are bruised, all flawed, all with secrets. I am thankful for second chances."

Group members hugged one another and gathered around the piano where they sang hymns and choruses to honor God.

On the way to the piano, John Law stopped Misty and John Mark and asked her, "Misty, would you please meet with me and two others Wednesday for lunch at noon. I will provide food from below my offices, the Bustos Family Mexican Restaurant. I assure you...it will be of considerable benefit for you to do so. And if you like, you could bring Mr. Cannikin with you."

Somewhat frightened, Misty asked John Mark, "Would you go with me?"

"Of course, I will. I'll come get you and we could walk there if you want," replied John Mark, and then he asked John Law, "Who else will be at the meeting?"

"You have met them," the attorney said as he pointed toward the ladies, "It will only be you two with me and Willa Sentry and Amanda."

As John Law put on his topcoat to leave, he handed an envelope to Ken Bond and said with a smile, "Be careful with this, you have been richly blessed!"

***

After the hymn sing all parted celebrating Thanksgiving by being thankful for one another and for how God had been at work in their lives and the community. Unlike the others, the Bonds went home to strange beds in strange rooms. When they got to the hotel, they met Lila Longdon, the night clerk, who had three rooms for them. The girls asked to sleep in one room with Mom and Dad. Since one room had a double bed and room enough for a rollaway to be added, Mom and Dad consented to their request. Lila was certain no one would mind the cancellation since the rooms were paid for with a voucher.

Lila recognized Ken Bond happened to be the man who took care of the newspaper stand, and she said, "You are the new pastor at my church, the little Church in the Glen. I've been going to church there, my daughter Sarah and I. We go there! And you must be Mrs. Bond… and the children. I am so glad to meet you."

"Thank you," Pastor Ken said, as he stretched out his hand and shook Lila's, "I'll look for you next Sunday."

"You'll see me before that. My house is the one just north of yours. When are you moving in?"

"Lila, we have been blessed. As soon as my husband finishes the paper routes and services the newsstands tomorrow morning, we are going shopping in Colorado Springs at one of those furniture warehouses."

"What fun! Be certain to eat breakfast before you go! It's on the house! And my daughter waits tables in the morning. Her name is Sarah."

"Do you have TV's in the rooms?" asked the girls.

"No, dear, we don't even have radios, but I've got plenty of towels, soap, and shampoo for you," Lila replied. "Come let's get a rollaway bed for you."

Although the girls thought the room to be very small, Kat convinced them it would be fun to stay there because they were on an adventure. Ken told Lila he would be leaving the hotel early to pick up his newspapers. He asked if she would be on duty early in the morning, and he wondered when the kitchen opened. Not before you leave Lila had told him.

The Bond family set up their room, moved in with their luggage, said their prayers, and turned in for a peaceful night's rest. Krystal said she was glad she didn't have to sleep away from her mom and dad in a different room. Kat conferred with Ken about his getting up as early as possible to meet the newspaper delivery truck near the interstate highway at the Ridge View exit. Ken said he would rise early and would do his job as quickly as possible, but he told her he would not cut corners. His customers counted on him to get the newspaper on the porch. Kat promised she would have the girls up in time to take a shower and eat breakfast before he got back, so they could leave promptly. She said he was not to worry that she would order something for him to eat, while she would drive them to the Springs.

Before turning out the table lamp, Ken rose from the bed and went to the coat rack where he had hung his jacket. Kat asked him what he was doing and Ken told her he had forgotten one thing. Krystal turned over and said, "What did you forget?"

Kristin sat up in bed and asked, "Why are you out of bed?"

As Ken reached in his jacket pocket and pulled out a large envelope he walked back toward Mom and said to the girls, "I have a sealed envelope I think Mom should open. Don't you agree, girls?"

"Oh yes Mommy, yes Mommy, open it!" said the girls in unison.

Taking the envelope, Kat said, "Ken, look how full it is!"

The girls hopped out of bed and onto the double bed, as Mom emptied the envelope in their laps, as Dad beamed! Kat wept and said, "This will take care of everything, everything we need."

Ken did as he said. He woke up before his alarm went off, and he dressed promptly and left the room without waking the girls. Kat had kissed him, said goodbye, rolled over, and went back to sleep on the lumpy mattress. While Ken delivered newspapers, the girls took their showers with hot water and washed their long curly hair. When they had said they were afraid someone would come inside the bathroom as they showered, Kat promised to wait for them outside the bathroom door.

Kat and the girls waited a few minutes outside the dining room on the bench opposite the telephone booth. Lila saw them before leaving her shift to go home, "My you really are early birds. Here comes my daughter. I want you to meet her."

"Sarah, look who is staying here!"

Sarah greeted them and said, "Hi, I have no idea who you are, but I'm pleased to meet you."

"The new pastor's wife, our new neighbors...Katarina Bond and her daughters Kristin and Krystal. They are staying at the hotel a few days, and they have a voucher to eat three meals here every day... no limit."

"You are kidding, really...no limit...my stars!"answered Sarah, "Butch has never done that before. I am pleased to meet you. Really!"

At first Kat did not make the connection, and she followed Sarah into the dining hall where Sarah asked them to sit toward the back in a booth. Sarah said she could serve them quickly from there, while she tended to her duties. She gave them the menus to look at, and then got them some water. They ordered bacon and eggs with hash brown potatoes and toast. Krystal asked for blueberry pancakes instead of toast, and Sarah said she could have a breakfast steak, if she wanted. The girls looked at each other and then at Mom, and said together, "Can we have chocolate milk?"

"Now we don't want to take advantage of someone's generosity," Kat said.

"Really, Mrs. Bond, take advantage of it. Enjoy yourselves, the cook said you deserve it for what you have been through."

Sarah left and came back with the chocolate milk, and said, "Mom, do you want a tall glass?"

"I do...it has been a long time."

From out of the kitchen, Butch brought the food and served them, "Will there be anything else? Ketchup? More bacon?"

"More bacon, please four more for me!" Kristin said.

"Why are you doing this?" Kat asked.

"Guilt, I'm glad you don't recognize me," Butch said.

Kat saw the opening and went for it, "No, I don't recognize you, but if you feel guilty, I encourage you to ask God to forgive you for whatever it was...He will forgive you and your sin will be removed from you. People might not forget, but God says your sin is removed and taken away as far as the east is from the west..."

"Sounds good..." Butch said, as he went back to the kitchen, "I'm a lost cause."

"We will talk again...oh by the way; my husband will want a break-fast sandwich to go, okay?"

"You got it, Mrs. Bond."

After serving his newspaper stands, Ken arrived at the hotel and met his girls before he could get out of the car. Kat handed him his breakfast sandwich and told Ken, "Move over. Buster, here's your sandwich. Here's your coffee! I'm driving. Eat and take a nap, so I can put the pedal to the metal without you knowing!"

"We'll watch her, Daddy!" said Kristin.

"Mama, I'll snitch on you if you get a ticket," said Krystal.

"I'm kidding, girls," replied Kat. "I'll be careful with you as my precious cargo!"

"Hit it, Mom, time's a wastin!" said Ken between mouthfuls of egg, cheese, and bacon between halves of an English muffin.

Kat looked at the two girls in the rear view mirror, and asked, "What are you thinking girls?"

"Me, first," Krystal shouted, "I'm thinking about what I had, what I lost, how nice Adam and all his men were to us. I'm thinking about everyone at the Blair House and how we are one big family there. And now we are going to be blessed with new furniture and live in a house made brand new, and Daddy's finally the pastor of a church."

And Ken said, "Well said Darling Daughter! What about you, Kristin, Lovely Daughter?"

"All of what Krystal said...and I'm thinking that God is good..."

And the Bond family chimed in, "All the time!"

***

John Mark arrived early Wednesday morning at the Blair House to escort Misty to her meeting with Attorney John Law at his offices located above Bustos Family Mexican Restaurant. He also looked forward to lunch catered by the restaurant. Uncharacteristically, Misty already had made herself ready knowing the beautiful and regal Amanda would be meeting with her. Oddly, Misty felt no ill will toward Amanda, and while their first meeting had been strained, all following contact had been pleasant and somewhat uplifting. Misty enjoyed being around Amanda, and the feeling had been mutual. Departing the Blair House, Misty took hold of the arm John Mark offered as they strolled down Main Street. While Misty had dressed well, John Mark had also. He wore a solid black suit with a vest, a red satin tie, and a tie bar with a leprechaun playing bagpipes on it.

When the couple rounded the corner of the restaurant onto the side street, they climbed the stairs to John Law's office. As they entered the lobby, Amanda rose from her seat behind the receptionist desk and came around to greet them. She said, "I'm so glad you are here! I've been terribly excited once I heard about our meeting."

After Amanda hugged Misty and shook John Mark's hand, Misty asked, "Do you work for Mr. Law...I mean you really must have an important job working for an attorney?"

"Thank you," Amanda said, "I find it exciting most of the time, and I get to meet interesting people. John is very good at what he does. I just love him."

John Mark added, "Everyone speaks well of him…that he is a man to be trusted."

"Not many are," said Misty, and then she sincerely added, "Few men are like you, John."

"Here, come right in, Misty…John," Amanda said as she opened the office door, "My mother is already here and John is chatting with her. Lunch will be here shortly. Have you eaten at Bustos'?"

"No, but Mr. Powell promised to take me there for dinner. Tim raves about the smothered enchiladas and chili rellanos," said Misty.

"Tim, the new waiter…do you know him?" Amanda asked.

"Yes," said Misty, "he lives at the Blair House. He is well liked by all of us!"

John and Willa ended their conversation as the three entered the room, and Willa embraced Misty, and said, "I am so happy to greet you. I held you and changed your diapers long ago…"

"You knew my mother?" asked Misty in a little bit of shock. John Mark took her hand.

"I did, but let me not get ahead of things. We have a lot of explaining to do," said Willa.

"I can't wait to hear!" said Misty excitedly.

"Please be seated and we will begin with lunch," said John Law, "and you too, Amanda."

"Apparently, someone invited Ezra Sr. to attend this meeting. Is it all right for him to join us?" said Amanda.

"Misty, did you invite Ezra to join our meeting?" John Law asked.

"No, unless you know of any reason he should not be here it is okay with me to have him join us," Misty answered.

Ezra joined the group and John asked Ezra, "Did someone ask you to attend this meeting, Ezra?"

When Ezra pointed his finger upward, John Mark said, "I'd say God has a purpose for him being here!"

Tim the waiter arrived with hot food and served them, "Today, we are serving beef enchiladas smothered in mild green chili. They are layered with cheddar cheese and onions, and served with refried beans and rice. Also, we have soft chili rellanos, not deep fried, and all beef tacos in crispy shells. Dessert is your choice of flan, fried ice cream, or stuffed sopapillas. If you will let me know which you would prefer, or I'll bring some of each for you to sample."

"Let's sample it all!" replied Misty.

After all were served, John Law gave thanks and then began, "Misty, we only told Amanda a little of what needs to be shared, so you would hear it at the same time. Amanda, it's not that we wanted to hold back information from you and I think you will soon understand. Willa, will you please begin."

"Yes, and in a way, I'm sad to tell you this..." Willa said, "John and I have been friends for years. He has watched over Amanda like a father or uncle. My husband died a long time ago, before both of you were born. I was there when you were born."

"Of course you were, Mother," said Amanda, as Willa took her hand, "I...am not the one who bore you and gave birth to you, but I am the one who changed your diapers and raised you."

"Oh, I don't understand what you are saying..." Amanda said, as her countenance changed to fear.

"I don't either! How do I figure into this? I'm a McNaughton and she's a Sentry." asked Misty.

"Please hear me out," Willa asked, "this is as hard for me to tell as it is for you to hear."

"There is more for you to hear that will change both of your lives for the better," said John Law.

"Believe it or not, I may have something to share that will clarify things," John Mark added.

"Really," John Law said testily.

Misty looked from John Mark to John Law and then at Amanda. Both Misty and Amanda were shocked by what was said and in their shock they bonded.

"In those days, I was a midwife. I helped deliver the babies in the absence of a doctor. Your mother..." said Willa Sentry.

"Whose? Mine or Misty's?"

"The two are the same. Amanda was born first and Misty came out second holding onto your foot. It was beautiful to see," Willa marveled.

"We are sisters? We are...sisters," Misty said, as she looked at Amanda, "I have a sister!"

"And you are twins...I knew it when I first saw Amanda. You are both beautiful twins!" John Mark said and smiled with enthusiasm.

"But you are my mother..." said Amanda, as anguish swept across her face, "you will always be my mother, won't you?"

"Yes, my dear sweet child..."

"We weren't raised together?" Misty said, "Why not?"

"No," said John Law, "and I'm afraid there is more to it that isn't totally clear. When Detective Jones began researching who owns the Asherah House Bed and Breakfast, he discovered some details I followed up on. You see, Misty was stolen one night from her crib. You had separate cribs, and apparently, the kidnapper didn't know there were two of you. Although a search had been made, the sheriff at the time failed to find you, Misty. Your mother died shortly after, which was twenty-five years ago."

"I'm twenty-five..." Misty stammered, "I thought...no I was told I was seventeen..."

"Willa took Amanda home after you were kidnapped. She insisted on having custody of her," John Law said. "The judge made certain that happened."

"Praise the Lord!" said Amanda, and then asked, "What was our mother's name?"

"Cristabel Elaine MacNaughten was your grandmother, and your mother was named the same, except her middle name was Amanda, so your mother's name was Cristabel Amanda MacNaughten," answered Willa, "and I must say I had a role in naming both of you."

"Thank you, Mother, and our father?" asked Amanda.

"I'm sorry, your mother would never tell me who the father was and I was her best friend."

"Question, if I may," asked John Mark to which all nodded, "What was the grandmother's maiden name?"

"Blair..." said John Law.

"As in Paul and Lydia Blair?" asked Amanda.

"Yes, and Paul may have been your mother's brother. We have no evidence, in hand, to prove that either way. Perhaps it is at the museum," stated the attorney.

"At the Asherah House, I was told to go by Misty McNaughton. I remember hearing the name Elaine as a little girl and I heard McClaren before too. According to John Mark, my name is Elaine McClaren, or so I have heard...Where does McClaren come in?" said Misty.

"Apparently, none of those who raised you...as it were...wanted you or anyone else to be able to trace you back to Cristabel or anyone else in the cemetery. So you were not given the last name of Cristabel's mother, you were told to go by McNaughton," John Law said, "and somehow that must be where McClaren comes in."

John Mark decided to not challenge the attorney's statement with what he knew.

Weeping Misty said, "I wish I had been raised with you, Willa...I knew I was missing someone and I've always wanted a sister."

"Me too!" said Amanda, "I heard you were raised at the Asherah House?"

"Ah, yes, the bed and breakfast...so that is why I never got to leave the house, why they wouldn't leave me alone..." explained Misty, "I was kept locked in my room, a prisoner all my life, and the ones responsible profited...and they made certain I participated in the Baal ceremony."

"You were forced to participate?" asked John Law.

"Oh, they didn't drag me by the arm, but I knew I had no choice. After all I only knew those at Asherah house. I had nowhere else to go and for all I knew I was under age."

"So you were raped..." asked Amanda.

"Yes, I guess and I guess others like Gloria Jones were raped too. And I know your next question is by whom," answered Misty, "so I don't know who the father is...he wore a bear skin during the ceremony."

"Perhaps just like our mother," Amanda speculated. "You say our grandmother's maiden name was Blair. There is more, isn't there?"

"And I have another question, if you please," asked John Mark, and when all nodded affirmatively, "What were their birth names?"

Willa answered, "Amanda is Amanda's middle name, and her real last name is MacNaughten, not the McNaughton as in Red McNaughton, but MacNaughten as in their grandmother Cristabel MacNaughten. Her first name is Elizabeth. And Misty, your real name is Elaine, your middle name is Cristabel. And you too are a MacNaughten."

"There's more...since the bank supposedly held the loan on your mother's property, banker Chauncey Brown has managed the property," said John Law.

"Chauncey Brown, city council member?" asked Misty, as she gripped the arms of her chair, clenched her teeth, nearly vomited, and said sarcastically, "Such a fine upstanding man..."

"Chairman of the Council...and more," said Willa.

"Were you able to freeze their financial accounts?" asked John Mark.

"Yes, and Mr. Brown immediately provided a summary of those accounts," said John Law, "and he did everything, acted rightly, to impress me that he was being above board, at least financially. I work with him on city council matters, so he knows quite well not to cross me."

"That's a laugh!" Misty said angrily. "He calls the shots for the McNaughton Corporation. He and Dr. Wood tell Red what to do!"

"Misty, you obviously have much to share about what happened to you at the Asherah House," said John Law, "but please, let us hold off on that for now. I promise I will help you deal with all of that."

"Yes, sir, I'm just realizing the scope of what has happened to me," Misty calmly said, "and I am grateful for the people at the church, and at Blair House, and especially John Mark. I just know Chauncey keeps two sets of books for the corporation."

"We will have to be careful, so we can prove what you just revealed, Misty. I'll call for a bank examiner to investigate," said John Law. "Chauncey Brown had the name of the original bed and breakfast changed to Asherah House from the Blair House Bed and Breakfast."

"Which means my sister and I are the rightful owners of the Asherah House?" asked Misty angrily.

"So any mortgage should have been paid off by now..." Amanda said.

"Yes, it is paid for and there are no tax liens," replied John Law.

"And there's another part of what I wanted to tell you," said John Law, "You are also co-owners of the Stage Stop Hotel. I have filed suit on your behalf with Willa's consent to make certain the two of you gain full control of your property as well as the proceeds from both businesses."

"Thank you, hasn't Red McNaughton been acting like the owner?" said Amanda, "And isn't his son Butch now managing the hotel?"

"Yes, Red, through Chauncey, has been managing the hotel," answered John Law. "Butch now manages the hotel, since he was fired from the sheriff's office."

"They have been sharing the wealth," said John Mark, "and they have been after the Blair House and its water and mineral resources too! My guess is they are behind the raves!"

"You are probably right," added John Law.

"I didn't realize the perversion," Willa added. "Chauncey removed the Blair name and brought in the pagan goddess Asherah and worship of Baal through the raves. Even if their worship was a fraud, it mocked the Blairs and the Church in the Glen."

"My mother is right, and I confess it really makes me angry!" Amanda said, and then asked, "I believe my sister and I need to ask, is there more?"

"I'm afraid there is...Red and Chauncey are under investigation by the Colorado Bureau of Investigation's Human Trafficking Task Force," said John Law.

"Absolutely, I can attest to that," Misty said, and then looked to see John Mark's response, "and you know Asherah included temple prostitution."

"That was then, this is now, you repented of your past," John Mark said, as he held her hand and put his arm around her, "and that is why Red McNaughton and the Night Riders have orchestrated two raids on the Blair House...kidnapping you again was the real purpose. I'll bet the attack to pollute the pond and destroy the bookstore and garden were diversion tactics as was the earlier one where Butch led the attack supposedly to rescue you and Hannah..."

"Kidnapping Misty again was really an effort to maintain what they had...I don't think they knew about me," said Amanda, as Misty wept.

"I am glad only one of us was caught in their web," Misty added with a tender smile toward her sister. "You need to know I had no choice."

"Something's missing," said John Law.

"Aye," John Mark shouted in his Gaelic dialect, "you are sisters. Sisters of a royal line! And you are the reason I am here," as he twisted a ring on his right hand.

"John Mark, whatever do you mean?" asked Attorney John Law, fearing for the worst.

"These lassies are why I am here," John Mark said, as he opened his wallet and unfolded a letter that he had read before speaking at the church meeting when he first had arrived. "I have been sent on a royal quest to make secure the daughter of the Blair line. Not just I, but also the Brothers called Tunnicliffe, which is why Coinneach and Drostan do not speak. They made a vow to secure the Blair grand-daughter of Cristabel to help her assume her lands and royal title, Lady Blair. None of us realized there were two of you...twins. I read the letter thinking Elizabeth was Elaine's middle name."

"What about Bear?" asked Misty, who was really Elaine.

"Brian the Bear Killer Tunnicliffe is a Brother like me," John Mark explained, "and you may think all of this is farfetched, as you may say, but I was assigned the quest to make secure the Lady Blair, and to watch over her should she decide to stay here and not return to Scotland. Bear was to handle the opposition, if any."

"Return to Scotland...to be kidnapped and taken to Scotland...to live...as Lady Blair," asked Amanda, who was really Elizabeth, "and you are on a quest to take us back to Scotland, Brother John Mark?"

"It would be by free choice for either of you to go, my Lady, I am not the one to escort you, but Drostan the Red and Coinneach the Fair. The brothers, both have made a vow of silence until the trek begins, and then they can speak. Ideally, Lady Blair will select one of them to be her escort," answered John Mark, "but there is more, my lady."

"Am I my lady as well, or is it just Amanda," asked Misty.

"Aye, my lady, you are my lady," John Mark replied more gently, more affectionately, and a smile spread over both their faces.

"What about Niall?" asked Misty.

"He too is on a quest, and Coinneach and Drostan helped him, and they went directly to the one who was keeper of the spreading tree, the Live Oak. Brothers of our order planted what you have called Freedom's tree. Real Baal worshippers set an Asher pole before it to worship there before the spreading tree like in *Judges*. But the Brothers chopped down the Asher pole, and sent a seed for another tree, a Live Oak tree. My guess is a remnant of the Baal worshippers remains in the valley. And the Brothers knew where to come...don't ask me how...but you, Amanda, found or had the oak sapling that Niall planted on the ridge where the fraudulent Asher pole and ceremonial table had been used," explained John Mark.

"The Asher pole the Night Riders burned on the ridge?" asked John Law.

"Not the Night Riders, but like King Josiah in *Second Kings*, Niall's quest was to destroy Baal worship in the valley if we found it, just as our forefathers had done. He chopped it down with his broad sword, broke the ceremonial table, and other implements, and then burned them and crushed the remains into fine ash."

"I heard there were no remains," said Willa.

"Aye, that was what was supposed to happen. We gathered the ashes and like Josiah, the ashes were spread over the grave of an innocent."

"You spread them over our grandmother's grave, didn't you?" asked Amanda.

"Yes, my lady," John Mark added, "over her grave and along the path which leads to her grave. I hope this pleases you...she too was of royal lineage."

"What happens next?" asked Misty.

"Since there are the two of you and since you have lands and property here as well as Scotland, you have choices, but we are to bring Lady Blair back with us by next summer, if you chose to go with us and assume your proper title and lands. Since there are two, one could go and one can stay, but both of you will be Lady Blair as long as you live," explained John Mark.

"And what about you if one of us chooses to stay here and take charge of our property," asked Misty.

"If Lady Blair decides not to go to Scotland, then I am required by my vow to make certain that she would be safe and secure here," John Mark answered with a smile.

"And John, what happens next?" asked Amanda.

"Well, Chauncey Brown, unexpectedly, was compliant when I mentioned lawsuit...he may have something he is hiding or not at all," said John Law, "but I believe he will be cooperative. He agreed to have the rightful owner, or...in this case owners, take charge of the property. I think it is time for you to make yourselves known."

"It would be nice to change the Asherah House sign, wouldn't it, sister?" asked Elizabeth, who was beginning to be comfortable with the idea of her name.

"Yes, it would, and to serve eviction notices," answered Elaine to her sister Elizabeth, "and John Mark, would you help us?"

"As you wish, my lady, I would be delighted, as would the Brothers, if anyone is still there."

"You think they may flee, or they may move to the Stage Stop Hotel, but before anything else happens, there is something I must do," said Elaine as she rose and walked around the table and first hugged her sister and then the woman who would become as a mother to her.

Elizabeth suggested she and Elaine confer before going any further, and they retreated to the file room where the other two saplings had begun to grow. After a few minutes, Elizabeth said, "Something is missing."

Elaine countered with, "Someone is missing!"

Together, they walked back to John's conference room, opened the door, and momentarily watched as Willa Sentry wept, and then Elizabeth told Elaine to do it.

Elaine said, "Come along, Mother, we need you..."

While the ladies and their mother conferred, John Law sought to press John Mark for more information to prove his authenticity. John Law asked him, "John Mark, you have only been here a short time..."

"Yes, I am a newcomer...you question my credentials as well as those of the Tunnicliffe brothers," said John Mark, "and well you should, as you said, something is missing."

"You have been referred to as a monk, a brother, and a knight, John Mark," the lawyer said, and then asked, "Have you been sent here from a priestly order? Will you become a priest?"

"Understandable questions," John Mark said, as he handed a letter to John Law. He removed his ring and handed it over as well. Next, he removed his shirt and turned around to reveal a tattoo on the back of his neck that matched the signet on the stationary and engraved in his ring.

Ezra emitted an appreciative moan, took hold of John Law's forearm, and removed his own shirt to reveal a similar tattoo on the back of his own neck. Ezra raised his long hair to expose the mark.

"They look the same, but there is only one difference, Ezra...we are from the same barony but different households, and I suspect that is why you chose to have someone from the Blair House to watch over your son and property," said John Mark, who continued, as he looked directly at John Law. "Neither Ezra, nor I, nor the Tunnicliffes are from or will be priests, but we are of an ancient brotherhood of knights, who may live in solitude like monks sometime do. To confirm all I have said, I will send for documents to verify our relationship with the McClaren, the Blair, the MacNaughten, and the Freedom households. The Tunnicliffes and I are knights of the Blair House, and all of our current quests are for its sake. It will also clarify the ladies' lineage. It will verify they are McClarens from the Blair House by way of the MacNaughten household. We often marry one with the other and when there were wars, we fought alongside one another. Our tartans bear the same weave and colors with only slight variation."

"It won't be necessary, John Mark," said John Law.

"Thank you, but I will send for it," said John Mark, "and you, Mr. Legal Counsel, I have a question for you...How is it you have allowed the likes of Red McNaughton and Chauncey Brown to do all that has happened at the expense of Elaine and Elizabeth McClaren?"

Ezra moaned...

"If you knew me, you would not have asked..." John Law answered.

"Of course, as a newcomer, I am at a disadvantage on some things, so you have a decision to make," said John Mark, as his eyes flashed emerald green. He continued, "The raves may be new to the community, but the storm gods and Baal worship are not, nor are the human trafficking and Canaanite rituals. We may have time to have further discussion, as we both help Elaine, Elizabeth, and Ezra."

"Good, and what decision is it you say I need to make?" asked John Law.

"Whether or not you want to have a newcomer as an ally or as an adversary..." answered John Mark.

"As an ally," replied John Law, who thrust forward the right hand of friendship.

John Mark thrust forward his right hand and grasped John Law's forearm just below the elbow, and said, "Then let us make right that which has been wrong. I will expect you to be transparent...and please know the Brothers Tunnicliffe and I seek truth and we are agents of justice!"

John Law looked at Ezra, who smiled and nodded affirmatively, and then both grinned at John Mark, as John Law said, "Welcome, we need and want your help!"

# Consequences

## CHAPTER 21

*"Do not quench the Spirit."*     *1 Thessalonians 5:19*

Consequences! For every action there was a reaction, and every action resulted from someone making a decision based upon a choice he or she chose. The leaders of the McNaughton Corporation either scattered by leaving the valley or they stayed hoping their lives would not fall apart. Both decisions produced a ripple effect in the lives of their associates.

Banker Chauncey Brown led the Jericho Springs City Council, while masking his role as a McNaughton Corporation leader. In both roles he profited for himself. He made or influenced multiple back room deals for his bank and the corporation. He wore one of the black bear costumes during the two known rave events. His life began to unravel when Chauncey underestimated the influence of a waiter who worked for him at the Cozy Corner Café. After Tim the waiter's inspirational encounter with John Mark Cannikin at the café, Tim moved into the Blair House. After Night Riders and others attacked Blair House, Tim volunteered to listen to conversations of the McNaughton Corporation members as he waited their tables, while they planned their misdeeds at the café. Tim chose to share what he had heard with leaders at Blair House, which meant they were forewarned and could prepare to defend themselves against those who coveted Ezra Freedom's gold and water. As a result the McNaughton Corporation began to unravel quickly like a ball of yarn batted around by a playful kitten. Chauncey fired Tim McNaughton, and the cook quit. In a town where jobs were at a premium, qualified candidates didn't apply to work for Chauncey, so Brown temporarily closed the café. The public learned Chauncey Brown owned the Cozy Corner Café. Angered, customers started dining elsewhere.

Detective Caleb Jones chose to share his research about the true ownership of the Asherah House and the Stage Stop Hotel with Attorney John Law, which caused the corporate empire to decline further. Jones told Law the bank had held the two properties in trust for the McClaren estate. He revealed the banker himself had managed the Asherah House Bed and Breakfast, while he had Red McNaughton manage the Stage Stop Hotel. Law chose to intercede for Amanda and Misty with banker Brown. John Law decided to hold Chauncey accountable for what he had done through his role at the bank. Chauncey chose to appear to be compliant by properly transferring ownership of the hotel and bed and breakfast to Elaine and Elizabeth McClaren. This included Chauncey disclosing his financial records concerning both properties. He chose not to disclose a second set of books that would have revealed the McNaughton Corporation's illegal activities through the raves and both buildings. For the time being, Chauncey and Red limited their activities to doing what each was supposed to do. When gossip circulated about Red and Chauncey and their connections with the unsavory activities at the Asherah House and the Stage Stop Hotel, the McNaughton Corporation appeared to be headed for total ruin.

Humiliated by his failed attempt to destroy the art work on Freedom's tree, Red McNaughton chose to leave town to recover from the wound he had suffered at the hands of Brian Tunnicliffe. Red acknowledged his encounter with Bear could have been fatal, so he withdrew to a safe place. He chose to heed his doctor's advice by entering a rehabilitation facility outside of Trinidad at the Stonewall settlement. He had already alienated his son Butch, who was in the midst of his own personal crisis. Many of Red's wranglers quit and moved on to other ranches outside the valley. They had been angry that Red had involved them in his unsavory activities. One of his paramours, Heather Ross, left town to visit her mother at her home on a ranch in Wild Horse. Since Irv and Ellis Moss worked for him at the lumberyard in Ridgeview, he asked them to run the business, while he was gone. He told them to ask Adam Claymore to watch over his herds. As a result Barnabas accepted the assignment, which did not include access to Red's house. Red closed his ranch house, or so it appeared.

When a grand jury investigation concerning the Night Riders ended, school district parents questioned Dr. Maurice Wood's involvement. Gossip linked him to both the McNaughton Corporation and the raves. He was thought correctly to be a member of the corporate inner circle. When Wood's wife found the bear costume he wore during at least one rave, she informed her former husband, the superintendent of schools, of her discovery. This meant Dr. Wood's employment with the school district became tenuous, as had his marriage to the former Mrs. Moss. When rumor spread to the teachers, Karen and others hoped Dr. Wood's contract would not be renewed. Dr. Wood bore little remorse, as he implemented an exit strategy to move on without his wife, the former Mrs. Moss, and her sons Ellis and Irving Moss.

Minor corporate leadership suffered the consequences of their misdoings. Sadly, wives of Van Allen and Seamus chose to file for divorce rather than endure public disdain because of their husbands. Van Allen faced possible jail time, and Seamus literally withered in fear of being linked to the corporation leadership. Ralph of Wolf City had already left the valley under pressure from Chief Strong Bull. Robert King asked for and received a transfer. Rumor had it he gained a transfer to Quail Point or Pueblo, but instead, he left the state with his children and former wife, who chose to leave with him. Irv and Ellis knew their father, Superintendent of Schools Moss, would not renew the contract of their stepfather Maurice Wood, the Assistant Superintendent. They chose to focus on doing a job well done for Red at the feed and lumber store as well as at Red's ranch under Barnabas' supervision. They knew their mother would divorce their stepfather Dr. Wood. While they hoped their mother and father would remarry, they knew it wouldn't happen. Only Buddy Smith had not tucked his tail in shame. Butch became strangely distant and quiet. He spent a lot of time writing.

Values had led to choices that resulted in decisions, which governed actions and each person's problem solving strategies. Truth had produced justice. The lustful efforts of the McNaughton Corporation to benefit from ill-gotten gain bruised many innocent people, who now hoped for second chances.

\*\*\*

In contrast, the other side had much to celebrate! Not only had Misty and Amanda been thankful for their many blessings, but also they were joyful that each had found the other. As Elaine and Elizabeth, they shared their free time by taking care of business at the hotel and the bed and breakfast. While Amanda worked fulltime at the law offices, Misty divided her time by helping at Blair House and by visiting the woman her sister called mother, Willa Sentry. Increasingly, Willa became very much a part of the sisters' lives, but the girls wondered about Amanda's brother, Roy Sentry, and the story behind his adoption. Sadly, Roy chose to distance himself from his home and family and his best friend Butch.

Although Adam's face had been scared, he relished how tender Karen's love had been toward him. Together they retrieved the boxes John Mark and the Tunnicliffe brothers had saved for Adam. Karen convinced Adam to move them to his ranch house where they could leisurely sort through them. Not only had she finished her first round of interviewing formal leadership in the valley, but also she had begun the second round. Happily, Ruth Browning continued to work some evenings privately by helping Karen compile the interview data. Impressed with Karen's work, the superintendent asked her to prepare a report and presentation for the school board and city council during February. Karen promised to share what she could with Caleb while maintaining confidentiality, as had Caleb with his investigations.

Others had found good reasons to rejoice. Izzy, Janine, and team rejoiced over having completed restoration of the inside of Blair House, except for perfecting a heating system. Burning wood and pellets in fireplaces had proven to be labor intensive. Hauling wood and emptying ashes consumed more time than originally anticipated, however, the workers enjoyed designing adjustments to the heating system. Restoring the outside became a springtime target. Ken, Kat, and the girls had enjoyed shopping to furnish their new home. They were pleased to speak well of their uneventful stay at the hotel and had no complaint about their benefactor Butch McNaughton, who provided food and lodging. Mercy had followed grace.

Once John Law gained eviction notices, Misty and Amanda, as Elaine and Elizabeth, happily took the offensive. First, they ordered new signs for the Asherah House Bed and Breakfast without telling where they would be posted. Of course, it had been easy to figure out. One sign read closed for remolding. Ellis prepared the signs at the lumber company, and then called Red about them in Stonewall. Red called the madam, who told the women their fate had been sealed. She told them to move now before eviction notices arrived. She told her girls she thought indictments might precede or follow the evictions. A few left on the next bus. Two others, who had no place to go, rented rooms at the hotel. They hoped justice would not catch up with them there. Since jobs were somewhat scarce, part timers hoped either to work from the hotel or out of a house they rented together. One decided to rent a small recreation vehicle, so she could work the truck stop outside of Ridge View and at rest stops along the interstate highway.

Next, Elaine and Elizabeth hired John Mark to remodel and update the bed and breakfast like he had done for Adam at his Rock Creek house. They wanted new appliances, new plumbing fixtures, a new paint job, new carpeting, and kitchen cabinets, and more. All furniture was destined for the dump. The sisters hired two Tunnicliffe brothers to both help John Mark and to install a new wooden fence which would surround the backyard. Also, they advertised for temporary help in *The Out Cry* to clean an old house and the hotel in Rock Creek. And then, they went to the Asherah House, accompanied by the brothers, expecting to find the enterprise fully functioning.

Misty picked up the signs from the feed and lumberyard in Ezra's truck, and then she waited for Amanda to get off work. She and Amanda prayed together, committed the Asherah House and the hotel to their Lord Jesus, and decided to go out as Elaine and Elizabeth McClaren. Followed by John Mark and the Tunnicliffe brothers, they drove to Rock Creek, where they parked directly in front of the bed and breakfast. Embolden by her escorts, Elaine approached the door by herself and knocked on it. No one answered. She looked through the windows and saw all was in disarray, so she called back to the others. "No one is here! Come on, let's go inside."

"Well," Elizabeth said, "they must have been forewarned, but I bet no one is here. I wonder where they went and what they are doing."

The others, who barely fit through the door, entered and looked around, as John Mark said, "It looks like they left in a hurry, but really it is not the pig pen I thought we would find."

"Me neither," said Niall, "let me start changing the locks on the front and rear doors!"

"Please remove the dead bolt lock to the corner room on the third floor, and turn it around so the room can be locked from the inside," asked Elaine.

The Brothers looked around as Elaine told the men what she and Elizabeth wanted them to do. Elaine escorted John Mark and the brothers around the first floor, then the second and third floors to her room at the back of the southwest corner. John Mark noticed the dead bolt on the outside of the door, stepped into the room, which had been well kept, and noticed bars were mounted on the outside of the windows, one on the south and another on the west.

John Mark moved next to Elaine and said, "You actually were a prisoner. You really were fearful the day we met when you said you would have trouble if they found you with me."

"Literally, the first time, at least I remember, that I made it outside on my own was when we met..." Elaine said and kissed him quickly, "and meeting you was what you call a divine appointment."

"Kissing you certainly was divine!" John Mark said, as he stole a kiss gladly returned.

"Keep that thought...you know they thought I would be back. I think that's why my room wasn't trashed or at least changed. I'm certain they thought the outside world would reject me, and I would come running back here to my cell."

Next, the team entered the front door of the Stage Stop Hotel and was greeted by Lila Longdon at the front desk and her daughter Sarah from the dining room. "We heard you were coming. Irv Moss called Butch from the feed store and told him you had bought signs for the bed and breakfast. The women left there like rats fleeing from a sinking ship. Misty, is it true you own the Stage Stop Hotel?"

"Yes, me and my sister, Amanda," Elaine replied, "Elizabeth, that's her real name and mine is Elaine, but we never knew it. Come meet these two nice ladies, everyone, I met them when I was out in the back yard at John Mark's house."

"Things are confusing, aren't they?" said Elizabeth.

"Aren't they always..." said Lila, "until the truth comes out. I am pleased to meet both of you... Will we continue to have a job?"

"You live right across the highway," asked Elaine, "Do you like your job?"

"It's all right," said Sarah, "I'm learning to ask God to change me in my circumstances from a book I bought from the counter pack on the check-in desk."

"It must be one of Kip Powell's consignments. Has anyone purchased a book from the counter pack? I think I filled this order."

"Mr. Powell, yes, he sure is a kind and gentle man. He said he might be able to bring in a spinner rack," explained Lila. "I'm not really certain what that would look like...I guess it's a metal stand of books that spin around."

"I see quite a few of my customers reading books, while they eat alone...especially when several of the girls from the Asherah House moved in," added Sarah. "Will we continue to have our job?"

"I'm sorry, I didn't mean to not answer you," Elaine said, "Hannah Rahab speaks well of you. She says we can trust both of you. Yes, you both can keep your jobs. We'll be making some changes, but not a lot."

"We should have a spinner rack or maybe a gift shop..."said Elizabeth.

From out of the kitchen, Butch McNaughton approached the women in the lobby talking. He said as he began to offer his hand to Elizabeth to introduce himself, then thought better of it and did not, "You must be whatever your real name is...I don't mean to be disrespectful...I just..."

Elizabeth mercifully thrust forward her hand and said, "I understand...you are, I presume, the cook and hotel manager, Butch McNaughton."

"I am," Butch said, as he gently grasped her hand, "I know this other lady, Misty or rather I hear your real name is Elaine. All I have heard are rumors. I don't know the full story, nor do I really want to hear it...I've already heard enough, did enough, to know I am sorry, I really am..."

As both Sarah and Lila watched Butch genuinely humble himself, Elaine responded with, "You'll have to excuse me...I'm shocked to see you...I do appreciate your cooking here. I hear you have done and continue to do good work."

"He's probably the best cook we have had for quite a long time, even better than his cousin Harper," added Lila.

"Thank you," Butch said to Lila, "I've bought and read some of the books from the counter pack. I've also read some our customers have left behind. I think they do that on purpose...my plan is to stay on cooking, until you make the transition. I don't mind helping you find your way around the management of things, the books and all, but I'll be leaving the valley soon to join the Marine Corps."

"Good for you, Butch, I'm impressed," Sarah offered.

"Hey, thanks, but don't let that fool ya, it's part of a deal I made with the DA, for me to get out of town and get out of what should really happen to me. I know I deserve worse. My uncle stepped up for me, which reminds me...I can't open tomorrow, because I have a meeting at sunrise with him tomorrow morning in Jericho Springs... at the tree behind the Blair House," said Butch.

Elaine cocked her head suspiciously, and said tenuously, "Really, which of us are you meeting with?"

Briefly laughing at her suspicion, Butch added, "Don't worry, Misty...I mean Elaine...what is your last name?"

"McClaren, but I'm a Blair by way of being a MacNaughten!"

"I know, we are not related. Mac not Mc, I meant no offense and you know I can be very offensive," as Elaine nodded, Butch continued, "I'm meeting at Freedom's tree with my Uncle Adam Claymore, and it's been cleared with Izzy and Ezra."

"You'll forgive me for not..."

"Trusting me," Butch inserted, "Hey, I get it. I wouldn't either, which is why I have to leave."

"Who do you have, or do you have someone covering for you?" asked Elizabeth.

"Yes, the cook at the truck stop outside of town in Ridge View has the day off and said he would work for me, if that's all right," Butch asked.

"The one who worked with your cousin Tim at the Cozy?" Sarah asked.

"The same," Butch replied.

"That works..." the women said.

"If I were you, I'd try to get the cook to replace me in the kitchen and Tim in the dining room. They both have a following, and a change of influence at the hotel would probably go along with what you want to do here."

"We would welcome that," said Sarah, as Lila nodded.

"I will be interested to see how things change for the hotel with the closing of the Asherah House," Butch said. "You will be surprised to learn how much business it brought into the valley."

"Does that include the raves?" asked John Mark.

"Yes, the raves brought a lot of newcomers to the valley. Many participants stayed at both the Asherah House and here at the Stage Stop Hotel. They ate their meals here," Butch said, as he nodded his head, "and they bought gasoline across the street."

"So regardless of other things," Elizabeth said, "the rave brought commerce to the valley."

"Indeed, not just to Rock Creek," Butch added, "we couldn't house or feed them all, so people stayed in the Springs and in Ridge View."

"They went to grocery stores and shops and all the other stores..." Elizabeth added.

"Yes, and you would be surprised how many came back to visit the Asherah House," Butch emphasized, "and I think you begin to understand what was going on. When the schools reorganized and the Interstate passed us by, many in leadership positions sought other ways to bring in business."

Waiting as Butch returned to the kitchen, Lila then added, "Butch didn't mention that trouble will come from those at the Tobacco Store and those who moved here from the Asherah House."

"It would be nice to have the detective living here again," said Sarah.

"Thanks for the heads up," said John Mark, "I may set up shop here, but what goes on at the Tobacco Store?"

"The owner of the antique shop used to have it, but he had to sell it to pay his taxes on his other properties," said Lila. "He sold it to someone who runs numbers and literally runs a gambling joint!"

"Not good," said Elizabeth, and Elaine nodded in agreement.

"We've scheduled one event you need to know about and put on your calendar. Circus performers will have a performance here on the deck sometime in the spring, unless the weather is too cold or snowy," said Elizabeth.

"Just so it's not in January when we usually have two weeks of sub zero weather," Lila answered, as she shivered and watched as the Tunnicliffe brothers entered the lobby.

Having overheard Amanda's comment, Niall added, "We are part of the play...as is our friend Chief Strong Bull and his mighty warriors!"

"Fascinating," said Sarah, as she studied the tallest of the Tunnicliffes.

***

The winter of 1979 had been bitterly cold, and valley residents feared another would follow the next year. Since the national forest had been ravaged for a few years by pine beetles, the supply of dead or dying timber seemed endless on federal land and Ezra and Adam's mountain properties. As a result Ezra produced a continuous supply of sawdust for the boys from Pryor to bag and use to make pellets for stoves to burn.

Blair House had been designed to be heated by wood burning fireplaces. Once the large rooms had been partitioned into smaller bedrooms, Paul Blair installed a new heating system that used thermally heated water from the pool on top of Huerfano. Unfortunately, the hot water system had been effectively destroyed by a rock-slide which cracked the outer core of the volcanic butte. The slide re-routed the water to form the hot springs pool south of the house. Izzy's solution was to install a pellet stove in the basement where there had been a coal bin. Izzy placed the stove before the inside entrance to the tunnel, which had been used as an escape route from the house during the Indian wars. With the boys' help, Ezra removed the board covering to the tunnel entrance and replaced them with a cinderblock wall, which sealed the tunnel and allowed smoke to vent safely outside through the tunnel.

When they finished construction of the project a week after Thanksgiving, the boys did not tell Ezra that they recognized the bear's odor in the tunnel. When they returned to school, Izzy assigned the boys from Pryor with the primary responsibility of maintaining the fire in the pellet stove. This meant they needed to maintain an adequate supply of wood pellets to burn. They not only got to start the initial fire, but also they had to open the outside cellar doors to the tunnel up on the hill where the bear lay asleep for the winter.

With malice and forethought the boys schemed to inflict further torment on the grizzly. Earlier, they had stolen two M-80 explosives that farmers used to frighten crows from newly planted fields. While at the feed and lumber store in Ridge View, the boys put an explosive in each front pocket with the intent of using them on New Year's Eve. They decided instead to use them on the bear that had killed the couple who had taken them in. With revenge as their motive, they thought little of how the explosions would affect anyone else. They hatched their plan first to light kindling and then the pellets in the pellet stove, and then to close the vent leading to the ground above. Instead, they set the flue to channel the flow of smoke up the tunnel to where the bear lay sleeping. Next, they had to hurry out of the kitchen to the entrance of the tunnel, and then open the tunnel doors, which hopefully would cause the smoke to rush out of the tunnel's entrance. Certain the bear would awaken at the pungent smell of smoke, the boys planned to ignite the fuses of two M-80's and throw them at the beast, while they ran in opposite directions. One would run left of the tunnel entrance to the house and climb the post where Ezra had fashioned footholds and the other would run to the right and up the butte to climb Freedom's tree.

***

Meanwhile, Adam arrived early at the Blair House and climbed the slope to the top of the butte and found Butch sleeping in a bedroll in the center of the dry pool. Butch awakened and rolled up his bedroll, but clutched a notebook in his hand. They sat waiting for the sun to rise, while Butch shared he had been busy managing the Stage Stop Hotel. He told Adam about his recent conversation with Elaine and Elizabeth McClaren, who were better known as Misty and Amanda. Butch confessed how he could see God's activity in all that was happening and that now he had hit rock bottom. He thanked Adam for interceding for him with the plea bargain which would remove him from the valley, while he got straightened out by the Marine Corps. Adam listened to his nephew, a boy he had led to the Lord and had spent countless hours to disciple him.

Butch said, "You did more for me, than my own father, and now I want to do something for you. I spent parts of a week writing things down in this notebook. I ask you do nothing with it until I am gone and in the Marines, out of here."

"Okay," said Adam, "what's in there that causes you to think you would need to be in a safe place, if the contents of your journal were revealed and made known to others?"

"It's about what my father and the leaders of the McNaughton Corporation have been doing and why. It's what they did before the corporation was formed, Adam. It's all about getting the Blair House and the land, so they could all become tremendously wealthy."

"As the saying goes, Butch, the love of money is the root of all evil."

"Adam, I know that has a scriptural basis, and there's more. And I know most of the people, who care, want to know who else wore the bear suits. Everyone knows Van Allen, Seamus, Robert King, and I were caught wearing them, but it's the other six that people don't know about."

"Who are they?"

"Sam Gelding who is dead, Ralph like Robert King has moved, the sheriff, my father, the assistant superintendent of schools-Dr. Maurice Wood, and the Chair of City Council-Chauncey Brown."

"I was afraid the sheriff had been involved, but I'm surprised Maurice and Chauncey would have risked so much. What about the raves?"

"They were all fake. At least in the discussions I was involved in, but I noticed something was different this time. I'm not sure what would have happened if you and your men had not stopped the rave. Before, it was what happened after the rave to the women who were involved. All of them went with the men in the bear suits. Some of those stayed on to work at the Asherah House. Heather Ross became a good friend of my father, Sarah continued at the Stage Stop and you know about Gloria Jones. Interesting isn't it how many became pregnant. Sam Gelding was in charge of tying up loose ends, like the girl in Quail Point. That woman who just came into a lot of money, a twin of Amanda, was kept prisoner at Asherah House, and I know Asherah is a pagan name, Baal worship. She was kept locked up to be used, and Betty Strong Bull was murdered."

"You mean she was pushed off the cliff on purpose?"

"They laughed about it afterwards, Adam!"

"Who was it?"

"I got them listed, Chauncey, Maurice, and...my father...I don't know when exactly it got so crazy...especially Red. Women like Hannah and Gloria Jones were snared into thinking they were something special, then we trafficked them, so we could finance the overall plan."

"Do you mean to get the water and mineral rights to the Blair House, or is there more?"

"My father became obsessed. You may have seen him or heard him growl like the bear. The human trafficking didn't just include prostitution, but also having sex slaves like Misty and selling the babies of women caught in the snare. Perhaps even murder."

"You saw this?"

"I list dates, times, who and where as best I could..."said Butch. "At first the plan was good. At least it sounded good...Red sold it on the idea of getting the land, the mineral rights and the water, then we were going to develop the land to counter the devastation the Interstate did to our valley when it by-passed us and the schools reorganized. The plan was to make up for that and to bring jobs, permanent jobs to the area with a ski resort, logging, gold mining on Ezra's property and more."

"Butch, those were good ideas. I was in on that, but everything changed."

"We knew everything was in trouble when three newcomers arrived in town on the Trailways bus."

"I remember...Karen's arrival has made a world of difference for me."

"Which is how things should be...and Izzy's return to restore Blair House. I thought how cool was that. A son had a chance to make things right for his father...that hit me hard, especially when we found out the old man, the wood carver, not only was the guy's father, but he had been living in the valley. We had no right. And the Brownings, everybody heard they had been on the verge of divorce, but they worked their way back..." said Butch, "but what really impacted me was when you defied what we were doing by standing at the inter-section and calling us out. And there was Rabbit standing guard at the door to the church, and Pilgrim shattered the Asher pole...I wanted to cheer...but I didn't know what to do if I did."

"Butch, you know Red won't be happy about you handing me this notebook."

"I know, and I won't be here to back up what was said, but I included a letter to you and I've initialed every page. Adam, in a way I'm doing this for Red. He has to be stopped," Butch said, "Go now before I change my mind...I'm going to sit here for awhile and look at the carving in the tree. I figured out it's about me making my choices, and I've made a lot of bad decisions. This isn't one of them, but like in the carving all heck is going to break loose, and the four hooded fig-ures around the alter or podium are the Tunnicliffe brothers, who are waiting to see what I do...oh, I know it's not really for me, but I think God has used it to help me sort things out...please go now, Adam."

"I love you, Butch, and remember God loves you more than anyone else."

"Me too, Adam, you've always been there for me, especially when Red wasn't."

"Butch, you did a really nice thing...I know you gave the gold nugget to the Bond family."

"You recognized it was the one you gave me when I was baptized in the creek behind the church..." Butch said, and continued, "Adam, did you ever meet my mother?"

"No, and the more I think about it, I wonder about the past," Adam said, "The raves are new, but I think the human trafficking is not. The Baal worship may have been happening in the valley for a long, long time."

"Then you think it is possible...my mother may have been someone...someone like Gloria, who Sam killed, after she bore a child or had an abortion," said Butch, while Adam had already started climbing down from the butte.

As Butch sat on the stump before the wood carving on the tree, he continued talking before he prayed, "What happened to my mother? Father God, I am so dirty with sin...sin that led to death for some and for others a life they may have wished they could escape by taking their own life. As a boy, I asked Jesus into my heart. I asked him to be my Lord and Savior. Your servant, Adam, discipled me. Please forgive me of my sin, once again. I know your word says my sin is removed from me...but do you love me? Please give me a sign if you will...tell me if I am capable of being loved..."

Adam did not answer Butch's question, but he left the butte to return home to Claymore Flats. He turned to wave at Butch, and noticed the sunlight descending on the mountain and to the tree where it seemed to linger. Butch had sat down on the stump of the Asher pole and looked at Ezra's carving. As Adam turned in the seat of his truck to back up, he had not seen the first wisp of smoke rising through the tunnel doors, nor had he seen the two boys from Pryor run from the back door of the Blair House to the tunnel entrance. Adam did hear the crash of the tunnel doors as they fell backwards and struck the ground, and then he had been startled by the unmistakable sound of the two M-80 explosions. Immediately, he turned to watch as the smoke billowed out of the entrance. He watched as one boy ran right and the other left of the tunnel entrance. One boy ran for side of the house and the other climbed the butte.

Enraged, the bear emerged from its sleep, shocked and angered, breathing heavily from the effects of its deep sleep and the smoke, but awake enough to see its tormentors. Inside Karen and others had been startled awake from the explosion and the roar of the bear. Karen sprang into immediate action by remembering Adam's words to not hesitate to kill the bear. She ran across the hall to Jill's room, opened the closet door and the door to the hidden stairwell, climbed the steps to the third floor bedroom where the staircase ended and where she had stored Pilgrim's rifle. In seconds she had made it to the top step, grabbed the Sharps rifle and burst into the room, while Coinneach was still in bed. Karen raised the window, knelt on the floor, rested the rifle barrel on the window sill, and pulled the trigger.

The bear had chosen to follow the boy who foolishly climbed the slope to the top of the butte. The boy bumped into Butch as he was rising from where he squatted on the stump. Butch, knocked off balance, sat back down only to rise again. He turned as the bear rushed him, and he tripped backward, as he heard the shot ring out. The bear fell forward on Butch nearly crushing him, were it not for the Asher pole stump where the bear's open jaws landed next to Butch's head. Butch let out a blood chilling yell, but stopped screaming when he noticed there was no eye where it should have been on the bear's head.

Adam grabbed his Winchester from the rifle rack in his truck and hurried back up the butte to Freedom's tree. Karen picked herself up from the floor and climbed out the third story window of the corner bedroom. Coinneach, who put on a bathrobe, joined her on the porch. One boy from Pryor continued climbing the tree, while the other continued climbing the pillars to the third floor porch. Sleepyheads appeared on balconies of the second and third floors to see Adam raise his rifle.

Waving at those at the house and seeing Karen holding the Sharps rifle on the third floor porch, Adam yelled, "The bear is dead...the bear is dead. Butch is alive. Karen killed the bear...Karen, my love, killed the bear. I dreamed she would!"

"He loves me! He loves me," Butch yelled at Adam, "He loves me...and I am forgiven...now please help get me out from under this beast! I'm alive and I'm forgiven. I asked God to show me, and He said He would!"

Adam waved toward those gathered on the porches below for them to join him and help free Butch, as he yelled, "Come help me!"

Men from the house climbed the hill with the women following after them. Butch asked Adam to make sure the bear was dead by sticking the end of his rifle in the bear's ear hole and shooting it, which Adam did. Getting Butch out from under the beast proved to be no easy matter.

Jerry Sunday commented, "Looks like it's true...God can use whatever he wants to do his will. Even the stump of an Asher pole!"

Morris Goodenough added, "He probably would have been crushed, if Butch had not fallen where he did."

Examining the bear, Adam took hold of a collar around its neck and said, "This was no wild bear. Look at the collar. Look here where I grasp its ear. A wedge has been cut from its ear for identification purposes. Chief Strong Bull told me that he and his braves found a flat bed truck near Pryor. The Chief traced it to a circus."

Izzy said, "And representatives from a circus and film company were here to meet with the chief. Bring the boys from Pryor up here. They have some explaining to do!"

Butch moaned and Hannah said, "Butch, I've never seen you look better, all covered with fur!"

"Hannah, please forgive me, God has and just now he convinced me that Jesus really did die for me too!" Butch said emphatically.

"What did Butch say?" asked Tim.

"It's what you said at the café, Tim. All have sinned and fall short of God's glory. I've earned a one way trip to Hell, but I've put my trust in Jesus, and just now I asked God to show me that he loves me…" said Butch.

"And he delivered you from certain death," Tim added.

While Caleb rounded up the boys from Pryor, the men and women from the Blair House formed a circle around Butch and the bear. Janine took pictures of the bear, Butch, the tree, and the Blair House team. She said, "This will make a great photo essay for *The Out Cry*!"

Adam led the group in prayer, and then they held hands and sang, "We are one in the Spirit, we are one in the Lord…"

Everyone helped remove the bear off Butch, as they rolled the bear off the top of the butte and down the northwest slope. The bear stopped just short of the two Live Oak branches that it had broken off Freedom's tree.

"Thank you all for rescuing the likes of me. I know I have offended all of you, and I'm sorry…hopefully you will one day forgive me…I've committed crimes against you," Butch confessed.

"All sin is sin against God," Karen said. "Each of us has a choice of whether or not to forgive Butch. I for one give up any right I might have for revenge against Butch in deference to what God has in store for him. I'd say God has already been at work!"

Butch brushed off his blue jeans, as the crowd began to climb down the side of the butte. He said to Adam, "I guess this is where you tell me to go and sin no more…"

Adam put his arm around Butch's shoulder and replied with, "Welcome home, Nephew."

\*\*\*

Caleb had Izzy join him with the boys from Pryor in the dining room, while the others went about their business. They sat down and Caleb looked the boys in their eyes and said, "You have been playing a game with all of us, and now it's time to come clean. You have tormented that bear before. It knew you and now it is dead…Deputy Candy has spent hours looking for your relatives with no success. It's because you were not the children of the couple you were living with in Pryor. What is the truth?"

"Okay, okay…all of what you said was true. You know about the circus that was here interviewing the Indians. I guess it's called an audition," said the oldest boy.

"And…" replied Izzy.

"Part of why they were here was because they were looking for the four of us. We stole the flatbed truck, the cage, and the dumb bear! We were with the circus as gophers;" said the oldest.

"When our parents died in a car crash, my brother and me ran away from home, so we wouldn't have to go to social services," said the younger brother.

"How long were you with the circus?" asked Caleb.

"This one for only a couple of months…" the little boy answered.

"This one…" Izzy said, "…then you have done this before."

"We kinda traveled with the bear. He changed hands a couple of times," the oldest boy said and then asked, "What are you going to do to us?"

"Truth and justice…grace and mercy…" Izzy mumbled, then said, "You can stay here, if your story checks out. If not, then you are out of here."

"Fair enough," both boys replied, as they raised their hands and slapped high fives with Caleb and Izzy.

***

Later Adam asked Karen to sit with him to watch the sunrise in chairs on the third floor balcony. He handed her a note card and said, "Look at this card some kind soul sent me...the author said the nicest words which really spoke to me."

"I received one too," Karen said. "What a blessing! Kind words are life giving. In Denver, I read a fortune cookie about kindness that said, kind words are memorable, they last three winters."

Adam asked her about shooting the bear and she said, "I sat on the floor of the room, rested the barrel of the Sharps on the window sill, and shot for the eye of the bear...but Adam, it looked like the grizzly paused before attacking Butch. He rose up and looked directly toward me, as if he were saying here I am, please shoot me. And then he fell directly on Butch but squarely on the stump, I guess..."

Adam smiled and said, "Did you know Ezra told me by sign that now the restoration of Blair House is finished, both physically and spiritually."

"That's one restoration of Blair House," said Karen.

"John Mark finished restoring Mary's house in Rock Creek, and a new pastor family has moved in. Mary's mother owned the house first and she was a Blair."

"That's two," Karen said, as Elaine and Elizabeth joined them on the porch.

"And the Asherah House is being restored...to what it was as Blair House Bed and Breakfast," said Elaine.

"That's three..."

"And the Stage Stop Hotel has been returned to us, as its rightful owners, as we are both of the Blair lineage..." Elizabeth announced, and also said, "You tell them sister..."

"That's four...what's next," asked Adam.

"Amanda and I are twin sisters, Elizabeth and Elaine, and we are each to be restored to our royal lineage as Lady Blair of Scotland to the McClaren lands."

"Do not share this, as more information is forthcoming, but it is official..." urged Elizabeth.

"Okay, Cinderella, that is five and that's too cool, but I too have been restored, cleared of any wrong doing in Quail Point," said Karen.

"Yea," said all three.

"And I have been healed of deep wounds to my heart," said Adam, as he held Karen's hand in his own, "and soon I will be free to make a new start..." That is a restoration, too.

Elaine, Elizabeth, and Karen began singing, "Falling in love again..." until Karen stopped short of finishing the song.

"A thought," Karen said. "That which was wrong has been and is being made right, because John Mark made the decision to be obedient to God's command to walk to the little Church in the Glen. His obedience caused him to speak words to Tim McNaughton that led to Adam prompting Tim to share the Gospel...revival in the valley began with Tim, but it was the result of an act of obedience by a newcomer."

Noticing how Adam and Karen were looking at one another, Elaine said, "I hear Rachael playing *How Great Thou Art* on the piano!"

"Let's go join the choir," replied Elizabeth.

Karen began to rise from the balcony chair when Adam placed his hand on hers and asked her to stay.

"Sure," Karen said as she sat back down.

"You have been precious to me as I have healed from my encounter with the bear. As I urged, you are the one who killed the bear..." Adam paused.

"And..."

"You have had such a positive influence on me and so many others in the valley, all of my wranglers too! No, it is more than that Karen...you brought out the best in me," Adam said as tears welled up in their eyes.

"What influence I have on you comes from my love for you," Karen sighed.

Adam moved forward, out of his chair, pulled something from his pocket and knelt on one knee before her, as he had seen the Tunnicliffes kneel before their ladies. He smiled and asked, "Will you, Karen Gustafson...will you marry me?"

Karen threw her arms around his neck with tears flowing from her eyes and said, "Oh Adam, yes, yes, yes, a thousand times yes!"

"Then let me put this ring on your finger," Adam said as he pulled her close and kissed her.

CPSIA information can be obtained
at www.ICGtesting.com
Printed in the USA
FFOW03n0550161217
44100798-43378FF

9 781545 615225